BROKEN SHELVES BOOK 4

CHOOSING A *forever*

DAISY WREN

Paperback ISBN: 9798991718943

Edited by Brittany Uller and Jen Bernacki at The Author Experience

Cover design by Brittany Uller at The Author Experience

For rights and permissions, please contact:

daisywren.author@gmail.com

Also by Daisy Wren

The Broken Shelves Series

Loving the Sinner
Living for Truth
Resisting the Temptation
Choosing a Forever

Novellas

More Than a Friend

This ones for my readers. Your support is what's kept me going.
And to those who love a teachable man (and might have a slight corruption kink) *wink*

Author's Note

Dear reader,

Tal and Mack gave me a run for my money. Their story changed quite a few times, but the one thing I could always count on was Tal's eagerness and zero chill when it comes to Mack. Tal was always going to be a golden retriever, eager to please, virgin mess of a man, and I love him. I hope you do too.

This book is not an accurate representation of the US healthcare system. I have taken creative liberties for the sake of the story.

Please check the trigger/content warnings and as always, enjoy!

Xoxo,

Daisy Wren

Content Warnings

This book is intended for people over the age of eighteen as it contains explicit sexual content.
Sexual content includes:

- Period sex

- Cum eating/swallowing

- Public sex

- Masturbation

- Watching porn

In addition to sexual content, it contains other themes that may be triggering for some such as:

- Religious trauma (Mormonism specifically)

- Mention of parental death (Not descriptive)

- On page ankle injury

- On page fire

- Mentions of infertility

- Mentions of self-harm and suicidal thoughts

- Mentions of STIs

- Sexual assault (in the past, not explicit detail, and not by the MMC)

- Body shaming/food shaming

988 Suicide and Crisis Lifeline
If you or someone you know is experiencing a mental health crisis, please call 988. There is help out there.

CHOOSING A *forever* PLAYLIST

"This Love (Taylor's Version)" by Taylor Swift
"Adore You" by Harry Styles
"All I Ever Wanted-Acoustic" by Dean Lewis
"Before You Go" by Lewis Capaldi
"Fifteen (Taylor's Version)" by Taylor Swift
"the 1" by Taylor Swift
"Guilty as Sin?" by Taylor Swift
"So High School" by Taylor Swift
"Teenage Dream" by Boyce Avenue
"If I Could Turn Back Time" by Cher
"arms" by Christina Perri
"Thinking out Loud" by Ed Sheeran
"Yours" by Conan Gray
"Till Forever Falls Apart" by Ashe, FINNEAS

Glossary

Ward: A local congregation where people gather to worship

Worthy Priesthood Holder: A man who holds the power of one of the three degrees of priesthood (Aaronic, Melchizedek, and Patriarchal)

Student Ward: A congregation where people gather to worship, generally on or around college campuses. Generally, people in this ward are not married.

Deconstruction: The process where people examine and question their religious beliefs

Apostate: When someone turns away from and/or denounces the principles of the gospel

Removing Records: When you get baptized into the Mormon church, you become an official member. Removing one's records is a legal process in which those records are removed and you are no longer considered a member.

Sacrament: A ceremony where they bless bread and water that is symbolizing the blood and the body of Jesus Christ.

Relief Society: The women's organization in the church. They're often the people called when there are philanthropic needs.

PROLOGUE

Talmage

15 years old...

Today's the day I've been dreading. I have to do it. It's the right thing to do. I mean, we both have a whole future in front of us. We can't exclusively date the entire three years of high school. We aren't supposed to exclusively date at this age, anyway—it's against the church's rules.

I have a mission to go on, and she'll probably go on one, too. Maybe by the time we both come home, we'll be ready for each other. We can have the future we've talked about and have a big family. I'll teach art, and she'll be a writer.

Maybe she won't go on a mission, though. Maybe she'll end up getting married right out of high school or before I can come home. If that's the case, then I know we aren't meant to be.

Holy heck, this is going to be hard. She's going to be so sad. I'm sad. Devastated, even if I can't show it.

Dread weighs on my chest like a lead balloon as I sit next to her on the bus like I always do. She gives me a wide smile, her green eyes shining in the afternoon sun, and her auburn hair glowing like an ember. I've always loved her eyes. They remind me of emeralds or the scales of a dragon in one of the fantasy novels I read.

"Hey, Tal! How was your chem test?"

My heart pounds in my ears as I try to process what she's asking. I don't want to talk about chemistry when I'm about to break her heart.

Her brows furrow, and she places her hand on my forearm as her nose scrunches the way it always does when she's confused. The touch sends a spark of electricity through my veins, and my face immediately turns red.

I clear my throat. "We shouldn't do this anymore." I want to take the words back as soon as I say them.

"Do... what?" she asks quietly. I think she already knows, but of course, she wants me to confirm it.

"This. Us. What we're doing. We both need to focus on school. I never should have kissed you or taken it this far because it's against the rules. I have to prepare to go on my mission, and we should date other people. Maybe when we're older and we—"

"Stop. Please, don't." Her voice wobbles, and her eyes fill with tears, but she blinks them away. "Don't give me hope of something in the future because you know I'd wait. If you're ending it, just end it. Don't give me hope."

My heart feels like it's being torn to shreds with a potato peeler as she dabs at the corners of her eyes with her fingertips to catch the few stray tears slipping out.

"Firefly, I'm sorry." I try to grab her hand, but she pulls away and grips her backpack with both arms, using it like a shield to defend herself.

"Please don't call me that anymore."

Ouch.

But I understand.

She'll need time and space to process this. The problem is, we have to see each other every day at rehearsals. If we make it into Chamber Choir next year, we'll see each other even more.

It'll be okay. This is the right thing to do.

But why does it feel so awful?

I'm sure I'm not the only one who feels like they're standing on the sidelines watching everyone else's lives move past them.

But dang does it feel like I am.

I have a career I love, a dog I adore, and hobbies I enjoy, but I can't help feeling like something is missing.

The people around me are getting married and having babies and buying houses while I go to work, take Siren for walks, and sit in a congregation of stuffy people on Sundays.

I used to love going to church. I used to love the community and the sense of belonging. The rules were there as guidelines to follow, not restrictions to keep me from living or keep me in line. I loved it so much, I spent two years knocking door to door and trying to get other people to join, too.

But now it feels like a cage that's too small, suffocating. The rules feel like walls painted with a realistic looking mural so I don't have to wonder what's on the other side. The people I thought were watching out for me, guiding me, now feel like overbearing entities, waiting for me to slip. Gossips waiting until it's my turn to be on the chopping block.

So I haven't slipped. At least not to the outside world.

On the inside? I've already removed my records and started living my life the way I want to.

Even if I don't know exactly what it looks like.

I thought I knew. It was a simple plan.

Graduate high school: check.

Serve a mission: check.

Go to school: check—even though I changed careers halfway through.

Find a nice girl and get married: well, I was halfway there.

I met a nice girl, and we were engaged, but she changed her mind about me. She said she wanted a husband with a career that's not so dangerous. She wanted someone with a regular nine-to-five who would be home at night.

That's fine, totally understandable. The minimal heartbreak I felt when she handed me back the ring was probably an indicator we wouldn't have been happy together long-term. It only took a week for me to get over it.

Maybe something's wrong with me because I haven't felt the kind of gut-wrenching heartbreak Taylor Swift writes songs about since I was fifteen.

Maybe that's because it was the last time you loved someone so deeply.

I can remember *that* heartbreak like it was yesterday.

I wish I could go back and tell fifteen-year-old Talmage not to let her go. Maybe he would have listened to me. Maybe then I wouldn't have a "one that got away."

Unfortunately, second chances are rare, and the likelihood of me getting one are slim to none.

CHAPTER 1

Talmage

13 years old...

I try not to let my eyes trail over to the girl a couple rows over, but I can't help it. She's just so...

Pretty.

I've never seen someone as pretty as her. Her auburn hair is twisted in two braids, and her long eyelashes are coated in mascara, making them look kind of like spider legs—in a good way.

But I don't think she even knows I exist. Sure, we were in the musical together last year, but we didn't talk. The cast was so big, we never really had a chance to do more than exist in the same area. Hopefully, we'll be in the musical together again this year, and I can get to know her. Until then, I'll sneak glances of her in math class.

A nudge on my arm brings my focus back to the teacher explaining the equations we'll be working on, and my face turns red as I look at Jacob next to me.

"Why are you so distracted?" he asks, looking behind me to find what I was looking at. When he sees her, he gives me a knowing grin. "Just talk to her, Talmage."

"No. We can't date until we're sixteen anyway, so there's no point."

"You can be friends with her, though."

The teacher clears her throat, giving us a look that tells us to stop talking. When she's done with her lesson, she tells us to work quietly in groups. I steal another glance at the girl I'm pretty sure I have my first crush on, and her brows are furrowed, her nose scrunched in an adorably confused way, reminding me of how a bunny wiggles its nose.

I wonder if she's struggling with what we're learning. I look at my already complete worksheet and wonder if I should ask her if she needs help, but the bell rings before I can make a decision.

The next time we're in class, the teacher tells us we have new assigned seats.

And she's sitting right next to me.

I try to keep my leg from shaking, but it's the only thing stopping me from standing up and shouting at someone—something very off-brand for me. I can't even pull out my phone and try to distract myself with something else because it would raise too many questions.

So instead, I smile when I need to. Nod when necessary. I scribble notes in my notebook that *should* be about what's being discussed, but it's actually just my grocery list and random doodles.

In my ward, I've been assigned as the ward mission leader. My duty is to coordinate meals for the missionaries and make sure they're following all of the church's arbitrary rules. Like if two missionaries want to go teach an unwed woman, another male member has to go with them. The rule doesn't make any sense because why would they not trust two men with a woman, but they'll trust *three*?

Most things don't make sense to me anymore, now that I don't have tunnel vision.

I hate my calling now.

Which is crazy; less than a year ago, I never would have said those words. I would have taken the title with honor and served happily without complaint. I would have come to this stupid ward council meeting and taken notes and enthusiastically offered my help and my perspective.

Now? I see these meetings for what they are: an opportunity to gossip and talk crap about members of the ward who are "struggling."

Little do they know, *I'm* one of the people "struggling."

When I moved back to Utah two years ago after spending some time in California, I couldn't help but feel like something was... off. I went to my ward in California when I could, but I didn't feel as much... *pressure* to go as I did when I was living in Utah.

I never realized how much the church was shoved down my throat until I came back to Utah and could see seven different temples in a thirty-minute drive and church buildings littering every street. Where there's a billboard bragging about the number of scripture copies sold each month.

When Grandpa Monson passed away four months ago, my cousins—Elli, Emma, Izzy, and Hannah—bluntly told me their personal issues with the church the night before the funeral. They had all left the church, and they seemed happier than ever. I wanted to know how they did it, if they were *actually* happy or if it was an act.

Emma's story about her rapist made me sick to my stomach. I have two younger sisters, and if they were treated the way Emma had been after such a horrible thing... I don't think I'd be seen as such a nice guy anymore.

I knew there were flaws in the church, obviously, but I don't think I wanted to believe what I knew deep down.

The church is a whole lot of bad wrapped in a whole bunch of money, pretending to be good.

I've asked myself over and over again why I don't just... *leave.* The only answer I seem to come up with is the church is familiar. It's what I know—*all* I know. For twenty-eight years, I've been neck deep in this organization. I haven't been given a chance to choose what I believe.

But the overwhelming question keeping me here is: what if I leave and I'm no longer happy?

But it also begs the question: am I truly happy *now?*

The short answer is yes. I'm happy.

The long answer is I feel like I'm moving through life on auto-pilot and something is... missing. I don't want to say it's a relationship, but sometimes it feels like my heart isn't complete without the romance love stories and poems are written about.

I *could* be married or in a relationship right now, but nothing ever seems to last.

Other relationships haven't worked out for various reasons, but the biggest common denominator is *me*. I want that once-in-a-lifetime love. The kind that feels like your soul is intertwined completely with hers. I want a love to consume me and the woman I'm with. To feel like my heart is being pulled out of my chest if I'm away from her for too long.

I want a fairytale ending. My happily-ever-after.

But I'm twenty-eight, and so far, I haven't had much luck with finding someone who makes my blood sing or my heart race. I haven't found the woman who makes me look forward to getting off of a shift instead of wishing I could work longer hours so I can socialize with actual humans instead of only having Siren to talk to.

I remember the excitement of my first crush as a teenager, and I remember the rush of knowing my crush liked me back. I remember the immediate smile that came to my face when I saw her. The way I'd find any reason to be close to her.

I guess maybe it's different as a teenager, but I want something like that. Something simple and sweet.

Something *real.*

Something like what I had with...

No. Best not to think about her. Besides, we were teenagers. Logically, how real could our feelings have been?

She's probably married to someone completely de-voted to her. They probably have a hoard of emerald-eyed kids to do family movie nights with and go to the farmer's market on Saturdays before spending Sundays together playing board games.

And she deserves that. She deserves a happily-ever-after.

Even if sometimes I regret I wasn't the one to give it to her.

The alarm blares through the station, and my blood immediately starts pumping.

Here we *go.*

I've been back with the Springville Fire Department for almost two years, and even though it's slower here than in California, I like it more. I worked one season with a hotshot crew—the firefighters who specialize in fighting wildfires—a few years ago and ultimately decided it wasn't my jam. Those guys are a different breed, and I'm just not cut out to be gone for weeks at a time at the drop of a hat. I like the rush of adrenaline from house fires or smaller wildfires I can help with. The danger of being a hotshot doesn't appeal to me.

Springville, Utah is small in comparison to the neighboring college cities of Orem and Provo, but it doesn't mean it's any less wild. Being near the mountains and close to Utah Lake, we have our fair share of accidents and house fires. It's December, so a good portion of our calls are due to the slick roads from the snow or the rain.

I swear, everyone in Utah forgets how to drive as soon as the first flake falls. Even if they've lived here their whole life.

According to dispatch, there's a three-car pileup on Main Street, but nothing fatal. Our job for smaller accidents like this is to create a safe work area, clean up any debris or liquid from the vehicles, and stabilize them if needed. It should hopefully be a quick and easy run.

When we get to the scene, there's a maroon minivan with a crunched front end, a small, blue sedan with a clipped rear, and a black SUV with damage to both ends blocking the traffic trying to come down Main Street.

It doesn't look like anyone is severely injured, but the EMTs are checking out the people involved while we help the police officers direct traffic and move the cars to the side of the road.

Once traffic is moving slowly but steadily past the scene of the accident, I walk over to the ambulance to see if I can help in any way.

There are a few officers taking statements from people. A flash of red catches my eye, and I turn. Something about the shade of the auburn hair falling past her shoulders feels familiar. She isn't wearing a coat, even though it's thirty degrees and lightly snowing. My eyes trail her curvy body, taking in the way she fits her jeans, and I have to look away before I stare at the curve of her hips too long. It would be inappropriate. I don't *ogle* women. Especially at the scene of an accident.

I shake my head lightly to put myself back into professional territory before I approach her.

"Excuse me, ma'am," I say as I tap her on the shoulder. "I was wondering if..." Anything else I was going to say dies on my tongue as she turns around and looks up at me with her piercing green eyes.

Green eyes that remind me of emeralds. Or the scales of a dragon. Or grass after it's rained, shiny and vibrant.

Eyes filled with tears because of me more than once in high school.

Eyes that look sad and distraught right now.

"Mack?"

CHAPTER 2

Mackenzie

14 years old...

Thank goodness I can use the temperature as an excuse for my heated face and not the fact that Talmage is looking at me like I'm something special.

It's making bees buzz in my stomach, and for the first time in a while I feel nervous around a boy.

I haven't felt this way since... No. He has no place here. Not after what he did and how he treated me.

How did I never notice the way Talmage looks at me before? Is this a new thing for him, too?

I can't remember the first time I really noticed him. When my crush started digging its roots in my heart. All I know is one day, my stomach flipped when he gave me his signature grin. Without him and Jacob, there's no way I would have passed that dang class. Math help turned into messaging on Facebook, and messaging on Facebook turned into organizing a group hangout session at the city's summer festival.

Next year, we'll be in choir and theatre together, so we'll be around each other even more often.

I can't wait.

Under the lights strewn across the little patio outside of the recreation building, his hand nudges mine.

Then his pinky wraps around my own. Sparks skitter across the skin he's touching, and my face heats further.

We stay like that, pinkies locked, as we listen to everyone else talk about what they've been up to this summer, what they plan on doing next year.

No fucking way.

Today has really gone to shit, and I'm ready to go home and cry in the bathtub with a pint of cookie dough ice cream smothered in hot fudge.

The day *was* going fine. Another tedious day in a long line of tedious days.

I work from home as a bid desk specialist for a tech company. I spend my days clicking "copy and paste" to send quotes for companies wanting to buy bulk products. I hate it, and it doesn't pay enough, so I work as a bartender part-time as well. Unfortunately, trying to find a job in Utah when you're heavily tattooed and don't have a college degree means your options are limited. Usually, I try not to work night shifts at the bar, but my manager needed me to fill in.

The twins are old enough to be home alone, but my best friend, Lizzie, was able to hang out with them tonight, so I don't feel as guilty about leaving them.

Except now, I have to ask Lizzie to take me to work and pick me up because some dumbass wasn't paying attention and rear ended the SUV behind me, which sent it into my car. Now I have a flat tire, and the suspension might have issues. I couldn't hear the tow truck guy explaining what was wrong with it over the rapid racing of my pulse.

I sure as hell hope it's only the flat tire and nothing more serious, or I have no idea what I'll do. My budget doesn't have the wiggle room for a car payment, and I don't have the savings to buy one in cash.

My entire body is vibrating with anxiety. My heart rate hasn't slowed since I felt the jolt of a car hitting my bumper, and even though it's hella cold outside, I can't feel it with the adrenaline coursing through me.

I'm lucky it's just a fender bender, but my nervous system can't tell the difference between a minor inconvenience and a catastrophic accident.

Thanks, PTSD.

I'm an overly cautious driver after what happened to my parents. I'm never on my phone unless it's to use my maps app. I try to avoid driving in the snow or heavy rain, and if I've had a single sip of alcohol, I refuse to get behind the wheel. I avoid being around semi-trucks if possible, and I never run red lights.

Apparently, not everyone is as cautious as I am. The guy behind me admitted he was on his phone to the officer at the scene, and if he hadn't been distracted, he would have noticed the brake lights.

Just as I finish going over my statement with the officer, I hear a voice I'd know anywhere—one I've heard in my dreams—and a tap on my shoulder diverts my attention. Shivers—not from the cold—zip up my spine as I mentally steel myself for the inevitable blast from the past. A blast I'm in no way prepared for.

Sure enough, I turn around, and there he is. Talmage *fucking* Monson. My first real love, my first shattering heartbreak, and the one guy I've never really gotten over—not that anyone knows besides Lizzie.

God, if you exist, fuck you very much.

I didn't even know he was still in Utah. Last I heard, he was in California about to get married. I stopped checking in on social media when he announced his engagement because... well, life sucks enough as it is, and I didn't need to see the man I've been secretly pining after for thirteen years living his best life with a woman who looks like a model.

He looks the same, but different. I can't tell under the coat of his uniform, but I've seen enough firefighters on social media to infer his body has bulked up a bit since we were in high school. His blonde mustache is neatly trimmed, and even though it should be off-putting—I've *never* found a mustache attractive—it actually makes my knees weak. His hair is faded on the sides and slightly longer on the top, neatly gelled away from his face. His blue eyes are still kind, but right now they're swirling with too many emotions to name.

I realize I still haven't answered when someone walks behind him, and he steps closer. I instinctually take a step back and almost fall into a small hole on the side of the road.

Strong hands grip my forearms and keep me from tipping over, and I mutter a quiet, "Thanks."

He steps back and removes his hands like I've burned him, and my heart sinks. It seems nothing's changed since we graduated.

"Where's your coat?" He looks around at all the people surrounding us.

"It's in my car." I wasn't thinking about grabbing my coat when I got out right after the accident.

He nods, then nods again. "Do you have someone you can call to come get you?"

"Yes."

"Okay. Well, yeah. You should do that. Call them, I mean. You should get out of the cold. I don't want you to get sick or something. Pneumonia or bronchitis would be terrible to deal with, not to mention the air quality isn't great today."

"Okay…" I don't know why he's rambling like he's nervous. The boy I knew in high school didn't get nervous. It's barely less than thirty degrees, I'm not going to get sick from it.

"You need to get checked out by the paramedics. Make sure you're not hurt or anything," Talmage suggests, nodding over the ambulance.

"I'm fine, I promise. My neck hurts a little but—"

"Then you should absolutely get it checked! We want to be sure you don't have whiplash or a sprain. It's protocol, really. They should have checked you out already or have you on the way to the hospital."

"I really need to get to work," I argue. I don't have time to be checked over, and I *definitely* don't have the time to go to the hospital. I swivel my head left to right and move it up and down. "I'm fine, see?"

"Please, just... for my peace of mind?" Talmage's blue eyes burn with what seems to be genuine concern.

"Fine," I grumble.

With a small smile, Talmage leads me to the ambulance where the paramedic asks me if anything hurts. I tell him my neck is a bit sore, but I don't think anything is wrong. He runs through a few motion tests, and the whole time, Talmage stands there with his eyes on me like some kind of watch dog. My entire body is tense with him so close.

"Take some pain medicine, and if you get severe headaches or the neck pain increases, see a physician straight away," the paramedic says once he's finished his tests.

"Got it. Am I good to go now?" I try to keep the impatience out of my tone, but more time here means less money on my next paycheck.

The paramedic gives me the all clear, and I turn to head back to the side of the road to can call Lizzie.

Talmage follows, his steps matching mine. "Are you sure you're okay?"

"I'm fine, really. I don't want to keep you from your job any longer. It was good seeing you, Talmage. Have a good evening."

His eyebrows furrow at my dismissal, and his lips tip down just a smidge before he rights them into his signature sunshiney smile. "You too, Mackenzie. Be safe out there. Maybe I'll see you around."

I sure hope not.

"Okay."

He turns around and walks back to the bright red firetruck I'm assuming he arrived in, and I shake off the weird emotions that have me feeling like I'm going to puke. Pulling my phone out of my pocket, I call Lizzie.

"Mack? Shouldn't you be at work already?"

"I was in an accident—"

"Oh my *God!* Are you okay?"

"I'm fine, Lizzie. I just need a ride to and from work tonight if that's okay?"

"Of course it's okay! Jesus. Drop me a pin, and I'll be right there."

"Thanks." I hang up and send her my location, then maneuver through the crowd of first responders to grab my purse and coat from my car.

Standing on the side of the road, I watch the first responders finish clearing up the minimal mess from the accident. My car is loaded on the tow truck by the time Lizzie arrives, and the driver gives me a card for the repair shop he's taking it to so I can check on it tomorrow.

I hop into the passenger seat of Lizzie's car, grateful she left the twins at home for this short trip because I can't stop myself from blurting, "Talmage is a firefighter."

Lizzie scans the crowd of firemen, and her lips pop open into an "o" when she spots him. "No *fucking* way, dude. Did he talk to you?"

"Yeah. He asked me where my coat was, then rambled about pneumonia and air quality? I don't know. Then he said, 'Maybe I'll see you around.'"

"No he didn't! God, what a douche!"

"I don't think he was trying to be a douche, I think we were both in shock. I mean, it's been almost eleven years since we graduated. Thirteen since he broke up

with me. He's clearly over it, and so am I. It was just...
unexpected."

Lizzie snorts. "Sure, Mack. I believe you. Not like
you've told me about the dreams."

I should have never fucking told her about them.
Almost every night since graduation, my mind creates
different dream scenarios where Talmage finds me and
declares his undying love for me. He says I'm the only
one he's ever wanted, he regrets ever breaking up, and
he's been trying to find me since graduation.

My brain is a cruel bitch.

Lizzie and I got drunk one night, and I told her about
the dreams. She's been a good friend and hasn't mentioned it.

Until now—the *worst* possible moment.

"Isn't he married?" she asks when I don't reply right
away.

"I don't know. I don't follow him on social media
anymore, remember?"

"Right, right. Well, good thing I have a free night
ahead to do some recon. FBI agent Lizzie Mikkelson at
your service." She gives me a little salute.

"God, please don't," I groan. "I don't want to see him
again. He's probably married to some pocket-sized Mol-
ly Mormon who has a penchant for baking bread and
canning in her spare time. They probably go to church
on Sundays and have regular family home evenings.
Hell, they probably have a gaggle of perfect blue-eyed,
blonde kids now."

Lizzie pulls up in front of Great and Spacious. A
ridiculous name for a bar, but it's a reference to Mormon
beliefs. Lehi, a "prophet" from The Book of Mormon,

had a dream where the "righteous" people held on to an iron rod—symbolism for the gospel of Christ—and there were people in a great and spacious building trying to "lure" them away from the path of righteousness.

The owners are ex-Mormons, and they thought it would be funny. I can't say I disagree.

"Well, I think everything happens for a reason, and maybe this is the universe trying to give you two a second chance." Lizzie waggles her eyebrows at me.

It's my turn to snort. "Yeah, right. That'll happen when pigs fly, and the U.S. gets universal healthcare. Thanks for the ride. Can you come pick me up at eleven?"

"Sure thing, bestie. Love you!"

"Love you, too."

I don't know what I believe about the universe or fate, but I *do* know Talmage Monson and I were never meant to be, and running into him was just a weird, cruel coincidence.

He's probably forgotten all about it by now, just like I need to.

CHAPTER 3

Talmage

14 years old...

I should be focusing on doing my homework, but I'm waiting for the little green dot to appear next to Mack's name so I can talk to her.

I've never hated the fact that I don't have my own cell phone until now.

I feel like I barely get to see her outside of school because we're both busy. I don't think I've ever missed someone the way I miss her when she's not around.

Every day after school, I walk her to the train tracks halfway between our houses. It's a longer path to my house, but I don't mind. I haven't gotten the nerve to touch her again, even though I really want to.

Sometimes, I can still feel the sparks from the time our pinkies touched.

I've never held hands with anyone before, so I'm nervous. How do I know when it's the right time to do it? What if she rejects me?

We're having a movie night at our friend Shaylee's house this weekend, and I hope Mack will sit next to me. Hope I can work up the nerve to finally hold her hand.

Part of me feels like we're breaking rules. Like we're doing something bad, since we're taught not to date until we're sixteen and never exclusively.

But we're not dating. We just have a mutual crush.

At least, I think we do.

I have a crush on her.

I think she likes me back.

A huge smile breaks out on my face when I see the green dot next to her name and three dots typing in the chat.

It's been a week since I saw Mack at the car accident, and she's been on my mind every moment since.

I haven't been able to stop thinking about her eyes, and the way they pierced through me. How sad they looked—more than just "I was in a car accident" sad. More than "this is a bad day" sad. A deep, to-the-bone sadness. A sadness I have an overwhelming urge to make better.

I haven't been able to stop thinking about the dip of her cupid's bow and the lovely pink shade of her lips.

I haven't been able to stop thinking about the look on her face when she recognized me—something a lot like hurt and shock. Wariness was painted all over her gorgeous face.

I haven't been able to stop thinking about the way she brushed me off and how it stung a bit when she didn't say she wanted to see me again, too.

I also haven't been able to stop thinking about the red of her hair or the gold rings piercing her nose. She looked so familiar but like a stranger at the same time.

I never would have pictured her with nose piercings.

But somehow, they suit her.

I've stopped myself from trying to find her on social media because what am I even looking for? A confirmation she's taken? To see how she's changed and what her life's been like post-graduation? A way to get back into her life?

We were best friends before we dated freshman year and into our sophomore year, so maybe I'm just feeling nostalgic about the relationship we had. How simple things were back then.

But a deeper part of me—the part I try to ignore—*knows* she's the one who got away, and it makes me want to reconcile and try again.

It feels like running into each other is a sign. A sign of what? I have no clue.

Maybe she's married, and this is just a chance for us to be friends again.

I hope it's not that.

I give in to my urge to look her up and type in her name, frowning when the profile I *think* is hers comes up as private. The picture is of a redhead with her hair in a bun facing away from the camera, a large moth tattoo is etched on the back of her neck. Would Mackenzie get a neck tattoo? I didn't notice any on her when I saw her, but she was also covered in long sleeves and pants, and her hair was down around her neck.

I request to follow her, then switch over to a different app and type in her name, but nothing comes up.

Huh. That's weird. I thought for sure we were friends at one point.

I'm already pushing it to get to family dinner on time, so I decide to investigate more a little bit later. I buckle my golden retriever into her doggy car harness and drive the short distance to my childhood home.

Siren barks when we arrive and darts to the door as soon as I have her unbuckled. Mom opens the door when she hears her furry grandbaby. Siren sits patiently on the porch until Mom gives her a head scratch and the okay to go inside.

"Hi, honey! How are you doing?" Mom greets me and wraps her arms around my waist, giving me a squeeze.

"Good, Mom. How are you?"

"Things are going. How has work been?" We step inside, and I take off my shoes, following her into the kitchen where she's stirring a pot of what smells like creamy potato soup.

She's still wearing her church dress, but she's exchanged her nylons for a pair of fuzzy socks and house slippers. Her graying blonde hair is pulled up with a clip, and her glasses are sitting perched on top of her head.

"It's been kind of slow. We've mostly been dealing with car accident calls this week, but luckily, nothing serious."

Mom sighs. "I don't understand how people who have lived here their whole lives forget how to drive in the snow."

"I don't know, but they've mostly been fender benders at least. Speaking of, last week there was an accident on Main Street, and Mackenzie Thorpe was involved."

I watch my mom for any sign of recognition. She wasn't really a fan of Mackenzie in high school, but I know she knows her parents.

Mom's stirring pauses before she slowly starts again. "Oh? I hope it wasn't too severe."

"No, she's fine. Did you know she moved back here?"

I watch Mom's head move with a nod. "After what happened, it would've been strange if she hadn't come back."

I furrow my brows. "What do you mean? After *what* happened?"

Mom lowers the heat of the burner and turns around to give me a puzzled look. "Her parents?"

My stomach starts to sink, and the hairs on the back of my neck stand up. "Did something happen to them?"

Mom's jaw drops open. "You don't know?"

"Obviously not." I want to scream, *If I knew, I wouldn't be asking.*

"The Thorpes passed away in a car accident five years ago. Mackenzie moved back to take care of her sisters," my little sister, Lauren, says as she enters the kitchen.

My jaw drops open. *How the heck did I not know that?*

Mom nods. "It was very tragic. A semi-truck driver had a heart attack at the wheel and swerved into the opposite lane of oncoming traffic. The Thorpes died on impact. I'm just glad they didn't suffer."

The story sounds familiar. I remember seeing something about it on social media or maybe the news, but I didn't know Mackenzie's parents were involved because

I never read the article, and no names were mentioned in the title. If I had known, I would have reached out. It explains the sadness in her eyes.

"Why didn't anyone tell me?"

Mom shrugs. "I figured you knew. It was all over the news and social media. I'm sure I mentioned it at some point."

My heart cracks in half. I had no idea something so tragic happened to her. No wonder she looked so shaken, even though the accident wasn't as bad as it could have been. Gosh, I can't even fathom how she must have felt or how hard it must have been to have to step into the role of parent after a tragedy like that.

"I guess I never realized it was *her* parents. That's terrible. I feel bad I never reached out."

"Well, why would you? It's not like you two were particularly close," Lauren adds, and I feel the weight of guilt grow heavier.

She's right, of course. After I broke up with her, we weren't even really friends. We were castmates at best. We got paired together a few times for dance numbers in musicals, and we went to dances with the same group of friends sometimes, shared choir classes and the occasional English class, but we didn't really *talk*. I remember thinking she always looked so sad after our breakup. Defeated, almost. It got particularly bad senior year, but I never paid much attention to the rumors going around about her. I had to keep my distance so I wouldn't give into the desire to beg her to give me another chance.

"We may not have been close friends, but I've still known her for years. This feels like something I should have given my condolences for."

"She probably didn't even realize you never reached out. She's clearly got stuff going on. I wouldn't worry about it or feel bad."

Why does that make my chest feel like it's burning? Did she truly just... *forget* all about me? I mean, I can't be upset if she did. I haven't exactly been thinking about *her* twenty-four-seven, but sometimes a song or a movie would remind me of her. She would pop into my head, and I'd wonder how she was doing.

This week, though, I've thought about her more than I have in the last ten years. I have this overwhelming *need* to see her. Even some of my drawings are starting to look like her, and I'm starting to feel like a freaking teenager with a crush again. I went to the grocery store and saw a flash of red hair and thought it was her, so I followed the poor stranger down the chip aisle until I realized it wasn't.

I don't say any of that to Mom and Lauren, though. I don't know if Mom still holds ill will towards her, and I don't need to have Lauren gossiping to Lacey, who goes to the same school as her sisters.

Conversation shifts as we sit around the table and start eating, but my mind never strays far from the girl who was my first love. My first kiss. My first real regret.

It takes all of dinner for all of us to give updates since there are five kids and my parents. My brother Thomas, who's two years younger than me at twenty-six, is finishing up his master's in civil engineering at BYU, tells us about his internship at the church headquarters where he's pretty much guaranteed a job after graduation.

Lauren's the next youngest at twenty-three and is just starting her master's program at BYU to be a music teacher. Mom asks her about her dating life, and—per usual—Lauren says she's not dating anyone. I don't know if she just doesn't date or if she doesn't tell anyone, but she's never brought anyone home, and I know my parents are worried she's too serious about school. I personally think it's good she's focusing on school instead of trying to get married, but I'm no longer blinded by the Mormon haze of thinking the only purpose in life is to get married and have babies.

The twins, Lacey and Timothy, are seventeen, and Timothy is on the track and field team while Lacey is in choir and theatre like I was. Tim is quiet and responds with one-word answers while Lacey could talk for hours if we let her. She's got a solo in the spring concert, and she hasn't stopped talking about it. I'm proud of her, though. I know sometimes her anxiety can get the best of her, and she gets stage fright, so this is a big step for her.

When it's my turn to give an update, I simply shrug and say nothing's new. Other than running into Mack, I don't have much I *can* tell them. Admitting I don't want to be a member of the religion I was born into isn't really something I can say over dinner, nor is it something I want to talk about in front of my siblings. Tim will be deciding whether or not he wants to go on a mission soon, and I don't want to be the reason he doesn't go, even if I think he could find a better use for his first two years out of high school.

"Well," Mom says as I help her serve dessert. "Sister Gleeson's daughter is moving back to Utah and was asking around for some eligible bachelors to date. I mentioned your name and said I'd see if you're interested."

I nearly roll my eyes. Mom means well, but I don't *want* to be set up with someone's daughter or grand-daughter or niece or second cousin.

While the pressure to get married isn't as heavy for men as it is for women, I still get a good dose of it because I'm almost thirty and single. It's not for a lack of trying, though. I just... haven't had the best luck finding some-one to match my energy. I can be over enthusiastic about my affection, and sometimes it's a turn off. I can't help it, though. When I want to be with someone, I don't do it halfway.

When I don't respond, Mom continues to tell me all about this girl. She's *twenty-two* and just graduated with a communications degree. She's moving back to Utah to work as a social media assistant to the Utah Polar Bears—our local ECHL hockey team. She's got blonde hair, blue eyes, loves to do Pilates, and—most impor-tantly—is looking for a "worthy priesthood holder" to be her eternal companion.

I can't tell my mom that just isn't me anymore.

"Mom, she's seven years younger than me. She's younger than *Lauren*."

Mom waves me off. "Only by a year. She seems like a nice girl! She comes from a good family and has a good job. Why won't you give her a chance?"

"She's too young!"

"Nonsense. Your cousin Hannah married a man ten years older than her. What's wrong with seven?"

"Hannah's prefrontal cortex was fully developed when she married Morgan, *and* she'd been married be-fore. She wasn't fresh out of college."

"Please, Talmage? One date." Mom's bottom lip wobbles, and I know what she's going to say before she says it. "I just don't want you to be alone anymore."

Aw, crud.

"Fine. I'll go on one date. Send me her number."

Maybe it won't be so bad. Maybe she's the one.

But even as I think it, I don't believe it because she's not a certain redhead from my past.

CHAPTER 4

Talmage

14 years old...

My hands are trembling as I sit next to Mack, trying to figure out how to be smooth about this.

She didn't hesitate to sit next to me on the couch, scooting over until our thighs were smooshed together. She said it was to make room for our friends, but I don't believe her.

She looks cute in her red skinny jeans and black and white shirt with a heart on it.

It's fitting, since I'm pretty sure she's stolen mine.

I put my arm down by my side, trying to nonchalantly move my hand closer to where hers is resting palm up, like she's waiting for me to make a move.

Taking a deep breath, I hover my hand over the top of hers.

She shocks me by meeting me halfway.

Our fingers intertwine, and my pulse picks up as sparks sizzle between us.

It feels so right.

Tayleigh is *not* the one. Just as I suspected.

But I did *try*, and I'm giving my all on this date. Tayleigh deserves my effort at least.

She's cute, I'll give her that. Long, blonde hair curled to perfection and blue eyes. She's got a bright white smile and perfectly manicured fingernails.

Honestly, if I didn't know better, I'd think we were related. Who knows, we might be somewhere down the line.

I decided to take her to a casual burger place for our date because I wanted to be able to talk and get to know her, and this place is really good. I thought it would be cute to maybe share a milkshake, but she told me she was "still recovering from the holiday fifteen" and didn't want to bloat from the dairy.

I can respect someone who wants to look after their health, but this feels like diet culture and not a health thing. What is the "holiday fifteen" anyway?

To further my suspicions she's under diet culture's grip, she ordered a salad with no dressing and refused to share an order of cheese fries—and the cheese fries here are the *best*. I assured her I wouldn't judge her if she wanted to eat something other than a salad, and she just brushed me off.

More cheese fries for me, I guess.

We're halfway through our meal, and so far, I'm not vibing with her. She's smart and knows a lot about current social media trends and how to get more engagement, but she still has so much life to live. I feel like we're at two very different places in our lives, which is blatantly obvious by the phrases she uses and her goals.

She talks about parties she's been to, the latest makeup trends, and her new job. All great things, but I'm not interested in parties. I'm interested in settling down and starting a family.

I'm determined to make the most of this date, even if I already know there won't be another one. I'm in the middle of telling her one of my stories from my brief stint as a hotshot when the bell above the door rings, and a flash of red hair catches my attention.

In walk Mack and her sisters. The three of them are talking quietly as they make their way to a table diagonal from where I'm sitting. As Mack sets her stuff down, she looks around the small restaurant, and her eyes snag on me. She does a double take, and I lift my fingers in a small wave. She hesitantly waves back, then turns and walks to the counter to order.

I don't know why my heart is racing so fast or why it suddenly feels like I want to burst into song, but I shake off the strange sensations as Tayleigh's voice pulls me back to reality.

"Talmage? Are you okay? You stopped mid-sentence."

"Yeah." *Does my voice sound high pitched?* "I just remembered I need some ranch for the fries. I'll be right back."

I get up and stand behind Mack in line. Her voice is soft but friendly as she orders, and for some reason, it gives me goosebumps.

When she's done, she turns around and startles when she sees me behind her. Her big green eyes widen, then blink up at me before she looks down, mutters, "Excuse me," and tries to walk around me.

"Hey, Mack. Did you get your car back?" I ask, desperately needing to hear her voice.

She turns halfway back to me before she says, "Yes."

"That's good. I'm glad... How are you?"

Her brows furrow, and she glances around like she's checking to make sure I'm talking to her and not someone else. "I'm fine, thanks. How are you?"

"Great, yeah. Can't complain." I don't know what else to say, but I want to keep talking to her. "Celebrating something tonight?"

She glances back at her sisters, and when she turns back her mouth is set in a small smile. "Kinsley made it to the state level for her science fair project, so we're celebrating."

I can't help the grin that spreads over my face. "That's awesome. What was her project on?"

Mack shifts from one foot to the other and scratches her head. "I honestly don't know how to explain it. Something with sugar energy, I think? She's better at explaining it. I've never been good at science stuff."

I hold back the nostalgic smile wanting to break free. Mack complained endlessly about biology our freshman year. That and math were her least favorite classes. "Nice. Well, tell her congrats."

"Will do. I'll, uh, let you get back to your date. Bye."

I honestly forgot Tayleigh was waiting for me, and it makes me feel like crap. Tayleigh and I may not be a good match, but she doesn't deserve to be ditched on a date.

"Right, yeah. See you around."

I head back to my table, and Tayleigh sets her phone down when I take my seat. "Did you get your ranch?"

"Huh?"

"Your ranch?" she says slowly. "The whole reason you went up to the counter?"

"Oh. No, they were out." Guilt swirls in my stomach at the lie. Tayliegh doesn't deserve lies either, but what am I supposed to say? *"I just wanted to talk to my ex-girl-friend because something is pulling me to her?"*

My eyes trail over to Mack's table as their food is brought out, and Tayleigh follows my line of sight.

"Doesn't she know it's not healthy to be eating stuff like that?" She shakes her head. "Her cortisol levels are probably insane. I think she'd be so pretty if she just lost the extra weight."

What?

My jaw goes slack, my hands pausing with my burger halfway to my mouth.

"I'm sorry?"

"I just mean she has a pretty face, but it's obvious she doesn't care about her health. She would be a lot prettier if she weren't, ya know, *big*. Or had those things through her nose. No man wants a woman who doesn't take care of herself."

"That's really, really mean. You can't know if someone is healthy or not based on how they look." I don't think Tayleigh would appreciate me telling her I think Mack is gorgeous as she is. Everything about her—from her eyes to her lips, to the messy waves of her hair and her generous curves—is absolutely breathtaking.

Tayleigh rears back as if I've slapped her. "You can't be serious. Look at what she's eating! Clearly, health isn't a priority."

"I'm eating more than she is. Does that make me unhealthy?"

Tayleigh's cheeks turn pink as her gaze wanders over me. "Well, no. You're a firefighter, so you're obviously very fit."

"Regardless of my job, you're not judging me for my food choices, so maybe you shouldn't judge her based on that either."

She looks like she wants to argue but doesn't. She just picks at her sad, bland lettuce and carrot mixture while I finish my burger.

When I take Tayleigh home, I tell her that while I had fun, I don't think we'll be seeing each other again. I don't kiss her goodnight or feel the excitement and anticipation when you have a crush.

When I get home, I take Siren out to do her business and spend the whole time thinking about Mack. She still seemed guarded when I was talking to her. Maybe it's because she wanted to get back to celebrating with her sisters, but I can't help feeling like it's something else.

Well, you broke her heart and haven't seen her in over a decade. You're not exactly BFFs.

Right, that makes a lot of sense.

Thinking about her *does* give me the excited anticipation you feel when you have a crush. I want to see her. I want to spend more time with her. I want to reacquaint myself with Mackenzie Thorpe and hear about what her life's been like the last ten years. Find out what's changed and what's the same.

When I finally get in bed, I check to see if she's accepted my follow request. I can't help but break out into a grin when I see she has. It looks like a lot of her posts are old, before her parents' accident. Pictures of her in tattoo chairs and showing off the designs she's had permanently etched into her skin.

I scroll until I get to a picture of her at the beach dated six years ago. Her hair is purple in the photo, and she's wearing an electric blue bikini that leaves very little to the imagination. My face flushes, and I know I should scroll past, but I can't seem to make myself.

I take in the softness of her round belly and the dips of her hips where the string of her bikini sits. I'm enthralled by the colorful artwork covering her thick thighs and the way her breasts seem to spill out of the triangles barely covering them. Her smile is wide and radiant, the nose rings glint in the sun, and her hair is thrown into two messy braids, her skin is pink from the sun and—

I throw my phone on the bed like it's on fire. I try to think of fire drills, the way my grandpa used to eat corn, and cleaning up Siren's poop.

When none of that works, I resort to singing hymns like I was taught to do on my mission to try to push away the arousal threatening to take me over. The trick works, but instead of lust I feel a slimy, icky sensation as the words pop up in my brain.

Even though I don't want to be part of the church anymore, some things are so ingrained in me it's hard to unlearn them. Masturbation being a sin is one of those. I've never given in to any of those urges—never really had them if I'm being honest—but the picture of Mack is tempting me to touch myself.

When I finally feel like I have control over my lust, I pick my phone back up and exit the app. No more scrolling through Mack's photos while I'm alone.

CHAPTER 5

Mackenzie

14 years old...

The breeze blows my hair across my face, and I use my free hand to tuck it behind my ear. Tal is walking me to the tracks halfway to my house, telling me all about the latest fantasy book he's reading.

I prefer a mystery or romance, but listening to Tal talk about the creatures and their powers is exciting.

Maybe it's because it's him, though.

He pauses to dig through his backpack and produces a lined piece of paper with doodles on it. The biggest sketch is of a dragon's body with three heads—a horse, a cow, and a pig.

A giggle bursts out of my throat. "What inspired this?"

He shrugs. "I don't know, I just wondered what a dragon with the heads of different animals would look like, so I drew it myself."

"You're really talented, Tal. This is a bit creepy, though."

His cheeks turn red. "I didn't think it'd look as weird as it does. Do you hate it?"

"Not at all. It's just a little... off-putting. But you know I like your art. Do you have anything else?"

Tal pulls out another paper, this one depicting some type of princess. The girl looks familiar, and—

My eyes shoot up to his. "Is this me?*"*

Tal nods, scratching the back of his neck. "I got a little distracted during science. They had us watch a movie since there was a substitute, my pencil kind of took on a mind of its own..."

Something soft and gooey flows through me at his admission. He's always doing simple, sweet stuff like this, stealing another piece of my heart every time.

I hold the paper to my chest. "Can I keep it?"

He gives me a dimpled grin. "Really?" I nod. "Of course, Firefly."

Talmage and I have existed in the same city for who knows how long, and I hadn't run into him once until my accident three weeks ago. But now? It seems to be a weekly occurrence for us.

First the car accident, then the burger place last week, and this week it's the grocery store.

I don't like talking to people in the store, so I wear headphones and go early on Sunday mornings to avoid the crowds. I've shopped at the same time every Sunday for over a year, and I've *never* seen the fire department here at the same time.

But there they are, dressed in their uniforms, with three freaking grocery carts full of food. I'm trying to avoid them, but they apparently like to divide and conquer, so every fucking aisle I go down, I find a firefighter, and my heart skips a beat every time wondering if it's him.

None of them have tried to talk to me, so I figured Talmage isn't part of the group.

I'm reaching for a box of cereal, and *of course* they moved it to the very top shelf. I'm only five-foot-five, so it's not like I can reach. I'm also not a small girl, so climbing on the shelves isn't a good idea.

I'm looking around for an associate or a tall person when a familiar blonde turns into the aisle with one of his buddies. I look away immediately but not before seeing Talmage's mouth twist into a grin.

Do I just leave the cereal and face the wrath of the twins?

Before I can answer my own question, there's a gentle tap on my shoulder.

I reluctantly take my headphones off and turn towards the two men.

"Hey, Mack. Fancy seeing you here. Do you need help with something?" Talmage asks.

I shake my head.

"You sure, doll? You looked like you were trying to get something on the top shelf. I'm happy to help you out," his buddy offers with a flirtatious smirk.

Now, I'm not immune to a man in uniform, and Talmage's friend isn't terrible looking with his slightly shaggy brown hair, light brown eyes, and clean-shaven face, but he's not my type.

Apparently, I only have it bad for blonde guys with mustaches and clear blue eyes.

"Enoch, stop flirting with Mack." Talmage smacks him on the shoulder.

"I was just offering her some help! Can't help I'm a natural flirt when it comes to pretty women." Enoch throws a wink my way, and to my absolute horror, my cheeks flush.

"Good grief." Talmage pinches the bridge of his nose. "Mack, is there something you need from the top shelf *I* can help you reach?"

I guess now I don't have to find a store associate. "Um. That cereal, please." I point to the box I want, and Talmage reaches up and grabs it with ease. His extra six inches makes all the difference, apparently.

"Thanks," I say, tossing the box in my basket. "Uh, happy shopping. See you around."

I start to push my cart towards the opposite end of the aisle when I hear Talmage call, "Mack, wait up!"

Heaving a sigh, I reluctantly stop and turn around.

"I was wondering if you'd like to go to dinner some-time."

Ummmm. What?

"Why?"

He reaches up and rubs the back of his neck, his cheeks pinkening. "Well, we haven't seen each other since grad-uation, and I think it'd be nice to catch up. Reminisce about high school."

I would rather saw off my big toe with a rusty kitchen knife than reminisce about high school.

"Uh, sure. I mean, my schedule is pretty busy, though, so it might be a while before I can find some free time."

Talmage's smile widens. "That's totally fine. Can I get your number so we can plan a time that works with both our schedules?" He pulls his phone out of his pocket and hands it to me.

I blink at it like I've never seen a cell phone in my life. *What is happening right now?*

First, he follows me on Instagram—I don't even want to think about why I accepted his request—and now he wants my number? I feel like I've entered some alternate timeline.

I put my contact information in his phone and hand it back to him.

"Thanks, Mack. I'm really excited. I'll text you soon, and we can make a plan. Enjoy the rest of your Sunday."

Then, he moves like he's going in for a hug but decides he shouldn't, so he kind of hovers in the air with his arms out before he brings them down and holds his hand out for a fist bump.

I bump my fist with his, he turns back to his friend, and I return to my grocery shopping.

I'm not expecting him to text me. He's probably just being friendly.

That is, until I check my phone when I get in the car, and I have a message.

> **Unknown:** Hey Mack! <smile emoji> This is Talmage. I just wanted you to have my number in case you need anything. I'll text you about dinner soon. Have a wonderful Sunday! <sun emoji> <smile emoji>

It's been four days since the run-in with Talmage, and he's texted me every day since. Sometimes, it's just a simple *hope you're having a good day!* Other days, he asks how I'm doing.

I don't know what to make of it, and I don't know what to do. I feel like I'm losing my mind.

It's almost 7 p.m., and I haven't heard from him at all. I feel like a fucking teenager again, checking my phone to see if he's texted me. Half hoping he hasn't so I can get my head on straight and half hoping he has because I like his attention more than I care to admit.

I don't think Talmage has a mean bone in his body, so I don't think he's playing mind games, but I've been wracking my brain trying to figure out what the *hell* his motivations are. Why is he so insistent now when there's been radio silence since we graduated? He barely acknowledged my existence before that.

The girls and I have already had dinner, and I'm settled in the bath with my Kindle and a mug of chamomile tea when my phone rings.

I'm expecting it to be Lizzie since she's the only one who ever calls me, so I don't look at the caller ID before I answer. "Hey, hot stuff, how's it going?"

There's a pause, and then the sound of someone clearing their throat.

Oh, no. No. No. No.

"Uhh hi, Mack," Talmage says with an awkward chuckle. "Expecting your boyfriend to call?"

I mentally slap my forehead. "No, I was expecting Lizzie to call. I'm so sorry."

"You and Lizzie are dating?"

Jesus Christ.

"Uhhhh no. We just answer the phone like that sometimes."

"Oh. I'm glad to see you two are still so close."

Lizzie and I have been best friends since our sophomore year of high school. Sometimes I forget she and Talmage know each other since we were all in choir and theatre together.

"Yeah, she's been a lifesaver." *Literally.*

"That's good. I was just calling to see if you were available Saturday night. I'm not working and was hoping we could get dinner."

"I'm actually working Saturday night."

"Oh? Where do you work?"

"Well, I have two jobs." *Why am I telling him this?* "I work as a bid desk specialist for a tech company during the week and then pick up shifts as a bartender at Great and Spacious."

"Oh." I don't like that I can't read his tone. Most Mormons get judgy when they hear I'm a bartender. Alcohol being against the rules and all that. "That's cool. What time does your shift start?"

"Uh, six?" I don't know why I pose it as a question. I know my own damn schedule.

"Well, what about lunch, then? Or breakfast? I'm free any time on Saturday." Why does he sound so eager? Why is he so hellbent on going out with me? What does he want?

Why is the universe being such a bitch? Haven't I been through enough? Can't I just... forget about my teenage love and move on?

Apparently not. And apparently, I'm a masochist.

"Lunch works, but I probably only have an hour or so. How about one?" That should give me enough time to have lunch, freak out about having lunch with him, then get ready for work while I dissect every single thing that happens at lunch.

"Sounds great! Is there anywhere in particular you want to go?"

My budget wants me to stay in and eat ramen. I can probably splurge a little on lunch.

"I'm not picky," I say instead of burdening him with my financial crisis.

"How does Valley Baker sound?"

"That sounds great." *And cheap.*

"Amazing. I'm looking forward to it. I'll let you get on with your night. Sweet dreams, Mack."

"Yeah, thanks. You, too, Talmage."

I hang up before he can say anything else, smacking my head lightly with my phone.

I chug the rest of the chamomile, hoping it will knock me out so I won't have dreams about the fireman with the shiny blue eyes and the brightest smile I've ever seen.

I know it won't work though. Even when I was taking sleep medication that was basically a tranquilizer, I couldn't escape the dreams.

Except, this isn't a dream. This is—somehow—my reality.

What does Talmage want from me anyway? Is this some kind of pity thing? I'm sure he's heard about my parents by now. It's been five years, though, so why would he be trying to get in contact now?

The sharp sting of grief hits me right in the chest like it always does when I think of my parents. Of how alone I felt when they died. How confused I was dealing with the funeral arrangements and stepping into a guardian role for the twins. How a small part of me wished Talmage would have reached out then, to offer his big bear hugs that always seemed to calm me when we were friends.

It's been thirteen years, Mack. You can't keep holding on to the past.

But how am I supposed to let go when the past has come back to haunt me?

CHAPTER 6

Talmage

14 years old...

Butterflies swirl around in my stomach as I wait for Mack at her locker. It's the last day of school before Christmas break, and I was up much later than I should have been so I could get this little project done for her.

I hear her laughter before I see her, and the nerves increase.

I hope she doesn't think this is weird.

The minute she turns the corner, her smile widens, and she skips over to me, wrapping me in a hug.

I melt into her embrace—something that's become a habit when we see each other. Hugging her is the best part of my day.

"I'll never get tired of your bear hugs," she says when she pulls back. "I should call you Bear, since you call me Firefly."

"I feel like bears would scare fireflies. Maybe even eat them. Do you think they eat fireflies?"

Her friend snickers, and Mack's cheeks turn red.

What did I miss?

"Um, maybe. I don't know what bears eat."

"Fair enough." I hold my hands out and give her the newspaper wrapped package. "Merry early Christmas, Firefly."

She gasps as she takes it. "Tal, I didn't get you anything!"

"I don't need anything. It's not much, obviously, but I was hoping it'd make you think of me over the break.

"I always think about you, silly. But thank you. Do you want me to open it now?"

"No, you can open it when you get home." I don't need her to open it in front of her friends and see the private, sappy things I've written to her—about her.

Or the drawings I've sketched of her as a princess again, only this time, I'm next to her, dressed as a knight.

My knee is bouncing uncontrollably, and my palms are sweaty as I wait for Mack inside Valley Baker.

I've had the biggest smile on my face since Wednesday night when she agreed to lunch. Enoch and Nathan have been teasing me mercilessly since our encounter at the grocery store.

Enoch pointed out that Mack looked... uneasy when we were talking, but if she were uncomfortable with me, she wouldn't have agreed to come to lunch with me.

Right?

She's probably hesitant because of our history and—

My leg stops bouncing as realization hits me.

Does she feel obligated to meet me? Am I just bothering her and bringing up more hurt by asking her to have lunch?

Shoot. Am I a bad person?

I'm about to text her to tell her she doesn't need to come if she doesn't want to when the front door opens and...

A literal angel walks in.

The sun shining behind Mack makes her red hair glow like an ember—it's how she earned the nickname "Firefly" when we were teens—and casts her in an ethereal glow. It may be chilly outside but seeing her makes my whole body heat up.

The breath is knocked out of my lungs—I need an oxygen mask stat.

I swear I've never seen someone so beautiful.

She waves at me with a tight-lipped smile, kicking me into gear. I shake off the way my pulse thunders in my ears and stride towards her, stopping myself short of wrapping her in a hug. I have the strongest urge to feel the curves of her body pressed against mine, but I have a feeling I need to take things slow so I don't scare her.

"Hey, Mack. It's good to see you. You look amazing."

She glances down at her body, at the black skinny jeans and denim shirt she's wearing underneath her winter coat, and she scrunches her nose in that adorable, familiar way. "Thanks? It's good to see you, too."

Gosh, she's cute.

"Ready to order?" I motion to the counter, and she steps in front of me. I *don't* look down at where the curve of her butt meets her thick thighs. Okay, maybe I do. Just quickly. Not in an objectifying way, I swear.

"It's been a minute since I've been here. What do you like?" I ask as she studies the menu board.

"I'm simple. I like the turkey and provolone with tomatoes and banana peppers. I love their twice baked potato soup, but they only have it on Wednesdays."

I make a mental note to pick up some twice baked potato soup for her on a Wednesday sometime.

Hmmm. I'll need to get her address so I can deliver it. I wonder if she still lives in her childhood home.

"It is pretty good. Only second to my mom's creamy potato, but I'm biased. Have you ever tried their breakfast sandwiches or their French toast?"

She shakes her head. "I've only been here a handful of times in a pinch before a shift at the bar, so I've only had their lunch and dinner options."

"We'll have to come back for breakfast sometime," I say without really thinking it through. I'd love to have a breakfast date with her, though.

I feel the overwhelming need to see her as soon as she wakes up. What does she sleep in? Does she braid her hair or let it be loose and wild across her pillows? Is she grumpy in the morning, or is she a happy riser? I bet she drinks coffee now. I wonder how she likes it. There are all sorts of fancy coffee drinks, right? I wonder if she likes her coffee fancy.

Mack doesn't respond as the cashier waves us forward and takes her order. She pulls her wallet out to pay, but I step up next to her and push her hand down with mine.

I swear there's a shock of electricity when our hands touch.

Maybe I'm just staticky. That happens when the weather is as dry as it is in Utah.

"We're together. Well, not *together* together but I'm paying for lunch."

Mack frowns. "Tal, I can—"

"I know you can, but I want to. Please." *She called me Tal!*

That's progress! It means she's not as uncomfortable as I thought, right?

Mack huffs and shoves her wallet into her pocket again, stepping away so I can order. I get a chicken salad sandwich and a bag of chips, tacking on an extra drink for Mack since she didn't order one.

The scowl on her face when I hand her the empty cup is so freaking cute, I have to bite my lip to suppress a smile. She's like a little ticked off kitten.

I don't think she'd appreciate it if I said that out loud.

We fill up our drinks and find a booth in the corner of the restaurant away from the people here for their Saturday lunches.

When Mack takes off her coat, I see her arms aren't covered by long sleeves, and I get to admire the ink I've only seen in pictures.

On her left arm is a hodgepodge of mushrooms, moths, and multitude of different florals filling in the blanks. On her right are delicate roses and leaves. Both arms are inked from her shoulder to her wrist.

They're stunning, just like her.

When I finally look up at her, her cheeks are pink, and she crosses and uncrosses her arms, rubbing her hands up and down them before placing them in her lap.

"They're gorgeous," I blurt out, startling both of us. I motion to her tattoos.

"Oh, uh, thank you. Lizzie did most of them." The pink on her cheeks turns darker.

"Oh, that's cool. Did they hurt?"

"Not really." She shrugs.

"What about your piercings?" I wave a hand in the general direction of her face.

"The one that hurt the most is my conch." She moves her hair and shows me a gold hoop through the middle part of her ear. "Well, no, that was the second most painful. My—never mind. Uh. They didn't hurt as bad as I thought they would. Each one gets easier."

I *really* want to know what she was going to say her worst piercing was. She has the two in her nose and a few in her ears. I didn't see her other ear, so maybe there's another piercing that hurt worse?

Maybe her belly button is pierced. That would probably hurt really bad.

"That's cool. I've never thought much about getting my ears pierced. What do you think? Could I pull off some shiny gold hoops?" I hold my hands up like I'm showing off my ears, and it pulls a small smile from her.

Win.

Her eyes dart around my face before she shrugs. "I think you'd look hot with a piercing."

Now it's my turn to blush. If I didn't work at a station that prohibited jewelry, I'd be looking up the closest piercing shop.

One of the workers brings over our food, and Mack and I tuck in. I feel like time is slipping by too fast for me to actually ask her any questions. I don't know if she'll agree to have a meal with me again. I need this to go well so she wants to hang out with me again.

"Why do you work two jobs?" I ask, then immediately regret it when she chokes on her sandwich.

After she takes a sip of her drink and is no longer choking, she gives me a sad smile. "Do you want the short answer or the long one?"

"The long one, obviously." I would listen to her talk for hours.

"Harper has Type I diabetes. Her glucose monitoring is expensive, plus the bi-annual doctor's visits. We had a little bit of money from my parents' life insurance policies and my dad's retirement, but we had to spend a good chunk of it to pay for the funeral. I want the girls to have good college funds and a nest egg for their futures. I work two jobs so Harper can *live* and have as normal of a life as possible."

My heart breaks for Mack. She's sacrificing so much for her sisters. I admire her resilience, but I wish she didn't have to work so hard.

"Doesn't your job offer insurance?"

"Yes, but it's not nearly enough to cover everything. The system kind of sucks for diabetics." Mack shifts in her seat, rubbing her hands on her thighs.

"I'm sorry, Mack. I can't even imagine what you must have gone through the last five years." I reach across the table and grab her free hand. "I'm sorry I never reached out when your parents passed. I didn't know about it until recently. I wish I had known sooner so I could have helped or-or—"

"It's okay," she interrupts with another sad smile. "If you didn't know, it's not your fault. I probably wouldn't have accepted your help even if you offered. Besides, we hadn't talked in nearly a decade. I didn't expect you to reach out."

I can tell she really, truly means that, and it stings a little.

She's right, though. I didn't reach out.

Not because I didn't *want* to. I just didn't *know.*

Why does that make me feel even worse? Does she really think she meant so little to me that I wouldn't try to reach out when she went through something so tragic?

Granted, I haven't reached out *at all.* But I think she's blocked me on Facebook.

"I'm still sorry. Is there anything I can do to help you now?" I ask, and when she pulls her hand away from me, I realize I was still holding it.

And I miss the touch of her skin as soon as it's gone.

"Unless you can magically change my insurance, no." She awkwardly chuckles. "But thanks."

"Yeah, of course." I smile, even though I hate that I can't fix her problems.

"Do you like working at the FD?" she asks, picking up her sandwich again.

"I love it." I tell her about being a captain and all the responsibility it entails. The training, overseeing station operations, heading emergency responses when I'm on duty. I tell her I tried to be a hotshot, but it didn't work out. There's still some adrenaline that comes with the job, but it's not quite as risky as fighting wildfires. While I liked the fast-paced energy of being a firefighter in California, the slower pace here is nice.

"Wow. That's really cool. I always thought you'd end up doing something with art, and I know you wanted to be a teacher at one point. How did you end up as a firefighter?"

My smile widens at her mention of my art. I used to draw the most random creatures that would pop into my head. Mack used to ask me to see them at the end of the day, and I'd explain what they were, and she always used to ask when I was going to draw her. I only sketched her a few times, but I never felt I could fully capture her beauty the way I wanted to.

I haven't gotten out my sketchpad and pencils in a while. Life's gotten in the way.

"After my mission, I went to school to be a teacher and realized it wasn't for me. I met Enoch and Nathan in the student ward. They told me I should come check out an EMS class, and I really liked it. The prospect of helping people appealed more to me than teaching bored teenagers the basics of drawing."

"That's really cool. Do you still draw, at least?"

"Not as much as I used to. Do you still write?"

She shakes her head. "I haven't had the time or the inspiration. I'm lucky if I can get time to read."

Mack used to always have her head bent over a notebook, writing poems or stories. I know at one point she wanted to be an author, but I guess it would be hard to do when you're working two jobs and trying to raise teenagers after a tragedy like losing your parents.

Mack's so strong. She's so brave and caring for taking over as guardian for her sisters when she could have easily said she didn't want to do it.

"What else have you been up to since graduation?"

"Well, I moved to Oregon about a year after and went to a community college in Bend for two semesters before I dropped out and moved to California. I lived there for four years before I moved back home."

"What were you studying?"

"Criminal Justice."

Hm. That was never something I thought she'd be interested in. "What did you want to do with that degree?"

"I wanted to be a victims' advocate."

"Is that still something you'd want to pursue?"

Mack shrugs. "Sure, if I had the time or money. When I dropped out to move to Cali, that dream kind of fizzled out."

She seems like she doesn't want to talk about this anymore, so I switch topics. "What part of California did you move to?"

"Bakersfield."

"Oh, cool. I was in the San Diego area for about two years. Kind of crazy we were in the same state. I wonder if we were ever in the same city at the same time and just missed each other."

"I mean, we've lived in the same small city for how long and haven't run into each other until recently."

I chuckle. "True. California is massive. What made you move there?"

Mack covers her face with her hands and groans. "Don't judge me, but I followed my then-boyfriend there. He wanted to make it as a musician, so I bartended to pay bills while he did... whatever he was doing."

My stomach swoops and drops to my butt at her admission, and something like jealousy sours in my gut.

Which is ridiculous. Of course she's dated other people. We're almost thirty. *I've* dated other people.

I hold up my hands. "No judgment from me. Did you like it there?"

"It was okay. Whenever I pictured living in California, I pictured the beach and endless sunny days, you know? Bakersfield wasn't like that, obviously." An alarm on her phone rings, and she quickly clicks it off. "I'm sorry, but I have to get going so I can get ready for work. It was really nice to see you, Tal." She gathers her trash, sucking down the last of her drink and standing to take it to the garbage.

I don't want her to go. I want to keep talking, keep getting to know the Mack she is now. I don't think we've even scratched the surface of what she's been up to in the last ten years, and I'm greedy for more knowledge. I want to know when she left the church—*why* she left the church. I want to know every story and detail about the ink on her skin. I want to know how I can help make her life easier. I want to put more smiles on her face and see if she laughs the same way she used to when we were teenagers—loud and uninhibited.

But I can't beg her to stay, and I can't ask her to call in sick. That would be selfish of me.

"Let me walk you to your car." I hold the door open for her after she puts on her coat, and I follow her to the same blue Camry she was in when she got rear-ended.

She unlocks it but doesn't get in just yet.

I open my arms, offering her a hug, even though I'm pretty sure she's going to refuse it. She hesitates for a minute, an emotion I can't place swirling in her green eyes before she tentatively steps forward and wraps her arms loosely around my waist.

With our height difference, my nose hovers over her hair. I don't know what shampoo she uses, but she smells so good—citrusy and sweet. I have to resist burying my nose in her hair to inhale more of her. Then, I have to resist the urge to plant a kiss on her forehead.

Too soon, she steps back. "I'll see you around, Tal."

"We should hang out again soon. I'll text you."

With a tight nod, she ducks into her car. I step back as she starts it and pulls out of the parking space, waving as she drives away.

This isn't the last time I'll see her.

I'm not even remotely close to satisfied when it comes to all things Mackenzie Thorpe.

CHAPTER 7

Mackenzie

14 years old...

T he minute I'm in my room, I rip the newspaper off of the gift Tal gave me.

Inside is a composition notebook, "Firefly" written in swooping, swirling letters on the front.

I open the front page and grin when I see his neat scrawl.

Merry Christmas! I hope you get what you asked for.

I know my wish has already come true by being your friend.

I can't wait to see you again.

Love,

Tal

Talmage is too sweet. My nose scrunches at the word "friend" because it doesn't feel like we're just friends. I don't know what we are, since all we've done is hold hands, but friends doesn't feel like a strong enough word.

I love him. Maybe it's puppy love or whatever adults say when you talk about your crush, but this feels like so much more than a simple crush or friendship. Tal's become *my best friend, the boy I'm in love with. Someone I can't imagine a future without.*

I turn to the next page, and my breath catches in my throat as I take in the sketch of us. Me, in a flowing gown with a tiara on my head, and Tal in a suit of armor. Even in the picture, he's looking at my character like she's precious.

I can't wait to see him after the break.

I truly thought after the awkward lunch with Talmage, he'd be done with whatever... reunion thing he was so adamant about, but no.

The man won't stop texting me. Not in a creepy way, but in a "hey, we were best friends and at one point dated, and I want to be friends again" way.

And I don't... hate it.

I hate that I don't hate it.

I hate that I want to let him back in. I hate that I want to confide in him and tell him everything about my day.

I don't want to long for the attention of my first love, but the teenager in me already has "Mrs. Talmage Monson" scrawled on her notebooks again. She's already started wondering what a wedding would look like and then pouted when I had to remind both of us this is *Talmage.*

Mormon golden boy and fireman heartthrob. Out of my league and too sweet for someone as jaded and broken as me.

Which is another reason I don't understand why he's so adamant about hanging out again. What could he possibly want with a burned-out, overworked guardian of teens?

A week has passed since our lunch, and he still texts me almost daily. He wanted to hang out today, which I thought was strange since it's Sunday, but I have another shift at the bar, so I had to decline.

Walking into Great and Spacious, my phone pings again.

Talmage: Hope you have a good shift! Let me know when you get home so I know you're safe. <smi-ley emoji>

Mackenzie: Thanks. Will do.

Am I being a bitch to him? Why does he care if I get home safe?

At the same time, my heart flutters, and the teenager in me sighs and swoons at how sweet he is.

"What's got a smile on that usually downturned mouth?" Joanna, the bar manager, calls from her position behind the register.

I shake my head and put my phone back in my pocket on "do not disturb." The only calls that will come through are from Harper, Kinsley, and Lizzie in case of an emergency. When I interviewed for the bartending position, I was transparent about my situation and how I'd need to have some type of accommodations in case something happens. Luckily, the owners, Gordan and Marie, were more than happy to oblige.

There hasn't been an emergency since I started here, thank goodness, but I still get anxious every time I have to leave my sisters alone for a shift. My mind swirls with anxiety thinking about Harper's blood sugar getting too low or someone breaking in and trying to kidnap them, and no one being there to protect them.

I know they're fifteen, and I'm not their mother, but I am their guardian. I'm still overly protective of them. They're the only family I have left, and I'm theirs. I don't know what would happen if we were to lose each other.

After putting the rest of my stuff in my employee locker and clocking in, I step behind the bar and start slicing limes and lemons next to where Joanna is still setting up the till.

"Well, are you going to answer me?" Joanna asks, shutting the register and turning to me.

Joanna is only in her early forties, but she still acts like a mother hen. She gives off major "don't fuck with me" vibes with her ice blonde, spiky pixie cut and dark eyeliner over her brown eyes. Her ears are filled with so many piercings I'm surprised they can hold them, and she's got a spiky black septum ring pierced through her nose.

I want to be her when I grow up.

Despite her outward appearance, the woman is a softie at heart and *lives* for gossip and drama.

She's been trying to get the lowdown on my non-existent love life since I started working here, and I haven't had anything to tell her.

Not that I have anything to tell her *now*. I'm not dating anyone.

I shrug while I quarter the lime on the cutting board. "Just a friend."

Joanna snorts. "Right. A *friend.* A friend who made your permanent frown turn into a smile. The only other person who's made you smile is Marie, and that's because she's the sweetest woman you'll ever meet."

She's right, Marie *is* the sweetest woman I've ever met. She's a petite, polite grandma type who makes quilts for the staff for Christmas and feeds stray cats.

She reminds me a lot of my mom, which makes me nostalgic and sad, but also comforts me when the days are darker than I'd like them to be.

I didn't even realize I was smiling about Tal's text. Now I'm even more upset with myself because I *shouldn't* be smiling over it. I should be annoyed he's somehow worked his way back into my life and is acting like a fucking gentleman, making me want to kick my feet and giggle every time he texts me.

I'm twenty-eight! I can't be acting like a teenager with a crush. Even if I feel like one.

"You're really not going to give me anything?" Joanna pushes her bottom lip out in a pout, and I shake my head. "Fine. Someday you'll have some juicy gossip for me, and I'll be ready and waiting with a shot of vodka."

Never gonna happen.

Sunday shifts are either hectic as fuck or slower than cold tar. Tonight, apparently, no one wants a drink before the work week starts, so I've been cleaning bottles and mixing new cocktails for our regular patrons to try.

Most of them are crotchety old men who stick to their whiskey or Bud Light, but they don't say no when Joanna tells them they get to be guinea pigs because they're scared of her.

I'm just setting down a Moscow mule made with jalapeño vodka in front of the men when the bell above the door rings. Joanna calls out she'll check IDs, so I wait while I watch them try their first sip.

Keith, the retired PD chief, chokes and coughs after taking a sip. "Mack, what in tarnation is this? You tryna kill me?"

That makes my lip twitch. "Come on, Keith. A little jalapeño never hurt anyone," I tease.

"You made this with that jalapeño vodka?" Randy bristles, pronouncing jalapeño "ja-lop-en-oh."

"I'm trying to add some new flavors to the menu. You guys don't like it?" I already know their answer. They don't like anything I make aside from their usuals.

They're not very good guinea pigs.

"Hell no! Get that shit away from me. All I need is a beer. Stop trying to expand my tastes, Mack. If I wanted that I'd go to the fancy-shmancy, hipster cocktail bar on Main," Keith grouses.

I don't take his grumpiness personally. I learned pretty quickly he's this way with everyone.

I grab their copper mugs and take them back to the kitchen, putting them in the dirty dish bin before heading behind the bar.

Joanna slides in next to me with a wicked smile on her face and a mischievous glimmer in her eye. A smile that says there's some hot gossip brewing, and I'm going to get an earful.

"You'll never guess who's here," she whispers.

I scan the bar for the new arrival, and as soon as I see who she's talking about, my entire body goes rigid.

Golden hair and a matching mustache, piercing blue eyes. He looks so out of place here in his white button down and suit pants. He looks like he just came from church and left his suit jacket and tie in the car. *What the hell is he doing here?*

She chuckles at my reaction. "And you'll *never* guess who Peter Priesthood asked to see."

I swallow down the urge to duck into the back room and pretend I'm not here. That won't work because I'm a shitty liar, and Talmage already knows I'm working tonight.

If I did that, Joanna wouldn't let me live it down, and I'd have to explain why just the sight of him makes me want to run for the hills.

"He's just a friend." I know it's the wrong thing to say as soon as I say it because Joanna's grin only grows.

"A *friend*, huh? The same friend who had you smiling at your phone?"

"No," I lie, which turns my face and chest red. *Damn my pale skin.*

"Right. I *totally* believe you. I'll man the bar; you go put your *friend* out of his misery and talk to him. He looked like an eager puppy who was about to pee on the floor when he asked to speak to you, and I'm not cleaning it up."

"Okay," I grumble, wishing I could take a shot of something to calm my nerves *and* erase the mental image Joanna just put in my head.

The walk from behind the bar to the table where Talmage sits scrolling on his phone feels like it takes ages.

Why is he here? *On a Sunday? In a bar? Asking for* me?

Nothing makes sense.

I clear my throat when I approach, and he immediately sets his phone down and jumps up from his chair with a beaming smile, wrapping me in a tight bear hug.

"Hey, Mack! I'm so happy to see you."

I tentatively wrap my arms around his narrow waist and try my hardest *not* to greedily inhale his scent. He smells like leather and cinnamon, and it makes me a little dizzy.

"You, too," I mumble against his broad chest.

I reluctantly step back. It was hard to pull away from him at Valley Baker, and it's hard to pull away now. "What are you doing here?"

Talmage's smile never falters as he shrugs. "I wanted to see you. I figured if I can't hang out with you outside of work, I could try to hang out with you *at* work. And I have something I want to talk to you about."

But WHY? I want to scream. *WHY ARE YOU SO ADAMANT ABOUT HANGING OUT? WHAT DO YOU WANT? Hasn't my heart suffered enough?!*

"Right. But... you don't go to bars."

Talmage tilts his head to the side. "Why would you think that?"

"Well, you're Mormon? And it's Sunday? And you're... *you*. Tal, you look like you just stepped out of church." I motion to his ensemble.

Talmage dramatically clutches his chest. "You wound me, milady. But you're not wrong. I did just step out of church, and I've never been to a bar until now. As for the Mormon thing..." He waves his hand in the air in a "so-so" motion, and my confusion only grows.

"Okaaaay. Wh-what does that mean?"

He waves his hand dismissively, and I snatch it out of the air. I ignore the way my stomach swoops when our hands touch and the way his eyes track to our hands. Does he feel the spark between us, too? "No, no. We're not breezing past that. What do you mean?"

With a heavy sigh, Tal motions for me to sit down. I glance back at Joanna, and she gives me an encouraging nod and another knowing smile. I know I'm going to have to give her a play-by-play after.

"I think—no, not think—I *want* to leave the church. I haven't figured out how to do it without breaking my parents' hearts, but I don't want to be part of it any-more."

Whaaaaat?

I pinch my thigh to make sure this isn't some type of dream. *Ouch.* No, not a dream.

"But... why?" I ask.

"Well, why did *you* leave?"

I shift in the wooden chair. No way in hell I'm getting into *that* with him right now. It's a long story wrapped in trauma and can only be told after at least two shots of tequila.

"Let's just say my reasons for leaving the church are probably way different than yours."

"Fair enough." He leans forward like he's about to share a government secret with me. "Do you know how much money the church hoards? Did you know Joseph Smith was a pedophile? Or that he lied about how he translated the *Book of Mormon*? Or that there's a whole secret temple ceremony the rich men can pay for that basically absolves them of all of their sins and guarantees them entrance into The Celestial Kingdom? Do you know how many sexual abuse victims—*children*—are swept under the rug because the church covers it up with their fancy lawyers?"

Tal's usual happy smile is nowhere to be seen. Instead, with every new question he asks, his lips turn down more. His eyes lose a little sparkle with every piece of information he shares. He looks genuinely distraught over these things.

"I know all of those things, yes."

I know from personal experience how the church treats the victims of sexual abuse and rape. That was enough for me to leave, but I learned the rest of it through ex-Mormon podcasts and videos. It only solidified my choice.

Talmage shakes his head. "I never realized how terrible it was. How sexist and racist and... dishonest. I only started learning last year, and in October, my cousins pointed out even more. I just... I'm in deep, and I don't know how to get out without blowing everything up."

I reach across the table and grab his hand again, giving it a gentle, reassuring squeeze.

"I wish I could tell you it's easy, but our situations are different. I can't tell you how it'll go, but…" I don't know if I'll regret my next words, but I say them anyway, "I'll be here if you need help."

Tal's answering smile is like the clouds parting on a cloudy day.

CHAPTER 8

Talmage

14 years old...

Mack doesn't see me. She throws her head back in a laugh, loud and boisterous, and my smile spreads across my face.

I didn't forget how beautiful she is, but seeing her again in person after two weeks makes me appreciate it even more.

As if she can sense my presence, her head turns to me, and she excuses herself from the group, rushing towards me with open arms.

"Bear! I missed you so much. Did you have a good break?"

"Missed you, too, Firefly. Yeah. It was fun. How was yours?"

"It was good. I have a late Christmas present for you." She grabs my hand and pulls me towards her locker, twisting the knob and pulling it open before she reaches in and grabs a familiar notebook from her backpack.

"I thought maybe we could start trading the notebook back and forth. You could draw in it, I could write in it, or we could just leave notes for each other."

"This is perfect."

She smiles again, wider than before. "Yeah? You don't think it's silly?"

"Not at all. I think it's kind of... romantic."

"Thank you so much, Mack. It means a lot to me." I didn't come here to tell her about my deconstruction journey, though, so I squeeze her hand again and clear my throat. "I mentioned earlier I have something I want to talk to you about."

"Oh, right. What's up?"

This next part is going to make or break whatever bond of friendship we've been mending. But I think it will help both of us a lot.

"I think I have a solution to your insurance problem. A way to help you so you don't have to work so hard."

She narrows her eyes at me, pursing her lips in a way that makes them look plump and biteable and—

Not the time, Tal.

"I'm listening..."

I take a fortifying breath, staring deeply into her mossy green eyes. "Marry me."

Her eyes bug out of her head, and her mouth gapes open before she starts cackling. Loud, uninhibited, true laughter that grabs the attention of the older gentlemen at the bar and makes me equal parts happy and embarrassed.

Is marrying me really this funny?

She must see the mortification on my face because her laughter stops almost immediately. "You're... you're serious?"

I nod.

I've been thinking about it since she told me about her financial issues. I've been wracking my brain trying to figure out a way to help her.

I started looking into my health insurance benefits and found my dependents would be totally covered. If Mack were married to me, since she's already the primary guardian of the girls, they'd fall under the same umbrella, which means Harper's pumps, insulin, doctors visits, and whatever else she needs would be covered. Mack wouldn't need to work two jobs in order to afford it.

"Why?" Mack asks, crossing her arms over her chest defensively.

"Because I get *really* good health insurance benefits, and if we get married, you and your sisters would be covered."

"Okaaaaaay. But what's in it for you? Why would you offer such a—a *commitment* to me when we haven't even talked in ten years?"

Excellent question.

The real answer is there's been a magnetic pull to her ever since I saw her again. I haven't been able to stop thinking about her since the accident—before, if I'm being honest. It's like she kickstarted my heart again, and all of the feelings I had for her as a teenager are coming back.

My religious upbringing tickles the back of my brain, whispering God put her in my path for a reason. Telling me it's a sign because none of my other relationships have worked out. She was the first girl I ever loved, and part of me is wondering if she's the last girl I *should* love. The only girl I have ever truly loved.

Another part of me wonders what would have happened if we'd stayed together all through high school. If she would have waited for me while I was on my mission, and we got married after.

Would we have kids? Would we have left the church and deconstructed together? Would I have still become a firefighter? Would I be drawing comics? Teaching?

Would we be happy?

There's no way to know for sure, but I want to know if we could have a future together *now*.

I can't tell her all of that, though. It would surely scare her away.

So I tell her a portion of the truth.

"My family has been on my case about being almost thirty and single. If I get married, then maybe they'll leave me be. Plus, then I can get out of the singles ward and maybe *actually* leave the church instead of feeling like I have to stay to keep the peace."

She scrunches her nose in the way she always has when she's confused, and a rush of affection flows through me.

"So your mom can blame me for being a bad influence again? No thanks. I'm sure your parents would rather you marry literally anyone else."

I grimace at that. I was hoping she'd forgotten about the things my mom said about her when we were in high school.

"It's been thirteen years. I'm sure she's over it." At least, I hope she's over it. It'd be weird if she still held a grudge with a teenage version of Mack.

Mack shakes her head. "I'm not the girl for you, Talmage. I appreciate you wanting to help, but I can't tie you down like this. You should be with some perky, wholesome girl who wants to have a million babies and will have dinner waiting for you after a long shift. Not someone who is barely scraping by, in charge of keeping two teenagers alive, and so exhausted she barely has the energy to reheat a frozen dinner."

But I don't want that. I want you.

Mack continues, "Besides, you deserve to marry someone for love. Not for... pity or whatever this is. You don't owe me, Tal, if that's what you're thinking. Whatever happened between us is in the past, and it should stay there."

Ouch. Her words slice through me, flaying me open. It's obvious she doesn't still feel something for me, even if I was hoping she did.

"It's *not* pity, and I don't feel like I owe you, Mack. Like I said, this would be helpful for me, too. Heck, you can even help me! You can teach me how to be an ex-mo. Drink coffee, drink alcohol, swear... that kind of stuff. Getting to help you is just a bonus."

Mack eyes me. "You've *never* said a swear word, have you?"

I shake my head. "Not even when I almost fell into an ash pit."

"Not even shit?"

"Not even... no."

"I think you should take some time to think about this. If this is just some impulsive decision—"

"It isn't," I interrupt. "I've thought about it. I've done the research on my insurance. I've spent the last two weeks trying to think of another way to help you, but getting married feels like the best option—for both of us."

This sounds crazy. It *is* crazy. But I feel calm and at peace with this decision. It feels like the jumbled mess that is my life is finally starting to arrange itself into pieces that make sense.

Marry Mack, leave the church, learn to be happy.

"How long do you plan on us staying married? Surely you have a time frame. Stipulations? Something."

I didn't think that far ahead. But of course, she wouldn't want to stay married after she no longer needs insurance. That gives us at least ten years together, right? Unless the twins get on their own insurance before they're twenty-six. After that, she'll probably want to leave Utah and find a guy who can curse and knows things about coffee and wants to get matching tattoos.

My heart already hurts thinking about us getting a divorce, and she hasn't even agreed to marry me. It still feels like a good idea, even if in my head I don't want it to end.

"Until you can either get a job with better insurance or a higher paying job. Or maybe until your sisters turn twenty-six or get a job with their own insurance? We can figure it out." It doesn't sound like a solid answer, but I don't have anything better at the moment.

Mack's lips roll into her mouth before she shakes her head. "I don't... I don't know, Tal. This seems like a crazy idea."

She's considering it, though. It isn't a "no." Hope flutters in my chest. There's still a chance.

"You don't have to answer right now. I can give you time to think about it. I think it would be good for you. You wouldn't have to keep working here and—"

"What's wrong with working here?" she snaps back.

"N-nothing! Nothing. I only meant you wouldn't have to work yourself to the bone just to buy Harper's stuff. I didn't mean it in a negative way."

"Sorry for snapping. People can be judgy about working in a bar."

"It's okay, Mack." My phone buzzes with my alarm—time to get to the station. "I'm sorry, but I have to get to work. I'll text you to set up another time to talk. Promise you'll think about it?"

Mack sighs and rubs her hands on her thighs. "Okay. I'll think about it."

I stand, offering her a hand to help her up from the chair and pulling her into a hug before she can scramble away from me. Having her in my arms settles some of the nerves in my chest.

"I'll talk to you soon, Firefly," I say against her hair. I feel more than hear her small gasp, and I wonder if I crossed a line using the nickname I gave her as a teenager.

She steps away and clears her throat. "Bye, Tal. Have a good day—or night, I guess—at work."

"Thanks, Mack. You, too. Text me when you get home so I know you're safe, okay?"

She nods, and I walk out of the bar.

That didn't go as I expected, but it's okay. There's still a chance she'll say yes.

Gosh, I hope she says yes.

CHAPTER 9

Mackenzie

14 years old...

"You guys have been going out for months *Mack, and all he's done is hold your hand. Are you sure he's not gay?" Tessa bites into her apple, and I scowl at her.*

"He made a promise to not kiss anyone until his wedding day." Do I wish he would break that for me? Yeah. But I know it's important to him.

"That's freaking weird!"

"I know." I sigh. "But I'm not going to be the one who pushes. It would be mean. Besides, we're going to get married. I just have to wait like... seven years. I can go seven years without kissing." I wince, realizing how long that actually is.

This is going to be torture.

Tessa rolls her eyes. "You know Kyle likes you, right? You should be kissing him instead of waiting seven years for Talmage."

"I thought you wanted to date Kyle?"

Tessa shrugs. "We're too similar. Besides, he's Austin's cousin, and I'm not dating my ex's cousin." She shudders like it's the worst idea ever.

"I don't know why you don't like Talmage."

Tessa's face softens. "I don't want you to get hurt again. After everything that went down with—"

"Please don't bring him up," I grumble. "He was a mistake, but Tal is different. He would never do anything to hurt me."

She sighs. "I hope you're right." After a beat, she leans forward and whispers, "Did you hear about what happened with Amber?"

Lizzie barrels through the front door, arms laden with more takeout containers than necessary considering it's only us tonight. Kinsley and Harper are at a sleepover party for one of the girls in the musical Harper's in. I know they're old enough to take care of themselves, but my stomach still swirls with anxiety every time I let them spend the night somewhere. I have Harper's glucose monitoring app notifications set at an extra high volume so I can be alerted in case she needs me to come get her.

"GIRL, you'll never believe who walked into the studio today!" Lizzie sets the bags on the counter and pulls out a pack of the fancy cream soda. She knows I don't like to drink when the girls are out in case there's an emergency, so I appreciate her thoughtfulness.

"Who?" I help her unload the takeout containers, my kitchen filling with the scent of kung pao chicken and sesame noodles.

"Amber Clements!"

I gasp. "No!"

Lizzie nods rapidly. "I swear. I don't know what she wanted because Alexi is the one who took her information, but I was flabbergasted. Pure, goody two-shoes Amber Clements walking into a tattoo shop? Now that's some gossip." Lizzie is a co-owner of a tattoo and piercing shop in Provo that's woman and LGBTQ+ owned and operated.

There was a lot of controversy when Medusa Tattoos opened, but they've been rated the best in the state the last two years. They do a fundraiser every year for victims of domestic violence and rape, and they offer free coverups for scars caused by DV, self-harm, or rape, and for victims of human trafficking.

"Are you sure she didn't just want another piercing or something? I know they changed the rules recently, and Mormons can have multiple piercings again."

"I wish they'd just stay consistent." Lizzie scoffs. "But no, her request was for a custom tattoo. I think I heard somewhere fine-line tattoos are okay now, too, but I don't know. People change. I mean, look at us." She waves a hand between us.

I chuckle. Yeah, we've changed a lot since high school. Lizzie didn't grow up Mormon, but all of her friends were Mormon. We say we're twins because we both have green eyes and a similar body type as well as birthdays two days apart. Now we have similar body types *and* bodies covered in tattoos and piercings.

While my hair is back to my natural auburn and down past my shoulders, Lizzie's is chopped into a bob and dyed pink.

Lizzie hasn't left my side since we bonded in high school. She's more like a sister than my actual sisters—only because they're so much younger. I literally owe this feisty woman my life.

"Yeah, people change," I say, my mind immediately going to Tal.

It's been almost a week since he asked me to marry him, and I still don't know what to do.

It's why I asked Lizzie to come over. I need her to be my voice of reason—to confirm it's a bad idea and doing this would be stupid.

Once we dish up our respective plates, we settle in on the couch.

"Alright, lady, spill. You have something on your mind, and I want to know what it is," Lizzie demands, pointing her fork at me.

I roll my eyes. "I always have something on my mind, Lizzie."

"True, but your vibes are different. Whatever's on your mind has your aura piss yellow when normally you're like a murky blue."

What a lovely visual. I don't understand what she means when she says she can see someone's aura, but I go with it because I love her, and she's never steered me wrong.

I take a long sip of my soda and then a deep breath. "Talmage asked me to marry him—"

Lizzie chokes on a piece of chicken, slapping the leather couch as she coughs and tries to swallow it.

"WHAT?" she gasps when she finally swallows, her face turning scarlet. "Are you fucking with me? Please say you're fucking with me! I didn't know you guys were even dating!"

"We *aren't*. We've gone to lunch one time and text occasionally, but you know that already. He showed up at the bar on Sunday and asked me to marry him so Harper can have full insurance coverage for her insulin."

Lizzie's mouth purses, and she tilts her head, processing the information.

"I know it's crazy."

"Definitely crazy," she agrees. "Especially considering you haven't talked to each other in over a decade. He just waltzes in and asks you to marry him after a singular lunch date? What's in it for him?"

"He says he wants to get his family off his back about getting married, and he wants someone to teach him how to leave the church."

"That's it? That's his only reason?"

I shrug. "It's the only reason he gave."

"That doesn't seem like a red flag to you?"

"I don't know," I grumble. "You know how I feel about him. My mind's not exactly in the best headspace when it comes to Talmage."

Lizzie nods, and I swear I see the wheels turning in her head. After a few minutes of silence she shrugs. "I think you should do it."

Now it's my turn to be shocked. "*What?!* Lizzie, you're supposed to be the voice of reason! You're supposed to say, 'Yeah, Mack, that's crazy and stupid. Don't do it.'"

Lizzie shrugs again and picks up a spring roll. "I mean, is it a little crazy? Sure. But think about it, Mack. You get coverage for Harper's insulin without having to find a new job, and you don't have to keep working yourself so hard. You could take a break, have an actual life. Plus," she gives me a sinister grin, "you can't tell me you're not at least a little excited for the chance to be married to Talmage. This is literally your teenage dream."

I shoot her a glare. "Key word being *teenage*. I'm an adult now, Lizzie. My dreams have changed."

"Oh, come on, you can't tell me you're not at least a *little* curious about the muscles underneath that uniform. Not to mention, if he's still in the church, it stands to reason he's a virgin, so you could teach him a few things." She waggles her eyebrows suggestively, and my face heats a million degrees.

"We would *not* be doing anything remotely sexual. We probably wouldn't even kiss. I'm not going to be accused of corrupting him—again."

"But you've thought about it!"

"I'm a woman who appreciates a man in uniform and hasn't had sex in over five years. Of *course* I've thought about it. But we wouldn't stay married forever. I wouldn't want to do anything to risk my already fragile heart."

Lizzie's face softens. "Marrying him *would* risk your heart, babe. I hate to say it, but we both know that—"

"I know, I know," I cut her off. I don't need a reminder that I've been harboring feelings for him for over a decade.

Fucking feelings.

I wish I could just turn them off. Shove them in a box and toss them into the ocean. Or set them on fire.

"You really think I should do it, though?"

"Hell yeah. Let him help you. Who knows? Maybe you'll rekindle the old flame."

"Not happening. I'm keeping my heart locked in a vault, thank you very much."

"Okay, keep your heart locked away but take the boy to Pound Town. Let him get his dick wet, and show him a good time."

"Elizabeth Marie Mikkelson!" I scold, but Lizzie is unaffected by it. She just cackles.

The conversation—thankfully—shifts to other things, but as the night goes on, my anxiety grows.

When Lizzie leaves and I'm left alone with my thoughts, I spiral. I should give him an answer soon.

But does the benefit of having Harper's insulin paid for outweigh the potential damage to my already barely hanging on heart? Is it selfish of me to say no simply because I don't want to give my heart another reason to get attached to him?

I've had over ten years to get over him, but for whatever reason, my heart's kept him close.

I don't know if I can handle another devastation when our marriage inevitably ends.

But this would be for Harper. To make sure she can get the best care possible and not worry that I won't be able to afford enough insulin next month.

I already know what I'm going to do, I just have to remember to keep my heart in check.

I open the front door, expecting a pizza delivery, but it's not a delivery driver. It's Talmage, soaked from head to toe because of the rain. His chest is heaving like he's been running.

"Talmage?" I whisper. "What are you doing here?"

He steps forward, close enough for me to see the lighter hues of blue in his eyes. "I'm here to tell you I love you, Mackenzie Thorpe. My heart has always been yours."

"Wh-what are you talking about? You're engaged."

He shakes his head. "I broke it off with her. I never should have been with her in the first place, it's always been you."

"I've been waiting so long, Tal," I admit through a sob. "How do I know you won't leave me again?"

"I'm sorry, Firefly. I promise, my heart is yours. I'm yours forever. Please, Mack, I need you."

"Kiss me, Talmage. Show me."

Talmage steps forward, his hands cupping my face and leaning in, his breath fanning across my lips as—

I jolt awake, my eyes shooting open. I glance at the clock and see it's almost 4 a.m., the normal time my brain comes back to reality after my dreams.

They always end before I can kiss Talmage.

Frustrated tears burn behind my eyes like usual after a dream where he's confessed his feelings. Where he swoops in like a knight to save me.

Before he came back into my life, my dreams left me sad and angry. Angry that my brain would betray me and give me a glimpse of a future I could have.

Now, it feels like a sick form of torture because he's back and offering a future where he's in it but not in the way I want.

If I say yes to him, he has the ability to crush my heart into a million tiny pieces.

If I say no, I'll most likely lose him again, and I'll have to keep working myself to the bone in order to keep me and the twins afloat.

Either way, my heart is at risk, and I don't have the strength to handle another heartbreak.

CHAPTER 10

Talmage

14 years old...

Now would be the perfect moment for a first kiss. The breeze is blowing her hair behind her shoulders, and the sun is casting her in a glow. Her green eyes are bright and vibrant and so open, honest.

I want to kiss her, but I made a promise to myself a long time ago I would only kiss my future wife on our wedding day.

Even if I plan on Mack being my wife, I can't break the promise.

Right?

Why is this so hard?

I never planned on falling in love so early on, and I never anticipated the waiting to be so difficult.

Mack's birthday is in a month, maybe it would be a good birthday present...

I don't know what to do. My friends have told me it's crazy to make her wait until we're married. That I should practice kissing in case something happens and we break up.

I'll never break up with Mack, though.

But will she break up with me if I never kiss her? I hear other boys talk about her. She doesn't know how many of them have crushes on her. Would one of them be able to steal her away?

I hope not. I hope our love is strong enough to stand the test of something like not kissing.

But what if it isn't?

I swear I'm going to vibrate right off of this bench.

Mack texted me this morning and asked when I'd be free to meet up, and I told her I was available all day. It's been exactly one week since my offer, and it seems she's ready to give me an answer.

She's given no indication as to which way she's leaning.

I hope she says yes.

I realize I don't have a solid reason for wanting to marry her, other than I just… feel it deep in my bones this is the right thing to do.

Everyone in the church always talks about promptings from "the spirit" and revelation from God, but I've never felt anything like that—and I've tried. I prayed and prayed and prayed when I was going to propose to Jamie. I went to the temple to try to get closer to God and see if He would answer.

Nothing.

I never felt a single thing in either direction. All I felt was a sense of disappointment God didn't deem me worthy of an answer. People in the church always say "no answer is an answer," but when it's a big, life-changing decision, sometimes it's not enough.

At the time, I figured it was because I was starting to question things, so I shoved my doubts aside and started praying more. I started reading my scriptures in earnest. I started going to the temple weekly. Even when I was coming off of a night shift and was bone-tired—I went.

I proposed to Jamie, and she ended things. So I figured maybe they were right: no answer *was* the answer. Maybe God *not* telling me I was making the wrong choice was His way of telling me I was making the right one.

Now?

I'm not even sure God exists.

And if He doesn't exist, then it was just my instincts that told me proposing to Jamie was a good idea. I wasn't taught to trust my instincts, so I don't know how to trust them outside of work. Clearly, they've been wrong when it comes to romance before, so why am I trusting them when it comes to asking Mack to marry me?

I want her to be able to go back to school if she wants. I want to help ease the exhaustion so clear on her face. I want to take care of her, give her time to rest.

There's a very real possibility this will all blow up in my face.

But I have to believe it won't. I have to believe this will all work out. Mack and I will get married, and she'll stop having to work so hard because Harper will have better insurance. Then we'll... I don't know—fall in love and have a real marriage, maybe.

I'm smiling to myself like a silly goose now, thinking about falling asleep next to Mack. Waking up next to Mack. Bringing Mack flowers on a random Tuesday. Writing a grocery list with her and telling her to stay in bed, I'll go pick up everything.

Ooo. Mack will wear the ring I *picked out for her. Everyone will see it and ask her about it, and she'll call me her husband.*

I'll get to come home from a late shift and give her a kiss on the forehead and snuggle up next to her warm body in bed. She'll tell me about her day while I trace the ink on her skin—I'll have the lines memorized in no time—and then I'll update her on what's happening at the station.

Yeah, it'll be perfect. This feels right.

I'm so caught up in my daydream I don't notice Mack sliding into the booth across from me.

Gosh, she looks pretty today.

Her long hair is in a braid over one shoulder, and she's wearing a black shirt that scoops low in the front—

I snap my gaze up to hers.

"Hi, Mack. You look good," I say, hoping she doesn't think I'm a creep.

"Hi, Tal, thanks. So do you," she replies, glancing around the shop.

We're at a different sandwich place since Valley Baker is closed on Sundays. I ordered for us already, and I slide the wrapped sandwich, bag of chips, and chocolate chip cookie over to Mack.

Her brows furrow. "What's this?"

"Your sandwich."

"Tal—"

"No, please don't argue with me. You need to eat."

She huffs. "I don't remember you being so bossy."

I grin. "I'm not bossy, Mack. I just want to make sure you're eating."

Mack sighs and opens her chips, crunching on one while I do the same. "Thank you."

"Of course. Anything for you." *ANYTHING.*

Anticipation rattles around in my stomach, and I want to ask her what her answer is, but I don't want to seem too eager—too pushy.

Mack doesn't touch her sandwich, but she does eat a few more chips before she wipes her fingers on her napkin and folds her arms in front of her on the table.

"So about your offer..." she says slowly.

My heart stutters. "Have you thought about it?"

"I have."

I hate that I can't read the emotion on her face. I hate that I can't tell what she's about to say.

"And..." She takes a deep breath before she looks directly into my eyes—directly into my freaking *soul*. "Yes, I'll marry you."

The wings of a thousand doves flap around in my stomach, and I swear the heavens open and light pours in through every window in this place—nevermind that the sky is filled with dark clouds.

Hope and joy light my chest, and I have the sudden urge to scoop her out of the booth and kiss her. Thank her. Make promises I have no business making.

Tears spring to my eyes.

"Really?" I croak, a grin threatening to take over my face.

Mack isn't smiling, though. She looks worried as she nods.

The doves stop flapping, my stomach dropping out of my butt as worry replaces the elation I felt for a brief moment.

I don't want this to be a sad thing for Mack.

"Are you sure about this? You seem..." I search for the right word, finally settling on "reluctant."

"It's not because of *you*," she starts. "This is all just so crazy. So fast. I mean, we barely know each other and—"

"Hey, we know each other! We've known each other for almost fifteen years."

Mack gives me a pitying smile I don't like. "I'm not the same girl I was at fifteen, Tal. Just like you're not the same guy. This new version of me has gone through more trauma than anyone should, and I'm not looking at things through rose-colored glasses. Fifteen-year-old Tal would have never dreamed of leaving the church, and you are."

But he dreamed of marrying you. We have that in common.

I don't say that, though. She's right, we're not the same people, but we're not complete strangers like she's making it seem.

"This just gives us a chance to get to know each other again. I haven't changed so much in the last decade."

"We could get to know each other *without* getting married, you know."

"Right, but if we get married, you have more free time. Plus, we'll be living together, so it gives us more opportunities to talk."

Mack's eyes widen. "I-I didn't think about that. Us living together, I mean. I guess we need to talk through logistics. You've clearly thought a lot about this."

I have. Every day for three weeks, I've thought about it. What it would look like, how things would feel. "Well, we'd have to live together to sell it, right? We could be charged with insurance fraud if someone suspects we're only getting married for insurance benefits, and it would be suspicious if we didn't live together."

"Right. That makes sense." She bites down on her lower lip. They look so soft. So kissable. They look fuller than they did when we were teenagers. I wonder if they feel the same. "So, we wouldn't tell anyone it's fake?"

"No. I think we'd need to keep it between us."

"And Lizzie," she blurts, her face flushing. "Lizzie knows you asked and why. She um, she told me to do it. So she would know."

"Do you trust she won't say anything?" I remember Lizzie from school. I didn't know her very well, but if Mack trusts her, I trust her.

"Yes. I trust her with my life."

"Great. We'll need a witness for the wedding anyway. Will you want to tell your sisters or...?"

Mack sighs. "I don't know. I don't like lying to them, but they're fifteen. They're either going to tell everyone or bully me about it. They'll probably bully me about it if I don't tell them it's fake anyway."

"Why would they bully you?"

"Well, I haven't dated anyone since before... you know. They've been up my ass about getting out there, but I always tell them I don't have time—which isn't exactly false. So if I come home and say, 'Hey, look! I'm getting married!' they're going to have very loud opinions and many, many questions."

She hasn't dated anyone in *five years?*

Has she really been going through all of the heartbreak and pain completely alone?

Well, I guess not completely alone if she's still close with Lizzie, but still.

Five years. Wow.

"Just tell them you didn't want to say anything until it was serious."

She snorts. "Right. I feel like marriage is a step above serious."

"Then tell them the truth. We're getting married so quickly so you can stop overworking yourself. It's technically true, it just leaves out the fact we weren't dating in the first place."

Mack studies my face for a minute. "You're so calm about this. Why?"

I shrug. "It feels right."

CHAPTER 11

Mackenzie

15 years old...

I don't know why I thought turning fifteen would feel like a big, life-altering event, but it does not feel that way.

Maybe sixteen will. Guess I'll find out next year.

My mom has always made me feel like the most special person on my birthday, so at least I started the day with a new shirt, crepes, and the promise of Red Lobster for dinner.

It only got better when I arrived at school and opened my locker to find a hand-carved rose from Talmage sitting there with a note and a drawing of a Firefly.

Happy birthday, Firefly. You "light" up my life.

Love,

Bear

I can't help the wide grin spreading across my face, and I look up and down the hall to see if I can find him. I'm sure he's waiting at our spot in the common area, so I place the rose and the note back in my locker and head in that direction.

What the *fuck* does that even *mean?*

"It feels right."

Okay, but *why?*

It takes me back to when I was still in the church. How people would tell you to just... *trust* if things feel right. "You'll know if things feel wrong," they'd say.

Well, I have anxiety. So I *don't* fucking trust my feelings. If I trusted my feelings, I wouldn't be alive right now!

But Tal looks so... vulnerable. He looks like he genuinely means it. When I first walked in, he looked like a puppy who had just found its owner, and dammit, it's endearing.

I don't think anyone has ever looked at me like they're excited to see me—at least not for a long time, and it made a brick in the well-constructed wall around my heart fall out and crumble to dust.

More than that, though, *I* was excited to see *him.*

I've made peace with my decision, and the teenager in me has been pushing to the forefront of my brain, giddy and elated to be marrying *Talmage fucking Monson.*

But it still doesn't feel real.

I guess because it's *not* real. This is a business transaction—or something similar. I still don't understand what he's getting out of our deal, but he's adamant about it and...

I could use the help. It would be nice to have free time and not have to scramble to pay the bills.

"When do you want to do this thing?" I ask instead of responding to his answer.

Tal pulls out his phone.

"We should set our date as soon as possible so you can start using the benefits sooner. How do you feel about a Valentine's Day anniversary? That's three weeks from Friday."

I scrunch my nose. "Valentine's Day? Really?"

He shrugs, giving me a sheepish smile. "It feels fitting, you know? Full circle."

I know he's referring to the Valentine's Day dance freshman year. When he kissed me for the first time. After swearing he wouldn't kiss anyone other than his wife on his wedding day, he changed his mind. We were slow dancing to "Arms" by Christina Perry, the last song of the dance, and it was like a movie moment, the way he tipped my chin and kissed me. He was so gentle about it—so shy and sweet. One of our friends came over to us after and said it was like watching a romance movie.

I guess maybe he remembers it because it was his first kiss, but does he think about the moment as often as I do? Does he ever think about the way his heart beat faster, the way the world around us blurred until it was just us in the musty junior high gym, the lights dimmed and music blaring from the speakers?

Or is it just me who thinks about it? Just me who has to skip that song because the memories are too over-whelming every time it comes on?

I swallow around the lump of emotion stuck in my throat. "Right, yeah. Full circle. But is it too cliché?"

Tal shrugs again. "I think it's kind of romantic. If you want, we can do it the week before, but I wasn't sure if you had plans since your birthday is that Sunday."

I blink at him. "You remember my birthday?"

"Of course I do. February ninth." He looks offended.

"I remember yours, too," I whisper. May twenty-seventh. I used to make fun of him for being younger than me, even though it's only four months. "I don't have plans. I think Lizzie wants to go out and celebrate since her birthday is only two days after mine, but we don't have anything set in stone."

Tal nods, his lips tipping into a small frown. "Well, which day would you prefer? We can do the seventh, then celebrate your birthday and our nuptials, or we can go with Valentine's Day."

It's a double-edged sword. I feel like my birthday *and* Valentine's Day will be forever ruined after we get divorced. Not that I celebrate either very much anyway. Hard to have a fun day of love when your only companion has been a vibrator for five years, and celebrating your birthday when you're overworked is just exhausting. Lizzie and I usually get takeout and watch horror movies to celebrate.

"Should we do it the day after Valentine's Day? Or do you want to get married on a Friday?"

"Right, you have a regular job." He chuckles. "We can do it the day after. I'll make an appointment at the courthouse and sort out the license."

Why does this feel like I'm scheduling a major, life-changing surgery?

"Okay, thank you. Um, when do you want to move in?"

"I figured I'd move in the same day. I pay month-to-month, so I can get out of my lease anytime. Oh, shoot. Do you have a fenced-in yard?"

"Yes. We were able to stay in my childhood home, so we have a fenced-in yard. Why?"

"Just wanted to make sure Siren won't be able to escape. Not that I think she would, but you never know."

I blink. "Who?"

"Siren's my girl!" As soon as the words leave his mouth he cringes. "I mean, my *dog*. She's a two-year-old golden retriever—high energy little thing, but I love her. She helps out at the station when I'm there and is being trained for search and rescue. She's almost done with her training."

"Oh, well, that's cool. I'm assuming she's not going to bite my hand off or anything?"

"Of course not, she's a good girl. Here—" He pulls out his phone and shows me a picture. Siren's lying on her back with her tongue lolled out to the side looking at the camera. I swear it looks like she's smiling.

You know when people say dogs look like their owners?

I never really understood, but Talmage and Siren have the same vibe. Same golden hair, same excited energy.

"She's cute. I love her collar."

Tal's face turns pink. "Thanks, I special order them from Etsy. She has a collar for every occasion."

God, why does his love for his dog make me want to melt?

It pulls a small smile from me. "That's adorable. Do you think she'll be okay changing environments?"

He nods. "Yeah, she'll be fine. I'm sure she'll love having an actual yard to run around in instead of staying cooped in the apartment until I can get her to the park."

"Good, good. I wouldn't want to cause her any stress." I've never owned a pet, so I don't know how this is going to pan out. Will she sleep on the bed with us—wait, are we sharing a bed?

Shit.

There are so many things we need to talk about. So many things are still up in the air, and I don't know how to bring any of it up. What are we doing about rings? Are we splitting the bills somehow? Will he bring his own furniture and mix it with mine? What about groceries?

"Mack, you good? Your face changed. Talk to me."

"Beds," I blurt. "And rings. Bills. Groceries. Where Siren will sleep. I just—there's a lot to talk about. Lots of logistics we haven't thought of."

"I'll pay half of everything—mortgage, utilities, groceries. Your sisters will most likely suspect something's off if we *don't* share a room, but you can make that decision. Siren sleeps in a crate. I already have a ring picked out for you, and I can buy my own if you want. I don't have any food allergies or preferences, but I enjoy cooking, so that burden won't fall on you." He reaches across the table to take my hand, rubbing his thumb over my knuckles in a soothing gesture. "I want to help take the burden off of your shoulders, Mack. I know this is a big change, but I've already thought some of it through. I'll get a storage unit for my stuff or sell it. I don't have much beyond the basics anyway."

"Okay, yeah, that sounds good." I stare at the place we're connected. My skin sizzles with every brush of his calloused thumb. Wait— "You've already picked out a ring for me?"

"Yeah. If you want to pick out your own—"

"No, no. That's okay. I can buy yours, too. Can you even wear a ring on the job, though? That seems like a hazard."

"I'll probably get a silicone band for when I'm work-ing, but if you buy me a ring, I will wear it proudly whenever I'm off the clock."

Why does my heart flutter when I think about him wearing a ring *I* buy him? Why does he have to be so fucking sweet and earnest?

"Okay. I can do that. Any color preference? Gold, silver, black?"

"Like I said, I'll proudly wear whatever you buy me. But if you want ours to match, gold would be best. That's the only hint about your ring you're getting, though. You'll have to wait to see it."

"Gold, got it," I say, almost robotically. My mind is too stuck on other things. What kind of ring does he envision for me? Does he know my heart is about to explode over how enthusiastic he sounds over all of this? He's practically vibrating with it, and it makes my nerves simmer down.

"Have a proper dinner date with me." He squeezes my hand. "Are you free on Saturday?"

I blink, trying to think if I'm scheduled at the bar. "Yeah, I'm free."

"Great! I'll pick you up at seven, okay? Nothing too fancy but not, like, jeans and a T-shirt. Is that okay?"

What the hell does he have planned?

"Yeah, sounds great."

His answering smile is blinding. I swear he's going to turn gold from all of the happiness pouring out of him. "Fantastic. Thank you for trusting me, Mack. I don't have the words to express how much it means to me." An alarm on his watch beeps. "I've got to run. I'll see you Saturday."

Automatically, I stand and follow him out the door. He wraps me in one of his big bear hugs, opens my car door for me, and helps me in, giving me a rapid wave before he gets into his own vehicle and drives away.

I slam my head back against the headrest. "What the fuck is my life?"

I picked up a mid-week shift at the bar so I could have a little extra money to buy Talmage a ring, and I'm regretting it now.

I swear Joanna has a sixth sense for gossip because she's been eyeing me all night like she's *waiting* for me to tell her.

The bar isn't as busy on a Wednesday, but some people come for the food, so the dinner rush is just dying down when she turns to me with her arms crossed.

"Spill it, Mack."

"I thought I wasn't supposed to purposely spill drinks anymore?" I try to joke, but her stern gaze blocks any levity from entering the conversation. I sigh. "I'm getting married."

Joanna throws her head back in a laugh, throaty and gruff. Tears trickle from her eyes as she continues to cackle, bent in half and slapping her knee like it's the funniest thing she's ever heard.

I don't know what to do in this situation, so I stand there awkwardly until her laughter dies down, and she sees the look on my face.

She immediately sobers. "Oh, shit. You're serious?"

I nod.

"I didn't even know you were dating anyone. Wait—" She holds up one finger and tilts her head like she's remembering something. "Oh, no. Mack, tell me it's not Peter Priesthood."

I bite my lip. I know she's talking about Talmage. I can't deny it, though. I can't deny it's him, and when she realizes it, she groans.

"I swear, kid. If I find out you've rejoined the cult, I'm kidnapping you and keeping you in the basement until you come to your senses. *Getting married? To him?* It's way too fast."

Defensiveness rises in my chest. "Talmage is a good guy, Joanna. Sure, he may be part of the church right now, but he wants to leave, not that it's any of your business. We've known each other since we were teenagers and—" I cut myself off before I confess I've been in love with him for just as long. "And it feels right."

Joanna studies my face again, like she's looking for a lie before she curses under her breath. "Damn it, you're down bad, aren't you? You'd tell me if you were being coerced into this or you were in trouble?"

No, I think. *I wouldn't tell you if I was in trouble. You don't know the half of the trouble I'm in.*

"Yeah, I would. But trust me when I tell you this is what I want. This is a good thing." I put on a small smile that doesn't feel as forced as it should, like I *truly* believe the words.

"Okay. I believe you." She sighs. "When's the big day?"

"The day after Valentine's Day."

"That's in less than a month! Why so fast?"

I shrug. "I'm almost thirty. No time to waste."

She rolls her eyes. "Well, show me the ring."

"I... I don't have it yet. It's getting resized." God, I hate lying to her.

"Hmm. Fine. I expect to see it as soon as it's back." She points a finger at me just as the bell above the door rings. "I'm happy for you if you're happy." Giving my shoulder a squeeze, she walks away to go check IDs.

I let out a long breath when she's no longer within hearing distance.

I don't know if I'd say I'm happy, but I can't exactly tell her that.

CHAPTER 12

Talmage

14 years old...

My hands are sweating as I sit in the bleachers, watching Mack throw her head back and laugh with her friends. I don't recognize the song playing—something about a clock, I think. I don't know. All I know is watching Mack dance is mesmerizing.

And I'm nervous.

Her birthday was last week, and today is the Valentine's dance. I've been waiting for our song to play, for the perfect moment to share our first kiss, but it's almost over, and they haven't played it yet.

Another song starts to play, and Mack takes a seat next to me to catch her breath. "Are you feeling okay, Bear? You look like you're ready to head out."

"I'm good, just taking a break. You know I'm not a great dancer."

Mack rolls her eyes. "That's not true, and you know it. Speaking of... I was wondering if you'd be able to come to my spring recital this year? I'm doing a solo, and I'd like you to be there."

"I'll see what I can work out with my parents, but I'd love to come." I reach over and give her hand a squeeze. She opens her mouth to say something, but the familiar chords to our song start to play. I stand and take her to the dance floor, placing my hands on her waist as hers wrap around my neck.

The smile she gives me is breathtaking.

And she has no idea what's about to happen.

Mack doesn't know it yet, but she's going to get a proper proposal. That's what tonight is for, and *boy*, am I nervous.

What if she says no?

I mean, she's already agreed to marry me, but still.

What if this is too much?

I open the little, gray velvet box for the hundredth time to inspect the ring. I have the shape memorized, but I can't stop looking at it. I knew exactly what I wanted to get her. I saw this ring in an ad when I was looking at more collars for Siren and *knew*.

It's a kite cut moss agate—it reminds me of her eyes—surrounded by tiny diamonds and leaves. I have a matching band I'll give her on our wedding day that really ties the whole ring together. It looks like something out of a fantasy novel, and the leaves remind me of Mack's tattoos.

I hope she likes it. I messaged Lizzie and asked for her ring size, and Lizzie was a bit too eager to help. I'm glad Mack's had her in her life. I get the feeling Lizzie would do anything for Mack and knowing she hasn't been alone all these years brings me a small sense of relief.

Siren trots over and sniffs the box in my hands. I close it and put it in my jacket pocket before rubbing a hand over her head, stopping to give her ear scratches.

"What do you think, girl, hm? Do you think she'll like it?"

Siren huffs and licks my hand, and I take it as an affirmation.

"In a few weeks we're going to have a whole backyard for you to play in. You'll have the twins to give you attention, too. Doesn't that sound fun?"

Siren woofs quietly, wagging her tail and panting.

Mack's concern for Siren's well-being was so endearing, it made me fall even harder for her. I already know Siren's going to get attached to Mack and the girls, and it'll be a harder transition to leave than it will be to move in.

But that's a problem for another time. Who knows how long it'll take for Mack to get a job with better benefits. It could be a while.

Selfishly, I hope it's a while.

I need time to show her I don't want her for a blip in time.

Which I know sounds crazy. Absolutely insane, but I can't help it.

I can't explain the burning in my chest or the way my stomach erupts when I think about her. It's like all the feelings I had as a teenager—the ones I thought were long gone—have multiplied tenfold in the last decade, and now I can't imagine a future without her, even if I've only had her back in my life for a month.

Even if she seems hesitant about opening up to me. I get the sense she's guarded her heart for so long, it's going to take a lot more than a month and a marriage born of necessity for her to trust me with the delicate organ.

Good thing I'm patient. I'll wait as long as it takes.

I give Siren one more good belly rub before I put her in her crate with a peanut butter treat and *Bluey* on the TV so she's not lonely.

"All right, girl. Time to go ask Mack to officially be your mom."

Mackenzie Thorpe is *gorgeous.*

The sky is blue, the grass is green, fire needs fuel, oxygen, and heat to burn, and Mackenzie Thorpe is the most beautiful woman I've ever seen.

These facts are ingrained into my psyche—things that will never change.

Mack is beautiful in jeans and a T-shirt. She was beautiful in her sparkly, purple choir dress and the shapeless, black dresses she had to wear for chamber choir. But she was a teenager then. Now, she's a woman.

And in a black dress that hugs every dip and curve of her body over an olive green lacy long sleeve shirt and paired with black tights and black boots that look like they were made for stomping on hearts?

Someone might need to cut off my oxygen because I'm about to combust.

I've been struggling to breathe since the moment she opened the door.

Her hair is down in sleek waves, one side tucked behind her ear, showcasing all of her shiny piercings. Her eyes are winged with eyeliner, her lashes dusted with dark mascara, and her lips...

Holy moly. The maroon lipstick contrasts so beautifully with her pale skin.

Smudge-proof lipstick is a thing, right? I wonder if it's what she used. I wonder if she'd let me test it... just a peck. To make sure it's as advertised.

If it isn't smudge proof, I'd wear the smeared color around my mouth as a badge of honor. Let everyone know this exquisite woman kissed me. *Me.*

Mack shifts from one foot to the other, folding her arms across her chest, then letting them hang at her sides, and I realize I've been staring at her mouth for longer than is appropriate.

"You look incredible." The words tumble out of my mouth like gravel, my voice rough and ragged in a way it's never been.

Mack's cheeks turn pink. "Thanks. You look really nice, too."

I glance down at my matching olive green chinos and light blue button up.

"Thank you." I hold my arm out for her. "Shall we?"

Her ring-clad fingers hesitantly grip my bicep in a loose hold.

Can she feel my muscles? Does she like them?

I put in a lot of work to get in shape to be a fireman. With no significant other, I've spent many nights running with Siren or lifting the few weights I have at home. I'm proud of the muscles I've gained to show how hard I work.

I subtly flex them, hoping to get a reaction out of her, but she just stares straight ahead at my little black Subaru Outback.

I open the passenger door for her, and she gets inside, buckling while I round the car and get in the driver's side, trying not to rush too fast.

I have to actively keep myself from staring at her and appreciating how much I like her in my car. How much I like her next to me. How much I want to reach across the console and hold her hand while we drive.

As I pull out of her driveway and out of her neighborhood, my nerves sizzle and spike again.

I once again remind myself she's already said yes to the marriage. To me. This is simply a formality. One I want to give her.

"How was your week?" I ask, glancing away from the road to steal another look at her.

"It was good. I spent some time applying for new jobs in my downtime, so hopefully something will come up. Maybe I'll get a new job, and we won't have to get married," she muses.

OOF.

Talk about an axe to the heart.

I don't like that idea. Not one bit. Does that make me a bad person?

"Are you having regrets saying yes to this?" I need to know. I don't want to force her into something she doesn't want to do. That would hurt her. I don't want to hurt her.

Shoot. Have I... manipulated her into this?

"If you feel like I've pressured you at *all,* I'm so sorry, Mack—"

"No," she interrupts. "You haven't made me feel pressured, I just... I don't like feeling like I'm taking advantage of *you.*"

"I'm sorry. But I promise, I don't feel that way. I offered. I'm not using the benefits. Someone should get to. Besides, you're helping me, too, remember? You get to teach me how to be the best ex-Mormon version of myself. I'm ready to enter my apostate era."

Mack shakes her head, but I see the slightest upturn of her lips. "You won't even swear, Tal. I don't want to feel like I'm corrupting you. Again."

"I want you to corrupt me!" I blurt. *Dang it. That sounds dirty.* "I mean, I *want* you to help me learn to break the rules I've been taught. I don't want to follow them blindly anymore, but it's hard to break them on my own, you know? I've gotten so used to them; it's a hard habit to undo. But we can talk about that later. Tonight, we're just a regular couple going on a date—" Mack snorts. "What's funny?"

"Tal, you look like a Hollister model or something, and I look like the poster child for Goths-R-Us. Complete opposites. No one is going to believe we're on a real date."

I don't like her insinuation that I wouldn't date her. Doesn't she understand how beautiful she is? "I think you look amazing. So what if you like black? It doesn't matter. Besides, people will believe what they want. All that matters is *we* know it's a date."

I glance over and see her looking at me with wide, shocked eyes. "I thought this was more of a formality thing or... something. I didn't—I didn't know you considered it an actual date..." Her voice trails off at the end, like she's embarrassed.

I'm not going to lie, that stings a little. I feel like I've been clear about my intentions, but maybe I've only been clear in my head.

Instead of showing her the hurt, I give her a beaming smile. "It's a date, Mack. I plan on wining—well, maybe no wine for me, but you can have some if you want—and dining you. Show you what you can look forward to as my wife. Besides, we need to be seen in public, right? No one will believe we're getting married so quickly if we haven't been out together."

"We were seen in public at Valley Baker and G and S. Joanna knew something was up immediately. I told her on Wednesday we're getting married, and she told me she'd kidnap me if she thought I was in trouble."

"Is Joanna the scary lady with the spiky hair and nose ring?"

Mack laughs. "Yeah, that's her. She looks scary, but she's actually a softie."

"I'll take your word for it."

We pull into the parking lot of Sorrento Groves in Provo—an upscale restaurant, popular for special occasions and date nights. I've heard great things about the food, but I've never had someone to take until Mack came back into my life. I knew immediately this is where I wanted to propose.

"Talmage," Mack gasps. "This place is too expensive."

"Nah. I'm a captain of the FD, Mack. The only thing I get to spend my money on is Siren. I promise it's not too much. Let me spoil you a little."

Mack shakes her head then sighs. "You're not going to be talked out of this, are you?"

"Not a chance, Firefly." I get out and round the car quickly, opening the door for her and offering my hand. "Let me show you off."

She takes my hand, sparks lighting up my bloodstream as our skin touches. I swear a shiver runs down my spine at the contact.

I expect my nerves to come back full-force as we head to the restaurant. The weight of the ring box in my pocket should be making me vibrate with anxiety, but I feel calm. It's like an anchor, keeping me grounded to reality.

The grass is green, the sky is blue, Mackenzie Thorpe is beautiful, and she's going to be my wife.

Facts.

CHAPTER 13

Mackenzie

15 years old...

The gym is full of teenage bodies swaying slowly as "Arms" by Christina Perri plays. Tal's hands are resting loosely on my hips and mine are around his neck. He won't look me in the eye, and my stomach fills with anxiety.

Is he breaking up with me?

Has he rethought whatever it is we're doing?

"Mack?" he whispers, and I look up to meet his eyes.

"Yeah?"

"I-I love you."

This is the first time he's said the words out loud. We've written them down and said it in a million ways, with and without words, but never have we spoken those exact words.

"I love you, too, Tal."

He licks his lips, and time slows down as he lowers his face to mine. The gym, our friends, everything fades away until we're in our own bubble, and then, it happens.

Talmage Monson kisses me. It's hesitant, just a brush of his lips against mine, feather light and so achingly soft. Hesitant and cautious, but perfect nonetheless.

I want to grab him by the back of his head and crash his lips against mine harder, but this is his first kiss ever, so I'll let him take the lead.

He presses his lips a bit more firmly against mine, and I swear I melt into a puddle. Someone is going to have to squeegee me off the floor.

The song ends, and the lights in the gym turn on since it was the last song. Our bubble is popped when our friend Austin comes over and starts gushing about how our kiss was the most romantic thing he's ever seen.

I wish we could stay in our bubble forever.

I don't remember the last time I was in a restaurant this nice.

When I was little, my parents used to take me to Red Lobster for my birthday, and I considered *that* nice, so maybe never? There was the one time my ex took me to a steakhouse in California, but it was basically just a glorified Texas Roadhouse. He said it was fancy, and maybe to him it was but definitely not fancy like *this*.

There are fake lemon trees creating a canopy over the dining room, the branches hold small rectangle lantern lights giving it a soft ambiance. Instrumental music plays quietly through hidden speakers. Each table has a single yellow rose in a vase in the middle of a crisp white table-cloth—except for ours. In the middle of our table is a large bouquet of pink calla lilies, my favorite flowers.

When I asked Talmage why ours was different, he shrugged and said, "They're your favorite."

I don't know how he remembers. I think I mentioned it to him once when I was fifteen. My taste could have changed, I could have a different favorite flower, but even if I did, I'd still be floored by him remembering something I said in passing over a decade ago and made a point to get them for me.

It nearly brought me to tears. No one's ever bought me flowers. Past boyfriends have always given excuses that they don't want to buy something bound to die, or they didn't know what flowers to get, even if I told them my favorite.

Tal and I are fake engaged. This is our first real date, and he's already raised the bar for future partners.

Ugh. Don't think about this ending before it's even begun. Don't ruin tonight.

Even though I could have used some liquid courage to calm my nerves, I ordered a strawberry lemonade to go with my dinner instead of a cocktail or a glass of wine so I could keep my wits about me. Who knows what I'd say after a little alcohol loosened my tongue. Tal ordered Brie en croute to share as an appetizer, and it's *so good*. I've never had fig jam, but the creamy brie balances the tart sweetness of it deliciously. I've never had anything like it before, and after subsisting off of mostly boxed and frozen meals, it tastes like heaven.

Tal has been peppering me with questions about my week, about my sisters, and sharing things he's been up to. He tells me about a group of preschoolers who came to the station for a field trip, asking a million questions about how they put out fires. Siren apparently loves field trip days because the kids give the best scratches.

It all feels so... normal. Like we've been doing this for years.

I don't—*can't*—trust the familiarity.

I'm having a hard time remembering that while we knew each other as teens, we've both changed. The same things that were true as teenagers aren't true now. My heart wants to pick up right where we left off, act like we weren't apart for thirteen years. But my brain knows it's not possible.

It would be easy to go back to how things were when I was fifteen. Before... everything else happened.

But I can't. I can't change the past. All I can do is move forward one step at a time.

Apparently, with Talmage.

God, my sisters were so annoying about him. I told them I was seeing someone, and Kinsley wouldn't leave me alone.

Who is he? Is he hot? Is he rich? Will he be sleeping over? Does he know you're boring? What does he do? Does he have any social media? Does he make thirst traps? Is he *boring?*

We had to have a chat about what is and isn't appropriate for her to be watching on social media, and thirst traps are in the "absolutely not" column.

She disagreed; it's a battle I'm not going to win, so I dropped it. I don't want to be a helicopter guardian, but I try to make sure they're being safe online.

Harper's not as nosy as Kinsley, thankfully. Or maybe she's just not as vocal about it. Not that Kinsley would let her get a word in. I don't know if Kins just... soaked up all the obnoxiousness in the womb, but while she gave me a thorough interrogation, all Harp asked was *"Does he make you happy?"*

And fuck me if that didn't make me want to cry. I told her he did, and she nodded in approval and said she hopes it works out before she turned back to the script she was studying.

I told Kinsley I would tell her about him after tonight because I don't know if Talmage has told his family, and Lacey is in the musical with Harper. I don't think Harper would gossip to anyone, but I don't need to cause any more issues with his family. His mom is probably going to blow a gasket about us being together as it is. The last thing we need is for Laurie to find out from her teenage daughter her oldest is marrying the girl she despises.

I understand *now* why Laurie thought I was bad for Talmage. She thought I was corrupting him, which... I guess in a way I was. I made him break his "no kissing until marriage" vow or whatever. But we never went past kissing and holding hands. The occasional cuddle at a movie night with all of our friends is hardly salacious.

I can only imagine how she'll feel about me now with my piercings and tattoos and him marrying me on a whim. She'll probably never know the real reason we're getting married. I almost wish she did, though. Then maybe it would soften the blow. Or maybe it would upset her even more. Maybe she'd tell me I'm using him and taking advantage of his kindness.

Joke's on her, I already feel that way about myself.

We each have our entrées now, and we've been eating them in relative silence. My scallop risotto is creamy, and the scallops melt in my mouth, but it's hard to focus on enjoying the meal when my anxiety is swirling.

"Have you told your parents about us yet?" I blurt out, unable to let myself sit with my questions any longer.

Talmage calmly sets down the knife he's using to cut his steak and swallows harshly. "I haven't. I plan on doing it soon, but I wanted to make things official first."

"What do you mean? We're getting married in three weeks. I don't think you should wait until then to tell them. I think that would—"

"That's not what I mean by official," he interrupts, rubbing his hands on his thighs.

"Then what do you mean?"

Tal clears his throat, stands from his chair, reaches into his pocket, and gets down on one knee in front of me.

My eyes probably look like saucers.

Is he...?

No.

Surely not.

He pulls out a gray velvet box.

Oh, God, he is!

"Mackenzie Thorpe," he starts, speaking loud enough he gets the attention of the whole restaurant. The music gets softer, and the hushed voices of the other patrons go quiet, listening intently to the absolutely *insane* man on his knee in front of me.

"When we were fourteen, I fell for the girl who was bad at math and scared of spiders. The girl who obsessively listened to Taylor Swift and would write love notes with hearts dotting the 'i's.' You once told me we were like Cory and Topanga from *Boy Meets World*. Our time wasn't then, but you knew we'd always find our way back to each other. We may have lost touch for a little while, but you were right. Our souls found each other again, and I'll forever be grateful they did.

"We may not be exactly who we were as teenagers, but now I've fallen for the woman who's strong, who will do anything to take care of those she loves. The woman who's been dealt a difficult hand in life but is resilient and hasn't let it consume her. You are the most incredible woman I've ever met, not to mention the most beautiful. I knew I wanted to marry you as a teenager, and I know I want to marry you now."

He opens the box, and my breath gets caught in my throat. Nestled against the padding is the most beautiful ring I've ever seen.

"Mack, will you make me the happiest man alive and marry me?"

My vision goes blurry. I'm so overwhelmed by his sweet words and the slew of emotions drowning my senses, all I can do is nod.

It's not real. My reasonable brain whispers, but I ignore it for now. I'll sob about the fact it's fake later.

Talmage's smile rivals the afternoon sun with how bright it is. There's a sheen of tears in his own eyes, making the blue irises glow as he slips the ring on my finger—a perfect fit.

He stands and pulls me into the tightest hug, whispering, "I'm going to kiss you now," in my ear. He pulls back slightly and cups my face.

I give an imperceptible nod, knowing a kiss will make this all more believable, even as I know it'll completely wreck me.

The restaurant erupts into cheers and applause as he wraps one arm around my waist, cups my face with the other, and brings his lips to mine.

Everything else fades away, though, and all I can see and hear and smell and taste is Talmage.

Talmage Monson is kissing me.

Gentle and cautious, our lips meet, and maybe I'm imagining it, but I swear he whimpers at the contact. Then he apparently decides to throw caution to the wind; he kisses me harder, more urgently, like he's worried I might pull away. His grip on my waist tightens, and his thumb brushes my cheek as his lips press intently against mine.

My senses return when a moan threatens to work its way up my throat, and I pull back, panting and blinking up at him. He didn't even slip me his tongue, and I'm hot and bothered.

No, no, no. I cannot be horny for my fake fiancé. It's just the first human affection I've had other than hugs from Lizzie or the twins in years, and my body is confused.

Tal's eyes are glassy as he stares into mine. Almost as if he's in a trance, he brings his thumb up to my lips and swipes it across them.

"Smudge proof," he whispers.

"Yeah," I whisper back.

"Mack, I—"

"Congratulations, love birds! That was *so* romantic. The manager would like to offer you a complimentary dessert to celebrate your engagement!" our waitress interrupts, and we both jolt a little.

"Oh, that's so kind. Thank you so much." Talmage says. "Can you actually take our picture really quick, please?"

The waitress nods, and he hands her his phone. He wraps his arm around my waist, and I bring my left hand up so the ring is on his chest. I give her my best smile, even though my mind is still reeling. She snaps a few pictures, then hands Tal the phone. He inspects them and nods his approval before giving me one last squeeze, and we take our seats again. "Do we get to choose the dessert?"

"Of course! What would you two like?"

Tal motions for me to go ahead, so I clear my throat. "We'll do the crème brulee, please." It's the only dessert I remember seeing.

She nods, congratulates us again, then leaves to—presumably—go put our order in. Talmage and I sit in an awkward silence.

My risotto is still half eaten, and Tal's steak is probably cold.

What the hell just happened?

"The ring is lovely," I finally say, breaking the silence.

Tal's eyes lock on my left ring finger, and a smile tugs at his lips. "I wanted to get you an emerald—to match the color of your eyes—but I saw this one, and it reminded me of your eyes even more. The different shades of green and the way they swirl together... I knew it was the one I wanted you to have."

"I love it. It's something I would have picked out for myself, if I were to choose my own. I figured you would have gone with a plain band or a simple oval diamond or something."

Talmage's eyes meet mine. "A simple diamond wouldn't cut it. You need a ring as unique and beautiful as you."

Chapter 14

Talmage

14 years old...

I can still feel the way her lips felt on mine, even as I'm sitting in church on Sunday.

All I've been able to think about all weekend is how perfect our first kiss was and how I can't wait to do it again. For the rest of our lives.

I feel bad because I can't tell my mom about what happened, when all I want to do is shout it from the rooftops. She doesn't seem to like Mack all that much, though I can't figure out why. So if I told her I had the perfect kiss with the girl I'm in love with, I think she'd be mad.

Saying those three words out loud filled me with so much happiness, I swear I thought I was going to burst. Something like peace settled inside me, and I finally get when people say "when you know, you know."

Because I know.

One day, Mackenzie Thorpe is going to be my wife.

Mackenzie Thorpe is my fiancée.

That's the first thought I had when I woke up.

Covered in... *stuff* from a wet dream.

A dream that feels wrong to have about my fiancée because she didn't give me consent to think about her like that. But I swear I didn't mean to. It's just...

I'm almost thirty, a virgin, and have only kissed five people in my entire life. I've never masturbated—ever. And that may be unbelievable to some, but it's been drilled into me forever that it's wrong. I was told masturbation could lead to damnation, so I've just... never done it. I've barely been tempted to.

Well, at least not since I was a teenager going through puberty. There were times my ex would try to initiate more, but I would shut it down fast. We were going to be married in the temple! I wasn't about to risk it just to get off.

Maybe that's another reason she ended things, now that I think about it.

But—and I hate to admit it because it makes me feel bad—I wasn't nearly as attracted to her as I am to Mack. Just remembering our simple kiss is making me a little bothered.

After we shared the best crème brulee I've ever had, I drove her home and walked her to her door. She didn't ask me to come inside, and we didn't kiss again, but it's okay. It was still one of the best nights of my life. A step towards the future with her as my wife.

I wish our first kiss after thirteen years wasn't in a crowded restaurant, but it felt right in the moment, and I wouldn't change it. Fitting, since our first kiss back then was also in a crowded space. A restaurant is much better than a gym full of sweaty teenagers, though.

I didn't want to pull back from our kiss. The feeling of her luxurious lips against mine made my brain melt and my blood boil in a way it hasn't before, and I wanted to keep kissing her forever.

It was probably a good thing she pulled away when she did, though, because we *were* in a crowded restaurant.

Am I a little disappointed I didn't get to kiss her good-night at her door? Yes. But do I also know she probably only kissed me because we were in public, and it was the natural thing after a proposal? Also yes.

I still have a bit of work to do before she fully understands—comprehends, accepts—I'm serious about her. About us.

As soon as I woke up—and took care of the mess—I texted Mack. I changed my lock screen to the picture the waitress took last night, and I grinned when I saw it first thing this morning. Mack's hand is on my chest, and her smile is wider than I've ever seen it. The best part is it doesn't look forced. She looks genuinely happy, and it makes warmth spread through my limbs.

We look amazing together.

> **TAL:** Good morning, Mack! <sunshine emoji> I hope you slept well. I'm telling my family about us today. Can I come see you after? <smiley face>

It's been two hours, and she hasn't responded. I've walked Siren, played fetch until my shoulder got tired and she was ready for a nap. Now I'm just sitting on my couch sketching until it's time to leave for dinner at my parents'.

I already knew I'd be skipping church today, and I feel like a rebel doing it without a legitimate reason.

I don't feel as guilty as I usually do, so that's progress. Maybe Mack is rubbing off on me already.

I'm so lost in my drawing of a dragon flying over a field of wildflowers that my phone buzzing startles me, and I snap the lead of my pencil.

I groan, not looking forward to sharpening it. But it's all worth it when I see who texted me back.

> **MACK:** Hey, I slept okay, thanks. You? What time did you want to stop by?

> **TAL:** I slept wonderfully, thanks. <heart> I was thinking 7, probably. Is that okay?

MACK: That's fine. I took Kinsley and Harper out to breakfast today and told them we're getting married.

TAL: How did it go? <peeking emoji>

MACK: About as well as I expected. Lots of questions. Be prepared for them to do the same to you.

TAL: I'll come prepared, promise. <winky face>

MACK: Good luck telling your family. I'll see you later.

TAL: Looking forward to it. <kissy face> <heart>

She doesn't respond, and part of me wonders if the kissing emoji was too much.

Dang it, now I'm thinking about kissing her again.

Smudge-proof lipstick.

Needing a distraction, I get off the couch and put my art supplies back in the drawer before taking a quick shower and putting on some nicer clothes than the sweats and Springville FD shirt I had on.

Why am I more nervous to tell my parents I'm getting married than I was to ask Mack to marry me? Maybe because my mom hasn't liked Mack in the past, and this *is* really sudden. But I'm an adult. I can make my own choices. They don't have to like them, but they do have to respect them.

I get Siren buckled into the car and drive to my parents' house. Time to face the music.

The clink of utensils hitting ceramic fills the air as we all dig into our food. I'm next in the lineup of updates on my life, and I think I'm sweating with how nervous I am.

Lauren is just finishing telling us about a guy in her master's program, a world-famous cellist who can no longer play to the same caliber because of a broken arm. He wants to teach now, and they're in a study group together. She doesn't say it with the cadence of someone who's interested in him romantically, but it doesn't stop my mom from pouncing on the information.

"Well, he sounds like a nice boy. Maybe you two can... study together," Mom says, and Lauren groans.

"Anyway, Talmage, you're up. What's new with you?" Dad asks, moving the conversation along.

I set down my fork and rub my hands on my thighs. "Well, I actually have some really big news. I'm getting married on February fifteenth."

A few forks drop, everyone's eyes turn to me, and my mom gasps.

"What do you mean you're getting *married?* To whom?" Mom sounds outraged and maybe a little hurt.

"Mackenzie Thorpe—"

"WHAT?" she yells. "That—that... *girl* who made you do things against your will as a teenager? The one who made you stray from the path? Talmage, please tell me you're joking!" Mom spits out the word "girl" like it's an insult, and feelings I'm not used to swell in my chest.

Anger. Defensiveness.

I'm angry my mom is already insulting my future wife, angry she's holding a grudge with a *teenager.* I didn't think she'd be singing Mack's praises or making plans to take her wedding dress shopping, but I also didn't expect her to be so mad, so hurtful.

I try to keep myself calm, even though I want to snap at her. "You're acting like I wasn't a willing participant in my relationship with her when we were teenagers, Mom, and that's not fair to her. Mackenzie didn't make me do anything I didn't want to do, but you've always thought she did."

Mom shakes her head. "She's bad news, Talmage. She doesn't go to church, she's got those tattoos, and not to mention the trauma she's been through. Who knows what kind of mental issues she has! Besides, I didn't know you two were even talking again! Now you're telling me you're getting *married?* It's just unbeliev-able."

"Well, believe it. It may be fast, but you're always telling me 'when you know, you know,' and I *know.*

Mackenzie isn't bad news. She's the woman I'm going to marry. The best thing to ever happen to me. I *love* her."

The weight of the truth of those words settles the anger in me, just a little. It's soon. It's crazy. But I don't really care. They're true regardless of the timing. I only wish I would have told Mack I love her before I told my mom, but I don't know how receptive Mack would be to those words right now. She's still a little closed off, and I know I need to give her time to be prepared to hear them.

I'll wait until she trusts me explicitly to tell her.

"Well, I can't support you not getting married in the temple, and I'm assuming you're not. This is the wrong choice, Talmage." Mom looks to my dad for support, and he just sits there with his arms crossed and shakes his head in disappointment.

My siblings all have their heads down now, avoiding eye contact with me or my mom, not wanting to get in the middle of this. I don't blame them. My mom can be scary.

"I'm not doing this to hurt you, and I'm sorry you don't feel like you can support me." I take a deep breath. It's time to go big or go home. "I guess I might as well rip off the Band-Aid and add that I'm leaving the church. And before you blame Mackenzie for it, you should know this has been a long time coming—before I even reconnected with her. She's just given me the courage to finally do it."

Mom's eyes fill with tears, and she covers her mouth like she's holding in a scream. "I knew you going to California—being around sin and hanging out with Emma—was a bad idea. But you wanted to spread your wings and try something different, so I didn't say any-thing. I hoped you'd be stronger than your cousins, but I guess Satan is stronger."

The anger comes back with a blazing vengeance, this time on behalf of my cousins. "Emma, Elli, and Hannah are some of the strongest people I know. You don't know half of what they've been through. I hoped you'd be more accepting of my decision, but I understand this is hard and you'll need time. I hope you'll change your mind because I'd like you to be there on my wedding day, but only if you're going to be happy for me."

I stand and take my half-eaten food to the sink, then whistle for Siren to come in from the backyard and get her in the car. All the while my mom's sporadic sobs and Dad's hushed words of comfort act as a soundtrack to my departure. No one tries to stop me, and it stings more than I anticipated.

Unfortunately, the dinner didn't go the way I wanted it to. But I still have a sliver of hope they'll come around.

At least the silver lining is I get to see Mack tonight. I just... won't tell her my mom's still holding a grudge with the teenage version of her. Mom will have to get over it if she wants to be part of my life.

Mackenzie is the most important person in my life now. My family—at least for now.

Forever if I can help it.

Chapter 15

Talmage

14 years old...

My nerves swirl around in my stomach when I get in the car with Mack's parents to head to her dance recital. She had to be there early to get ready, so I'll be alone with them on the short drive.

"Talmage. How's it going?" her dad asks when I get in the car. Her twin sisters are blabbering away when I squeeze myself between their car seats to sit in the very back row.

Do her parents know Mack and I are in love? Has she told them anything?

I feel like it'd be pretty obvious with how much time we spend together, and the fact I'm going to her recital. But has she said it out loud? If she has, they're a lot more chill than my parents. They wouldn't be cool about it.

"I'm doing well, Mr. Thorpe. How are you?"

"No need to be so formal, son, Lyle is perfectly fine."

"Sorry, force of habit." I feel my cheeks redden.

"No need to be nervous, Talmage. We're not going to bite your head off, I promise." Her mom, Angie, turns to *give me a smile. Mack got her wide smile and red hair from her mom, and it fills me with a little bit of comfort. "Mackenzie told us you two were planning on singing together for your term performance, is that still the plan?"*

"Yes, we have a practice scheduled with her voice teacher in two weeks, I think."

"That'll be so fun. You two are going to be great together, I just know it. Mackenzie's been happier than ever since you two became such good friends." Angie gives me a wink.

They have to know.

And they seem okay with it.

It makes me feel good, knowing Mack isn't going to be in trouble.

I only wish my parents were as accepting.

I hope Mack's okay with me showing up an hour early. In my hurry to get out of my parents', I didn't think about texting her, and the ten minute drive to her house passed in a blur.

Now, I'm sitting in the driveway of the little blue house, contemplating whether I should take Siren home or not.

Before I make a decision, the front door swings open, and two girls who look similar to Mack but with different colored hair stand there. One of them grabs the other by the arm and tries to pull her inside, but she's too fast and yanks her arm from her then sprints towards me.

I'm not even fully out of my car before the one with dirty blonde hair starts hurling questions my way at a million miles an hour.

"Are you Talmage? You're Lacey and Tim's brother, right? Your brother is so *cute.* Oh, shit, don't tell him that. *Awkward.* What do you do? How are you so fit? Are you sure you want to marry Mack? *Why* do you want to marry Mack? Is this like some Make-A-Wish shit because of the whole dead parents thing? Do you make thi—"

"Kinsley! Will you shut up?" her twin hisses. She turns to me, cheeks aflame and shakes her head. Her hair is more of a strawberry blonde than her sister's. "I'm sorry about her."

I open my mouth to speak when Siren barks once from inside my car, pressing her nose to the window like she's trying to smell the twins through the glass.

Kinsley—the one with all the questions—*squeals.*

"Oh my *God!* Is this your dog? Hi, puppy, what a cutie-wootie!" She wiggles her fingers at Siren through the glass.

Harper cringes at Kinsley's puppy voice.

I chuckle, opening the door and letting Siren out. She immediately runs around the girls, sniffing their legs. She's trained not to jump up on people, but I can tell she likes them already by how rapidly her tail is wagging. She lets out a little *woof* when she sniffs Harper before plopping down at her feet while Harper gently pets Siren's silky fur.

"This is Siren. Do you think your sister will mind if I let her wander around the backyard?"

Kinsley gasps, kneeling on the cold driveway and scratching Siren's ears. "No fur-niece of mine will be cast to the backyard like a commoner. She can come hang out in our room while you and Mack talk or... whatever you do." Her nose crinkles like she smells something bad. "You guys aren't going to like, kiss and be gross all the time, are you?"

My stomach flutters at the thought of kissing Mack again. I *hope* we kiss all the time. That would be a dream come true.

"I—"

"Kinsley, I swear to God. I'll make you eat school lunch for a week if you're bothering Talmage." The voice of my dream girl floats through the chilly air, sending a shiver down my spine. Siren barks and runs up to Mack, giving her a thorough sniff-spection. Mack squats and rubs behind Siren's ears, a small smile on her face.

Kinsley rolls her eyes but heads back towards the front door. Harper and I follow.

"I wasn't bothering our future brother-in-law. I was just making sure his intentions are pure. Harp and I are going to take Siren to our room while you two talk. C'mon, girl."

Siren looks at me and tilts her head like she's waiting for my permission.

"Go on, go get some attention from your new aunts," I say as I reach the threshold of the door. As soon as Siren and the girls are out of sight, I let my gaze meet Mack's.

She looks cozy in an oversized gray sweatshirt and leggings, her hair in a messy bun. She's not wearing any makeup, and the bags under her eyes make my chest ache. I still think she's the most beautiful woman I've ever seen, but I hate how tired and worn out she looks.

Not for long. My wife will be well-rested and rejuvenated if I have any say in the matter.

"Hey, Mack. Hope it's okay I'm early."

"Of course. Come on in." She steps into the house, and I follow. I didn't get to see inside when I picked her up for our date yesterday, and I'm eager to see what Mack's space looks like. When we were teens, I never saw the inside of her house.

The door opens into a little entryway. To the left is a set of French doors leading to a space with a piano and shelves full of books, and to the right is what looks like a half bath. We walk down the hall into an open-concept kitchen and living room. There's a plush looking brown leather couch, matching armchair, and a TV mounted to the wall. More bookshelves hold DVDs, and pictures line the walls. All the walls are painted a light gray, and the flooring is light oak. There's a large multi-colored floral area rug in the middle of the living room.

The kitchen lights are off, but from what I can see, the cabinets are painted a pale yellow with silver handles and matching stainless steel appliances. The countertops are white and gray marbled granite that pair nicely with the color scheme. It looks... bright. Happy. It makes me wonder if Mack picked it out or if this was her parents' doing.

"Your house is nice," I comment as she motions for me to sit down on one end of the couch.

Her smile is sad when she replies, "Thanks. They'd just finished remodeling the upstairs about six months before... well, you know. Mom was so happy to finally have her yellow kitchen."

"I'm sorry, Mack."

She shrugs. "Thank you. How did it go with your parents?"

I blow out a long breath. "Not... great. My mom is really upset, and I think it'll take some time to mend our relationship. I also may have blurted out I was leaving the church, so..."

"Oh, no, Tal. I'm so sorry." She reaches across the couch and grabs my hand, giving it a comforting squeeze.

I scoot a little closer to her and flip my hand over, intertwining my fingers with hers—a perfect fit.

My heart flip flops when I realize she's wearing her ring. I like seeing it on her finger way more than I thought I would.

"It's okay. I'm sure she'll come around, and if she doesn't, then... I'll cross that bridge when I come to it. If she can't be happy for me, then I don't need her in my life."

Mack's frown deepens. "I don't want your family relationship to be ruined just so Harp can have better health insurance. I'm not worth all the pain and trouble."

She doesn't realize I'd walk over a bed of nails for her. I'd trudge through a building on fire with no gear, if I needed to, just to get to her. I'd do *anything* to keep her in my life and make her happy.

"You're more than worth it, Mack. Like I said, I'm sure she'll come around. She just needs to get over the initial shock of... everything. I would have to tell her anyway when I eventually left the church—and it would have happened with or without you. We would've had the same argument. The only difference is, now I have you."

Mack chews on the inside of her cheek. "For now," she mutters.

Yeah, the reminder makes me itchy. I don't like it. Not one bit.

I scoot even closer, so our thighs are touching. Then, I cup her cheek. "Then I'll have to make the most of the time I've got."

I start to lean in, but she turns her head. "I don't think we should kiss again. Other than like, on our wedding day, you know? We need to make sure we don't cross any lines so it's not as hard when this ends."

I scoot back, and instant regret floods my body. "Right. You're right. Sorry. I got caught up in the moment." I don't agree with her, though. I think whether we kiss or not, it'll be like ripping off a limb when we get divorced. It'll feel like losing half of my soul.

"It's okay. So, are we all set for the fifteenth?"

I nod. "Did you ask Lizzie if she wants to be a witness?"

"Yes. She said I didn't have to ask because it's the best friend law that she gets to be one. Are you asking one of your friends?"

"I thought I'd ask Enoch or Nathan."

"Are you okay with Harper and Kinsley being there, too? Kinsley told me it was illegal for them to *not* be included since they're my only family. She's convinced me to get us all new dresses for the day, too."

"Kinsley's a feisty one, isn't she? Yeah, they can come for sure. I'm going to reach out to my siblings and ask if they want to come, too, but I don't know if they'll be willing to go behind my mom's back."

"Yeah, Harper may be the one in theatre, but you'd never know it because Kins has all the drama. I hope your siblings come."

Me, too. It would be nice to have my family there for my only wedding—and it *will* be my only wedding if I have any say. Maybe once Mack realizes we're kismet, we can have a big wedding do-over with the cake and the flowers and dancing surrounded by family and friends.

Hannah and Morgan had a small, intimate ceremony at the courthouse last year, and they'll be having a party in April to celebrate their one-year anniversary. It's not totally unheard of to have a belated celebration.

"Our appointment is for two o'clock. I'll come pick you guys up at one-thirty, then we can go to an early dinner after to celebrate."

"Oh, no, it's okay. I can meet you there, and there's no need to—"

"There is absolutely a need to celebrate. Let me take my wife and sisters-in-law out. If you want to drive separately, that's okay. I can pack up my stuff so it's ready to move in that night, then get the rest on Sunday."

"I think it'd be best to drive separately. Everything else sounds... good."

"Perfect. Are you still planning on us sharing a room?"

Mack's face heats up, turning red like an adorable strawberry, and I don't understand why. "Yeah," she says. "I have a king bed in my room downstairs, so it should be fine. We're adults. We can share a bed and be cool about it."

"Of course we can. Wanna show me? That way I can plan accordingly for what needs to be put in storage."

"Sure. Don't set your expectations too high, though, it's nothing fancy." She stands from the couch, and I follow her downstairs.

The basement is one large living area with brown speckled carpet and tan walls. There's a TV on one wall and four bookshelves filled to the brim on another. A desk is set against a wall with a large office chair in front of it. I assume it's where Mack works when she works from home.

"Are all these books yours?" I ask, inspecting the spines. Some are bright, playful colors with swooping lettering. Others are dark with crisp, clean words. Some have titles that sound like they'd be fantasy novels, while others are clearly rom-com types.

"Yeah. Books are the only thing I allow myself to buy that's not a necessity, but I haven't been able to buy any new ones in a few years—for obvious reasons. I usually stick to my Kindle."

"Do you mind if I read some of these? They sound cool."

"Ummm. Sure? You might not like them, though. They're not just standard fantasy novels. A lot of them are romantasy."

I shrug. "I'm not worried about a little romance in my fantasy."

She opens her mouth like she's going to say something but shuts it as if she changed her mind. "Okay. Well, enjoy."

She walks to the door on the opposite side of the living room and opens it, revealing a decent sized bedroom. The walls are painted a soft pink, and the bed is covered in unmade floral sheets. There's still plenty of space, even with the king bed. There are no pictures on the walls, though, just a mirror propped against it next to a set of doors.

I whistle. "This is nice."

"Thanks. After the twins were born, my parents didn't want me to have to keep going upstairs to use the bathroom, so they made this into another primary suite. The bathroom is through that door, and the other doors are the walk-in closet. I'll clear out some space for you in there and in the dresser."

"Thanks, Mack. I know this is a big change. I can always sleep out on the couch if you need me to. I don't want you to be uncomfortable."

Mack shakes her head. "I don't want to risk Kins or Harper seeing you on the couch if they come down here. It'll all be okay."

She sounds like she's trying to convince herself more than me, and my chest pinches. I don't like that she's uncomfortable.

I make a vow to myself to do everything in my power to make her as comfortable as I can—to make this transition as easy as possible. I'll prove to her I can make her life better and not be a hindrance.

CHAPTER 16

Mackenzie

15 years old...

I'm not usually nervous before a performance, but knowing Tal is going to be here watching a dance my teacher and I choreographed to a song I've dedicated to him in my head?

I feel like I'm going to throw up.

What if he hates it? What if he doesn't think I'm good enough? What if he hates my costume? The song choice? That it isn't as complicated as the other dances?

I don't think I'm bad at dancing, but my body isn't as flexible as some of the other girls on my team, and sometimes it feels like I'm not good enough because of it.

I run my hands over the lavender halter dress. The skirt flows out from my hips and looks lovely in my spins, and the color pops against my skin. My hair is pulled back in a half-bun, curled, and hairsprayed within an inch of its life.

I feel *pretty*. But will he think I am? Mom always says to dress for yourself and not for anyone else, but I can't help it. I want Tal to think I'm beautiful.

The song the six-year-olds are dancing to ends, and the audience claps, bringing the nerves back with a vengeance.

I walk to the center of the stage and strike my opening pose, then the music—Boyce Avenue's cover of "Teenage Dream"—begins, and I let the music take over as I perform the routine that's embedded itself into my muscles, thinking about Talmage the entire time.

I'm getting married today.

Fuck, I'm getting married today. To Talmage fucking Monson.

Since he left the Sunday he told his family we were getting married, we've seen each other in person at least twice a week and text every day.

It's been…

Nice.

Except for my poor heart. She's been through the wringer. Every time he texts, she beats a little faster. My stomach hasn't fared any better with the way it gets tied up in knots when he's around or the way the butterflies take flight when he looks at me with his warm grin and kissable lips.

Telling him we shouldn't kiss because it'll blur the lines was the smart thing to do, and yet… I find myself regretting it more often than not. I find myself thinking *just once. One hit, so I can memorize the feel of his mouth. To learn the way he kisses now.*

It's obvious he's gained some experience since we last kissed. I can't stand to think about it, though. Knowing some other woman has felt his lips makes me want to stomp my feet and throw a tantrum. I've kissed other people, had *sex* with other people. He was engaged, of course he's kissed other people.

We're going to have to kiss today. That's what you do on your wedding day, it would be weird if we didn't. It would raise too many questions from the twins and his friends, and I don't have a valid excuse not to do it. I've been mentally psyching myself up all day. Thank God no one will ever know whether or not we consummate our marriage because if we had to...

I would simply pass away.

I would *not* survive making love to Talmage Monson. No, no, no.

My body, though? She wants it—wants him. The first time he came over in his Springville FD T-shirt, contoured to the subtle bulge of his muscles on his arms and the expanse of his chest...

I'm deeply ashamed to admit my vibrator got a workout that night, imagining what those arms would feel like caging me in. Imagining what his mustache would feel like tickling the dimpled skin of my inner thighs. I want to feel the rough calluses of his fingers tracing the sensitive peaks of my nipples.

Yeah, I'm fucked. Maybe not literally but metaphorically for sure.

It's three hours before our appointment, and I'm sitting on a kitchen stool while Lizzie twists a curling iron around my hair and Kinsley and Harper chatter away about... something.

I wish I could pay more attention. But all my brain power is trying to wrap my head around the fact I'm marrying the first boy I ever loved—probably the only boy I've ever truly loved.

How did I get to this point? What am I *doing?* Is this a huge mistake? Is it worth it to—

"Earth to Mack!" Lizzie's fingers snap in front of my face, bringing me out of my thoughts.

"Sorry. Zoned out. What's up?"

Lizzie's hot pink painted lips turn down into a frown. "You don't seem like a joyous bride today, babe. What's up?"

I look pointedly at my twin sisters, hoping Lizzie can understand my unspoken message of "not in front of them."

"All right, twinsies. I need to have an adult chat with your sister. Go... get dressed or something. No eavesdropping." Lizzie points at each girl individually.

Harper nods and scurries off to her room, while Kinsley rolls her eyes. "You're not the boss of me. And I'm almost an adult! I should be included."

"Three years does not almost an adult make, Kinny-poo. Unless you want to hear all about how sloppy of a kisser Talmage is then—"

"EEEW, okay, I'm going. Gross. Keep that shit to yourself." Kinsley covers her ears and runs out of the kitchen.

Lizzie turns back to me with a triumphant grin. "All right, Mack, spill it."

I chew on my bottom lip. I'm glad Lizzie knows this is all fake. I don't know how I'd explain my anxious mood otherwise.

"Am I making a huge mistake? I mean, Tal's relationship with his parents is ruined, and he's really not getting anything out of this. I'm already starting to get attached to him, and I feel *so* selfish—"

Lizzie holds up a hand. "Nope. Gonna stop you right there. You're *not* selfish. You've been working your ass off to make ends meet so Harper can have the medicine she needs to *live*. It's not selfish to accept the help offered to you."

"But a whole-ass *marriage?*"

"Marriage is a piece of paper. It's a social construct and an institution rooted in control. But I don't think that's what you'll be entering into with Talmage because he doesn't seem to have a controlling bone in his body.

"Besides, we live in a no-fault state. You can divorce him for whatever reason at any time, and no one will think less of you. Well, okay, *that's* not true because society is still misogynistic, and Tal is a hot man with an honorable career, so people *might* judge you for not staying with him, but if it's not making you happy then you have options. You said once you find a job with better benefits, you can divorce him, right?" I nod. "So you're not *stuck*. Tal's a big boy who can make his own decisions. He wants to marry you. So take the help and accept this is what he wants."

"You're right, you're right. I need to believe he knows what he's doing." I take a deep breath—in for a count of four, out for six—and give Lizzie a small smirk. "It's not like it'll be a hardship for me to be with him. He's pretty easy on the eyes."

She barks out a laugh. "Talk about a glow-up. He's a far cry from the boy who used to wear knee-high socks with his cargo shorts and long sleeves under his dad's button ups."

A genuine smile spreads across my face when I think about teenage Tal and his lack of fashion sense. His quirky style was one of the things I loved about him. He didn't care what other people thought about him, and I found it admirable.

I didn't mind the knee-high socks and cargo shorts, just like I don't mind the muscles and tight T-shirts now.

"My mom would like that I'm marrying him. He was always one of her favorites." I've been feeling a deep sense of devastation that my parents won't be here. I always pictured my dad walking me down the aisle and my mom sobbing into a tissue as I said my vows. I pictured her here to help me get ready and give me advice about marriage. Their marriage had its ups and downs, I'm sure, but I don't ever remember them fighting. They were always hugging or holding hands, so in love, even twenty years in. I used to be disgusted by their blatant affection, but I miss it now.

"I know you wish they were here. I'm sorry they're missing this. If it helps, I know they'd be so fucking proud of you."

I hope that's true. "Thanks, Liz. We should get my makeup on before I start crying."

"On it! Let's make you into the most beautiful blushing bride."

CHAPTER 17

Talmage

14 years old...

I don't know much about the technical terms of dance, but I know I'm mesmerized watching Mack spin and leap across the stage. The way her movements flow together?

Breathtaking.

She looks beautiful in her costume, and I can't stop staring at her.

During her first group number, I tried to watch the other girls, but they never held my attention for more than a few seconds because Mack is the only one I can focus on.

I love her so much.

I've heard the song she's dancing to before but not like this.

Did she think of me when she picked this song?

I hope so. Because I'll be listening to it on repeat and thinking of her.

My teenage dream.

When the song ends and she walks off the stage, I crane my neck to get every last glimpse of her I can.

"Isn't she incredible?" Her mom's voice is filled with pride. Even the twins are watching their sister with rapt attention.

"Incredibly incredible," I say, then cringe at how silly that sounds.

"She's been working so hard. Dancing in the living room, downstairs in the family room, staying late at the studio. She said it needed to be perfect because it's important to her."

"Well, she nailed it. I would give her a twenty out of ten if I were judging."

Angie and Lyle chuckle, and Lyle reaches past Angie to pat me on the shoulder. "You're a good one, Talmage. Thanks for treating her so well."

I'm getting married today.

To Mackenzie Thorpe.

My first kiss, my first love, and the girl of my dreams.

I just wish my parents could be here to see it—to support me.

My mom called me a week after our disagreement and asked if I had changed my mind about marrying "that Thorpe girl."

I told her no, I'm confident in my decision, and I hoped they could come and be supportive. Be happy for me—for *us*.

She told me she was disappointed in me, and she hoped I got my head on straight soon and thought about the eternal repercussions. To think about what I want my forever to look like.

I told her I've never had a clearer head. I know what I want from my life, and I'm finally going after it. My life doesn't revolve around the arbitrary rules of the church anymore.

She hung up after, but that's okay. I still think she'll come around after she has some time to process. I can only imagine how hard it is when your oldest son leaves the only religion he's ever known and marries a girl you're not a fan of—which I don't fully understand. I don't get why she's still holding a grudge.

It's just a shame she and my dad won't be here for what's sure to be the greatest day of my life.

Today, I get to marry the love of my life with my best friends and her sisters by our side. I reached out to Thomas and Lauren to see if they wanted to come, but they both said they weren't sure if they wanted to deal with the blowback from Mom.

I expected it, but it still stung a little. I'd hoped they'd want to support me.

That's okay, though. I'm sure things with them will calm down, too. As soon as Mom comes around, everything will go back to normal.

I'm standing in the lobby of the Utah County Passport and Marriage Office with Nathan and Enoch, and I'm wishing we planned for a different location. This doesn't exactly scream "romantic" with the drab wood floor, gray walls, and fluorescent lighting.

Mack and I *will* have a bigger, better ceremony or party later on. I'm going to make sure of it.

The front doors open, and—like every time they've opened in the last few minutes—my eyes track to the entrance hoping to see Mack.

Only, it's not Mack who enters. It's her sisters, dressed in identical pale pink dresses with the hem falling to their knees in a flowy material and the sleeves cuffing at the wrists. They look cute, like they're going to a school dance with their hair in braided crowns around their heads.

Lizzie walks in next in a simple black slip dress with a lace undershirt and hot pink cowgirl boots that match the shade of her lipstick and the pink of her hair.

"Dude. Who is that?" Enoch whispers, smacking me on the shoulder.

"Mack's best friend, Lizzie."

"She looks like she'd *absolutely* destroy my heart. I think I'm in love."

"Please don't. I don't want to have to pick my wife over you if things go wrong. And they *will*. You two are total opposites."

My best friend scoffs, running his hand through his shaggy brown hair, leaving it looking tousled in a way I know women go crazy for. "You'd pick your wife over me?"

"Any day of the week," I trail off, because I see her. My wife.

Looking like a literal angel.

Her hair is in soft waves with half of it pulled back away from her face, and her make up is simple but elegant, the shimmery eyeshadow on her lids makes her eyes glimmer in the light.

But the dress...

The dress!

The bottom half of it looks like plain white satin flowing over her wide hips and down to her nude-colored flats, but the top...

The *top.*

It has long sleeves with white lace, floral beading accents on the cuffs, and beading over the bodice. The front dips down between her breasts in a way that makes me think she's not wearing a bra.

Don't think about that. This is a pure, happy, innocent moment. She doesn't have to wear a bra if she doesn't want to. Don't be a creep.

I have to swallow the lump in my throat three times before I can finally speak, and when I finally do, it comes out hoarse. "Mack, you look..."

"It's too much, isn't it? I told them this was too much for a courthouse ceremony, but it was on sale and—"

I gently grab her hand, halting her rambling. "*No.* No, you look... *breathtaking,* Mack. That's not even a strong enough word for how incredible you look."

"Thank you," she says breathily. "You look... really good, too."

I'm wearing a simple black suit with a green tie that matches the shade of her ring. I look like I'm wearing casual clothes compared to her.

"EW. Can you two stop looking at each other like that?" Kinsley punctuates her question with a pretend gag.

Mack rolls her eyes.

"Get used to it, they're going to be eye-fucking each other twenty-four-seven, kid." Lizzie chuckles, nudging Kinsley with her elbow.

My face flames—both at the casual use of the curse word and the mental image it conjures.

Harper covers her mouth and giggles as Kinsley groans. Nathan's face is as red as mine, and Enoch is staring at Lizzie with hearts in his brown eyes.

"Is the Monson-Thorpe party ready?" a woman at the front desk of the courthouse calls.

I offer my arm to Mack, and she places her hand on my bicep. We lead our little group towards them.

"We're here," I announce.

The woman glances up from her clipboard. "Great. Follow me."

We follow her down a carpeted hallway to an open door. "Deputy Clerk Higgins will be performing your ceremony today. Who are your witnesses?"

Lizzie and Enoch step forward.

"Great, we'll get your signatures after the ceremony."

The room looks like your standard conference room with a big table and a few rolling chairs. At the front of the room stands a tall, gangly man with dark rectangular glasses and a very pronounced widow's peak. He's wearing a blue sweater over a white collared shirt and a pair of khakis. Not exactly what I imagined our officiant to be wearing, but that's okay. All that matters is by the end of this, Mack will be my wife.

He gives a beaming smile when he sees us enter the room. "You must be the happy couple! Let's get this going so you guys can get out of here and celebrate. If you'll just give me your full names, I can jot them down in my little speech."

"Talmage George Monson and Mackenzie Thorpe," I answer.

"Great!" He scribbles our names on the little paper he's holding. "Your party can take their seats in the vacant chairs, and I'll have you two stand here, and here." He points to either side of him, and we all take our spots.

Mr. Higgins clears his throat. "We're here today to witness the union of Talmage George Monson and Mackenzie Thorpe in marriage. Today, you begin a new life together, founded in love, laughter, honesty, respect, and friendship. The promises you make to each other today should not be taken lightly. A marriage is more than a ceremony or a piece of paper—it's a lasting and lifelong commitment."

My stomach drops. This marriage technically *isn't* one founded in love and honesty. Mack's lips turn down, and I know she's thinking the same thing.

Our officiant continues, unaware of our thoughts, "The future promises many happy days ahead, filled with adventures and challenges. Through trust, love, and unwavering support for each other, you will be able to weather the inevitable ups and downs to come.

"Do you, Talmage George Monson, take Mackenzie Thorpe to be your spouse and to live as one team, to treat her with love and respect, and build a marriage that grows stronger and more loving as the years pass?"

Why do I want to cry right now?

"Absolutely, without a doubt, yes," I croak out, hoping tears don't fall from my eyes.

He turns to Mack. "Do you, Mackenzie Thorpe, take Talmage George Monson to be your spouse and to live as one team, to treat him with love and respect, and build a marriage that grows stronger and more loving as the years pass?"

"Yes, I do," Mack whispers, staring me directly in the eyes. Her own are wide and vulnerable, and I wish right now I could read what's going on in her head. Is she regretting this? Surely not, since she said yes. Right?

"If you have rings, please take them out now."

Lizzie stands and hands Mack a ring, and Enoch hands me the band I bought for Mack.

"These rings represent the promises and potential of marriage. It has no beginning and no end, just like the love and commitment you have pledged. As you wear your rings, let them remind you of the love you feel for one another. Mackenzie, please place the ring on Talmage's finger, and repeat after me: I give you this ring as a symbol of my love and devotion. As we join our lives together, today, tomorrow, and for as long as our love will last."

Mack's shaking hands slip the gold ring on my finger as she repeats the promises, and my heart swells to the point of pain. When she removes her fingers from the ring, I feel like I'm about to have a heart attack because it's not just a plain gold band.

There's a small sliver of moss agate in the middle of the band—an exact match to the gem in her ring.

I look between my ring and her, and she gives me a small shrug as if to say "no big deal." But it *is* a big deal.

Hope floats around in my chest and inflates my lungs. She could have picked a generic ring, but she picked one that matches hers and has *meaning.* You don't do that for a marriage you don't want to last.

Maybe there's a real chance for us after all.

"Talmage, please place your ring on Mackenzie's finger and repeat the same vows."

I slide the gold band on her finger, and it sits perfectly on top of her other one, just like I knew it would. I say the same words Mack said to me, my voice cracking from the sheer amount of emotion I feel.

"True marriage is more than a piece of paper. It is a lasting bond joining two lives—two hearts—forever. May you always find strength in each other, laugh with each other, and find safety, comfort, joy, and love in each other's company. Celebrate the highs and support each other when things are difficult. Continue to grow closer with each year.

"By the authority vested in me by the State of Utah, I now pronounce you married. You may kiss! Congratulations."

As soon as the word "kiss" is said, I practically lunge for Mack.

She doesn't hesitate at all as our lips meet in a kiss that feels like sealing a promise. Her lips are soft against mine as I cup her face and pour every emotion I'm feeling into the kiss.

I hope she can feel the love I have for her, the silent vow I'm making to never give up on us. I meant every word that came out of my mouth. This isn't a deal born of convenience, but something I've been searching for my whole life.

"All right, you two. This is a public building. I don't think Deputy Clerk Higgins wants to arrest you for public indecency." Lizzie breaks the haze of our kiss, and I force myself to pull away from Mack.

Even though my face is flushed with embarrassment at getting carried away, I still shrug with as much nonchalance as I can. "What can I say? I can't get enough of my wife."

CHAPTER 18

Mackenzie

15 years old...

Tal and I are sitting behind the school, waiting for rehearsals to start and sharing a pack of gummy worms.

"Which temple do you want to get married in?" he asks, and I tilt my head while I think about it.

"I think the Provo City Center Temple. I've never been inside, but I think the outside is really pretty."

He nods. "I like that one, too. What season?"

"Fall. I love the colors."

"I like that, too. Then it's not close to either of our birthdays, either. I'm thinking maybe the end of September or the beginning of October?"

I smile when I realize he's planning our wedding and not just making small talk. "That sounds good to me."

"What kind of cake are we having?"

I tap my chin. "I think a combination. You like funfetti, but I like red velvet, so maybe we do a layer of each?"

"I like that idea. Best of both worlds. Just promise you won't shove the cake in my face?"

"I won't if you won't." I hold out my pinky, and he wraps his around mine before giving me a quick kiss.

"Deal. I can't wait to marry you, Mack."

"I can't get enough of my wife."

I'm Talmage Monson's wife.

And apparently... he can't get enough of me.

Signing the certificate, leaving the municipal building, and getting in the car is a bit of a blur since my mind is still reeling from the fact I'm *married*.

I wasn't expecting to feel the cocktail of emotions swirling through my stomach. Everything from guilt, sadness, relief, hope, and... love.

I felt like we were lying to the Higgins guy. His speech was sweet and heartfelt, and even though he probably uses it with everyone, it felt genuine—like it was meant just for us.

And it made me feel guilty.

Because this marriage isn't built on love—at least, not entirely. I've loved Talmage for over a decade, but there's a slim chance he reciprocates those feelings. Whatever this is, it's built on mutual benefit and America's shitty healthcare system. It's built on desperation and Talmage's kind, selfless nature.

But you'd never know this marriage is a sham based on Tal's reactions. I saw the way his gaze traveled over my body when I walked in. I saw the tears he was blinking away during the ceremony, and the genuine surprise and awe on his face when he realized I got him a ring to match mine.

I don't know why I did it. A sense of possession, maybe? Just something small to show he's *mine.* I doubt people will look too closely at our rings, but I still wanted to know for *myself* that our rings match and symbolize our union even if it doesn't last forever.

Tal convinced me to ride in his car with him to the restaurant. Nathan and Enoch are in one car, and Lizzie and the twins are in mine. We're going to Brazão, a Brazilian steakhouse where they cut the meat at your table. I argued it was too much, but Tal reminded me this is a celebration, and nothing is too much when it comes to celebrating our marriage.

Hard to argue with him. Especially when he sounds so earnest.

The car is filled with a heavy silence. Tal's hands grip the steering wheel at ten and two, and I can feel him glancing at me every few seconds, like he's trying to make sure I'm actually here.

The back of his car is filled with bags and boxes, a reminder that after dinner he'll be moving in. Tonight, we'll share a bed. Tomorrow, we'll have breakfast together and possibly lunch and dinner—I don't know his work schedule. We'll be sharing a *life* just like the officiant said.

I've never shared a life with anyone. Sharing apartments with my friends or my workaholic ex-boyfriend didn't feel as life-altering as sharing a space with the boy I've loved since I was fourteen.

We get to the restaurant first and sit in silence for a minute. I watch happy couples celebrating a belated Valentine's Day hold hands and walk around with big smiles on their faces, hearts practically coming out of their eyes.

"How are you feeling?" Tal breaks the silence, turning to face me.

"Overwhelmed," I answer honestly.

Tal's lips kick up on one side. "Same. It was... a lot. Are you... do you have any regrets?"

I roll my head on the headrest to look at him. The sun glints off of the gem in his ring, catching my attention before I look at my husband. He looks dashing in his suit. The tie matches the moss agate in our rings—intentional, probably. His mustache is freshly trimmed, and his face has clearly just been shaved. His skin looks so smooth, my hands itch to feel it. His dirty blonde hair is neatly gelled to one side, but a stray strand has escaped, flopped on his forehead.

My eyes automatically drop to his lips, and—maybe unconsciously—his tongue pokes out and licks a path across the pillowy surface.

"No regrets." I look in his eyes—safer territory than anywhere lower.

Or not, if the heat I see in his blue depths is real and not my imagination.

"Me neither. In fact I—"

A knock on the window startles both of us.

I really want to know what he was going to say, but I guess I'll have to wait since our entourage is standing in the brisk wind and motioning for us to get the hell inside.

I give Tal an apologetic smile and go to open my door.

"Wait! Let me open my wife's door." He hurries out, rounding the car and opening my door for me. I take his offered hand, and he helps me out of the car, our bodies pressing close together. His eyes roam around my face

"You look beautiful," he whispers, just for us to hear.

"You already complimented me," I whisper back.

"I'll compliment you for the rest of my life, Mack."

The butterflies erupt, flying around in my stomach as he takes my hand and turns to lead our group into the restaurant.

I really want to believe him.

I'm only half listening to the conversations going on around me. I'm still staring at the massive bouquet of red, pink, and white roses. A ring balloon and a heart-shaped one stick out of the vase, nestled between the flowers.

Tal looked sheepish when I turned to him with wide eyes. He just shrugged and told me he couldn't *not* get me something for Valentine's Day.

Then, he produced a wood-carved rose painted gold. Another callback to our first—and only—Valentine's Day together in ninth grade. The rose he carved at fourteen was misshapen and lumpy and not painted. Clearly the work of someone who'd just barely gotten into wood carving, but I still cherished it until we broke up and looking at it hurt too much. I threw it away—which I regretted later.

This rose looks almost professionally done. It's got crisp cuts and smooth surfaces, the gold paint is evenly spread, and there are no chips or blotchy spots to be seen.

How long did it take him to do this?

Kinsley and Harper "ooo'd" and "aww'd" over the flowers and the gold-painted rose. To them, this is just a sweet gesture to celebrate our marriage and Valentine's Day. Lizzie gave me a look that said *you're fucked*.

I am. My heart is fucked, and we've only been married for two hours! Because the wooden rose means so much more to me than he could ever know. It represents a time when things were simple, and I was in love with a boy who promised me forever. It reminds me of late-night texting and early mornings at school, walking around talking about everything and nothing. It's stolen kisses backstage between rehearsals and notes passed between classes. A reminder of a time before life flipped me upside down.

I tune back in when another server comes back over with their sticks of meat and pineapple. I really want more of the pineapple, so I ask them to cut me off a few slices.

"Preparing for the wedding night?" Lizzie whispers in my ear from beside me.

I roll my eyes. "You know that's not what this is."

Lizzie shrugs, stabbing a piece of chicken with her fork. "The way that man was eye-fucking you when he saw the girls sitting so pretty? I wouldn't be so sure." She motions to the way my dress hugs my tits, pumping her eyebrows suggestively.

"Lizzie!" I hiss. "He was not! Don't say shit like that."

"Why? You're married. He *should* want to fuck his wife."

"You know that's not going to happen," I murmur, hoping no one else can hear our conversation. How mortifying to be embarrassed about fucking your husband.

"Maybe not, but don't count it out, babe. I still think you should keep an open mind about this. I think this could be the start of something beautiful." She leans away from me and says, loud enough for the table to hear, "Twinsies, you're having a sleepover at my house tonight so Tal and Mack can... get settled."

Woah, what?!

Tal chokes on his cheese bread, and Enoch starts patting him on the back.

Kinsley points her fork at Lizzie. "Will there be popcorn and movies?"

Lizzie rolls her eyes. "Obviously."

Kinsley nods her approval and goes back to eating her food. I'm shocked at her lack of argument.

"Dude," Enoch says. "You're finally going to lose your virginity!" He holds his hand up for a high five.

Talmage socks him in the arm.

Enoch starts wailing about the pain. "Lizzie," he pouts. "I need you to kiss it better."

"I would, but I wouldn't want to over-excite you and have you come in your pants at this nice restaurant," my best friend says, not sparing him a second glance.

"I love it when they're mean," Enoch groans.

What the hell is happening right now?!

Lizzie—bless her—helps shift the conversation by asking Kinsley about her science project, and Nathan, Enoch, and Talmage ask insightful questions. The rest of lunch goes by quickly, and before I know it, Talmage is paying the bill—despite my protests—and we're making the half-hour journey back to my house.

Where Tal will be moving in.

With me.

And we'll be alone tonight.

Nothing's going to happen.

Even if part of me really, really wants it to.

Chapter 19

Talmage

14 years old...

"Don't you think you're too young to be planning a future with someone?" Jacob asks quietly over our biology worksheet.

"Everyone always says you'll know when you find the one, so why shouldn't I know Mack's the one, even if we're young?"

"You don't even want to try to date other girls? You know when we get to high school there will be so many more options. You'll have the girls from the other junior high to interact with. What if you meet someone else you like more than Mack?"

I shake my head. "Not possible." There won't be anyone I like more than Mack because I love her. It's not possible to love someone more than I love her. The fact he keeps bringing it up is starting to irritate me.

"I'm just saying, I think it might—"

"Please stop before someone else hears."

"I don't want either of you to get hurt. You're both my friends, and it would be awkward if things ended and I had to choose a side."

"Good thing nothing's going to end, then."

I could castrate Enoch for the ridiculous comment at lunch. Acting like he's not also a freaking virgin.

I'm so embarrassed he said it in front of Mack, even though I'm sure she deduced I was a virgin already. If I can't even say a swear word, there's no way I broke one of the cardinal rules of the church and had sex before marriage.

Am I a loser? Does that make me bland? Boring? I hope it doesn't change her opinion of me.

Mack looked just as mortified as I was, though, and I can't help but wonder if sex with me scares her. Is it a turnoff that I don't know what I'm doing?

I would be more than happy to learn! I'd love to spend hours learning exactly what she likes—

Nope. Lose that train of thought.

If she doesn't even want to kiss because she's worried about blurring the lines, then doing anything more intimate would for sure be off the table.

Too bad the logical part of me recognizes that, but the rest of me doesn't. I want to explore Mack's curves. Create a roadmap over the hills and planes of her body. Figure out what other tattoos she has and learn the stories behind them. I want to press our naked skin together and bask in her warmth. If it never led to sex, then I'd be perfectly content, but I'm dying to know how her skin feels against mine—

Praise to the man who communed with Jehovah, Jesus anointed that prophet and seer...

The hymn barely works to stop the flow of blood down south.

We're almost back to Mack's house, and we haven't talked much the whole ride. Lizzie and the twins are stopping to pick up the girls' things for their sleepover, but when they leave, it'll just be me and my wife.

My wife. My wife. My wife.

I back into the slanted driveway so I can easily transport the boxes from the back.

"Let's go in and change, then I'll help you move boxes." Mack unbuckles and gets out before I can protest. I quickly snag my duffle bag from the back before following her up the porch steps.

"I thought I could change and grab Siren, if that's okay? She's been in her kennel a little longer than I usually like to leave her."

Mack nods. "Sure, of course. I cleared out a spot by the back door for her kennel and bowls, but if you need a different place, we can move it. Just let me know."

She unlocks the front door, and I follow her through the living room over to an area next to the back door where the table's been turned and slid over.

"Is this enough space? We don't use the dining table often, so we can just put it somewhere else if she needs more space."

Affection for my wife turns my heart to mush. "This is perfect. Thank you, Mack."

"It's nothing, really."

I knock her shoulder with mine, even though what I really want to do is wrap her in a hug and kiss her silly. "It means a lot."

The front door bursts open, and Mack's sisters don't spare us a glance before they're rushing to their room.

Lizzie walks in and gives us a knowing grin before she produces a wrapped box from her purse and tosses it to me.

"Happy wedding day, lovebirds. May your love prosper and grow and yada yada."

"Lizzie, what did you buy?" Mack tries to grab the box from me, but I hold it away from her.

Lizzie grins like the Cheshire Cat. "Just something every newlywed couple needs."

I unwrap the box, revealing... *oh my goodness.*

"A forty-count pack of condoms?! Lizzie! What the hell?" Mack whisper-shouts.

Lizzie shrugs. "I know you can't get pregnant, but it's still important to practice safe sex. I even bought the variety pack so you have options. They have ultra-ribbed, her pleasure, and double ecstasy. Oh!" She rifles around in her bag again. "I also got you this, Mack, but don't open it in front of Tal. You can surprise him later." She tosses Mack a wink and hands her a tissue wrapped bundle.

Can't get pregnant? What does she mea—

"Lizzie," Mack warns through clenched teeth, a flush crawling up her neck.

"It's okay, Mack, I know she's just joking around. You'd probably be better off with this box than I would, though." I hand it back to Lizzie.

She rolls her eyes but takes the box from me. "Ugh. You guys are such prudes. You're married now! The Mormon rules don't apply anymore. Might as well make the most of your time together. Share some pleasure."

She has a point...

I look over at Mack who's shaking her head.

Guess she doesn't agree.

I clear my throat. "Well, thank you for being there for us today. I should go change so I can go get Siren."

"Thank you for lunch."

I give her a nod, then take my duffle bag down.

When I'm halfway down the stairs, I hear Mack's frustrated tone and stop to listen, even though I know I probably shouldn't.

"What in the actual hell, Elizabeth? You can't just give him a box of condoms and me lingerie! You *know* that's not what this is! We literally *just* talked about this. Not to mention you can't just go around telling people I can't get pregnant. I'm not even remotely ready to have that conversation with him."

"I'm sorry I brought up the pregnancy thing. But come *on,* Mack. Let's not pretend you don't want to know what he's packing underneath that suit. You told me yourself you've had dreams—"

"And you promised not to bring those up again! Doing... *that* with Talmage would cross so many lines, and my heart can't handle the fallout. This was a bit too far, Lizzie."

"I'm sorry, Mack." Lizzie's voice sounds genuinely remorseful. "I just want to see you happy, and having him back in your life—"

"Is temporary. I can't let myself get attached because he'll leave eventually, and then *you'll* have to deal with the aftermath."

I don't hear what Lizzie says next because I book it to Mack's room—our room?—to process the information I've just learned.

Maybe I'm just being hopeful, but it almost sounds like Mack *wants* this to be more, be real. Has she thought about what it would be like to be intimate with me? I've actively tried to avoid thinking about what anything more than kissing would be like with Mack but sometimes my dreams...

My groin stirs, and I shake my head, quickly changing out of my suit and into a pair of joggers and a Springville FD hoodie. I trade my dress socks for regular crew ones and take my tennis shoes upstairs where Mack is standing in the kitchen, scrolling on her phone.

"Are the twins gone?" I ask, startling her. "Sorry, I thought you heard me."

"It's okay. Yeah, they left. I'm sorry about Lizzie and her... *gift*."

I shrug. "No big deal. Like I said, I know she was just joking around. I'm sorry it made *you* uncomfortable."

"Still, it was a boundary she shouldn't have crossed, you know? I promise she won't do it again."

"Seriously, it's all good. I'm going to go grab Siren. Do you want me to pick anything up on my way back?"

Mack shakes her head. "No, but thank you. I've already cleared a section of the closet out for you and a few drawers so..."

I step towards her and open my arms, hoping she'll take my offered hug. My pulse leaps when she does, wrapping her arms around my waist.

"Why don't you go take a bath or something, relax for a little bit. I know today was a lot, and you probably could use some time to yourself."

She sighs, her breath warming the spot just below my shoulder. "Okay. Thank you. I'll see you when you get back."

I give her one last squeeze. "See you soon."

CHAPTER 20

Mackenzie

15 years old...

"*So you're going to spend the next seven years just kissing?" Tessa asks—again—as we paint our nails.*

I roll my eyes. "Yes. I'm perfectly fine with it. Happy, even. As long as in the end, I get to marry Talmage. I'd never jeopardize his mission eligibility or our temple marriage by pushing things further."

"But you said you don't want to be part of the church anymore. After—"

"I'll stay for Talmage," I interrupt. I still don't want to talk about him.

"You know it's normal for teenagers to have sex, right? Most people lose their virginity before they turn seventeen."

"Not me. Not Talmage. Not most Mormons."

Tessa rolls her eyes at me, and I'm starting to question if she's as good of a friend as I want to believe she is. She seems so adamant that I end things with Tal before I get hurt, and I don't understand where she's coming from.

We're never breaking up. We're forever.

"What are you going to do all summer when he's at Scout camp?"

I shrug. He won't have a phone, so we can't text. No computer access either. I guess we'll write letters.

"I'll be busy with all of my camps, so I'm sure it'll fly by."

I still can't believe Lizzie gave Tal a Costco sized box of condoms. And blurted out I can't get pregnant. Talmage is going to have so many questions, and I don't blame him, but I don't want to relive the reasons why.

I shake my head and sink deeper into the bubbly water. I'm supposed to be relaxing, not wondering if I can put a curse on my best friend so every time she's about to have sex, her vagina turns green. There would be nothing wrong with her medically—I'm not *that* mean—but it would be pretty off-putting to have a green vagina.

Another wave of embarrassment washes over me. Why the fuck would she do that? She knows we're not going to have sex. This isn't that kind of marriage. We're not having a sex marathon for our wedding night like a normal couple, and even if we were, I...

I wouldn't want to use condoms.

I would want to feel every bare inch of him.

Stop it. You're going to get yourself worked up for nothing, and then you'll have to share a bed with him.

I grab my Kindle and fire it up, opening it to where I left off in the second chance romance I'm reading.

How ironic.

But this isn't a second chance for me and Tal, is it? Life isn't a romance novel. People don't fall back in love decades later and live happily ever after. The man who broke my heart as a teenager isn't still harboring feelings for me and wishing I'd give him another opportunity.

Men as sweet and lovely as Talmage Monson don't fall for shattered, broken girls like me.

This story sort of mirrors ours, though, and it's a mind trip.

High school sweethearts who broke up and went their separate ways, only for a tragedy to bring them both back to their hometown. He's an ex-Marine with experience in first response, and she's a trauma nurse. They get thrown together on a taskforce to help the victims of a hurricane after it wreaks havoc on their town.

I'm at the point where the tension has built so much, if they don't kiss soon, I'm going to want to throw my e-reader in the bathtub. The way he thinks about her is so fucking sweet, and she has no idea he's still head over heels in love with her. She thinks his flirting is just what he does—that he's a playboy who doesn't want to settle down.

I relate to her character because she's been burned before and doesn't want to open her heart again. She's scared to let the feelings consume her and then be shattered when he leaves.

But his point of view shows he wants another chance with her. He wants it all, and he'll do whatever he can to prove it.

Eventually, the characters and their descriptions don't matter anymore. My brain puts me and Talmage in their places. The words said between them become things I wish would be said between us, and that's when I know it's time to call it quits. It's a slippery slope to heartbreak if I continue thinking Tal and I could have a real second chance.

The water's gone cold, anyway, so I get out of the tub and dry myself off, cursing when I realize I forgot to bring clothes in with me. I listen for footsteps but don't hear anything. Talmage must not be back yet, so I should be safe to walk out and grab clothes.

I wrap the towel around myself as best as I can, but these towels aren't big enough to cover everything. There's a two-inch gap at my side, and the towel barely covers half of my ass.

Good thing Tal's not here. I don't know what I'd do if I had to walk out there barely covered. He'd probably be scandalized by my nudity or disgusted by my body.

I've always been on the bigger side, even when I was dancing for fifteen hours a week in high school, but my body has changed since then. I'm rounder in my stomach, and my thighs are riddled with cellulite and stretch marks. Working so much and dealing with the aftermath of losing my parents made it so I barely thought about my body the last few years. I wasn't dating, so I didn't have to worry about what anyone else thought about me, either.

But now, I have a husband who will be sleeping next to me, and I'm suddenly feeling very self-conscious.

I peek around the door just to be safe and find the room empty. I rush over to the dresser and pull out a long sleeve shirt and flannel pajama pants. I usually run hot at night and sleep in an oversized T-shirt, but I don't want to flash Tal in the middle of the night. I'll just have to suffer and sweat and hope I can get some semblance of sleep.

Ha. As if. I'll be lucky if my body relaxes at all.

I've just hung up my towel and turned to put my clothes on when the door swings open, and Tal walks in with a duffle bag in one hand and a suit bag in the other.

His mouth drops open, and the duffle thunks onto the floor. I squeal, trying to cover my body with my arms. It doesn't fucking work, though, because my tits are too big to be covered by one arm and the other one is trying to cover my vagina.

Talmage drops the suit bag like it's on fire and immediately turns around and covers his eyes. "I'm so sorry. I didn't think to knock!" he squeaks out.

"It's okay. I should have changed in the bathroom." I scramble to pull my pants up and shove the shirt over my head, cursing when it gets caught on my breasts. Of course I'd end up picking the only skin tight shirt I own. It shows every lump and curve and the peaks of my nipples. He'll for sure be able to see the barbells through the tight fabric, but I don't have time to change now.

"I'm dressed, you can turn around," I whisper, crossing my arms over my chest.

Tal turns around, his face as red as a tomato. His Adam's apple bobs as his eyes travel across my body, so slowly it makes me want to squirm. "Sorry again."

I shake my head. "No need to apologize. I didn't hear any footsteps upstairs, so I thought I was in the clear. I'll make sure to change in the bathroom from now on."

Tal rubs the back of his neck. "I was outside letting Siren get acquainted with her new space. We've been back for about half an hour."

"I must have been too lost in my book to hear you."

"Oh, what's it about? It must be good if you got lost."

I shift my weight from side to side. "It's uh, a second chance romance. Two high school sweethearts find their way back to each other."

Tal gives me a boyish grin. "Sounds familiar."

I let out an awkward laugh. I need to change the subject. We're not getting into this right now.

"Are those your clothes?" I nod towards the duffle and suit bag.

"Yeah, and toiletries and such."

"What else do we need to get moved in tonight?"

Tal shrugs. "Nothing, really. I didn't realize how little I had until I started packing. My furniture is all in storage, and I only had a few books and my art supplies. Most of the stuff was Siren's to be honest."

"No family heirlooms, mementos, or pictures to hang up?"

"I keep all of the important things in a fireproof safe, and I don't have pictures to hang up. Anything important to remember is either on my phone, an external hard drive, or in here." He taps his head.

"Cool, well, do you want some help unpacking? I was going to go make some macaroni and cheese. I'm a little hungry now."

Talmage shakes his head. "It won't take very long. I'll just unpack, then hop in the shower really fast."

"Do you want some food, too? Are you on a special diet? I think I have some lettuce or something. I usually go grocery shopping on Sundays, so my fridge isn't well stocked right now."

Tal grins. "I'd love some mac 'n' cheese. I'm not on a special diet. We can make the list together when I come up after my shower."

"Okay. I'll leave you to it."

"Thanks, Mack."

This is my life now. I share a room with a boy—no, a man—and we're going to make a grocery list together.

Good luck keeping yourself unattached.

Chapter 21

Talmage

14 years old...

I should be paying attention to the instructions from our teacher about the field trip, but I can't stop staring at Mack. The dress she's wearing must be new, and it looks so beautiful on her, I don't know how I'm going to pay attention to the musical we're going to. I only want to look at her.

A feeling low in my gut starts to stir, something unfamiliar to me, and I don't know if I like it.

If it's what I think it is, it's something I shouldn't *be* feeling. Not until I'm married.

I snap my face forward so I can focus and pinch the side of my thigh, willing my heart rate to slow down.

The church warns spending too much time with someone of the opposite sex could cause lustful thoughts, but I thought Mack and I were in the clear. We've been spending a lot of time together, sure, but never alone. We never go past kissing. Our hands don't roam to forbidden places.

My face heats as I remember the kiss backstage last week before they turned the lights on.

No more kissing in the dark.

We make our way to the buses, and—to my relief—the teacher says boys have to sit with boys and girls with girls.

Mack and her friend Tessa sit in front of me and Jacob, but we hold hands between the gap in the seats as we make the journey. Her touch lights up my bloodstream, but I don't want to let go.

I think my brain is still buffering. Still trying to process the expanse of skin I saw. The whorls of ink etched onto Mack's body.

I'm sure I've seen a naked woman before. I must have in my twenty-eight years. Right?

If I have, every memory is now erased and replaced by the image of my wife's naked butt and lovely breasts.

After I quickly unpack my clothes and place them in the drawers or in the closet, I make my way to the bathroom.

It still smells like whatever bubble bath or soap Mack uses—only it smells more like lavender and vanilla than her usual citrus scent.

The bathroom is spacious, with a separate shower stall and large bathtub. White marble countertops and white painted walls with a large black vanity beneath a big mirror. There are plenty of drawers underneath, and I find an empty one to put my toiletries in before I strip off my clothes and turn on the shower. I grab a clean towel from beneath the sink and sling it over the shower door before stepping inside.

I'm surrounded by Mack. Her shampoo, conditioner, and body wash. Her loofah and face wash.

Images of Mack washing herself flash behind my eyes, and I shake my head to try to clear them. She hasn't given me permission to think about her in this way.

But still, the images come in rapid succession. The image of her ample backside is burned into my memory, and my body responds accordingly.

All the blood rushing south makes me dizzy.

My brain recalls what Lizzie said. *The Mormon rules don't apply anymore.*

Now that I'm officially married, masturbation is up to the discretion of the couple. If Mack and I aren't going to be intimate, there's nothing wrong with touching myself.

Right?

I look down at my penis, hard as a steel rod, and for the first time in my life, I give in to the urge to touch myself.

I pump some of Mack's body wash into my hand, and I swear I get even harder as the scent meets my nostrils. My erection pulses with need.

An unbidden whimper escapes my throat as I wrap my hand around myself and tug once.

This feels so good, how have I gone this long without doing it?

I have to brace myself with a hand on the tiled wall when my knees buckle at the sensation. All I see when

I close my eyes is Mack's body. Her lips. Her smile. The swirls of green in her mossy eyes.

It doesn't even take a whole thirty seconds of thinking about our brief kisses before I'm shooting white ropes onto the floor of the shower and watching it wash down the drain.

I expect to feel relief. Satisfaction. I just orgasmed *on purpose* for the first time in my life. But I don't feel satisfied. All I feel is... hungry.

Not for food.

For Mack. For her kisses. Her affection. For... more.

I want her in all the ways a husband and wife can have someone. I want her to be the first—and only—person I make love to.

I want to know what it feels like to have someone else's—*Mack's*—hands on me, not my own.

But she's made it clear it's not what she wants. And I'll respect her wishes.

I guess my hand and I will be getting *very* acquainted.

Hopefully purposeful masturbation will put an end to the wet dreams.

I quickly rinse myself off and get out of the shower. I dry off and start to put on my usual underwear of the church issued garments when I pause.

This day signifies new beginnings. A chance for me to start living how *I* want and not how the church tells me to.

I haven't worn regular underwear in ten years—I don't even own any. But I can buy some tomorrow. I can go commando for a few hours, right?

I slip on my gray sweatpants and a long-sleeved shirt before I grab the rest of my garments from the drawer and take them upstairs.

Mack's standing at the stove, stirring something in a pot.

"Do you have a pair of scissors?"

Mack turns around, and when she sees the pile of white cloth, her eyebrows shoot up. "What are you do-ing?"

I plop them on the couch. "I'm starting my new life! The first step is to get rid of the garments. I need to cut the symbols off."

Mack tilts her head. "You know if you just... throw them away, nothing bad will happen, right? They teach you to cut the symbols off because they think people will use them for evil."

Huh. That never occurred to me. "You're right. I guess I *don't* have to cut the symbols off. Should I just go toss them in the trash?"

Mack shrugs. "They make excellent cleaning rags if you'd rather get some use out of them. There are scissors in the drawer by the fridge. The food should be ready in about ten minutes."

I grab the scissors and start cutting my garment tops into rectangles. It feels symbolic to be doing this. Like cutting them up is cutting the last ties to the religion that has caused so many people harm.

I know it's not true because I have to remove my records, but still. It's cathartic, and I feel lighter with every piece I cut.

When Mack tells me the food's ready, I'm about eighty percent through my pile, so I stop and sit next to her at the island.

"Will you help me pick out underwear tomorrow? It's been a long time since I've worn something other than garments, and there are so many options, I don't know what I'll like."

Mack's head whips to me. "Are you... not wearing underwear right now?"

I shrug. "No. I didn't want to put the garments on, and I don't have any other underwear. I figure I'll be fine until tomorrow morning."

Mack blinks her big green eyes at me. They dart down, like she's trying to verify, but the counter blocks her line of sight. Blood rushes south at the idea of her checking me out.

She clears her throat and turns back to her food, shaking her head slightly. "Right. Yeah. Okay. Sounds... good. I can definitely help you shop for new underwear."

I grin. "Thanks, Mack. I appreciate it."

Once I'm finished with my food, I place my bowl and spoon in the dishwasher and find a pad of paper and a pen. "All right, wifey. Let's make a grocery list."

CHAPTER 22

Mackenzie

15 years old...

With the school year ending, Tal and I have been spending every minute we can together.

I'm anxious about this summer. What if he decides he doesn't want me anymore? What if he realizes I'm not as great as he thought? What if he meets someone else?

Everything will be fine. We're meant to be.

It's almost his birthday, and I have a gift I hope will keep him thinking about me all summer. I've written him ten letters, one for each week he'll be gone. Hopefully it gives him something to look forward to.

We're having our cast party for the musical tonight, and usually these things make me happy, but this one is bittersweet.

This party signifies the end of junior high. I didn't get into the musical at the high school like Tal and some of our friends did, and it's been a hard thing to come to terms with.

I heard they're incorporating a dance company, though, so hopefully I can be part of it. I don't know what I'll do with my time if I don't have the musical.

It felt like a bad sign when I wasn't on the cast sheet, but I'm hoping it means there's something bigger that'll happen for me—something better.

I didn't sleep a wink last night.

I was overheated from wearing too many clothes, and then I got even hotter with Tal's body heat in the bed when I'm used to being alone.

Not to mention how hot and bothered I got knowing he wasn't wearing any fucking underwear. Him going commando shouldn't be so hot.

He said it so casually. Like not wearing underwear in front of your fake wife isn't a huge fucking deal.

And maybe it wouldn't be if the circumstances around it weren't so bonkers. Cutting up his garments was a big deal and asking *me* to help him pick out underwear?

That's *real* wife stuff. Not fake wife stuff.

The men's underwear section is our first stop when we get to the store. Luckily, we came early enough it's not crowded, and Tal is acting like we're at Disneyland instead of Wal Mart.

"Woah. There are a lot of options," he murmurs when he sees the wall of men's underpants.

He starts reading the descriptions, feeling the fabric through the little hole, and occasionally asking for my opinion.

I'm not sure why he thinks I'm an expert, but I guess I know more than him.

"Do you want them to fit like garments?" I ask.

Tal nods. "I used to buy garments a size smaller and in "short" so they weren't so long and baggy. I'd like something similar, but shorter. Hoochie daddy season is approaching, afterall."

"Where did you learn about 'hoochie daddy season?'" I balk. But the image of him in those little shorts...

Yeah. I can't deny it'd be hot.

"I'm on social media, Mack." The implied "duh" makes me want to roll my eyes.

"Right, and you want to be in your slutty little shorts era?"

"Sure. I'll have to buy some of those next."

Who is this man? This is a side of Talmage I never thought would exist.

"Maybe I should custom order some underwear with Siren's face on them," he muses, picking up a pack of slim-fit boxer briefs in varying colors.

"Please, no." I tap the pack he's holding. "These would probably be the most comfortable for you, but you might have to keep trying different styles or sizes until you find one you like."

"All right, I'll trust your judgment. But I still might order some with Siren's face on them. Maybe I'll get us matching pairs." He tosses a playful wink my way, and this time I *do* roll my eyes.

"Come on, let's get the rest of the groceries before it gets busy." I make to grab the cart, but Talmage tosses the pack of underwear into it and bumps me with his hip, taking my place.

"A lady should never have to push her own cart," he says by way of explanation.

I huff out an exasperated laugh through my nose but don't fight him.

"Okay, where are we starting with the list?" Tal asks, grabbing it from his pocket. He's completely commandeered my grocery shopping, and I don't know how to feel about it.

Last night, while I finished my dinner, we made a *meal* plan. I can cook, don't get me wrong, but I kind of just... go with the vibes and cook whatever seems easiest that night.

Tal, though? He's prepared. He gave me a calendar with his schedule for the month and made sure to jot down when Harper has late rehearsals and Kinsley has chemistry club so he could make sure they would have food when they came home. Then, he proceeded to ask for our favorite meals and looked up recipes for each, jotting down ingredients as he went.

It was nice, not having to figure out everything on my own. Kinsley and Harper never know what they want to eat, so it's like pulling teeth to decide on dinner. Most of the time, they're gone with school stuff or holed up doing homework and make their own food, so I end up heating up a frozen dinner and calling it a night. Their lunches consist of PB&Js or turkey and cheese sandwiches with a bag of chips if they take one, or they use their small allowance to go out to lunch with their friends. They refuse to eat school lunch, which is fine. I never ate it, either.

Tal's excitement surrounding cooking is a breath of fresh air.

I'll just have to make sure I don't get used to it since this isn't going to last forever.

We're halfway through our list when we turn down the bread aisle and see two men standing at the end of the aisle looking at the loaves.

"Oh shoot," Tal whispers, looking behind us.

"What? Do you know them?"

"Yeah, they're from the singles ward. I know *of* them, but we're not, like, best friends."

"Maybe they won't recognize you—"

"Brother Monson! How's it going?" the taller one with sand colored hair shouts. The other one has blonde hair so light it looks white. They both approach, and Tal's demeanor visibly changes.

"Hey, guys. Bread for the sacrament?" Tal nods his head towards the two loaves they've got.

The blonde man chuckles nervously. "Yeah, bro. I know we're not supposed to be shopping on a Sunday, but I think The Lord would rather us take the sacrament, right?"

"The Relief Society was supposed to bake it this week, but the president got the flu and cancelled the activity." The sandy haired guy nudges his friend and rolls his eyes.

I clamp my lips closed to keep myself from saying something that would hurt their feelings.

Tal cringes. "Right, yeah. That's... sad for her. I hope she's okay."

"Ah, you know women. They bounce back fast. We'll have fresh bread next week, guaranteed." The blonde guy looks at our cart, then zeroes his gaze on Tal's left ring finger—where his wedding ring sits. His eyes narrow. "You no longer part of the ward, Brother Monson?"

I glance over at Tal to see his reaction, and his smile is soft as his gaze meets mine. "Nope. Got married yesterday. This is my wife, Mackenzie."

I know it's proper and polite to shake hands, but they look like they don't wash theirs for anything other than to break the sacrament bread—maybe not even then—so I just give an awkward wave.

Both men appraise me, their gazes like slugs slithering on my skin as they inevitably pick apart every flaw and "sinful" thing about me. From my makeup-less face, to my pierced nose, to my round body. They can't see my tattoos due to the hoodie and leggings I'm wearing, but I'm sure that's not what they'd find most unappealing about me. Their faces morph into something like disgust mixed with incredulity.

"*This* is your wife? I didn't even know you were dating anyone," Sandy Hair practically sneers.

Talmage puts a protective arm around my waist, his thumb rubbing soothingly up and down on my hip. "It was a sudden thing. High school sweethearts who fell apart, but when we reconnected? It was like everything fell into place. When you know, you know, and I knew the minute she came back into my life I couldn't let her get away again."

Why does he make it sound so dreamy?

The two dudes share a puzzled look before Bleach clears his throat. "Well, congratulations, I guess? We should run. Wouldn't want to be late for the sacrament meeting. People are counting on us for their salvation, after all."

Gag.

"Yep. Bye." Sandy and Bleach turn and scurry down the aisle like if they stay next to us a minute longer, they'll become apostate by proximity.

"Well, that was fun." Talmage gives my hip a squeeze, then releases his hold on me and pushes the cart forward, stopping in front of the bagels.

I can't help the snort that comes out of me. "Yeah, nothing like a good old-fashioned judging on a Sunday morning."

"I think it went as well as it could have gone. They'll probably just go to church and forget all about it."

I gape at him. "Tal, are you kidding? They're about to walk into those meetings and tell everyone they know Talmage Monson married a harlot or some shit. You're going to become the new boogeyman." I lower my voice like I'm a man. "'Talmage Monson is an example of what happens when you stray from the teachings. Do not let temptation lead you astray.' They're going to use you as a lesson now. I'd be surprised if the bishop doesn't call you personally to make sure you haven't been possessed by a demon."

Tal's eyes go wide. "Oh, sh-*shit.* They're totally going to do that." He tilts his head in thought before shrugging. "Oh, well. I can't change it now, can I? They're going to talk no matter what. Their opinions on how I live my life don't matter."

"Tal! You swore!" I gasp. "First the garments, then grocery shopping on a Sunday, and now swearing?" I shake my head, but I can't stop the small smile. "Who even are you right now?"

His smile is so wide, so proud, it makes my heart beat a little faster. I want to kiss him.

"I guess becoming your husband was the first step to becoming who I want to be. I always knew great things would come from being married to you."

With that nugget of praise, he continues shopping as if he didn't just dislodge another brick from the wall around my heart.

Chapter 23

Talmage

15 years old...

This is it. The last big event before the last day of school.

I never thought I'd dread a dance, but something about it is making me feel like it's the end of more than just the school year.

Not me and Mack, obviously. We're solid.

She looks gorgeous in a fifties style, black dress. She has a little gray silk jacket over it which matches my tie—unintentionally.

Mack's been a little sad after finding out she wasn't cast in the musical with me and some of our friends. She's been trying to put on a brave face, but there's an inherent sadness surrounding her.

I'm hoping they play our song again, and it'll bring a smile to her face.

I'm nervous to leave her this summer, but I need the money I'll make from working at the camp to save up to go on my mission, so I couldn't turn it down when I got in.

I know I won't forget her after the present she gave me.

I just hope she doesn't forget me.

She'll be at a few different camps with other guys. What if one of them grabs her attention? What if she finds someone she likes more than me? Someone willing to do more than just kiss her?

I have to believe that won't be the case. That she's as committed to this—to us—as I am. She hasn't given me any reason to think otherwise.

When we got home after grocery shopping—where I *insisted* on paying even though she argued she had the money—I started meal prepping for the week.

Cutting up vegetables and putting them in individual snack containers for easy access, marinating the steak for our dinner tonight, and mixing up some overnight oats.

Mack says she's never had overnight oats, but they're an easy, hearty breakfast I hope she and the twins will like. I don't want to sound judgmental, but there's no way they're staying full very long with only a bowl of cereal in the morning.

I insisted on making vegetable and steak skewers tonight so we can have a proper meal with the twins, so I've been cutting up zucchini and onions while the wooden skewers soak in warm water.

I want to grill them, but Mack's never touched the grill—her words, not mine—so we don't know if it even works. She doesn't remember the last time her dad used it, so it could be housing a family of squirrels for all we know. I plan to check it out as soon as I'm done chopping the vegetables.

"Really, Tal, this is too much. The girls will be fine with a frozen lasagna or spaghetti or—hell—even turkey sandwiches."

I give her a *get real* look. "We're celebrating! You all deserve a good, home cooked meal you don't have to do any work for, so quit arguing with me and let me feed you, please."

"I'm perfectly capable of making a good meal," she grumbles.

I gently set down my knife and round the counter to where she's standing with her arms crossed defensively.

I hesitate to wrap her in a hug, but the desire to comfort her and feel her in my arms wins out. I wrap my arms around her shoulders and rest my head against hers.

"You've been taking care of everyone else for so long, Firefly. It's time you let someone else take care of you." I pull back, and she tips her chin up so we're eye to eye. We're so close, it would take nothing at all to lean in and kiss her.

"You don't need to take care of me," she breathes.

I know I don't *need* to. "But I *really* want to. Please, let me?"

Our gazes are locked, my pulse is racing, and I think about bulldozing over her no kissing rule. She looks like she wants me to so I slowly lean in and—

The front door bangs open, and the chittering of Harper and Kinsley—well, mostly Kinsley—breaks whatever spell we're under.

The clomping of feet on the hardwood has me stepping back, feeling like a teenager caught with a girl in his room—not that I know what that's like. I never broke the rules. The twins and Lizzie come in, looking between Mack and I.

"Eeewww. Were you two *kissing* in here? That can't be sanitary." Kinsley's nose crinkles, and I catch the quick roll of Harper's eyes.

I grin. "Nah. You'd never be able to tear me away from her if I were kissing her. We're just working on dinner prep."

Kinsley looks at her phone. "But it's eleven in the morning."

"I'm making shish kebabs. Takes time to marinate."

Kinsley's eyes narrow on me full of suspicion. "Why? Are you trying to bribe us or something?"

Surprise makes my eyebrows shoot up to my hairline. "What? No. I'm making dinner because one, I live here now, so I'm doing my part. And two, so we can sit down and get to know one another better. We're going to be seeing a lot of each other, so I want to make sure you girls are comfortable with me. I know it'll take more than one dinner to earn your trust, but it's a start."

"Thank you for making dinner, Talmage, that sounds great. Let us know if you want any help. We need to go... do homework," Harper pipes up, giving Kinsley a warning look before dragging her sister down the hall.

Mack shakes her head and lets out an exasperated sigh before she nods at Lizzie. "How was last night?"

"Oh, you know, the usual. I gave them matching princess crown tattoos on their asses and taught them how to shoot vodka without gagging. It'll really come in handy at college, and I want them to be prepared," she deadpans.

I'm not entirely sure if she's joking. I look over at Mack with wide eyes, and Mack just grins and shakes her head.

"So you watched the first three *Pirates of the Caribbean* movies and fell asleep halfway through the fourth one after too much popcorn and ice cream?"

Lizzie snaps her fingers and points at Mack. "Exactly."

Mack chuckles. "We can teach them to shoot vodka next weekend."

Lizzie's eyes land on me, and she gives me a sinister smile. "How was *your* night? Anything *big* happen?"

Her emphasis on the word *big* makes heat swirl around my face. Is she implying *I'm* big? Is that something you can tell by simply looking at someone? I've never really compared myself to other men, so I think I'm probably average. Should I be looking it up? I don't—

"Tal here said his first curse word this morning at the grocery store," Mack states proudly.

Lizzie does a slow clap. "My man! What was it? Damn? Shit? Ooooh, please tell me it was 'fuck.'"

"I said 'shit.' You guys are acting like me swearing is a bigger deal than me not wearing garments anymore."

Lizzie gasps. "Talmage! Not wearing garments is way bigger than swearing! Mack, lead with the important stuff next time."

Mack shrugs. "I don't want to talk to you about my husband's underwear choices. That seems like a personal thing."

My husband.

I like the sound of that way too much.

Lizzie rolls her eyes. "You're so boring now that you're a married woman. You used to tell me about KC's personal business all the time. Remember when his Prince Albert got infected and—"

"Lizzie!" Mack hisses. "We don't need to talk about that. Besides, Tal is *right here.* If you want to know about him, ask *him.* Don't be rude, bitch."

This side of Mack isn't one I've seen in our time back together. The more playful side. It's both endearing and heart-wrenching because I want her to feel comfortable enough with me to open up and be playful.

Lizzie's phone beeps, and she sighs. "I'll have to interrogate you about your choice in underwear later, Tally. There's an emergency at the shop, and I need to head in. I'll text you later, Mack. Love you, byyyee." She blows us a kiss and heads towards the door.

"Love you, too!" Mack shouts at her retreating form. When the front door closes, Mack still has a small smile on her face.

"I like her," I state, resuming my chopping.

"Yeah? I would have thought she makes you uncomfortable. Lizzie sometimes doesn't know when to keep her mouth shut."

I shrug, removing the seeds from the last bell pepper. "I don't mind. I'd rather someone speak their mind than keep things in, you know? Besides, she makes you happy. You seem lighter, more comfortable with her."

Mack nods, examining her nails. "She's one of the only people in my life I know I can count on. She's been by my side through my lowest times. I wouldn't be here without her."

I feel like she's not just talking about her parents' deaths. Something in the back of my mind whispers whatever it is, it has to do with the rumors circulating about her in high school.

Did something else happen? Something so bad, it made her run from home and go to Oregon? I'm racking my brain trying to remember *something* about it, but I tried not to get involved in high school gossip. Especially about her. My heart couldn't handle it.

"I'm really happy you've had someone to help you. I hope you know she's not the only one you can count on now."

Mack gives me a sad smile, like she may not fully believe me. "Yeah. Thank you."

CHAPTER 24

Mackenzie

15 years old...

Today is the last time I'll see Talmage until school starts again next year. I've been holding back frustrated, hurt tears because I don't want our last day together to be filled with sadness.

He already feels bad enough for leaving, and I don't want to make him feel worse.

We're walking hand in hand towards the gas station about half a mile away from school. We're trailing behind our group of friends, and Tessa keeps looking back at me with a pitying expression, making me feel even worse.

"We're going to be okay, right?" Tal asks quietly.

"Yeah. You have Scout camp, and I'll be busy with vocal performance camp and girls' camp. It'll fly by." The words taste like acid, and I know they're a lie. Tal must know, too, because he just hums in reply.

We get our Slurpees, then follow our friends to the park next to the gas station, talking about our summer plans. Tessa's moving an hour north. The news made me even more nervous about next year because I won't have my *friend to help navigate high school. Our friendship is fiz-zling out, and we've been drifting apart, though, so maybe it's for the best.*

The thought of high school is daunting and scary, espe-cially since I'm not in the musical with my friends. I don't like change. I don't like not knowing how things are going to go.

When everyone separates and heads in the direction of their respective houses, Tal follows me to the train tracks. They've always felt like an invisible barrier between us, but today, they feel like a stone wall. Once I cross over, will our relationship still be there?

When he wraps me in his arms one last time, I can't stop the tears from falling.

"I'm going to miss you so much, Firefly. But I'll be back before you know it."

"I'll miss you, too," I sob, swiping the tears before they can fall.

He bends down and kisses me gently. "I love you."

"I love you, too."

By the vibes at the table, you'd think we were holding Kinsley and Harper hostage and waterboarding them for information instead of having a delicious dinner so they can get to know my husband.

My husband, who is genuinely the sweetest man I've ever known. Who fixed up the rickety grill and made one of the best meals I've had in years.

The beginning of the dinner was silent. Forks scraping on plates, glasses being picked up and put down, and the occasional murmured praise for Tal's cooking.

But I think Tal had enough of the silence, so he started asking the twins questions. Not just standard get-to-know-you questions, either. Insightful, personal questions that made them open up.

Kinsley has been talking in depth about her science fair project for the last ten minutes, explaining the different variables and constants and her method of testing various types of sugar and sugar substitutes on yeast energy output.

I wondered why we had so many different kinds of artificial sweeteners in our cupboard and why she needed to buy yeast when we don't bake.

It's not that I'm uninterested in her science project, but to them, my role is still as their older sister—not their parent. Sure, I pay the bills and run the household, but they don't see me as a parental figure they want to go to for help. I'm just the grouchy older sister who won't let Kins pierce her belly button. I tried to ask Kins about it once, and she told me she didn't want to have to explain it to me, so I let her be.

Guilt over not trying hard enough with her—with either of them—makes the tender meat in my mouth turn to ash. I should have asked again. I shouldn't have waited for them to come to me. I should have tried harder. I've been in survival mode for so long I didn't stop to think about how it was affecting our relationship. They each attend therapy, which is helpful, but is it enough?

"That's why artificial sweeteners like stevia won't activate yeast," Kinsley finishes her monologue with a flourish.

Tal nods. "That's fascinating. I never considered the possibility of using something other than plain sugar or honey to activate yeast. It's really cool you qualified for the state level for your project, Kinsley. You should be proud of yourself."

For the first time in a while, Kinsley looks almost bashful. "Thanks, Talmage."

"Hopefully Mack and I can come support you. When is it again?"

"My presentation day is on March eleventh. If I win, then I'm eligible to go to the International Science Fair in San Antonio in May. I-if we can afford it. I'd have to pay for the plane ticket out there, but they cover the cost of the hotel and food." She looks at me hesitantly.

I want her to be able to go if she wins, and maybe now that I won't have to shell out hundreds of dollars a month to big pharma for Harper's medicine, I can send her.

Tal nods. "Oh, that's cool! My cousin Izzy lives in San Antonio with her boyfriend, and her sister, Elli, lives in San Marcos with her fiancé. Maybe we could all make a trip, I'd love an excuse to visit them. I've never been to Texas."

Harper, Kinsley, and I all pause our eating and blink at him. The last family vacation we took together was when the twins were seven and I was twenty. I met them in Seattle, and we visited all the touristy spots. It was rough because they were still young and didn't want to do all the grown-up things I wanted to do. When they were nine, they came to visit me in California after they went to Disneyland. I had to work, so I couldn't go with them. It was the last time I saw them before...

"We've never really been on a family vacation," Kinsley blurts out.

"Well, no better time to start, then! It'll be fun. Even if you don't get into the international competition—which I think you will—we should plan a summer trip. Your birthdays are in July, right?"

Harper and Kinsley nod. How did he know that? I don't remember telling him.

Tal grins. "We can go somewhere to celebrate your sweet sixteen! Unless you'd rather have a party. We can talk about it when it gets a little closer. I have another cousin in San Diego, though, and I'm sure she'd be ecstatic to meet you all, if that's somewhere you'd want to go."

"Can we go to The Observatory North Park if we go to San Diego? Or Balboa Theatre? Or The Old Globe? I've always wanted to see a show there." Harper's eyes are wide and excited, something I don't see often. She doesn't get hyped about things the way Kinsley does, but her passion for theatre gets her talking more than any other subject.

"Oh my gosh, Balboa Theatre is *stunning*. We'll have to go." Talmage nods, matching her enthusiasm.

Kinsley's nose crinkles. "If we go to the theatre, we have to go to the Fleet Science Center."

Tal chuckles. "It's for your birthday, of course we'll do something each of you wants to do."

My head is spinning. He's making plans for five months from now? I could have a job with better benefits by then. We could be starting our divorce proceedings. We agreed *not* to get attached, and now he's planning a fucking family vacation?

How much money does he make if he can afford to be talking about a vacation to San Diego, anyway? I have no idea what a firefighter makes, and he's a captain—whatever that means. Does it come with a big pay raise?

By the time I come back to the conversation, Harper is talking about the latest musical drama. She's more animated than I've seen her in a long time, and the guilt comes back.

Have I not been giving them what they need emotionally? Have I been a bad sister, a bad guardian? I thought they didn't want to talk about their personal lives, but they're opening up to Talmage in a way that makes me think *I'm* the problem.

"...and they told me I was going to be paired with this boy I really like—" Harper clamps her mouth shut, and her fair skin turns scarlet.

Oh God, they're going to start dating soon! No! I'm not ready!

"No, no, continue. Tell me about this boy. You know, your sister and I were paired together during many of our school musicals."

Harper's eyes dart to me, and I give her an encouraging smile. I'm determined to make sure they feel comfortable talking about this stuff with me. I want them to know they can come to me no matter what.

"W-well, his name is Jeremy. He's in the same grade as me. He's talented and funny, and he's very kind. He checks in with me to make sure my blood sugar levels are good and even offered me a Capri-Sun when I was low one day." Harper looks how I imagine I did when I was her age talking about Tal: googly-eyed and wistful, with a lovestruck smile on her face.

"Are you going to ask him out?" Tal asks.

"What?!" Harper shrieks. "No! Absolutely not. It would be mortifying to be rejected and have to see him every day. To date someone in the cast and then break up and have to see them every day for the next two years? Talk about awkward."

I nearly laugh. Yeah, it is fucking awkward. It was so difficult, I almost quit theatre and choir because of it. I don't want Harper to go through what I went through.

Tal shrugs. "Not every relationship is meant to last, but I think they can all be a learning opportunity."

"Can we please change the subject?" Harper mumbles, shuffling her food around her plate, cheeks still red.

Tal's dimples peek out as he smiles. "Sure thing. Let's talk about how things will be different now with me living here—and before you freak out, I'm not trying to be your parent, okay? I just want you to know I'm here if you need me. Any dinner or snack requests, you let me know because I'll be taking over some of the cooking duties so Mack can have some free time. I don't want you guys to feel like I'm encroaching on your space, okay? I'm just an extra set of hands to help out."

"We have really busy schedules, so family dinners like this might not happen often," Kinsley hedges.

"Oh, don't worry. I'm not expecting big family dinners all the time. But I want to earn your trust, and that comes from spending time together sometimes. Deal?"

The twins share a look, using their twin-telepathy to have a conversation before they both look at Tal and nod.

"Thanks for being so cool with how quick this was, ladies. I hope I won't disrupt your lives too much. There may be some nights I come in later because we rotate our shifts, but I'll try to be as quiet as I can so I don't disturb you."

"Does Siren always go to the station with you?" Kinsley asks, looking over to the dog bed on the floor behind the couch.

Siren perks up at the sound of her name. She's been really calm all day, probably because while Tal was fixing the grill, she ran around the yard like a maniac. It was adorable.

"Yeah, she usually comes with me. But you're more than welcome to snuggle or play with her when she's here. If you want to give her treats, just make sure you limit them. I don't usually give her human food unless it's for special occasions, so just make sure you run things by me, okay?"

Kinsley and Harper nod rapidly.

After the girls and I cleaned up dinner and they played fetch with Siren, we put her in her crate and went our separate ways for bed.

Tal and I both work tomorrow, so we took turns showering—I didn't forget my clothes in the bedroom this time—and now we're lying in the dark trying to fall asleep.

I'm wearing another long-sleeved shirt and sweats, and I'm sweltering. I don't have any blankets on me, but I still can't get comfortable. I'm trying not to toss and turn too much, so I don't disturb Talmage.

It doesn't help that I can't stop thinking about what Tal's body might feel like pressed against mine without the barrier of fabric. I'm still thinking about our almost-kiss in the kitchen earlier and wondering if he would have kissed me nice and slow or if there would be an urgency to it. Would he ravage my mouth and take what he wanted, or would he let me lead?

"Mack," Tal whispers in the darkness. "Are you okay? You don't seem comfortable."

I let out a sigh. "I'm a little hot. I don't usually wear long sleeves and pants to bed."

"You don't have to change the way you dress on my account. Go put on what you usually sleep in, I want you to get your rest."

I want you to put your mouth on mine.

Ugh. Why can't my brain function? I must be ovulating. That's the only reason I'm so horny for my fake husband.

"I don't want to make you uncomfortable."

"Do you want me to change into what I usually sleep in? Will that make you feel better?"

No. Yes. Fuck, I don't know.

"If you want. I want you to be comfortable, too."

Tal pats my shoulder. "I'll go change in the bathroom, and you can change in here, then we'll both feel more comfortable and be able to sleep."

"Okay."

He rolls off the bed and heads to the bathroom, then I get up and grab my tank top and shorts from the dresser and quickly change into them.

The cool air kisses my overheated skin, a nice reprieve from the suffocating heat I was experiencing. I might be able to get some rest, after all.

Tal opens the bathroom door and comes out in nothing but a white shirt and royal blue boxer briefs so tight they look strained on his muscular thighs.

Or maybe I won't get any rest, after all.

Not when I have to actively keep my gaze from glancing down at his—

Nope. No.

Seemingly unaffected by the change in wardrobe, Tal gets back under the covers, so I follow suit.

"Good night, Mack. Sweet dreams," he says.

I click off my phone light.

"Good night. You, too."

God help me, I am so fucked.

CHAPTER 25

Talmage

15 years old...

The car is quiet as we drive up to the Scout camp about three hours away. I can tell my mom wants to say something to me by the way she keeps drumming her fingers on the steering wheel and sighing.

Finally, after what feels like an eon of waiting, she turns off the music.

"Talmage, your father and I wanted to sit down and talk to you together, but we didn't know how. So we decided I'd talk to you alone when I took you to camp."

"Okay... About what?"

"We know about the Thorpe girl."

My heart plummets to my stomach.

What does she know? Does she know... everything?

"What do you mean?" My voice comes out shaky.

"Well, Brother Linswell was out in his backyard one afternoon about two months ago and came around the front and saw you and her embracing. He didn't think much of it, until he saw you *kiss* her before you went your separate ways. He was concerned there might be something more going on, so he called us and let us know to keep an eye on you. Your father and I didn't want to believe what we were hearing, but Brother Linswell texted us multiple times after saying he saw you kiss her again."

"Wh-why didn't you and dad say anything?" I can't even wrap my mind around what I'm hearing. Mack and I got tattled on like children by an old man? It's not like we were out there naked or touching each other inappropriately. We've only kissed, nothing more.

"We thought you would come to your senses and confess. We hoped you'd end things with her and repent for your sins."

"I don't have anything to repent for, Mom. Mack and I never did anything more than kiss and hold hands. I don't want to end things with her. I love her."

Mom scoffs, and for the first time ever, I feel anger towards her. We've always had a close relationship, but right now it feels like she doesn't trust me.

"You don't love her, Talmage. You're too young to know what that means. And you may not have done anything more, but you know you aren't allowed to date until you're sixteen, and you shouldn't have a serious relationship until you come home from your mission. You've been lying to me and your father."

"I haven't lied. You never asked. Mack and I are best friends, and I've been open about it." I don't want to get into the fact she thinks I'm too young—how many times will I hear that regarding Mack?

"I don't think she's good news, Talmage. She seems... lost. There's something dark inside her, something sinful, and I don't want it to tarnish your light."

How can my mom think that about her? How can she say Mack would tarnish my light when I've never been happier than when I'm with her?

Mom continues before I can even begin to protest, "You need to make a choice, Talmage. You need to either break up with Mackenzie or potentially ruin your future. One mistake is all it would take to undo all you're working towards. No mission, no temple marriage, no Celestial Kingdom. Don't throw it all away for some girl. I hope you make the right choice."

Mack's not some girl. *She's everything.*

But... is my mom right? Am I risking the future I've been working towards forever if I keep spending time with Mack the way I have been? If I continue to date her, will I ruin my chances at eternal salvation?

I've been living with Mack for a little over two weeks, and I'm losing my mind.

I had to look up how often is considered "normal" to masturbate because I've been doing it twice a day, and it still doesn't feel like I'm getting any sort of relief.

After the first night Mack admitted to being uncomfortable while she slept, she's been wearing what I assume are her regular pajamas, and my hormones... they can't take it.

I want my wife. Badly. I'm in a constant state of desire for her.

It's not even about sex, I just want to hold her and feel her skin on mine. I want to kiss the tip of her nose and inhale her scent first thing when I wake up.

There was one night last week when I woke up at two in the morning and felt like I was boiling, only to realize Mack and I had somehow met in the middle of the bed, and her soft, lovely body was pressed right up against mine, her front to my back.

Thank goodness I was facing away from her, because one movement from her against my erection would have had me coming immediately.

When I woke up in the morning, though, she was back on her side of the bed, not touching me. Accidental cuddling hasn't happened since.

I'm a little sad about it.

Other than my growing need for her, things have been nice. We've gotten into a good routine. If I'm off when she's working, I make lunch and dinner for us both, and she cooks when I work.

She hasn't let me do her laundry yet, and I'm still trying to figure out the system she and the twins have when it comes to the way their cupboards are organized, but I think I'm getting the hang of things.

I'm trying not to dwell on my disappointment at not being able to kiss her goodbye or snuggle her when I've had a long day, and I'm ignoring my body's eagerness to be close to her unless I'm in the shower, surrounded by the scent of her body wash and shampoo.

Siren's bark pulls me out of my thoughts, and I turn to see Enoch and Nathan enter the kitchen area in the firehouse.

"How's married life, brother?" Enoch gives me a slap on the back as he walks past me to the fridge.

I shrug. "Can't complain. What's new with you two?"

Enoch shakes his finger at me. "No, no, we're not doing that today. You've avoided talking about Mackenzie for weeks, dude. It's time to spill. Let us lonely bachelors live vicariously through you."

I roll my eyes. "I don't have much to tell. Mack and I are both busy, but it's nice having someone to come home to. I love having someone to cook for and talk to about my day. I like having a partner."

"And how are the *marital activities*?" Enoch pumps his eyebrows suggestively.

Nathan smacks him on the chest. "Dude, don't ask shit like that. It's personal!"

Nathan didn't grow up Mormon, and his casual use of curse words used to be jarring but not anymore. It's nice to not feel like I have to cover my ears to keep the "bad words" out.

"I want to know if the waiting is worth it!" Enoch argues.

Enoch *did* grow up Mormon, and from what I understand, is still active in the church.

How honest can I be with them right now? Do I tell them I don't *know* if it's worth it? It would be kind of suspicious if I haven't made love to my wife after getting married so quickly.

Enoch studies me for a minute before his jaw drops. "You're still a virgin, aren't you?"

"Will you be quiet?" I hiss at him, checking to make sure no one else is around us. "Yes. I'm still a virgin."

"Why?" Enoch cries.

"Dude! Not cool." Nathan sends Enoch a warning glare.

I groan, regretting admitting it.

"I can't tell you why, so stop asking."

Enoch frowns. "Not that I'm trying to be crass about your wife, but how have you kept your hands off of her? I would have torn her dress off as soon as we got home if I were you."

A sound close to a growl—something I didn't know I was capable of—rips out of my throat. I don't want to imagine anyone but *me* doing anything with my wife.

"Don't you fucking dare say anything like that about my wife again."

Enoch's eyes go wide, and he holds up his hands. "S-sorry, man. Didn't mean to be disrespectful."

Nathan's eyes narrow at me. "Did you just say 'fuck?'"

"Yes. I did."

"But you don't swear."

"I do now."

"Since when?"

"Since I left the church," I blurt out, and both of them gasp.

Nathan grins. "Congratulations, bro. That's a huge step. How has it been?"

This is a safer conversation. One I'm happy to have with them. "It's been really good. Freeing. I mean, it's new, but I can't complain. Instead of dreading Sundays, I look forward to them, and not having to follow the arbitrary rules has been nice."

"Wait, wait, wait. So you're saying you're married, left the church, and you're *still* not having sex?" Enoch's voice drips with disbelief.

"Oh, for the love of—life isn't all about sex!" I nearly shout at him.

"I'm just saying when I left, sex was—"

"Wait, what do you mean? You left the church?"

Enoch shrugs. "Yeah. About a year ago. I'm not open about it, but I'm not really hiding it either."

How did I not know my best friend left the church? What signs did I miss? Now that I think about it, I haven't noticed his garments peeking out of the collar of his T-shirts anymore.

"And you're not a virgin?" Nathan gasps dramatically.

Enoch grins. "Nope. As soon as I submitted my request for my records to be removed, I lost my virginity. Best two minutes of my life. Don't worry, I last longer now."

"I wasn't worried, but thanks for the information. Good for you for leaving, man. But why didn't you say anything?" I ask.

"Probably for the same reason you didn't. I didn't want the judgment or to risk losing our friendship."

"Well, now I feel like we should celebrate!"

"Hell yeah! Maybe if I get some alcohol in you, you'll tell me why you haven't fucked your wife."

I sigh. "Can you please drop it? It's not—we're not... It's complicated."

"Fine. I'll drop it. But just know, if you need some advice, you can ask me."

I will not be asking him for advice on this particular subject. It would mean I'd have to explain the whole fake marriage thing, and it would open up a can of worms for even more questions.

"Thanks, but I—"

The alarm in the station blares at level three, and we jump into action.

The fire's at an older house on the outskirts of town. According to the neighbor who called it in, the elderly couple living there has mobility issues, making it difficult for them to get out on their own. Nathan and I are tasked with helping them.

We're already suited up in our turnout gear, all that's left is put on our SCBA masks.

The fire looks like it started in the living room, so instead of going through the front door, we rush around to the back but find the door locked. I give it a few swift, powerful kicks, and the old wood splinters on the hinges and opens for us.

Thick gray smoke fills the kitchen and beyond, and sweat pours down my back as the heat from the flames permeates the air, getting closer to this area of the house. The fire is spreading quickly, so we need to work faster.

Nathan and I follow the sound of faint coughing and the frail voice of someone calling out for help. In the hallway, we find an older gentleman passed out on the floor, his cane two feet away. Nathan scoops him up and, with a nod to me, carries him out of the house while I try to find his wife.

There are three doors in the hallway, one leads to a bathroom, the second looks like a guest room, and the third is where I find the wife lying on a bed, covering her mouth with a handkerchief.

I take note of the wheelchair in the corner and her foot in a cast. She must have had some type of injury preventing her from moving on her own. I don't have time to grab the wheelchair.

I take off my SCBA mask and place it on her face, just in case. "I'm going to lift you now, ma'am. Let me know if I need to reposition you so I'm not causing any pain."

She nods weakly, loosely hooking her arms around my neck while I lift her bridal style. It's not ideal, but I don't want to cause any harm to her legs.

I hear the cracking of wood, the heat increasing as more smoke fills the room. I silently pray to whatever higher being there is that the flames haven't made our escape route impossible. I open the door slightly and see the flames at the entrance to the hallway, blocking our way out.

I need to find another exit

I spin around to the double-pane window which looks big enough for me to carry her out. The house is only one story, so the ground is close enough. My team must have had the same idea, because Nathan and Enoch are on the other side of the window with a gurney at the ready.

I set the woman on the bed, quickly shove the dresser away from the window, and open it.

I scoop up the lady and gently carry her to the window where Nathan helps me get her outside.

She rips off the SCBA mask as soon as she's outside. "My Jerry! My Jerry is in there!"

"No, ma'am, we got your husband out. He's with the EMTs now," Enoch says calmly.

"Jerry is our dog! Our baby! I can't leave him!" She tries to sit up but can't. Her eyes fill with tears, and she starts crying hysterically.

I know if Siren were in a fire, I'd want to get her out. The pain of losing my furbaby would be gut-wrenching, and I can't let this woman experience that.

"Do you know where he is?"

"In the bathroom. He likes to hide in the tub."

"Cap, you can't. We haven't gotten the fire under control yet," Nathan warns.

"I can't leave him. Give me the mask."

Reluctantly, Nathan hands me my SCBA. I fit it back onto my head and turn around, before making my way through the bedroom and into the hall. I get down on my belly and crawl the few feet to the bathroom. The flames are working their way through the house, closer to where I am. Something crackles and crashes too close for comfort, so I pick up my speed, entering the small bathroom.

I pull back the curtain to find a small white dog shaking in the corner.

"It's all right, Jerry. I'm just going to pick you up and take you to safety," I coo, reaching for the dog.

Jerry barks and nips at my hands, but I don't feel it through the gloves. I get him secured in my arms as best as I can before I rush out of the bathroom—straight into the path of the flames.

Fuck.

Jerry panics and twists out of my arms, running towards the bedroom. I chase after him, but my foot gets caught on a rug, and I twist, toppling over. A popping sound followed by pain from my right ankle makes me howl in pain.

Fuck, that's not good.

I see Jerry jump up to try and get to his owner through the window. I grit my teeth and scoop up the little dog and hand him to Nathan, who takes him to the older lady.

I hoist myself out of the window, grunting when I land on my bad ankle, which gives out, and I crumple to the ground.

CHAPTER 26

Mackenzie

15 years old...

My stomach swirls with anticipation. I'm nervous but also excited to see Tal again. We didn't get to talk much this summer, save for a few messages when he was home for a weekend in July.

I've missed him terribly.

I feel pathetic for it, but my life's not the same without seeing Tal's smiling face all the time.

As I wait by the bus stop, I see his familiar head of blonde hair in the distance, and butterflies erupt in my stomach. He's tan from all the time spent in the sun, and his hair looks lighter.

When he glances up from the ground and sees me, I lift my hand in an enthusiastic wave. He returns it, but his smile doesn't reach his eyes.

Is he not excited to see me?

As he crosses the street, I stay rooted in place, not wanting to come off as too eager.

When he's standing right in front of me, he hesitates for just a second before finally wrapping his arms around me in a hug.

I feel his sigh of relief, and he can probably feel mine.

"I missed you so much, Firefly. You look beautiful," he murmurs against my hairline.

"I missed you, too. Thank you." My cheeks flush. I'm not wearing anything special. Just a pair of turquoise skinny jeans and a plain black babydoll top.

He steps back as the bus approaches, and we don't talk as we get on and take a seat next to each other.

"How was your summer? How are the twins?" he asks, sliding his hand on the seat between our bodies with his palm facing up.

I take the invitation and waffle our fingers together. The familiar spark of electricity that sizzled between us before the summer is still there, and my anxiety settles.

"They're good. They're getting sassier by the day. Summer was a little boring. Vocal performance camp was fun, I got a solo during the showcase."

Tal squeezes my hand. "That's awesome, Firefly. I'm so proud of you."

"Thank you." I squeeze his hand. "How was Scout camp?"

"It was alright. You know, a lot of boys being boys. I earned my watersports badge, though, so that's fun."

I don't know anything about Boy Scout badges or what it takes to earn them, so I don't know what to say other than, "That's cool. Did you get your schedule?"

"Yeah, I got it when I went to get my ID last week. Want to see if we have any classes together?"

I nod, and we both pull out our schedules. We compare classes and find we'll be in the same theatre class this semester.

My heart pinches when I see the musical class on his list, but I try not to let my disappointment show. It's not his fault I'm not in it.

"This year is going to be great," he says as he puts his schedule away.

I hope so.

My heart races as I rush through the emergency room doors and to the front desk. My ears are ringing as anxiety threatens to consume me.

"How can I help you?" the woman at the front desk asks, typing on her computer.

"Talmage Monson. He—he came in with the fire department."

"Are you family?

"I'm his wife."

She clicks a few times. "I'll have a nurse come grab you in a moment to take you back to him."

She's far too calm about this. He's injured! Can't she tell I'm losing my mind with worry over here?

I take a seat and try to count the ceiling tiles to calm my frayed nerves. I hate hospitals, but this hospital makes me especially itchy with anxiety. It's the hospital I was taken to after—

I take a deep breath and shake my head. Thinking about it will only send me into an anxiety spiral.

I almost didn't answer the call from the unknown number earlier, but something in my gut told me I needed to, just like the night my parents died.

It was Enoch, Tal's friend, letting me know there was an incident at a fire, and Tal was being taken to Mountainside Memorial.

I didn't even hesitate to message my manager and get to my car. I white-knuckled the entire drive, tears blurring my vision. Enoch didn't have time to give me any more information on how serious it was, so my mind immediately went to third degree burns and life-altering damage or worse, death.

I don't want to lose him when I just got him back.

He's already embedded himself into my life, burrowed under my skin. I can't lose the love of my life again.

Not when I haven't even told him I love him. I've been too much of a coward to give in to my feelings because I'm worried he'll reject me again.

You're so stupid.

The rejection would hurt, yes, but can I live with myself if I let him slip away for a second time? Can I survive it?

Tal has been tattooed onto my skin since I was fourteen years old. Even when I tried to cover it up, he was always there underneath the surface. Now, he's engraved onto my fucking soul. Losing him in any capacity will be like ripping out a vital organ.

But am I strong enough to lay it all out there again? To risk my heart?

"Talmage Monson's family?" a nurse in blue scrubs calls from the doorway to the back of the ER.

I stand, and out of the corner of my eye, I see a familiar woman do the same.

Oh great. Talmage's mom is here.

Laurie Monson looks the same as when I was a teenager, though her hair is a bit more gray than blonde now, pinned back in a neat ponytail.

Her face pinches into a frown. "What are you doing here?"

"I'm his wife. I came to make sure he's okay."

"Well, *I'm* his emergency contact."

"He must not have updated it yet. Either way, I'm going back there to make sure my husband is alright," I snap.

The nurse clears her throat. "If you ladies will follow me."

The nurse leads us to a curtained off area, directing us to go inside. Tal gives me a sheepish grin as he sees me. He has a tan wrap around his left ankle, and he looks exhausted but otherwise unharmed. I want to go to him, give him a hug, sob uncontrollably with relief that he's okay—

"Oh! My baby!" Laurie wails, pushing past me and throwing her arms around his neck.

Tal's grin falls. "Mom? What are you doing here?"

"I'm your emergency contact, they called to let me know you were injured." She tries to stroke his face, but he gently bats her hands away.

He looks at me. "I was going to change it tomorrow when I talked to HR about benefits. I'm so sorry, Mack."

"You don't need to apologize. I'm just glad you're okay. What happened?" I motion towards his ankle.

"I have a grade two sprain. I got tangled in a rug and went down trying to save a dog."

I let out a long, relieved breath. A sprained ankle is painful but not life-threatening. All of this for a dog?

"Oh my goodness! Do you need to stay at my house so I can take care of you? I don't want you to be alone," Laurie coos, and Talmage looks annoyed.

"No, Mom. I live with my wife, who is more than capable of helping me. I just have to stay off of it for the next few weeks and use crutches, then I'll have to go to physical therapy."

Laurie glares at me like I'm controlling what Talmage says.

"There's no one more fit to take care of you than your mother."

"My wife does an excellent job taking care of me. I think it'd be best if you leave. I want Mack to take me home so I can rest."

"You're not still upset—"

"Oh, I am. You haven't apologized for the way you spoke to me the last time we talked, and I'm too tired to deal with it right now. If you'd like to check in on me, you can send me a text, but until you're ready to apologize, I want some space."

Laurie's eyes well with tears. "Fine. I'll be praying for you."

Then, she storms out.

Tal motions for me to sit on the chair next to his bed, so I do.

"I was so scared when Enoch called me," I whisper. "He didn't give me any information other than you were at the hospital." My voice cracks, and a tear slips out. He may be okay, but my body is still shaking with fear.

Tal reaches over and grabs my hand, interlacing our fingers. "Damn it, I'm so sorry, Firefly. I wish he would have told you it wasn't anything serious. Nothing life-threatening. I may be off of work for two weeks, but I'm okay. I'm here, and I'm safe. I'm not going anywhere."

"Don't be sorry. It's not like you did it on purpose." I sniffle. "I know you didn't have control over this. I just... I d-don't want to lose you, Tal."

"You're not going to lose me, Mack. Hey, look at me." I lift my chin to look at him through my tears. "You have me, for as long as you want me. I'm not going anywhere."

I want you forever.

CHAPTER 27

Talmage

15 years old...

It's been three weeks since school started. Three weeks of riding the bus to and from school with Mack. Three weeks of all the old feelings I had for her rushing to the surface.

I need to break up with her. I can't keep this up. My mom keeps asking if I've ended things, and I keep telling her I will. She's getting irritated with me, and the tension between us hurts.

I've never disappointed my parents before, and I hate the way it feels. I hate the strain it's put on our relationship. I know what I need to do in order to make them proud, but I know it's going to be hard.

Mack stayed behind a few days last week to audition for the dance company—which she got into. I'm happy for her; I know how badly she wanted to be part of the musical, and now she will be.

But it also means we'll be spending even more time together, and it makes breaking up even harder.

I had a lot of time to think about it over the summer. I studied my scriptures and prayed for guidance, but I don't feel like I ever got a clear answer. It felt like Heavenly Father was just saying, "You know what to do."

And I do.

But it's going to hurt.

Something's shifted between Mack and me in the week since I was injured.

She's been both more open and more reserved. I don't know how to explain it. She talks to me about her day more, and I've been able to pull more smiles from her than I have before, but she still goes a little quiet sometimes when things turn serious. Something in my gut tells me she's holding back from saying something, but I don't have a single clue what it could be.

She's been an angel helping me with my recovery, cooking for me and making sure I have everything I need so I don't have to get up. She's acting like I broke my entire leg instead of just spraining my ankle, but I'm basking in her doting attention, and I don't want to give it up.

I got bored of TV, so I've been working my way through some of her books.

Books I didn't realize had explicit sex scenes. Dirty, filthy scenes that have my imagination running away.

I thought I was picking up a nice, fun fantasy novel about dragons and fairies with a sweet little romance where the two main characters fall in love.

And that *is* what it's about. But I didn't realize halfway through the male main character would say "fuck it," pin his love interest against a wall, and stick his head up her skirt.

I had to sit on the couch for half an hour to will my erection to go down because Mack was behind me working, and I didn't know how she would react.

I went to find some other reading material, but I think *all* of Mack's books contain scenes like that.

Some of them, she put little sticky tabs in, like she wanted to remember where the scene was so she could come back to it later. Those are the only parts of the book with sticky tabs, at least from the four I looked at. I didn't want to keep looking at them and make her wonder what I was looking for. I don't want her to feel ashamed for what she likes.

Does she... *touch herself* to these scenes?

Oh no, that's a dangerous thought. Nope. Don't go there.

But if she does...

It must mean she likes that stuff in real life, right? Reading the marked scenes would be like a how-to guide for pleasuring my wife.

Not that she's given any indication she *wants* me to pleasure her, but if the chance arose...

I should be prepared.

Mack has a team lunch today, so she'll be out of the house long enough for me to snoop without being questioned and give me time to take notes.

"Are you sure you're going to be okay?" she calls from the bedroom.

"Yes, Mack. I'm feeling a lot better. I just need to..." I trail off as she comes out in those freaking black skinny jeans and a black shirt with billowy sleeves. Her lips are painted the same color as the night I proposed to her, and my heart leaps into my throat as I remember our kiss.

"Need to what?" She tilts her head, her hair falling over one shoulder.

What was I saying? "Need to make sure I stay consistent on my pain meds and keep it iced. I should be fine to go back to office duty next week."

Mack nods. "Text me if you need anything."

"Okay. Have fun at your lunch. I l-like the outfit. You look amazing."

Mack's face flushes. "Thank you. I'll see you later."

As soon as I hear the front door close, I hobble over to her bookcase and grab a stack of books with the most sticky tabs.

I spend the next hour reading through the tabbed sections. One book has seven scenes marked, and it's...

Hot.

I'm not entirely sure what the book is about, but the sex scenes start five chapters in and seem to happen every couple of chapters. He... licks her in his office on his desk, then ties her to his bed at his house. He uses a vibrator on her and puts clamps on her nipples.

I had to look up if nipple clamps are safe because it sounds *painful*, but apparently, they're very, very pleasurable if used correctly.

There are so many things I don't know, and I'm suddenly ravenous for more information.

She fingers herself in front of him, then he takes over and makes her squirt. I had to look up what that means and a diagram of the vagina to see if I can figure out what spots they're talking about because they don't use the anatomically correct words.

It's a rabbit hole from there.

I abandon my book research for articles and videos of how to best pleasure a woman, and my penis is rock solid the entire time, imagining doing all of these things to Mack.

I've never once wondered what it would be like to put my mouth on a woman's vagina—er, pussy?—but now it's all I can think about. I want to know what she tastes like. I'm desperate to know if I can bring her the same amount of pleasure the men in her books bring their partners.

I know some people may find it hard to believe, but I've never once looked at porn. I've never had the desire. According to the internet, porn isn't always the most accurate depiction of sex, but since my sex education was pretty much "don't have sex until you're married, then you can have it whenever you want," I don't know what I'm doing.

That's how I find myself on a porn website, watching video after video of people getting... *fucked.*

Some of it looks so fake it's a turn off. Others, the women look so young and the men so old I'm wondering if it's even legal. There's one video, though, that looks homemade. A man is sitting behind a woman with a similar body type to Mack, his fingers buried deep inside her; I can't look away.

The woman writhes against his hand like she's trying to get away from the pleasure but wants more of it at the same time.

Her vagina is hairless, so I can see the arousal glistening on her skin as her body tenses, and she comes. Then it switches angles, and the man has her on top of him.

My eyes close, and suddenly it's not the strangers in the video, but Mack on top of me.

As much as I tried *not* to look when I accidentally barged in on her naked, I still caught a glimpse of the tops of her creamy breasts and the way they sat, heavy and full.

I didn't see her nipples, but now my mind is full of questions about them. What color are they? Are they the shade of her lips when she doesn't have any lipstick on? Or are they darker? More pink or brown?

The thought of having her weight on top of me, feeling the warm wetness of her enveloping me makes my erection twitch.

I groan, grabbing myself through my sweats. There's a small patch of wetness where I've leaked through my underwear. I'm ten seconds away from coming, all it would take is—

"Tal? Are you okay?"

I let out an embarrassing yelp, accidentally tossing my phone on the floor trying to cover my lap with a throw pillow.

Shit. I was so lost in my fantasy, I didn't even hear her come home.

"Yeah." My voice comes out lower than expected, so I clear my throat before I continue, "Just in a bit of pain."

Mack checks the time on her phone. "Have you taken your afternoon pain meds? It doesn't look like you've... moved..." Her eyes narrow on the stack of books next to me, and her head tilts. "Wh-why do you have all of those next to you?"

ABORT. ABORT. DANGER, DANGER.

"Just doing some light reading," I answer.

She walks around the couch and picks up the books, running her fingers across the tabs. "Right, yeah. Okay. Um. Cool. Reading is... fun. Have you eaten yet? I can go make you a sandwich so you can take your meds."

"I can make my ow—"

"No, no. I've got it. You just relax and—" she swallows harshly, "finish your *reading.*"

She sets the books back down next to me, avoiding looking at me. Then she picks up my phone, her eyes widening when she sees what's on the screen.

Oh, no. No. No. This can't be happening.

"Here's your phone." Her voice is tight as she practically throws it at me and rushes up the stairs.

Sure enough, the scene continued, and now the man has the woman's hair in his grip as he enters her from below. Her pale body is flushed in pleasure, but my brain isn't registering the couple's faces.

In my head, all I see is me and Mack in that position. Would she like it? The thought of having her body weight on me makes a new wave of lust roll through me.

Is she upset I'm watching this? I can't imagine why she would be, unless she's against porn and feels it's like cheating as some people do?

I don't want her to feel like I'm cheating, even if our marriage is fake.

I stand, cursing the wet patch which has only grown and hobble to our bedroom to change out of my underwear and sweats before I limp up the stairs to the kitchen.

Mack's just turning around holding a plate with a bomb looking sandwich and a bag of chips. She jumps a little when she sees me.

"Tal, what are you doing? I said I'd bring you your sandwich."

"I'm not cheating on you!" I blurt out. "I mean, I-I don't want you to feel like I'm cheating on you."

Her brows furrow. "I didn't think you were? What are you talking about?"

"The porn. You seem upset, and I want to have a conversation about it. I don't want to hurt you, and if you're hurt—"

"I'm not hurt, Talmage," she interrupts. "I'm just... I was shocked. To see it on your phone after seeing what you were reading... I mean, you're an adult. I don't think porn is a bad thing as long as a relationship isn't compromised for it, it was just... surprising. Besides, we're not... *you know*. You probably have needs. So it makes sense you'd be..." She waves her hand around in the air and makes a vague jerking off gesture.

"I've only started since we got married," I murmur.

"What?"

"I never... masturbated until we got married."

CHAPTER 28

Mackenzie

15 years old...

I should have known when I woke up late this morning that today would be crappy. Nothing's gone right. I got an F on my physics homework, and I spilled chocolate milk on my light pink shirt at lunch, so I've been walking around with a brown patch all day.

Now, Talmage is walking towards me on the bus looking like he'd rather be anywhere else.

I paste on a smile. "Hey, Tal! How was your chem test?"

He sits frozen like a statue, like he isn't processing what I'm saying. I touch his arm, and his face turns beet red.

Is he okay? Should I call someone?

He clears his throat. "We shouldn't do this anymore."

My ears start ringing as soon as the words register.

No, no, no. This can't be happening.

"Do... what?" I whisper. I want him to say it. I need to know for sure he's saying what I think he's saying.

"This. Us. What we're doing. We both need to focus on school. I never should have kissed you or taken it this far because it's against the rules. I have to prepare to go on my *mission, and we should date other people. Maybe when we're older, and we—"*

"Stop. Please don't." My eyes fill with tears, and I blink them away. "Don't give me hope of something in the future because you know I'd wait. If you're ending it, just end it. Don't give me hope."

I would say no to every person who asks me on a date between now and when he comes home if it meant we'd have a chance.

"Firefly, I'm sorry." His face is pinched with hurt as he tries to grab my hand.

"Please don't call me that anymore." I hug my back-pack, hoping it can act as a shield. I want to ask him to move spots. To leave me alone, but the bus is already moving, and the driver will yell at him if he gets up.

Talmage and I don't speak for the rest of the ride home. I put in my headphones and let the tears fall silently.

I walk home from the bus stop, wiping my nose as the tears fall faster, and when I'm finally home, I crumple into a heap on my bed.

I thought I'd already experienced heartbreak. I thought I knew what true agony felt like, but it's nothing compared to the way Talmage Monson has ripped my heart to pieces.

The saddest part is, I still love him. Still want him.

I think I always will.

Tomorrow, I'll have to get on the bus with him again.

Tomorrow, I'll have to go to school and pretend I'm not dying on the inside.

Tomorrow, I'll have to answer questions about why Talmage and I don't sit next to each other anymore.

But tonight, I'll cry until I don't have any more tears.

Surely, I must have heard him wrong.

Talmage went *twenty-eight years* without masturbating? Is that even *healthy?*

I truly don't know what to say, what to think.

He was so turned on by you he couldn't control himself anymore! The hopeless romantic in me who refuses to die and has read way too many romance novels squeals.

Noooope. No. I can't think like that.

But damn it. Seeing what was on his phone and the books he had out didn't upset me. It turned me on a little.

Okay, a lot.

It's like once I finally admitted to myself I am—still—in love with my fake husband, my body started gearing up to be fucked. The occasional horny thought I used to have when I read something spicy has turned into a full-body *need.* Even though we haven't so much as kissed in over three weeks. I haven't seen him naked. We've barely even touched.

God, the kiss on our wedding day feels like a lifetime ago.

I haven't had time to get myself off because we've been stuck in the house together most of the last week—which has only amplified my desire for him.

I'm not the kind of girl who can get herself off standing up in the shower. I have to have something to read or listen to while I do it, or I can't focus, and I need the space to spread out so I can enjoy myself.

"You're telling me you've never touched yourself? In your entire life? Not once?"

Tal nods rapidly. "Not until we got married. You know what the church teaches. It was one of the rules that scared me the most, but when we got married, I figured, good enough. I could... *do that* and not feel like I was breaking any rules because I was married."

I blink at him, still trying to process. "So, you've never... *orgasmed*... until three weeks ago?"

Tal gives me a sheepish grin and shrugs. "The body will find a way to get a release if it needs to, but I've never actively sought out an orgasm."

I tilt my head, confused. How can he have had an orgasm without—*oh.*

Ohhhhhh.

"Got it. Right. Yeah. That... makes sense." I clear my throat. "Like I said, I was just shocked. You can look at or read whatever you want. If you decide you want to go find someone to—"

"No!" he practically barks, then takes a deep breath. "No, I don't need—or *want*—to find someone to do anything with. If I'm not going to be... *intimate* with my wife, I sure as hell am not going to go out and find someone else."

Good lord. Is it hot in here?

I want to ask him if he *wants* to be intimate with me. I want to ask him if he's thought about me the way I've thought about him.

My entire body flushes as I conjure an image of Tal, his strong frame leaning against the wall of the shower, his cock in his hand. Is he a moaner? I feel like he'd make so many noises of pleasure. Would he whimper and beg for me to make him feel good? I bet if I wrapped my hand around him, he'd be putty in my hands, and I could make him come in two minutes. Or if I put him in my mouth...

Do I have a corruption kink?

I don't necessarily *want* to corrupt Tal, but I *do* want to give him the overwhelming pleasure no one else has.

You can't even admit out loud you've got real feelings for him, don't complicate things, Mackenzie.

"Mack? Are you good? You kind of zoned out." Tal's voice brings me back to the present, and it's then I realize I'm still holding his sandwich.

"Yeah, yeah. I'm good." I set the plate on the counter and slide it towards one of the stools. "Eat your sandwich. I'll go grab my laptop so I can work up here."

Tal's eyes roam my face for a second before he limps over to the stool and sits down. He picks up the sandwich and takes a bite, letting out a groan of appreciation, and my nipples harden.

Thank fuck I'm wearing a bra.

"This is really good. Thank you for making it for me." He takes another bite.

"No problem," I squeak. "I'll be right back."

Before he can say anything, I rush downstairs. My eyes snag again on the books on the couch, the ones with the tabs marking scenes that make my blood heat. That's the only kind of annotation I do. If the spice is enough to make me need a break, it gets a tab.

The clothes I'm wearing are making me too hot—at least that's what I'm telling myself. I duck into our room to change, shucking off my pants and shirt. Before I toss my shirt into my laundry basket, something in Tal's basket catches my eye.

These were the sweats he put on this morning.

Don't. It's none of your business.

Ignoring the logical voice in my head, I pick them up and notice the wet patch on the front.

Where I imagine the head of his dick would sit.

Oh god, he got so aroused he soiled his pants.

A helpless, needy sound expels from my throat before I can stop it, and I toss the pants back in the laundry so I don't do something creepy and inappropriate like smell the wet patch.

I quickly pull on leggings and an oversized T-shirt then grab my laptop and make my way back upstairs.

I hope I can keep my body in check.

I could not keep it in check.

Everything was fine, I made it through the rest of my workday and dinner with no salacious thoughts of my fake husband.

But then we went downstairs to get ready for bed, and he hopped in the shower, and now my mind is running away with itself.

My clit is pulsing and begging to be touched as I imagine him in there.

Is he touching himself?

I'm straining my ears, trying to hear something, but the bed's a bit too far away.

I feel like a lunatic, creeping to the bathroom door and gently pushing my ear against it.

But I don't hear anything other than the steady drumming of the water hitting the tiles and the—

"Mack."

I jump back as if I've been caught, but the door is still closed, and the shower is still on.

I press my ear against the wood harder.

"P-please, Firefly. Want you to touch me," Tal whimpers. The use of my nickname makes my core clench around nothing, emphasizing how empty I feel.

Now that I know he's doing what I hoped he was doing, I can hear the subtle slap of his hand moving along his cock.

Move away from the door. You're invading his privacy.

Right. Yes. I should move. I should leave the room, maybe the fucking house so I can get my head on straight.

But I don't.

I can't make myself do it.

"Mmm, I'm coming, Mack. You make me feel so good. *Shit.*" His voice is laced with so much desperation, it only serves to turn me on more.

I can't stop myself any longer, I dive for the bed and lie on my side, facing away from the door before I shove my hand in my pajama shorts and start rapidly rubbing my clit.

I usually like to ease into it, work myself up, use a toy, but I know I don't have enough time, and I'm so amped up I don't think I need to, anyway.

I bite my pillow to stop myself from moaning out loud as I continue to get myself off. Listening to him made me so wet, my fingers keep slipping.

The shower turns off, and I know I have less than five minutes to get myself there, or I'm going to have to go to sleep even more hot and bothered than I was before.

The sounds he was making ring in my ears, and I imagine Tal's tentative fingers rubbing my clit. He'd be a little clumsy, but that's okay. I'd guide him, teach him everything he wants to know.

I hear the buzz of his toothbrush and work my fingers in faster circles, bringing my free hand under my shirt to pluck and pull at my nipples to add to the sensation.

My body tenses, and my pussy clenches, my orgasm sizzling through me just as the bathroom door clicks open.

I pull my hands from my pants and bring up social media on my phone so it looks like I was just lying here scrolling, but my breathing is rapid, and I'm sure my pale skin is flushed.

I hope he doesn't notice.

I sit up and give Tal what I hope is a friendly smile, quickly scanning his underwear and T-shirt clad form. I'm quick so he doesn't catch me staring, but his eyes are locked on my chest so he doesn't notice.

I follow his gaze and find my skin red and splotchy, and my flush turns redder as embarrassment washes over me.

I can't believe I did that.

Tal licks his lips and brings his eyes up to mine. "Are you okay?"

"Yeah," I croak. "Just... hot."

Tal nods, a strand of slightly damp hair falling onto this forehead. "Do you want me to go turn the heat off?"

"No, no. I'll be fine."

"Okay." He limps over to his side of the bed and gets under the blanket, grabbing his own phone.

I roll off the bed and rush to the bathroom to do my business and wash my hands. The bathroom is still a little steamy, but that's not what has my skin feeling hot.

No, it's the scent of *my* body wash permeating the air. I showered before Tal, so it shouldn't be as strong as it is, which means...

Does he use my body wash to jerk off?

I clench my thighs together at the thought.

I finish washing my hands and leave the bathroom, my mind swirling with possibilities.

Is it unethical to want to fuck your virgin fake husband who you're deeply in love with?

CHAPTER 29

Talmage

15 years old...

Mackenzie looks like she hasn't slept in weeks, and I feel like it's my fault.

I dimmed the bright light in her eyes. She doesn't even look at me anymore.

I hurt her.

And I hate myself for it.

My parents are proud of me, though. Whatever was straining our relationship is fixed and everything is back to normal.

Was it worth it?

I don't know.

I've kept my distance from Mack. It's more difficult than I thought it would be, but I was stupid because we run in the same circles. We have the same extracurriculars.

And apparently we have the perfect height difference for dance numbers because I keep getting paired with her.

Every time, she looks like she would rather jump off the stage.

I don't blame her.

I keep telling myself this will all get better—easier.
Hopefully, I'll believe it soon.

Before I'm even fully awake, I know something is off.

I'm too warm and sticky.

Sticky?

Oh no.

My eyes shoot open. Mack's got her front pressed up against my side, her large breasts pinning my left hand to my body, one of her hands on my chest.

I can't even appreciate the feel of her hand on me because I'm embarrassed. I can feel myself throbbing beneath the blanket. I'm just glad her hand is nowhere near *it*.

I reach under the covers to tuck my dick into my waistband, and I'm met with the somewhat familiar, sticky sensation of my cum seeping through my underwear.

I had a wet dream in Mack's bed.

And I'm still *hard*.

This has never happened before. I've had morning wood, sure, but I've never had a wet dream and woken up with an erection at the same time.

Shit. This is so embarrassing. She's going to know as soon as I sit up what happened. She's going to think I'm a pervert.

I went to sleep already half-aroused from the flush on Mack's chest when I came out of the shower. It reminded me of the way the woman's skin in the video flushed with pleasure.

That led to a very vivid dream once I fell asleep. The dream comes back to me in flashes. Mack on top of me, my face cradled between her thick thighs, Mack's mouth around my—

Mack shifts and sighs as her eyes flutter open. She gives me a sleepy smile so stunning the urge to kiss her overpowers the feeling of embarrassment.

"Good morning," I rasp.

She blinks, looks down at where her hand is, and shuffles to sit up. "Good morning, I'm so sorry if I infringed on your space last night. I-I didn't mean to."

"I'll never complain about cuddling with my wife. Maybe next time I can get my arm out from between us, though," I joke, shaking my half-asleep hand.

"I'm not usually a cuddler," she mumbles.

"I know. We've shared a bed for almost a month, and we've only ended up pressed together a few times—"

"We have?!"

I chuckle at the way her voice rises in surprise, about to sit up until I remember my predicament. Luckily, since we're in the basement, there's not much light in the room, so hopefully she won't notice.

"Not often. I don't know who scoots which way, but we've ended up cuddling a few times. I thought you knew but didn't want to acknowledge it, so I never brought it up. Like I said, though, I'll never complain about getting to cuddle you."

Mack sighs. "Why are you so sweet to me?" Then, she straightens her spine like she didn't mean to say it.

"Because I care about you, Mack," I answer, even though I don't think she's actually looking for one. It barely scratches the surface of how I feel about her, but I know I need to tread lightly. We're making slow progress, and I don't want her to retreat because I can't keep my mouth shut.

Mack gets out of bed and turns on the bedroom light, both of us blinking to adjust to the change. She comes back and sits cross-legged on the bed facing me.

I sit up, too, because her face looks serious. Unfortunately, I momentarily forget about my sticky situation, and the blanket falls, revealing the wetness seeping through my light gray boxer briefs, and the outline of my erection.

"I didn't pee my pants, I swear," I blurt out as Mack's gaze lands on the mess.

Her nose scrunches. "I didn't think you did. Is that...?" Her eyes widen.

"Yeah." I rub the back of my neck, my entire body heating with shame.

"You're still hard," she whispers, something akin to awe in her tone.

"Yeah, this has never happened before." *Why are you telling her this?*

Mack's eyes are still locked on my groin, her gaze curious and... heated? My length twitches, excited by her perusal.

"Mack, if you keep looking at it like that, I'm going to have an even bigger mess to clean up," I whisper.

Mack's eyes shoot to mine, and she licks her lips slowly.

My eyes trace the movement, desperate for it to be *my* tongue. Morning breath be damned. I'd kiss her after she ate an entire bulb of garlic if it meant feeling her lips on mine again.

"You think you can come just from me looking at it?" she rasps.

"Yes," I answer honestly. Logistically, I don't know how it would work, but I'm so keyed up, and I want her so *severely,* I think it could happen.

"Do you want me to leave so you can take care of it?"

No! I want to whine. *Please don't leave me this way. Help me, touch me, kiss me, love me. Let me worship you. Teach me how to make you feel good. I'd happily walk around with an erection all day if it means I know what it feels like to please you.*

But she said she doesn't want to get attached. She doesn't want to make things harder than they need to be, and I'm not going to push it just because I want her more than I need air.

"It'll go away on its own, but I should get cleaned up and change the sheets," I admit sheepishly.

"Right." She shakes her head and gets off the bed. "I'm just going to brush my teeth. Then I'll go get breakfast started, and you can... take care of that." She rushes into the bathroom before I can respond. I wait for her to come out and head upstairs before I move.

Gingerly, I get out of bed and use a washcloth to clean myself before slipping on a new pair of underwear and some basketball shorts. I brush my teeth and splash my face with cold water before combing my mustache.

Then, I strip the bed and toss the sheets into the basket, before remaking it with clean sheets.

This morning gave me a bit of whiplash, and I need to make sure my head is on right before I go upstairs and see my wife again.

Does she want me? Her reaction seemed like she did, but I don't know. I can't read her as well as I'd like to.

I *want* her to want me.

She was opening up to me, but one wrong move could have her shutting down again, and I don't want that.

My feelings for her are growing and expanding in my chest, and eventually they'll have to be let out, or I'll explode.

As I make my way to the stairs, the melody of a song floats down, and I pause halfway through my ascent to listen to Taylor Swift's voice singing about feeling guilty for things she hasn't done. I've never paid much attention to the lyrics, but for some reason, it makes me pause.

Chills run up and down my arms as I keep listening to her sing about bed sheets being ablaze and screaming someone's name.

About the way he holds her being what's *actually* holy.

Why do I suddenly feel like crying? This song, the lyrics, are saying things I haven't been able to put into words. Feeling guilty for something I haven't even done, for touching someone I've never touched in a sexual way.

As I reach the top of the stairs, I find Mack bobbing her head to the beat and flipping pancakes.

The blinds are open, the early morning sun shining through and casting her in an angelic glow. She's so beautiful my breath hitches, and a rightness settles in my chest.

This. *This* is what I've been waiting forever for. Casual mornings with the love of my life.

Tell her now.

Oh, how I want to. I want to wrap her in my arms and tell her this is real for me. This is what I want. The forever I'm choosing is with her, and I hope she'll choose me, too.

The song changes, and my heart rate speeds up as I recognize the guitar string intro immediately, even though it's a song I actively avoided for years because it brings me too much pain.

Mack's back stiffens, and she reaches for her phone—

"Please don't," I blurt out, startling her.

"Jesus H. Christ, Talmage! I didn't even hear you come up." Her hand slaps her chest in shock.

"I'm sorry." I wish my ankle wasn't hurting so I could walk faster, but I hobble in her direction anyway. "But please don't change the song," I whisper.

"I don't listen to this song anymore," she admits quietly.

"Why?"

She swallows and shakes her head. "I just... can't."

"Don't shut me out, tell me why. *Please.*"

Her eyes search my face, for what, I don't know. But eventually, she turns back to the griddle, and I assume she's not going to answer.

"I haven't listened to it since you broke up with me. I tried to, but it brought me to tears every time. I can't bring myself to block it from my app, but… I skip it every time," she admits softly while she plates the pancakes and some bacon.

She still skips it fourteen years later? Maybe Mack's feelings aren't gone like I thought, not if the pain is still real. If she'd moved on, she would be able to listen to it no problem. If she didn't have feelings for me, the song wouldn't bring her such pain.

I step beside her and put my hand on her arm to grab her attention. Her head tilts up to look at me, and the emotions swirling around her green eyes make me want to fall to my knees.

Fourteen years later, but the pain I caused her still exists—still *hurts*—and it makes me feel like shit.

"Mack, I—"

"I hope you made chocolate chip!" Kinsley's voice interrupts what I was about to say—about to confess.

Probably for the best. Mack deserves more than a hasty kitchen confession. She deserves the grandest of grand gestures. A romance-novel-worthy moment, and I intend to give it to her.

I step away from Mack and let her put the plates in front of her sisters. "Of course I made chocolate chip," she deadpans.

The girls inhale their pancakes and bacon, then Mack slips on her shoes and a sweatshirt, and the three of them leave so the twins aren't late for school.

I take care of the dishes, grateful for the silence to think about what I'm going to do. I have fourteen years' worth of romance to make up for.

But first, I need a favor from Lizzie.

Chapter 30

Talmage

16 years old...

Finally, the school year is over. I never pictured having to mend a broken heart my sophomore year while adjusting to high school life, but I hope it means I get to have an easier junior year.

After the musical wrapped, Mack and I saw each other in passing in the hall but rarely spoke unless we had to co-ordinate during a dance number in rehearsal. We ended up in the same group for the Sadie Hawkins dance, but luckily, it wasn't too awkward.

She still looks sad, but I know she was dating one of the military academy guys, so maybe they broke up, and it's not my fault anymore.

We'll be in the musical and chamber choir together next year, so hopefully we can be cordial and friendly to one another.

I'm heading back to Scout camp, hoping to finish my Eagle Scout this summer.

Things are looking up.

I'm relieved to be back at work this week, even if I am resigned to desk duty for the next little while. Siren's relieved, too, even though she got to come in with Enoch a few times while I was off. Having a backyard to run around in at home helps. The twins were really helpful, too, playing with her and taking her on walks. They even offered to feed her if I couldn't make it up the stairs.

When we got here, she started running around begging everyone for scratches like she's been gone for an eternity instead of two weeks.

Now, she's thoroughly inspecting all of the equipment—what she's looking for, I have no idea—while Enoch, Travis, and I talk about what I missed while I was gone.

According to Enoch's text, the fire I got injured in was caused by two candles that had fallen over and lit the viscose rug on fire. Since the house was almost a century old, the wood used to build it was more flammable. That, paired with modern-day furniture being built with highly flammable materials, caused the flames to spread too quickly. The house is considered a total loss, condemned by the insurance company.

The couple is fine. Other than a little smoke inhalation, they should make a full recovery. Their dog, too, which is good.

My heart aches for them, losing all of their personal belongings and their home is tragic. I think it's one of the hardest parts of this job—seeing the damage one tiny flame can cause.

Since I've been out, they've only been called to a few accidents and one minor fire in a field caused by a still-lit cigarette being discarded. The dry grass catches so fast, but luckily, they stopped it before it did any real damage.

"How are things with the wife?" Enoch pumps his eyebrows at me, and I shoot him an unamused glare.

"They're good. She was really helpful with my recovery."

"That's good, but did you get to play sexy nurse with her?"

I scowl at him.

Enoch chuckles. "I'll take that as a *no* then."

"I'm not discussing my sex life with you. I've already made that clear."

Enoch clicks his tongue. "Can't discuss something you don't have anyway. Travis, how's Samm? You two good?"

Travis' eyes go wide as he nods. "Yep. All good. We're good."

"Enoch, if you're so eager to talk about someone's sex life, why don't you tell us about yours and leave Travis alone?"

Travis—still a rookie and not used to Enoch's antics—gives me a grateful nod. He's a good kid, and I don't want Enoch to scare him off with his big mouth.

Enoch crosses his arms and puffs out his chest. "I'll have you know I'm on a self-imposed dating break until I can get my dream girl to go out with me."

Oh no.

"You're not talking about—"

"Lizzie? Hell yeah, I am, brother. I knew the minute I saw her I wanted her. Love at first sight. She's playing hard to get, but I'll win her over. I've got a tattoo appointment scheduled for May—a big piece—so we'll be spending *lots* of time together."

I pinch the bridge of my nose. "Isn't there some type of ethical code or something that says she can't date clients? Like nurses or doctors?"

Enoch shrugs and waves me off. "I don't know about a code, but I'm just getting the one from her, so it won't be a problem. I'll charm her while I'm in the chair and impress her with my pain tolerance. Then, when it's finished, I'll ask her out, and wham! She'll be my wife."

"*Wife?* That's a bit of a stretch, isn't it?"

"Nah. Besides, we'll be brothers-in-law if I marry her. Don't you want me in your family?"

"I don't think that's how it works," Travis interjects quietly.

Enoch glares at him, and I chuckle. "He's not wrong. Lizzie and Mack aren't *actually* related."

"Semantics. Either way, we'd be seeing a lot more of each other."

"Just what I want," I deadpan, and Enoch rolls his eyes.

Chief Johnson comes stomping into the break area before Enoch can respond, and both men shoot to their feet. I gently stand, giving Chief a nod.

"Gentlemen, Relief Society is usually reserved for Sundays. What gossip could be so good it's keeping you from cleaning the bathrooms?"

Did I mention he's kind of a misogynistic asshole?

"Nothing of importance, sir, but we've already done all the tasks on the list today," I pipe in. As Captain, I take it upon myself to advocate for my crew, and even though Chief is technically in charge, I won't let him bully my men.

Chief's signature frown remains in place as he opens the fridge, probably checking for moldy food. He won't find any, though, because we keep our kitchen tidy and organized.

"Monson, when are you off of desk duty?" he barks.

"I should be back in two weeks, sir. I just need to be signed off on by a physical therapist."

He gives me a curt nod. "Good. You've been missed. Now, no more chitter-chattering. Find something to do. Monson—no more tripping over rugs, got it?"

"Yes, sir."

With a final nod, he stomps out of the break room and down the stairs to his office.

"Well, I guess I'll go... double-check the fuel levels," Travis says, scurrying off without waiting for our reply.

Enoch shakes his head before checking the time and heading towards the kitchen. He's on lunch duty today, but I won't be sticking around since I have an appointment.

"Hey, Tal?" Enoch calls from the fridge.

"Yeah?"

"I know I tease you about your sex life, but I'm not trying to be a dick. Truth is, I'm rooting for you and Mack. I guess I'm just... I guess I'm jealous."

I make my way over to one of the barstools and sit down. "Jealous? Of what?"

"The way you two look at each other. The love be-tween you two is so obvious, it's nearly palpable. I know I talk a big game, but I'm kind of terrified I'll never find a love like yours, terrified I'm doomed to die alone."

Enoch and I may be best friends, but I don't usually see this side of him. The vulnerable side he hides behind jokes and lewd comments.

"It'll happen, man. When you least expect it."

"I hope so."

My phone beeps with my alarm, I have about forty-five minutes until my appointment, and I need to get going. "I've got to run, but if you need to talk about something, text me. You know I've got your back, bro."

"If you could put in a good word with Lizzie if you see her..." he trails off, giving me a smirk.

I roll my eyes. "You and I both know nothing I say is going to convince her if her mind's already made up."

Enoch sighs. "Yeah, I know. Worth a shot, though."

After dropping Siren off at home—still weird I get to call Mack's house *home*—and changing into basketball shorts, I make my way to Provo and park in front of the little strip mall where the sign boasts "Medusa Tattoos."

Lizzie graciously agreed to help me with the first step in showing Mack how I feel, and I'm grateful she could fit me in on such short notice.

I walk through the door and am immediately mesmerized by the dark green wallpaper engraved with little gold snakes. Everything is in shades of green, black, and gold. Normally, I think I'd be a little put off by the vibes, but everything feels cozy and welcoming. The wall of Pride flags should clash with the dark décor, but it only adds to the comforting vibes.

I wonder if Emma knows about this place. This seems like something she'd appreciate.

There's a person at the front desk with a shaved head dyed to look like cheetah spots, and they give me a curious onceover after welcoming me into the shop.

I can imagine what they're thinking. Clean cut, golden Mormon boy in a tattoo shop? I must be lost.

Luckily, I don't have to explain anything because Lizzie comes to the front. "Hey, Talmage. Ready to get inked?"

"Sure am," I say confidently. I can handle a little bit of pain.

Lizzie and the other person share a look I don't understand before Lizzie chuckles and grabs a paper and a clipboard for me. "Men are always so confident when they walk in, but let me tell you a secret, Tal. I could power this whole building if it ran off of men's pain."

"That's... scary." I take the clipboard from her and fill out the information, unease worming its way up my spine. Is this a bad idea? Am I making a mistake?

"You'll be fine. It's just more painful than people think sometimes."

"Well, you and Mack have a bunch, so how bad can it be?"

Lizzie purses her lips like she wants to say something, but she just shakes her head. "We have different pain tolerances. Come on back, let me show you the design I came up with."

I follow her to a curtained off area. There's artwork on the walls depicting different goddesses, but they're all plus size. There are crystals and decks of tarot cards on little shelves. A premade design board catches my attention, and I'm intrigued by the details. Depictions of goddesses, intricate tarot card designs, florals, and nature scenes. There are some pin-up style girls in different costumes and a few animal designs.

Lizzie's extremely talented. I made a good choice asking her for help.

Lizzie taps a few times on her iPad and turns it around to show me what she's designed.

My breath hitches, and tears well in my eyes. "It's perfect."

Her face softens. "And you're sure you want this on you forever? What happens if—"

"I'm sure," I cut her off. "I don't plan on going anywhere."

She rolls her lips into her mouth and nods. "Let me get this printed then. Have a seat."

After a few minutes, she comes back, shaves the area we're tattooing, and places the stencil on my skin.

After she gets me situated in her chair the way she needs me, she starts the tattoo machine and holds the gun over my thigh.

"Hold on tight, Talmage."

CHAPTER 31

Mackenzie

17 years old...

I'll forever be grateful for finding Lizzie as a friend. Without her, there's no way I would have survived sophomore and junior year. She's distracted me with movie nights and held my hand while I've cried.

I would be lost without her.

I've had to watch Tal date the other girls in choir. I've had to dance with him in the musical. I've had to sit and listen to his melodic tenor voice and watch him give his golden smile to everyone but me.

It's been terrible.

I thought I could erase the hurt by kissing more people, going on more dates. Out of sight, out of mind. Moving on.

Every date, every "hang out" with someone who wasn't him ended up enhancing the fact Talmage is the best I'll ever get, and being with anyone else is settling.

Which is rude of me, I know, because I've had two boyfriends since he broke up with me.

But neither of them felt like home the way Talmage did. Neither of them looked at me like I was something special and precious.

So I'll keep trying to find someone else, even as my heart holds on to the hope that one day, Tal will change his mind.

I'm embarrassed to admit the amount of letters I've written to him, begging him to come back to me. I'm pathetic.

Worthless.

Stupid.

Just like Brock used to say.

I shudder just thinking his name, and tears well in my eyes.

Another mistake in the long line of them on my list.

Tal's been acting weird for the last week. He's been wearing basketball shorts to bed instead of just his boxers, and part of me wonders if it's because of his... sticky situation.

Does an extra layer make it less likely for a wet dream to happen? I don't really know how it works.

All I know is I can't stop thinking about that morning. What I saw, the overwhelming heat that sizzled through my body. The way I wanted to pull away his boxers and clean up the mess he'd made.

I only saw the outline through his soiled underwear, but from what I could tell, Tal is *well endowed.*

I can't stop imagining what it would feel like. I want to know what he tastes like. How the weight of him would feel in my hand—in my mouth, in *me.*

But I think my blatant staring scared him because he's been careful not to touch me, especially during the night. We've had surface level conversations but haven't ventured into anything deeper.

Or maybe I'm just projecting because *I* scared myself.

My feelings are too strong. My desire for him is becoming overwhelming, I find myself zoning out at work and playing out "what if" scenarios. I try to read, but all I can picture is Tal and me in the place of the main characters.

And not just during the spicy scenes.

During the big gestures and love confessions, all I can picture is Talmage saying those things to me.

I can't take much more of this. It's our one-month anniversary, and every day that passes, the tension ramps up higher.

It's almost two o'clock in the morning, and I can't sleep. My mind is racing, trying to find a justifiable reason to give in to the pull between us. I feel like I need a plausible excuse to fuck my husband, and I can't think of a single one.

Logically, I know it would just cause me more pain. It would hurt to have him in such an intimate way and then have to end things, but Goddammit, I don't think I've ever been so needy in my life.

On Monday, Tal let me know he had an appointment after work and wouldn't be back until well after dinner.

The girls had their clubs in the afternoon, so I took some time to myself. I got in the bath, read a spicy scene, and brought my trusty rose with me.

I was able to come, so I thought I was good and could handle seeing my husband without wanting to jump his bones, but *nope.*

The minute he came downstairs and hit me with his golden smile, my vagina perked up, acting like we haven't been touched in years—which isn't wrong.

I shift, ready to roll out of bed and make a cup of tea, when Tal mumbles something in his sleep. I pause, not wanting to wake him. I haven't heard him talk in his sleep before, but I've been sleeping much deeper since we started sharing a bed, so maybe I've just missed it.

"Mack," he mumbles, rolling onto his side to face me.

"What?" I whisper, still unsure if he's actually awake.

"Need you to touch me." He moves his hips in a thrusting motion. "Please, Firefly."

My entire body freezes. His eyes are closed, so I don't think he's awake. I don't want to wake him up and ruin the dream but...

Fuck. I don't know what to do. I can't lie here and listen to him moan my name. I don't want him to wake up embarrassed again.

I reach over and poke his shoulder. "Talmage. Tal. Bear. Wake up."

Tal jolts and blinks awake, the whites of his eyes barely visible in the dark room. "What's wrong? Are you okay?"

"Everything's fine. You um... you were having a dream. Talking in your sleep."

"Oh." He's completely silent for a second, and I think he's fallen back to sleep until he says, "Sorry if I woke you up."

"You didn't. I was awake."

"Have you slept at all?" I hear the worried frown in his voice.

"Not really," I admit softly. "But it's okay. I don't have any plans tomorrow, so I can sleep in... if I ever fall asleep."

Tal shifts and sits up in the bed. "How can I help you? Can I get you some tea or something?"

I'm glad he can't see me because I'm sure my face is beet red with the thoughts of how he can help me. All of them are rated R.

"Can you just hold me? Maybe?"

"Of course. You don't have to ask me to snuggle. Come here."

I lie down and scoot towards him, my back to his front, regretting this suggestion immediately when his clean scent and warmth envelop me.

He tosses an arm over my hip while I lay my head on his bicep, but I notice his body is arched in what's probably an uncomfortable position.

"Why are you arched like that?" I ask, but as soon as the words are out, I realize why.

He's trying to make it so I don't feel... *it.*

God, I want to feel him.

"I don't want to make you uncomfortable," he murmurs.

"I'm fine, Tal. Don't worry about me."

Talmage makes a pained sound but shuffles until the front of his thighs meet the back of mine, and—

There it is.

Hot and hard against the curve of my ass, and I swear I feel it twitch. My instincts are telling me to grind back, but I fight them with everything in me.

Not hard enough, apparently, because I move back, just a little bit and press myself against him harder.

"*Mack,*" Tal groans, gripping my hip to stop me from moving. The heat from his palm sears my skin through my clothes, and I just barely hold back a whimper.

"I'm just trying to get comfortable," I feign innocence, but I don't believe myself with the way my voice comes out breathy and thick with need.

"I get that, and you should be comfortable, but *please.* You're killing me here. I'm trying really hard not to cross any lines."

Maybe it's the exhaustion from keeping my emotions in check, or maybe it's the blanket of darkness making me feel brave, but I find myself asking, "Do you want to cross them?"

I feel more than I hear the deep breath Tal takes. "Yes."

Bless his blatant honesty. I don't know why I find his restraint so attractive—probably because of my past—but it only makes me want him more.

I'm tired of fighting the pull I feel towards him, and he seems to want me just as much, so what's the harm in finding some mutual satisfaction with each other?

"What if I told you I want you to cross them?" I whisper, shifting my hips back again.

"I would ask if you're sure. I would tell you I'll follow your lead, do whatever you want. I would say I don't know what I'm doing, Mack, but I'm willing to learn.

Anything you want, anything you need. I'll give it to you. I'll give you *everything*."

Goddammit. His eagerness is so hot. Hotter than it should be.

"What do you want to learn first, Tal?" I flip over so I'm facing him. I can barely make out his features in the dark, but I think his eyes are pinched shut.

"I want to taste you," he whimpers. "Teach me how to make you feel good. Please."

I sit up and lean over to turn on the lamp, blinking rapidly while my eyes adjust.

"Are you sure this is something you want?" I look him directly in the eyes. I need to be sure.

"Yes," he answers immediately, determination in his tone.

I lie back down on the bed and take off my shorts, discarding them on the floor. "Have you ever seen a pussy in real life before?"

Tal shakes his head, his eyes planted firmly on my face, like he's scared to look down.

"Well, you'll have to look in order to taste, Tal." I don't know where this confidence is coming from. My need for my husband is overpowering any insecurities or hesitancy I may have. Maybe it's because he's inexperienced, and I need to take the lead. Maybe it's the way his eyes are greedily taking me in, making me feel more beautiful than anything else ever has. Whatever it is, I don't hate it.

His eyes get stuck on a tattoo on my hip. One that hasn't been visible until now.

One of the few Lizzie didn't do because I knew she'd refuse.

It's a simple line drawing of a teddy bear with hearts on the bottom of its feet. To anyone else, it wouldn't seem like anything special, but Tal's eyes whip up to mine, swirling with questions.

He must sense my apprehension to talk about it because instead of asking, he lies down on the bed, his face inches from my pussy. I let out a breath of relief.

"Wow," he whispers reverently, his stare locked on my exposed cunt. I don't wax, just give myself a bit of a trim every so often, and while I should feel self-conscious, it's hard to be when he's looking at it like it's a rare piece of art. After a moment, he looks up at me over the swell of my stomach. "Can I touch you?" His voice is huskier than I've ever heard it, and my pussy clenches greedily.

"Yes."

"Will you tell me if what I'm doing doesn't feel good?" He sounds hesitant.

"I will, but I don't think it will be a problem." I think if he finds my clit, I'm bound to detonate immediately. It's been so long since someone else has touched me, and the fact it's *Talmage*, the one boy I've never gotten over? I'm ready to combust already.

He's not a boy anymore. My brain supplies through the lustful haze.

No, he's definitely not. He's all man. Broad shoulders and thick biceps. Sharp jaw and—

He trails a slightly shaky finger through the wetness at my entrance, letting out a groan when he feels my arousal. I let out a moan at the minimal contact, my eyelids fluttering closed. Tal trails his finger up and down a few times before he brings it all the way up to my clit and presses down slightly.

I jolt as shocks of pleasure shoot through me.

"That's your clitoris, right?" he rasps. I open my eyes to look at him, but his gaze is firmly on where his finger is circling the firm bundle of nerves.

"Yes," I croak as he increases the pressure.

"Can you come from just clitoral stimulation?" He finally looks up at me, his eyes glassy and filled with so much desire.

"I—" *Where did he learn that?* "Yeah."

Tal just nods, his eyes once again falling to where he's touching me.

"Can I taste you, Firefly?"

"*Please.*"

Tal doesn't waste any time shuffling forward and licking quickly up through my lips. His mustache tickles me as he does, heightening the sensation.

"*Fuck,*" he mumbles against me before his mouth is on me in earnest, kissing and licking me like I'm his favorite dessert. He's a little sloppy, a little uncoordinated, but honestly? It's hot as fuck to feel him making out with my pussy.

When his tongue traces a path up to my clit and circles it a few times, my hips lift off the bed, and my hand shoots to his hair to give it a gentle tug.

"Use my face to make yourself come, Mack. Tell me what else you need to get there. Teach me how to please you."

"Two fingers inside me, please. Tongue on my clit."

Tal doesn't hesitate. He laps at my clit and works two thick fingers inside me, thrusting slowly. I'm about to tell him to crook them up, but he does it himself, and I cry out my approval, "*Yes.*"

Tal somehow finds the spot inside me only my toys have reached and sets a steady rhythm, while his tongue never stops its relentless pace on my clit. I grip his hair, keeping his face where I want it while I selfishly take my pleasure.

My eyes roll back as my orgasm crests. "I'm going to come," I warn, crying out Talmage's name as pleasure sizzles through my veins. My thighs tense hard around his head, I'm worried I'm going to squeeze his brains out.

But he still doesn't stop after I relax.

I watch him as his tongue, greedy and swift, licks up the arousal around my pussy lips. When he pulls his fingers from me, he sticks them in his mouth and licks them clean, moaning the entire time.

"Thank you," he mumbles around his fingers. "That was the best experience of my life."

Surely, that's not true. "But you didn't come."

The tips of Tal's ears turn red as he stands from the bed. "I did, actually."

Sure enough, there's a wet patch on the blue basketball shorts.

"Eating me out made you come?"

"I came the second I tasted you, Mack," he admits without an ounce of shame. Like it's a normal thing that happens all the time.

I'm still processing his words when he says, "I'm going to change in the bathroom. Don't move, I'll bring a washcloth to clean you up. Actually, we should change the sheets. I uh... I made a mess."

I sit up, see the wet spot on the sheets from where it's leaked through his clothes, and find I'm once again talking myself out of smelling it.

That's weird fucking behavior, Mackenzie.

"Right. I'll change the sheets while you get cleaned up." I give him a nervous smile.

Tal turns like he's going to go, then spins back around and rubs his neck. I stand from the bed to change the sheets, but Tal grips me by the hips gently and turns me towards him before crashing his lips against mine.

I'm stunned, so it takes me a moment to kiss him back, and he must take it as a rejection because he steps back.

"I'm so sorry. I should have asked. I just thought—never mind. It doesn't matter. I'm so sorry." He blindly grabs things from his drawers and rushes to the bathroom, locking himself inside.

I stand there, tracing my lips with my fingertips. The faintest hint of my arousal from his mustache lingers on my lips, and it only makes my belly swoop with more desire.

I put my shorts back on, strip the bed and am in the middle of remaking it when he emerges from the bathroom in fresh basketball shorts and a new T-shirt.

He helps me put the sheet on, then I go to the bathroom. When I come out, he's already lying down with his back to me.

I don't like how awkward this feels.

I tap his shoulder, which causes him to turn over before I lean in slowly, so if he wants to move away he can. When he doesn't, I gingerly press my lips to his. It's a chaste, quick kiss, but I think it's enough to have him relaxing.

"Good night, Bear. Sweet dreams." I turn off the lamp and settle under the covers.

The bed shifts, and I feel him scoot close and put his arm over my waist.

"Good night, Firefly." His breath fans the back of my neck, and goosebumps rise along my arms.

Feeling comfortable and relaxed, I drift off.

I swear I hear him whisper, "I love you," before sleep overtakes me.

Chapter 32

Talmage

17 years old...

"Did you hear Mackenzie had to miss rehearsal today because she had to go to the hospital?" one of the girls next to me in choir whispers to her friend.

My ears perk up at the mention of Mack.

Things between us have been cordial. She rarely looks at me if she doesn't have to, but I don't blame her.

I've heard she's dated a few other guys. I've seen her pictures with them on dates or at dances on Facebook.

I'm happy she seems happy.

Except sometimes, I wonder if she's actually happy, or if she's putting on a really good mask. She's looked tired lately and has missed a lot of school.

We're choreography partners again for the spring musical, and not having her at rehearsal makes it difficult to do the right steps.

Something must be really wrong if she's at the hospital, and worry slithers up my spine.

I can't hear the rest of the conversation, but I make a mental note to ask her if she's okay at our next rehearsal. Not that she'll tell me anything.

There's been another shift since I had the honor of tasting Mack a few nights ago—since she kissed me tenderly, and my lips haven't felt the same.

We sleep curled together now, and I've braved giving her kisses goodbye, but we haven't done anything more. Slight brushes of hands here, a peck on the lips there.

I'll go at whatever speed she needs, but the craving I have for her has only increased. I've done more research on how to bring her pleasure, eager to make our next time even better for her.

Every morning, I wake up with an erection so hard it's almost painful after being pressed against her soft body. I'm constantly buzzing with anticipation in her presence—what do we do next? Does she want more?

The way she's looking at me right now across the dinner table makes me think she does, but I'm too scared to ask.

I worked an early shift today, getting home in time to make a nice dinner for us. Harper and Kinsley are home, too, so we're having a rare family dinner.

Siren is lying on the floor by Harper's feet, probably hoping someone will drop a piece of chicken.

Last week was Kinsley's state science fair presentation, and she knocked it out of the park, just like I knew she would. Mack and I were there when she won her award, and Kinsley sought us out in the crowd. I think I even saw Mack's eyes well with tears.

She got invited to the fair in San Antonio in May, and I overheard her talking to Harper about what an amazing opportunity it would be. Mack hasn't brought it up, but I'm sure she's stressed about how she'll afford it.

I clear my throat, getting everyone's attention. "All right, let's talk about San Antonio. Kins, do you still want to go?"

Kinsley nods immediately.

"Good. Harper, Mack?"

Harper nods but looks a little nervous about it.

"I don't know how we can afford it," Mack admits softly.

"I didn't ask if you can afford it, Firefly, I asked if you wanted to go."

Mack's cheeks turn pink as she nods, and I can't help but chuckle.

"Great. Kinsley, send me the details of the event, and I'll get everything booked and squared away with flights and hotel. Elli and her fiancé will be here in a few weeks for Hannah and Morgan's party, so we can talk to them about fun stuff to do while we're there."

Mack opens her mouth to say something, then quickly shuts it.

"And my cousin Emma, the one who lives in San Diego, will be here, too, so we can talk about going there for your birthday in July."

Kinsley's mouth drops open. "Really? We can do both?"

I shrug. "Why not? You only turn sixteen once."

"Tal, we can't afford—" Mack starts, but I reach over and place my hand on hers.

"Mack, I promise we can. Let me do this for you. Please." Mack bites her lip, drawing my attention to her mouth as she nods.

We talk about things the girls want to see and do while we're in San Antonio and San Diego while we finish dinner, then the girls offer to do the dishes since I cooked.

I start to protest, but Mack gently shakes her head and motions for me to follow her downstairs.

"Goodnight, girls!" I call as I follow, and they both call out a simultaneous, "Goodnight!"

The minute we're downstairs, Mack whirls on me. "What are we doing, Talmage? What are *you* doing? Planning trips and offering to pay for them? Are you nuts?"

I hold my hands up in surrender. "I—"

"I don't know whether I want to kiss you and get on my knees to thank you for being so generous or smack you upside the head for spoiling us."

Oh no, the image of Mack on her knees *thanking* me is making me hard. I don't think I'd last even a second if I got inside her pretty mouth.

Focus.

"What's wrong with spoiling you? I *want* to spoil you, Mack. I already told you—I don't have anything else to spend my money on. I have so much saved, and I have a good salary. Let me spend it on you." I step forward and wrap my hands around her waist, and I see the fight leaving her just as quickly as it came. I lean down and whisper in her ear, "Think about it: sandy beaches, a fruity drink in your hand, the ocean. Good food. Relaxing. No work to worry about."

Mack makes a disgruntled sound. "Fine. That sounds nice. But what if your cousins hate me?"

I shake my head and barely hold back a laugh. My cousins will love her. "Elli and Emma are two of the nicest people you'll ever meet. Hannah, too. Oh, by the way, I kind of RSVP'd to their party for us, so I hope you're okay with going."

"They're not going to judge me because I'm covered in tattoos and have piercings?"

I shake my head. "Elli's fiancé has tattoos and piercings, and so does Emma. Hannah left the church and is super chill, so don't worry."

"Okay. Do I need to wear anything fancy? When is it?"

"Third week of April, but I'll send you the invite. It's cocktail attire, I think."

She nods, then looks up at me through her lashes while biting her lip again. On instinct, I bring my hand up to her face and pull her lip from between her teeth with my thumb. Then, I lean down and gently press my lips against hers. She leans further into me, fisting my shirt and deepening the kiss. Her tongue sweeps into my mouth, and I groan, mirroring the action.

She pulls back, breathing heavily. "Sorry, I—"

I cut her off with another kiss, wrapping my arms tighter around her. "Don't apologize. I've been dying to make out with you for years. *Years,* Mack."

"I feel like we're blurring the lines. Setting ourselves up to be hurt when this ends."

Her words are like a bucket of ice cold water washing over me. I release her and step back. I don't understand. Was the other night just a release for her? Was it a spur of the moment, rash decision?

I could have sworn she was looking at me differently. Opening up to me more, starting to trust me, but maybe it's just wishful thinking.

Her shoulders slump forward, and something that looks a lot like disappointment flashes across her face.

"You asked earlier what we're doing, Mack. And I... I don't know exactly, but I know I want you. I know I haven't stopped thinking about the taste of you since the other night. Sleeping next to you makes me sleep deeper than I ever have in my life. I know being with you feels *right*."

I almost tell her I'm in love with her. Almost tell her if this ends, no matter what lines we cross or blur, I'll be hurt—devastated. But I don't know if she's ready to hear it yet.

Mack opens her mouth to say something, but my phone rings and cuts her off.

I pull it out of my pocket, and my brows furrow when my mom's contact flashes across the screen.

"I need to take this, Mack. I'm sorry," I say as I make my way to the bedroom. "Hello?" I answer as anxiety swirls in my chest. Why would she be calling? She hasn't reached out since the hospital.

"Hi, Talmage. How are you healing?" I'm taken aback by how... *normal* she sounds. Has she forgotten we haven't spoken in almost a month?

"I should be back to full duty in a week or two."

"Good, good. I'm glad to hear it." I hear her rustling around in the background, and then she sighs. "Look, I wanted to invite you... and Mackenzie and her sisters over for dinner on Sunday."

"I don't know if that's a good idea, Mom, you haven't apologized—"

"I know. I owe you—and her—an apology. I may not agree with the life choices you've made or who you've chosen to spend forever with, but..." She sighs again, and I can picture her pinching the bridge of her nose. "You're my child, and I want to support you. Your siblings miss you—your dad and I miss you. We want to get to know your wife and her sisters."

I want to believe her—trust she's not going to turn around and do the opposite of what she's saying. She took the first step, after all.

"I'll talk to Mack and the girls, but if she's uncomfortable with the idea I'm not going to force her."

"I understand. Let me know."

"I will." After a few more pleasantries, we hang up, and Mack knocks on the bedroom door. "You're good to come in," I say.

"Everything okay?" she asks, sitting next to me on the bed.

"My mom wants us and the twins to come over for dinner Sunday..."

"Why?" she hedges.

"She says she wants to apologize. She may not agree with my choices, but she wants to get to know you since we're married..." I trail off and look at her, wondering if the words affect her as much as they affect me. If she wants this as much as I do. From what she said, it sounds like she doesn't, but something in me doesn't fully believe her. Something in me wants to keep trying.

Her throat works on a swallow, and she nods once. "Okay. Um, we can go. Promise you won't leave me alone with her?"

I intertwine our fingers. "I promise."

There's so much we need to talk about—so many things I need to say to her. I need to lay my feelings out for her and figure out if she wants the same things.

Keeping them in isn't an option any longer.

I'll need Lizzie's help again.

CHAPTER 33

Mackenzie

17 years old...

The bed dips as Lizzie lies down, and the simple fact she's here makes the tears that stopped only two hours ago come back full force.

I didn't know I had anything left to cry, but I guess the body does what it wants.

Her arms wrap around me, but she doesn't say anything as sobs wrack through my body.

I'm tired of crying. I'm tired of the pain. I'm tired of feeling like a burden to everyone around me. I'm tired of being here.

"I can't do this anymore," I whisper into the darkness. "I don't want to be alive, Lizzie. It hurts too much."

Lizzie's arms band around me tighter. "You've been through so much, and I know you're tired. I know nothing I say can change your mind, but know that I'd miss you. You're my twin, Mack. My sister in all the ways that count. It'd be devastating to lose you. Your parents would miss you, too. And the twins."

I sniff. "The twins wouldn't even realize I was gone."

"They would." She strokes my hair. "If you'll let me, I'll be strong for you until you can be strong for yourself. Just... please stay. At least until graduation. Don't let him win. Don't let him take any more from you."

Screw school.

I don't want to see my classmates or hear people whisper about me and listen to the rumors spread.

"He already won. He didn't have to be rushed to the hospital. He didn't have to be poked and prodded and told he might not be able to have kids. I'm seventeen, Lizzie. No man is going to want me when I'm this—this broken. *"*

"You're not broken, Mackenzie. You went through something fucking traumatizing, and you got dealt a really shitty hand. Some day, a man will come along and love you for everything you are."

"What if I want kids, though?"

"Then you adopt. Or have a surrogate. Pregnancy isn't the only way to have kids."

"You're right." I sigh. I'm only seventeen. I don't need to worry about it now.

Lizzie changes topics—bless her—and I try to focus on what she's saying, but my mind keeps straying to blue eyes and golden hair.

There's no chance of a happily ever after for us.

Especially not now.

I should have known something was up when Lizzie asked me to come shopping with her.

First, neither of us like shopping on Saturdays. Everyone else is out, and the crowds are terrible.

Second, there are only two stores in the Orem mall with plus size clothing, and neither of them are her style. She usually shops online or thrifts, so the fact she drove us all the way to the mall is suspicious as hell.

At least it gave me a chance to find something more... *appropriate* to wear to Tal's parents' tomorrow for dinner. Something that says "meeting the in-laws" and not "I'm going through my teenage goth phase at twenty-nine."

Once I found a dress, she insisted on taking me to lunch. Which *isn't* abnormal. Lizzie's a giver, always has been. She likes to spoil the people she loves, and usually I don't feel like there's an ulterior motive.

Today, I feel like she's fishing for something. She kept pointing out things she thought Tal would like and making comments about how we can double date if she finally finds a partner she can stand for more than two weeks.

I keep reminding her Tal and I are temporary—even if it feels more and more like a lie—but she keeps brushing it off.

Halfway through our lunch, she gives me a scrutinizing look, making my skin pebble. It's the look she gets before she reads you like an open book.

"Your sexual aura is a mix of violet and orange today," she states.

I roll my eyes. "All right, holy one, what does that mean?"

Lizzie sits back and crosses her arms. "Well, usually, your sexual aura is barely prominent, my friend, so the fact I can see it at all speaks for itself. I get the feeling something's happened, something's changed, and you want to seduce your husband. You want to make love to him. You want to feel your souls connecting in an irreversible way."

What the fuck? How does she do that?

I squint at her. "What do you know?"

Lizzie shrugs. "I just know what your aura is telling me, babe. And since *you* won't tell me the truth, I have to rely on my intuition, and my intuition is rarely wrong."

She's right. I wouldn't say she's psychic, but Lizzie's always had the third-eye-knowing-things-be-fore-they-happen sense I wish I had. It's the only reason I told her about what happened to me in high school. She stuck around until I caved and spilled my guts to her. When she discovered tarot and crystals and started reading auras, it only got worse. I don't know how she does it.

"Fine, we've been intimate, he... I don't want to go into the details, but I will admit, I *really* want to fuck my husband. But I'm not going to, and you already know why. So please, just drop it."

Lizzie shakes her head. "Nah, babe. I'm not going to drop it anymore. You need someone to give you per-mission to give in, to let *go*, and that's what I'm do-ing. You're hurting yourself by keeping your feelings locked away. You've been trying to keep the lid closed on your box of emotions surrounding Tal for over a decade, Mack. It's not healthy. What's the worst that could happen if you open them up and let them loose again?"

Frustrated tears burn behind my eyes, but I blink them back. "Our marriage is purely transactional—"

"Don't give me that bullshit excuse again. You know damn well Talmage wouldn't have married you out of pity. And you didn't agree just because he offered."

"He's going to leave eventually! And then what? I'll have to pick up the shattered pieces of my heart *again* and try to move on. I barely survived our breakup when we were fifteen, and I didn't have the same experience I do now—didn't have *him* the way I do now. I can't keep losing everyone I love, Lizzie."

Lizzie's eyes soften, and she reaches across the table to grab my hand. "I don't think he's going anywhere, Mack. You don't see the way he looks at you because you're too scared you'll look at him the same way, and he'll know."

"How does he look at me?" I whisper.

"Like his whole world revolves around *you*. He couldn't take his eyes off of you during your wedding, and all through lunch, his focus was solely on you. Talmage is down bad, and you're hurting both of you by not giving in to your feelings."

"What if you're just seeing things, and he doesn't actually feel that way?"

"If I'm wrong, I will personally supply all the alcohol you'll need for a breakup bender."

"I'm scared," I admit quietly.

"I know you are. But just... trust me on this, okay?"

I nod, at a loss for what else to say. I do trust her, but I'm not sure I'm strong enough to open up first.

If Talmage were to admit to feeling something more, maybe then I'd feel like I could voice my own feelings, but I don't see it happening anytime soon.

The house is eerily quiet when I get home, which isn't odd, but I know Kins and Harper don't have any extracurriculars today, and they didn't mention going out with friends.

I double-check my phone to make sure there are no new notifications, but my screen is blank.

Panic slithers up my spine, but I tamp it down. They can't drive yet, so if they're not here, maybe they just forgot to tell me they were going out. Talmage's car is here, so he must be downstairs drawing or something. I'll just text the twins to make sure they're okay.

MACK: Are you two home? Where are you?

KINS: OMG we're fiiiineeee. Tal took us to Tylie's house for a sleep-over.

HARP: We thought Talmage told you, sorry if we worried you.

> **MACK:** It's okay. Text me if you need something.

> **HARP:** We will. Have a good night <heart emoji>

> **KINS:** Yeah, a REALLY good night <winky face>

Okay...

I hang my jacket in the closet and pad downstairs, my jaw dropping open when I get to the bottom.

Tal is standing in the middle of the room with a bouquet of white calla lilies and pale pink roses. The room is lit with fairy lights, all the furniture has been pushed to the sides, and a mattress with an array of pillows and blankets sits in the middle of the floor.

"Wh-what's all this?"

Tal gives me a shy smile. "Date night. I have *A Walk to Remember* queued up and your favorite snacks at the ready."

I blink at him. "You did all of this?"

"Of course. Think of it as a belated one-month anniversary celebration."

"But... why?"

He steps forward, setting the bouquet on one of the side tables before he stands right in front of me. "I know it's not much, but I wanted to do something special for you. To show you how much I appreciate all you've done for me since I hurt my ankle and..." he trails off, takes a deep breath, then looks me in the eyes. "I want to make up for the years we lost because of me."

My breath hitches. "You have nothing to make up for."

He shakes his head. "I do, though, Mack. You can't even listen to our song, and it's my fault. I'm the one who ended things years ago and—"

"Tal, we were *kids*. I don't blame you for not wanting to be serious with the first girl you thought you loved. We probably wouldn't have worked out anyway, so you were just—"

"I never *thought* I loved you. I did love you. I *do* love you."

My heart hammers against my rib cage. "Wh-what?"

Tal tentatively cups my face. "I only broke up with you because it's what I thought was supposed to happen. The church and my parents made me think I was doing us both a favor, but I see now all I did was hurt us both. I've never, *never* loved someone the way I love you, Mackenzie. I've never felt a pull so strong towards another person. Before you came back into my life, I felt like I was sitting on the sidelines waiting for something to happen, and that something was *you*."

"I don't understand. Our marriage—"

"Isn't fake for me. I haven't been totally honest with you, and for that I'm sorry. I wanted to marry you to help you out, yes, but I also wanted another chance for us, and I didn't think you'd give me one, not after how we ended. I can give you more than just pleasure, Mack. If you let me, I'll give you the whole world."

My head is spinning from his confession, and I feel like I'm dreaming. For fourteen years, I've dreamed of him saying something similar. For fourteen years, I've been hoping he'd come back to me, but now that it's actually happening, my mind can't comprehend it.

It feels too good to be true.

"But you barely know me anymore," I whisper. "I-I'm not the same girl I was at fourteen. I have baggage and trauma you don't know about—things that could make you change your mind."

"Hear me, *believe* me, when I say that there is *nothing* you could tell me that would make me love you less. There's nothing you could tell me that would scare me away or change my mind."

I worry my bottom lip, the anxiety and stress of the last decade bubbling in my stomach and threatening to spill out of me. He just confessed his *love* for me, and I can't even bask in my dream come true because he *doesn't know.*

"Hey, hey. I didn't mean to upset you." Tal swipes away a falling tear. "You don't have to tell me now or at all if you don't want to. But just know I'm here for you when—if—you're ready."

"I love you, too, you know," I murmur, and his answering smile is luminous.

"Yeah?"

"Yeah."

"Can I kiss you now? Please?" His gaze drops down to my lips with the plea, and as soon as I nod my agreement, he's pressing his lips to mine.

Our kisses at the restaurant and on our wedding day were for the benefit of other people—to sell the story of our love.

This kiss?

It's purely for us.

Tal's lips are sure and firm as they press against mine, and for the first time in years, I feel... happy.

So happy, the tears of anxiety have morphed into tears of happiness, and the salty droplets flavor our kiss.

Tal pulls back and presses his forehead against mine. "I missed you so much, Firefly. Everything feels right now with you back in my life."

"I missed you, too, Bear."

CHAPTER 34

Talmage

18 years old...

Graduation day doesn't feel as monumental as I thought it would. Maybe leaving for Canada on my mission will feel more significant.

I can't stop my eyes from veering to Mack as we sit in the choir seats. She looks beautiful, and for once, her smile looks like it reaches her eyes, even if there's a lingering sadness in them.

I still don't know what happened to her earlier this year, but when she came back to school, she seemed... despondent. Instead of laughing and smiling with her friends like usual, she just nodded along, offering smiles every so often. It was like her body was there, going through the motions, but her mind was somewhere else.

I never did end up asking her if she was okay. I didn't feel like it was my place, especially since she flinched whenever I touched her for our number in the musical. I thought I'd hurt her at first, but she assured me she was fine.

So it must have just been me. I made her flinch.

It's been almost three years since we broke up, and I thought maybe she had gotten over it, but I guess not. She still hates me.

It's okay. Now that we don't have to see each other every day for hours on end, we can both move on and be happy.

The sentiment still stings but not as much as before. I know what I need to do, and I'm excited to get out there, serve people, and bring them to the church. When I get home, I can think about dating again.

She loves me.

Maybe she never stopped, just like I never stopped loving her.

Her hands wrap around my neck as she brings my mouth back to hers, and I grin as our lips mold together. I can't help it, I feel more... *alive* than I have in years.

The kiss turns heated as my hands grip her hips, and she pulls me closer. Our tongues caress and tangle, a little messy, but so perfect. My heart pounds against my ribcage, and a sense of peace washes over me.

I'm finally where I'm supposed to be, with the person I was always meant to be with.

Mackenzie Thorpe—Monson, if she wants to change her name—is it for me. This is forever. *She* is my forever.

My contentment intertwines with lust as she rolls her hips, giving friction to my erection, and I groan against her mouth.

"I want you, Tal," she whispers.

"I didn't do all this to get in your pants, Mack."

"I know, and it makes me want you even more."

"Go change into something more comfortable. Let's watch the movie and snuggle. See where the night leads us." I give her one final peck, then use all of my willpower to step away.

She pouts but nods her head and takes her shopping bag to our room.

I let out a long breath and reposition my dick so it's not tenting my sweatpants. As much as I want Mack, I want to take it slow with her. I've waited this long to have sex, I can wait a little bit longer.

Mack comes back out in an outfit I've never seen before. Lace barely covers her breasts, and the skirt hem reaches mid-thigh. The black material looks enticingly soft, and I want to rub my hands up her sides and test the texture.

Maybe I can't wait.

I shake my head to hopefully free it of the lustful thoughts of my wife—*my wife*—and settle on the mattress, propped up against some pillows. I open my arms for her, and she nestles into my side as I press play on the movie.

Her body is soft and pliant against mine as she rests her hand on my abs and her head on my shoulder. I wrap an arm around her waist and pull her in as close as I can. Now that I know she feels the same way, all bets are off. I'm not keeping my hands to myself anymore. I'm going to be touching her all the time. I have over a decade to make up for.

As we watch Mandy Moore and Shane West's journey of falling in love, I can't focus. My attention is solely focused on the heat of Mack's body pressed against my own. The way her curves mold to me, the way her breasts rise and fall with every breath in that freaking outfit.

I try not to look, but each time I glance at her face, I get a clear view down her top, and my dick hardens further.

Her hand trails dangerously close to the waistband of my pants. When I look over at her, her gaze is firmly on the screen, but there's a flush to her cheeks.

"Mack," I whisper. "What are you doing?"

"Hm?"

"Your hand." I swallow. "It's close to... you know."

"It can't be comfortable to be this hard for so long, Bear. Can I please take care of you? Let me return the favor from the other night."

I'm shaking my head before she even finishes her sentence. "It wasn't a favor. If anything, you letting me taste you was the favor. It was a dream come true, Firefly. I don't need anything from you."

"What if I've dreamed of tasting you? What if I'm dying to know what *you* taste like?"

I feel myself leaking at the thought of having her mouth anywhere near me. My voice is strained when I reply, "Are you? Dying to know what I taste like, I mean."

"Yes." She doesn't even hesitate.

"Mack, if you put that gorgeous mouth anywhere near me, I'm going to come in five seconds and embarrass myself again."

"The only way to boost your stamina is to practice." Her hand trails down and brushes over my erection, and

I let out a pathetic whimper. "I won't push you, Tal, but I want to do this. I want *you*. I'll go at whatever speed you need. Please don't worry about being embarrassed. I just want you."

Turning my face to look in her emerald eyes, I see the desire and truth in them. I see how serious she is, and I'm helpless to deny my wife anything. I can't exactly complain about her wanting me.

I cup her face and take her mouth in a needy kiss, pouring all of my eagerness into it. Her tongue parts my lips, and the wet patch in my underwear grows at the taste of her.

"I'm nervous. You're clearly experienced, and I'm—"

She cuts me off with a kiss. "I may have more experience, but I can guarantee you whatever we do will be the best thing I've ever done."

"You're sure you want to do this?"

She nods enthusiastically. "Lean back, Bear. Let me take care of you."

I lie back on the pillows as the movie plays in the background, all but forgotten. She helps me take off my shirt before kissing me once, then trailing her soft lips down my chest and my stomach, leaving a trail of goosebumps in her wake.

When she reaches my waistband, I lift my hips as she slides off my shorts, leaving my underwear on.

She licks her lips when she sees the wet patch on them, then her eyes snag on the swirl of ink on my right thigh. Her eyes dart up to mine, curious and full of questions.

"Tal... is that—"

"Yeah."

"When did you get it?" Her fingers trace around the ink of her name and the delicate image of a firefly. The ink is still slightly raised, but it's healing well.

"Almost two weeks ago."

Her eyes widen. "Before you..." her cheeks flush, and so do mine when I think about the night I tasted her.

I swallow, wanting to tell her the truth. "Yes. I wanted to get 'mine' in your handwriting, but I didn't know how to ask you, so I asked Lizzie to come up with a design."

"Like the Taylor Swift song?"

"Exactly like that. That song resonated with me, and I wanted to show you how serious I am about you."

"It's bad luck to get the name of your partner tattooed on you. What if we break up?" she whispers, still staring at the ink.

I lean forward and cup her face. I want her eyes on mine when I say what I'm about to say.

"I'm not going anywhere, Mackenzie. I'm in this, till death do us part or whatever the afterlife holds. I've wanted you for over a decade. Nothing in this world could possibly tear me away from you. I love you, Firefly."

"I love you, too, Talmage. So much." She clears her throat as her voice wobbles. After a deep breath, she gives me a sultry look, glancing up at me through her lashes. "Where were we?" she asks before leaning down and running her tongue along my dick through the material.

Oh shit.

A sound I've never made before rips itself from my throat as she peppers kisses along my covered length. A feeling I've never felt sizzles through my body, potent and heady. My legs stiffen to try and keep myself from coming immediately.

Is this what pleasure is supposed to feel like? Why would anyone think this is wrong?

How does this feel so good already? I'm not going to last long enough to feel her mouth on me at this rate.

As Mack hooks her thumbs into the elastic band of my boxers and pulls them down, her eyes never leave mine.

When my dick springs free, her mouth parts in awe. The head is an angry shade of red, and the tip glistens with my arousal. More precum leaks as her eyes take me in.

"Oh, Tal," she sighs. "Your cock is so pretty. The perfect size. It's going to feel so good inside me... Does it hurt being this hard?" She wraps her hand around me and swipes her thumb across the tip, smearing my precum.

A garbled moan comes out of me as I nod, unable to say anything through the sheer pleasure shooting up my spine just from having her hand on me. It's overwhelming in the best way.

"I'll take care of you. You just relax and enjoy," she murmurs, leaning down and kissing my tip.

"Oh fuck," I whimper then cover my mouth with my hand as embarrassment stains my cheeks.

"I want to hear you enjoying it, Bear. Don't be embarrassed."

I don't get to reply because her mouth envelopes me, all warm and wet and gentle, and I just about lose it.

Pleasure unlike anything I've ever felt before sizzles down my spine and spreads through my veins as she takes me deeper into her mouth, and I can feel it. My orgasm is fast approaching.

"Mack," I try to warn her, but it comes out as a greedy moan instead. I squeeze my eyes shut because watching her mouth wrap around me is too much.

She bobs her head and brings her hands up to lightly cup my balls, and that's it. That's all it takes. I don't get to warn her to pull off because my cum shoots into her mouth as I sob her name like a prayer, thanking her repeatedly for giving me this pleasure.

I expect her to be grossed out and pull away when the first rope hits her tongue, but she doesn't. She drinks it down like it's the only thing that will quench her thirst, and it only prolongs my orgasm.

I shudder when I'm finished, and she pulls off of me with a wet slurp. My eyes are still closed as I catch my breath, and when I finally regain the strength to open them, I watch Mack's tongue trace her lips, then she dabs the corners of her mouth and sucks off the remnants of my arousal.

She gives me a proud, satisfied smile as I sit up, my head dizzy with lust. Gratitude. *Need.*

"You okay there, champ?" she teases, then does a double take when she sees I'm still hard. "How..."

I can't help it, I tackle her, pushing her body back and hovering over her while I take her mouth in a frenzied and demanding kiss. I taste myself as I stroke my tongue against hers, and the want to know what we'd taste like mixed together becomes an overwhelming need.

"When it comes to you, wife, I fear I'll always be hard."

Mack's heavenly thighs come to bracket my hips, her nightdress rucking up around her hips. On instinct, I thrust myself forward and am met with—

"Mack, are you not wearing underwear?"

She bites her lip and shakes her head.

I groan and thrust forward again, feeling the heat radiating from her pussy as the head of my cock hits her entrance.

"Are you going to fuck me, Tal? Finally consummate our marriage?"

I shake my head. "No, Mack. I'm not going to fuck you."

Disappointment flashes across her face, but she nods. "I understand, I—"

I shake my head again. "No, you don't. I'm not going to fuck you, but I am going to make love to you." I cup her face. "I've waited too long for you. I'm going to cherish you—*worship* you—the way you deserve."

Mack's face softens. "I'd love that even more."

"Can I take this off of you? Please?" I tease the hem while I wait for her answer.

When she nods her consent, I don't waste any time pulling it over her head, relishing every creamy expanse of skin revealed to me.

When her breasts are exposed, my eyes home in on the silver bars pierced through her peaked nipples.

"When you said your conch was your second most painful piercing..."

"I was talking about these, yes." She brings her hands up and pinches them, moaning at the contact.

"Why do it if it's painful?" I can't stop looking at them. I want to know what they feel like on my tongue.

She shrugs. "It hurt at first, but now it just amplifies pleasure. Are you going to use them to make me feel good, Talmage?"

I nod, leaning down and giving each jeweled nipple a quick kiss before swirling my tongue around them. The sensation of the piercings on my tongue is strange at first, but I get used to it pretty quickly, and I refuse to stop when Mack's moaning because of something *I'm* doing.

One of Mack's hands threads through the hair on top of my head while the other cradles the back, and she arches into my mouth as I alternate.

Who knew nipples would be so fun to play with?

I cup her heavy breasts in my hands, flicking the jewelry and causing her to whimper.

"I love the way your tongue feels, Tal. So good. Don't stop."

I pull back and give her what's probably the most love drunk grin. "I'll do this any time you ask, Firefly. My mouth is yours to use as you please."

CHAPTER 35

Mackenzie

18 years old...

I'm sitting in the back row of the crowded chapel, the cold metal of the folding chairs against my thighs grounding me in my anxiety.

Lizzie couldn't come with me today since she's working, but I needed to be here. Needed to see him one last time before whatever ties we have are well and truly severed.

I was supposed to be leaving for college next month, starting my new adult life, but after everything happened, I can't move yet.

I glance around and see some familiar faces—former castmates and choir members, mostly. I know many of the guys have already left on their missions, but the few who haven't are sitting up front.

No one's talked to me, which is fine. I chopped my hair, dyed it purple, pierced my septum, and I'm wearing more makeup than I usually do. Maybe I'm too unrecognizable.

I don't look like I belong here and anyone else would agree.

I haven't stepped foot in a church in almost two years. My parents were disappointed at first, but I couldn't handle the pressure put on me by the young women leaders to lose weight or stay pure when I knew I was already tainted and tarnished.

The sacrament portion is done, and I know from the program currently crumpled in my lap Talmage is speaking first.

After the bishop announces the speakers, Talmage stands at the pulpit and begins talking about the importance of staying on the path of righteousness. How Satan will throw temptations in our path to make us stray but to focus on God because He knows all.

Tears burn behind my eyes, but I hold them back. His voice, so familiar, used to be a comfort. Now, it's reiterating the fact I was nothing more than a trial on his way to salvation.

When he's done talking, I get up and quietly leave the church building.

As soon as I'm in my car, the tears stream steadily down my face.

This was a good thing.

Now I can finally let Talmage Monson go.

This is the best night of my life.

After pining for Talmage for years and spending the last month wishing I could have him like this, it's better than any of my fantasies.

Sex has always been transactional in the past. Yes, I've enjoyed it and have had a few good experiences with past hookups, but nothing compares to the connection Tal and I are forging right now.

It has nothing to do with him being a virgin or the fact I've been pretty much celibate for the past five years.

Even if he had more experience or I'd been having sex in the recently, being together for the first time like this would be life-altering and soul-changing. The connection we share, the invisible string tying us together even when we were apart is too strong to ever fully break, and it heightens everything. Every kiss, every touch of his tentative fingers, every swipe of his eager tongue is amplified because this has been fourteen years in the making, and the fire is burning brighter than ever now that we've acknowledged the flames.

His lips keep tipping up in the corners as his tongue traces the curves of my breasts and the silver balls on the ends of my nipple rings. I don't think he realizes his hips are slowly thrusting, the head of his cock nudging my pussy with each pass, and I know if he just pushed a *tiny* bit harder, he'd slip right inside.

The sounds of pure bliss coming from his mouth make me wetter than I've ever been. Watching him—*tasting him*—fall apart in my mouth was the hottest experience of my life. I can't wait to watch him fall apart while inside me.

"I want to taste you, Mack. Can I taste you again? I'm thirsty for it. Let me feel you come on my tongue again."

God, he's so eager, and I hate to deny him, but if I don't have him inside me soon, I just might perish.

"I need to feel you inside me, Tal. I feel so empty without you."

He swallows harshly as his eyes track to his cock and how close to my pussy it is. "Co-condoms. Do we have any?"

"Yes. But I-I can't have kids. Um, and I haven't touched anyone in five years. I know you haven't either, so I was hoping..." I trail off, hoping he doesn't ask for any clarification.

A half whimper, half moan rumbles in his chest. "No barrier. Okay. Not that I know the difference, but I've heard it feels even better. If you're sure..."

"I want to feel you, all of you, Talmage. Make love to me," I whisper the last part, cupping his cheek and pulling his face down to kiss me.

I snake one hand between us and grip the base of his cock, guiding it to my entrance until the head notches at my opening.

"Ooooh gosh, Mack. You're so wet. So warm. *Shit.*"

"Take it as slow as you need to, Tal," I coo, rubbing my hands up and down the straining muscles on his back.

His eyes pinch shut as he thrusts forward just the tiniest bit. The head of his cock stretches me the perfect amount, and I moan softly. "I want you to feel good, too," he grits out.

"Anything you do will make me feel good, Talmage. Don't worry about me, okay? This is about you right now."

His eyes pop open, glassy and alight with so many emotions it forms a knot in my throat. He hangs his head, watching where we're connected and in one smooth glide, thrusts all the way inside me until his pubic hair tickles my clit. I moan again, my eyes rolling to the back of my head.

It's cheesy and cliché to think, but I swear, Talmage Monson was made for me, and I was made for him. He fills me perfectly, I already know nothing and no one will ever compare to this.

"Oh-sh-fu-*damn* it, Mack. You feel incredible—ah!" I clench around him, and he whimpers. "D-don't do that again or else I'll come."

"Come inside me, Tal. You've already left your mark on my heart, now claim me as yours by filling me with your cum."

"You have a dirty mouth," he gasps, pulling back and thrusting in again.

"Does it bother you?" I moan when his head drags across my G-spot.

"No—*oh shit*—I love it." Talmage glances up so he's looking me in the eye. "I love *you*, Mackenzie Thorpe."

Tears burn behind my eyelids as the weight of what this means settles inside of me. There's no going back now. We're together, for real, for however long we live. "I love you, too, Talmage Monson. I never stopped."

He turns his face and kisses my palm. "I'm going to start moving faster now, is that okay?"

"Do whatever feels best, Bear."

He takes a deep breath, pulling out and thrusting into me, gradually increasing his pace, chasing his orgasm. It's a little uncoordinated and a bit choppy, but I've never experienced greater pleasure than Talmage Monson losing himself in sex.

I use two fingers to circle my clit, giving myself the extra friction I need as our moans fill the room, and our desire becomes one.

"I'm going to come, Mack."

"Give it to me, Tal. Give me your cum," I moan, increasing the speed of my fingers so I can finish with him.

He chants my name as sweat beads on his forehead, and when his motions become jerky and uneven, I tip right over the edge with him, feeling him spill everything he has inside of me.

I expect him to collapse on top of me from the exertion, but instead, he stays seated inside me and crashes his mouth against mine, twisting our tongues together in a sloppy tango.

"Can I taste you now?" he whispers against my lips.

"But you just—"

"I need to know what we taste like together."

I've never been with a man who wants to taste his own cum, let alone one who sounds so *eager* to do it, so I just nod.

Tal pulls out, and I feel the rush of cum leak from me. I thought since he already came—twice—he'd be spent, but I was wrong.

He kisses down my body, flicking my nipple rings again—I can already tell it's going to be a common occurrence—before he settles between my thighs.

God, the mere sight of him between them has me aching to come again. I'm afraid now that we've crossed this line, we're never going to be able to keep our hands off each other.

I can't wait.

Tal's thumb swipes through the cum leaking out of me before pushing it back inside. He looks like he's in a trance, mesmerized by the way it looks to be full of him.

I wish I could see it. I have half a mind to ask him to take a picture so I can keep it as a memento of our first time.

Without any warning, Talmage swipes his tongue up my slit, moaning as our combined flavor hits his tongue. "So good," he groans before doing it again, this time taking the time to swirl his tongue around my clit.

"Oh, fuck, Tal. Feels so good." I reach down and grab at his hair, needing to feel him in every way possible.

I'm greedy now that I've had him. I'll never get enough.

He looks up from between my legs. "Do you want to know what we taste like together?"

I nod rapidly. I've never been one to crave the taste of cum—I actually think it's kind of gross—but swallowing Tal's? It was euphoric. I wouldn't trade the experience for anything. I can only imagine how perfect we'll taste mixed together.

Tal puts two fingers inside me, caressing my walls and making me whimper before pulling them out and putting them to my lips.

I don't waste any time sucking them into my mouth. I moan when the flavor hits my taste buds. Tal was right, we taste good together. Perfect.

"I need to make you come, Mack. Can I?"

I sit up to reassure him I don't need to come again, and that's when I see it.

He's hard *again.*

Still?

"Tal, you're still hard?"

The tips of his ears turn pink, and he looks at me with a sheepish expression. "Well, can you blame me when you look like *that* and we taste so good together? How can I *not* be ready to go again?"

I shake my head and giggle. How someone can be so sexy and so sweet at the same time, I'll never know.

"Can I show you my favorite position?" I ask, and he nods. I flip over so I'm on all fours, glancing back at him over my shoulder.

"Uh, Mack? I may not be super experienced, but I don't think I can just... stick it in this hole. Won't that hurt?"

"What? Oh! No, Tal. I mean, we can try anal another time if you want, but you can reach my pussy from back there. Just trust me."

"If you say so."

"Just kneel, scoot a little closer—there you go, now grab the base of that glorious cock and find the—*yessss.* That's so good, Tal. You fill me so perfectly." He presses in slowly, tentatively, and at this angle, he hits that perfect spot head on.

"You feel even tighter like this, Firefly. How is that even possible?" he grits out, clearly trying to keep it together. I'm hoping since he already came twice, he can last just a bit longer so I can come on his cock again.

"I know you wanted to make love, Tal, but I need you to fuck me hard in this position, okay?"

"I don't want to hurt you."

"You won't, I promise. It'll make us both feel good."

He pulls out, leaving just the tip in before slamming back into me, and the pleasure fizzing through my veins is unlike anything I've ever experienced.

"*Yes.* Fuck, yes. Right there, don't stop."

"Couldn't if I tried. You feel too good. So right. So perfect. I love you so much."

"I love you, too, Bear. *Please.*" I don't know what I'm begging for, but Tal must understand because he keeps a steady pace as he thrusts inside me. My ass bounces off of his abs, and my nipples chafe deliciously against the blanket, adding to the sensation.

Tal's hands grip my hips, and I know he'll feel bad if he leaves marks, but I want them. I want proof of our first—well, second—time together etched in my skin.

"Tal, I'm right there. Please don't stop."

"Give it to me, Firefly. You said I marked you as mine, but I've been yours all along. I've got your name tattooed on me forever, and it's still not enough. I need your pleasure, too. I love you so damn much it hurts sometimes. You're so perfect. So beautiful. Being with you in this way is the holiest experience I've ever had, and not a day will go by that I won't want to worship you the way you deserve."

His heartfelt words are what send me spiraling off the cliff and have tears slipping down my cheeks. My orgasm feels like being baptized—all the hurt I've been carrying is washed away, leaving me open to receive the love Talmage is willing to give me.

CHAPTER 36

Talmage

20 years old...

I scan the rows of people, smiling when I find familiar faces. I'm looking for one in particular, but I haven't seen her green eyes yet.

I try not to let my shoulders slump in disappointment at the realization Mack's not here. She didn't come to welcome me home.

Why would she, though? Just because she came to my farewell doesn't mean she's going to show up now after two years of no contact.

I thought about reaching out to her a few times on my mission, but I didn't know how, and we're told to shut outside distractions out.

Every time I thought about Mack, I would open my scriptures and lose myself in the words of past prophets to get my mind on track. I had people to serve and gospel to teach.

I guess she's well and truly moved on, and that's great for her. She deserves to be happy.

The organ blares behind me, and I open my hymn book to the opening song, shaking off the slithering feeling coating my skin. I should be happy to be home. I had a good number of baptisms and conversions on my mission, and I worked hard. I should be feeling happy, fulfilled.

So why do I feel like something's missing?

This time, instead of speaking about the hopes I had for my mission when I left, I recount the things I saw and the people I met.

I talk about how strongly I felt the presence of Christ with me.

And for the first time, a slither of doubt creeps in if what I'm saying is true.

Last night, after Mack clenched around me so tight I thought I'd be locked inside her forever—which would be a dream come true—we took our spent and exhausted bodies to the shower.

I slid my dick between Mack's juicy thighs, our soapy bodies sliding together while nudging her clit with every thrust until we both came again.

Then, we tumbled into bed naked, and I slept deeper than I ever have. I woke up to my hard dick nestled against Mack's ass. She spread her legs, and we had slow, sensual morning sex while we kissed and caressed before I came inside her again.

I swear I'm never going to get enough of her. I feel feral—like if I stop touching her I'll die.

Is this what marriage is like? I can't recall anyone I know exhibiting this kind of behavior. Maybe they do feel out of control, but they're good at hiding it in public.

I hope I can keep it together long enough to have dinner at my parents' house.

I have some questions now that I'm not drunk on Mack and hazy with lust. What did she mean when she said she couldn't have kids? I feel like it's something we should discuss since we're together for real now. I know it's expected of us to have children, and my parents will probably ask about it, but truth be told, I've never really thought about having kids of my own.

I love kids, and I think Hannah's babies are adorable, but if Mack didn't want any, I would be perfectly content to live out the rest of my days with just her.

The twins should be home in an hour, and Mack's in the bathroom getting ready while I wait for Enoch to bring Siren back. I didn't want anything to interrupt us last night, luckily, he was willing to watch her so she wouldn't be neglected.

The doorbell rings, and I open the door to find my golden girl tippy-tapping on the porch. I drop to a crouch and give her head scratches, cooing about how much I missed her.

Her tongue laps at my face, and her tail wags with excitement at being back home.

I motion for Enoch to follow me inside while I let Siren out in the backyard so she can get some zoomies out.

"Congratulations, man." He pats me on the shoulder with a big smile on his face.

"Um, thanks? What for?"

"Finally losing your virginity!"

I shush him. "Will you keep your voice down? Jesus, dude. How do you even know?"

Enoch shrugs. "You've got that post-orgasmic glow and a dopey smile on your face."

I chuckle and shake my head. "You're full of it, Smithe. I'm not talking about my sex life with you."

Enoch's smile becomes teasing, and he practically vibrates. "Oooh, so you have a sex life now, eh? I *knew* it. Like I said, congratulations."

I roll my eyes but still can't stop the smile on my face. "Thanks."

He crosses his arms over his broad chest. "Now, tell me all about—"

"No."

He nods. "Off limits. Understood." Enoch leans in and whispers conspiratorially, "It's fucking awesome, isn't it?"

"What's awesome?" Mack asks from the top of the stairs.

Oh no, that dress is... I'm in trouble.

I think she was going for something a little more modest, but the way the bust of the dress holds her breasts, tying in a pretty bow between them and cinching in at her waist before flowing down to her ankles; it's downright sinful.

The pale green fabric looks stunning against the ink on her skin, and her makeup is subtle and simple. Her hair is loose, straight and sleek down her back. My little fairy.

She looks... different. And it's a bit concerning because I want her to feel comfortable enough to be herself, but I won't point it out in front of Enoch.

"Uh, not going to church on Sundays," Enoch lies, his cheeks turning red as he studies Mack—a little too long for my liking.

"Stop staring at my wife," I bark, startling all of us. I've never felt this... possessive of someone before.

Mack's green eyes blink at me as a small smile tips her lips, and Enoch laughs.

"Sorry, man. I didn't mean to stare. But can you blame me?" Enoch tosses Mack a wink.

"Don't flirt with her, either. What the hell's the matter with you?" I stride over to her and wrap my arms around her from behind, taking in her citrus scent.

Oh no, I'm going to get hard in front of Enoch. This was a bad idea.

Mack tips her head back and gives me a chaste kiss on the lips, one I'm dying to turn deeper but won't because Enoch would probably like it, the weirdo.

"Don't worry, Tal, I only have eyes for you," she whispers, stroking my cheek as I melt into her.

"Stop it, you two are too cute, and I can't stand it. I need to get out of here before I start crying about dying alone." Enoch pretends to wipe tears away.

I roll my eyes again. "Thank you for taking Siren last night. I owe you, man."

"Nah." He waves me off. "You know I love spending time with her. The ladies love a dog dad." He pumps his eyebrows, and Mack snorts. "I'll see you later, love-birds."

With a salute, he walks out the front door.

"Your friend is odd but nice," Mack says, still wrapped in my arms.

"He's got a thing for Lizzie."

Mack snorts again. "Oh no, Lizzie would chew him up and spit him out. Besides, I don't think she's had a serious partner in a few years since she's so busy with the shop. She's very particular about who she dates, too."

"He's determined to make her his wife, but we'll see if it wears off after getting his back piece done."

"He's getting a back piece from her? That seals it. Lizzie doesn't date clients."

"That's what I said, but he said he's going to wear her down and get her to agree to go out with him after it's done."

"Well, I wish him luck, but he shouldn't hold out for her." She turns fully, her arms wrapping around my neck, and my hands rest just above the curve of her butt. "Do you like my dress?"

"I love your dress, Firefly, but..." I trail off, unsure if I want to ask.

"But... what?"

"But do *you* like it? I've never seen you dress like this, not since we were teens, and I want to make sure you're doing it for you and not because you're trying to impress my parents."

Her smile is soft, grateful, and stunning. "I'll admit, I haven't dressed like this in a while, and I *did* pick this dress to fit in with your family, but I like it. It's comfy, has pockets, and for the first time in a long time, I feel...

pretty. Not just like a dark shell of a person trying to get by."

I want to dive deeper and ask her what she means. Obviously, the trauma of losing her parents would have an impact on her mental health. Not to mention the way she had to step into a parental role for her sisters—one of whom has health issues that have caused a financial strain...

Damn. Have I been so selfish in wanting to get closer to Mack that I haven't paid attention to how she's doing mentally? Have I missed some signs or misread things?

And now I'm going to add more stress to her plate by taking her to a potentially hostile environment at my parents' house.

I don't want to get into all of it right now, especially when we've just taken a huge step forward, so I stick a pin in the idea for now, and I'll circle back later—after we get through dinner.

"As long as you're comfortable, Firefly. That's all I care about. I love your clothes."

"Thank you, Tal."

I dip my head and kiss her, getting lost in the gentle glide of her lips and the soft caress of her tongue as it swipes across my lips.

We pull apart only because the front door swings open, and Kinsley and Harper come barreling in as Kinsley talks a million miles an hour.

"I *told her* you called dibs! But the little slut can't let anyone else have *anything*. Let me rip her a new one, Harp. Please? You know she deserves it."

Harper's eyes are wide, bouncing between Kinsley's scowling face and me and Mack still locked in an embrace.

Finally, she looks down and shakes her head. "It's fine, Kins. I'm not... He didn't want me anyway or he would have asked."

Kinsley stomps her foot with her hands balled into fists. She opens her mouth to say something, but Mack beats her to it. "Woah, woah, woah. What are we talking about? Why are we so heated? Kinsley, we don't slut shame, okay? That's purity culture bullshit, and we don't subscribe to it here."

Kinsley scowls, scoffing as she rolls her eyes and crosses her arms. "Ashlynn Nelson was posting stories with Jeremy Newsom talking about how he asked her to prom!"

Who?

"Okay..." Mack starts, "and these people are important because..."

"*Jeremy Newsom*? The guy Harper was paired with in the musical? The one she has a *huge* crush on? The one who gives her Capri-Suns when her blood sugar is low? Ring a bell?"

I cough to cover my laugh. Is this how Mack and I acted at this age? Was everything the end of the world?

"Right. Harper, I'm sorry Jeremy asked Ashlynn to prom but—"

"You don't get it! Jeremy told Michael who told Charity who told *me* he was going to ask Harper, but *Ashlynn* snagged her claws into him first and promised if he took her, she'd let him soak on prom night."

Oh my gosh. What is happening right now?

Mack pinches the bridge of her nose and shakes her head, then opens her mouth to speak, but Kinsley looks at me. "Soaking, if you didn't know, is when a guy puts his—"

"Nope. I don't want to hear you explain it." Mack holds up her hand and shakes her head, visibly cringing at the explanation.

I clear my throat. "I'm old but not *that* old, Kinsley. I know what soaking is." I turn my attention to Harper. "I'm really sorry Jeremy is a bit of a douche. It sounds like he's not the kind of guy you want to go to prom with, anyway."

Harper shrugs, tracing the toe of her sneaker on the hardwood floor. "It's not a big deal. It's not like he was my boyfriend."

"But it can still hurt, Harp. And your feelings are valid. I know it probably feels like the end of the world right now, but like Talmage said, he's a bit of a douche. Next year, you'll find someone even better to go to prom with," Mack says, walking towards Harper with her arms open.

Harper only hesitates for a second before she wraps her arms around Mack's waist in a tight hug. Harper's face is to me, and I see a single tear track down her cheek.

Kinsley, clearly feeling left out, hugs Mack from behind. "I'll kick him in the balls if he ever hurts your feelings again," she whispers, making them all laugh. Kinsley lifts her head up and turns to look at me. "Get in here, Tal. This is a family group hug."

Tears burn behind my eyes as I walk over and wrap all three girls in an embrace. Another puzzle piece settles in my chest as warm contentment spreads through me.

Whatever happens today at my parents', whatever the future holds, these three are my family now, and I'll do whatever it takes to make sure they're happy, healthy, and thriving.

CHAPTER 37

Mackenzie

19 years old...

The sting of the needle makes me jolt, and Lizzie scoffs from the chair next to me.

"You're such a baby," she teases.

"Oh, please. You almost passed out when you got your helix pierced!"

"Yeah, well, that's different. The needle went through my ear. It wasn't just a surface scratch."

I roll my eyes, but a smile tugs at my lips. Lizzie and I have kind of gone overboard on body art since we graduated. Lizzie needs the practice, and I have plenty of blank skin for her to use as a canvas.

For me, it's a way to separate myself from the girl I was and the woman I want to be.

Whoever the fuck she is.

I leave for Oregon in a month, despite my parents wanting me to stay. They haven't been pushy, luckily, but I can tell they're sad I'm leaving.

I don't like upsetting them, but I can't stay in our small town with all the memories, good and bad.

I can't move to Provo or Orem and go to college there because I risk running into him, *and I can't handle the anxiety.*

No, moving states will be the only way I can find some peace. It's the only thing that can help me move on.

Leaving my parents, the twins, and Lizzie will be hard, but I know it's what I need to do.

I'll be happy in Oregon. I'll thrive. I'll get my business degree and hopefully land a good job which will allow me to travel. I'll fall in love and get married and have my happily ever after.

Life will be great.

After our group hug, the twins took turns showering before we had to leave for Talmage's parents' house.

Every inch closer to their place ramps up my nerves, and my leg won't stop bouncing from the passenger's seat.

Tal's palm lands on my thigh, and he gives it a gentle, reassuring squeeze. "Everything will be fine. They invited us, remember?"

I nod, taking a deep breath. I still remember the things Laurie said about me to another theatre mom when she didn't know I could hear her. I was already in a bad headspace, and hearing the mother of the boy I still held out hope could love me was...

Devastating.

"Why does your mom not like Mack?" Kinsley—nosey little bugger—asks from the backseat.

Tal tosses me a quick, questioning glance, and I shrug. I don't want to explain it.

"Mack and I dated before we were technically allowed to back in junior high, and my mom kind of blamed Mack for um, corrupting me, I guess is the best way to explain it. Mack and I never did anything more than kiss, but to my mom, that was unfathomable."

Kinsley hums. "Your parents are still part of the church? Even though you aren't?"

"Yep. They still believe."

"Well, I promise to be on my best behavior and rave about how great Mack is, then. Hopefully earn some brownie points for her so they like her again."

Oh God, no.

"Kinsley, please just be polite. No need to talk me up, okay? Just... answer their questions and make conversation. Talk to Lacey about school or ask Tim about track, I don't know."

"Oh my GOD. It didn't click Tim will be there! Oh no, I'm going to be sick. Take me home. Siren, you're getting fur all over me!" Kinsley whines. I hear Siren panting from where she's strapped into the car, not a care in the world about shedding on Kinsley's dress.

I roll my eyes. "You'll be fine, Kin. We're not going home. Everything will be fine." Maybe if I tell myself enough times, I'll actually believe it.

Before I'm ready, we're pulling into the driveway of Tal's childhood home. A home I used to drive by more than I'd care to admit, trying to get a single glance of him during the summer months.

I've come a long way since the pathetic, pining teen I was. *We've* come a long way. Instead of feeling dread because I'll have to put on a show and pretend we're married for reasons other than financial, I can be genuine. Touching Tal casually doesn't fill me with longing, only peace, now that we've confessed our feelings for one another.

Tal opens the car doors for all of us, and he holds out his hand, interlacing our fingers as we follow Siren up to the front steps with the twins tagging along behind us.

I didn't ask them to, but they both wanted to look a little nicer for dinner, so they're in dresses they wear when they have presentations or choir performances. Kinsley told me my dress made my waist look "snatched," so I'm feeling pretty good about myself.

The look in Tal's eyes helps boost my confidence, too. Pure adoration with a smidge of lust. I swear, my libido has been higher in the last twenty-four hours than ever before, and I'm already ready to get out of here so I can make love to my husband.

The front door opens, and Laurie bends down to give Siren scratches, talking in a baby voice about how much she missed her and how she has special treats for her. Siren's tail wags rapidly, eating up the attention. Laurie tries to guide her inside, but Siren turns around and sits at my feet, like she knows I need a little boost of support.

Laurie stands and nervously wipes her hands on her apron as her eyes bounce between Talmage and our intertwined hands.

"It's good to see you, Talmage. Mackenzie. Please, come in."

Talmage follows his mom in, dragging me behind him, and I motion for the twins to follow. We slip off our shoes just inside the door, Siren never leaving my side.

I bend down to give her a kiss on the head, whispering, "I'm okay, girl. You wanna go outside?"

She pants, tilting her head like she's assessing me before she quietly huffs and saunters around the room, giving everyone else a warm greeting.

Talmage clears his throat. "Thomas, Lauren, Tim, Lacey, this is my wife, Mack, and her sisters, Kinsley and Harper."

The twins and I wave, and Lacey bounces over to me. "Hi! Welcome to the family. I'm so happy you're here." Wow, she's energetic. I love it. "I know Harper from the musical! Do you guys want to come listen to the new Wes Jones song with me?" she asks the twins.

Harper and Kinsley look to me for an answer, and when I nod my head, they smile and follow Lacey down the hall.

"Dinner will be ready in about ten minutes, girls! Please be out by then," Laurie shouts after them, shaking her head. "I don't like that she's listening to Wes Jones. He's got tattoos, and his ears are pierced and—" Laurie's eyes widen, and she clamps her mouth shut. "I just think he's too old for them."

I internally roll my eyes. *Good to know she hasn't changed too much.*

Tal clears his throat. "Well, if he's good enough for Elli to marry, he can't be that bad of a person. His music is really good, Mom. You should listen to the song he wrote for Elli. It's beautiful."

My jaw drops open. "Your cousin is married to *Wes Jones*?! Why didn't I know?"

Tal's eyes light up with humor. "They're not married yet, but yeah. The wedding is supposed to be sometime next year, I think. My other cousin is married to Morgan Fowler."

I scrunch my nose. "Am I supposed to know who he is?"

"He's a famous football player. Played for the Denver Mustangs."

I can't help the unladylike snort that comes out of me. "Do I look like a sports fan?"

"No. And I love that about you." He leans in for a kiss but must snap back to reality and remember where we are because he focuses back on his mom. "Do you need any help with dinner?"

Laurie's eyes—a darker blue than Talmage's—volley between us again, wide and curious. Like she's unsure what to make of our relationship.

"No, no. I'm just waiting on the rolls to be done. I hope there are no dietary restrictions, I forgot to ask." She sounds almost... sheepish.

"Harper has diabetes, but she'll just need to input what we're eating so she can get the right amount of insulin," Talmage supplies before I can. Did he research? How does he know that?

"Oh. I'll be sure to make something more diabetic friendly next time, then."

"Thank you," I whisper. It's kind of her to offer, and a small part of me lights up with hope that there *could* be a next time. Maybe this is a step in the right direction for us.

Laurie nods before rushing off to the kitchen, and Talmage guides me over to the couch, sitting us on one end, my thigh squished up against his.

His dad reaches over and extends his hand. "Welcome to the family, Mackenzie. I apologize it's a bit of a delayed welcome."

"Thank you, sir. I'm honored to be part of it. I love your son very much."

He waves me off. "Call me George. I'll wait to pepper you with questions until we're at the table, otherwise Laurie will just ask them again, and I don't want you to have to keep repeating yourself."

"I appreciate it."

"Dad, how's business going? Any new projects?" If I remember correctly, Tal's dad is a landscape archi-tect and does a lot of business planning out the temple grounds for the church.

"It's going well. We will start on the gardens for the Lehi temple soon, since construction will start in about six months. How are things at the station? Your ankle all healed up?" George points his chin to Tal's ankle.

Tal nods. "I'm almost one hundred percent. I should be back to full duty soon, after I get approval from my physical therapist."

"Glad to hear it."

"Dinner's ready!" Laurie calls at the same time three giggling teenage girls come bouncing down the hall.

I'm glad the girls have already connected with Lacey. I hope—if things can be mended with Laurie and George—it means they'll have a lifelong friend in their... sister-in-law.

Ew. Kinsley has a crush on her brother-in-law.

Thank God nothing will probably come of it. Tim hasn't spared her a second glance, and I think she's too wrapped up in whatever Lacey is talking about to notice.

After the ordeal with Jeremy, the last thing we need is Kinsley getting her heart crushed by someone we'll have to see often.

We sit around the table, Tal to my left and Harper on my right, and George asks Thomas to say a prayer.

I haven't prayed in a *long* time, but I bow my head anyway. I turn to peek at Tal, who I find already staring at me.

"I love you," he mouths, squeezing my thigh under the table.

"I love you, too," I mouth back, resting my hand on top of his and squeezing back.

After everyone mutters, "Amen," we pass each dish around the table and scoop up what we want. Once everything has made its rounds and everyone starts eating, Laurie clears her throat. "So, Mackenzie, tell us about yourself. What do you do for work?"

I swallow the bite of mashed potatoes I just put in my mouth, dabbing the corners of my lips with a napkin. "I'm a bid desk specialist."

"Oh? I'm unfamiliar with that job title. What is it you do?"

"I put together quotes for companies wanting to purchase tech equipment. We work with anyone from schools to government entities to software developers. We generate discount codes and things like that. It's mostly a lot of copying and pasting."

I hate explaining my job because it sounds so unimportant. I mean, it kind of is, but it's the first one I found when I needed one, and the company's been decent so far. The schedule is flexible, and the pay is okay. All I cared about was my ability to be home for the girls in case of an emergency.

"That sounds like a boring job," Lacey pipes up.

I shrug. "Yeah, but it pays the bills." *Mostly.*

Talmage's family takes turns asking me and the girls questions, and as the night goes on, I feel slightly less anxious. No one's made any snide comments or back-handed remarks, and I'm feeling hopeful Tal can reconcile with his family.

"All right, kids. Favorite time of the week. Tell me what's been going on in your lives," George says once the interrogation has ended.

Laurie and Lauren clear the plates as Thomas starts off, and it takes all of dessert and then some before we get all the way around the table.

At the end of the night, Laurie gives me a gentle shoulder squeeze and a Tupperware full of leftovers to take home, and I'm feeling lighter than I was when I got here.

Maybe, just maybe, the girls and I will be accepted into this family.

Chapter 38

Talmage

24 years old...

I don't remember when Emma left the church or when she started getting tattoos, but she looks like she feels lighter, freer.

It doesn't match the way the leaders of the church say people who leave will never know true happiness.

Once again, I wonder if the church is lying.

I think about some of my other cousins, Hannah and Elli. Hannah got married young—right out of high school—and the last time I saw her, she looked miserable. Her smile never quite reached her eyes, and there was a sadness about her I don't remember being there when we were kids.

Elli's always been a bit more reserved, but the way she's shrunk in on herself makes me think she's not as okay as she wants to be. That was almost a year ago, though, so I don't know if she's doing any better.

I think about my girlfriend, Jamie. She's happy. We're happy. So happy I'm going to be picking out a ring for her soon, and we'll be planning our wedding.

The thought should fill me with unabashed joy, but it doesn't. There's a small spark of excitement, but it's not an all-consuming happiness or rightness I wish I felt.

Contentment is good. Safe, happy, healthy relationships should be the goal, and it's what I have with Jamie. We go to church on Sundays and don't do anything more than hold hands and kiss. One time she ended up in my lap, but I was able to stop her before she started grinding on me.

I'm not about to ruin our chances of an eternity together just because of lust.

Even if there is a small voice in the back of my head whispering maybe the rules aren't worth following.

After Mom gives Mack the Tupperware of food, she asks me if I can stay back for just a second to talk about something.

I send Mack and the twins to the car, promising I'll be out soon. I follow my mom back to her bedroom, where she's wringing her hands nervously.

This conversation could go one of two ways: either she'll berate me again for my life choices or she'll apologize.

I'm hoping for the latter.

"Talmage," she starts. "I'm sorry for how I reacted when you told me you were leaving the church and getting married."

"Thank you. I appreciate your apology."

"I just... Your father and I raised you to be a certain way, and watching one of your children stray is... difficult. You'll figure that out when you and Mack have children."

I hold back my wince. I knew she'd bring up kids, but I'm not going to dive into that conversation right now. Not before I know what's up with Mack.

She continues, "It's clear to me you're happy with her, and even if I don't agree with the choices you're making, I want happiness for all of my kids. I hope one day you'll see the truth and come back to the church—"

"No," I cut her off. "I'm sorry, Mom, but that's not going to happen. You can hope, but I want to give you realistic expectations about this. I'm not coming back to the church."

Her face falls, disappointment and hurt painted all over it, and she sighs. "I want to be part of your life, Talmage. Can we put aside our differences in order to still be a family?"

"You promised you'd apologize to Mack tonight, and while you were kind to her, you didn't. If you want to be part of my life, you have to apologize—and *mean* it. Mackenzie and the twins are my family now, and I'll choose my wife every time. You can't be part of my life without being part of hers."

A single tear slips from her eye, and I clench my fists. I understand she's hurting from our disagreement, but she didn't have to react the way she did. She could have apologized weeks ago, but she hasn't, and she hasn't kept up her end of the bargain today.

"I understand. I didn't want to apologize in front of your siblings and raise more questions. Can we plan a lunch or something with just the four of us? You, me, Mackenzie, and your dad?"

"I'll talk to Mack and see what she wants to do, then I'll let you know. I should get going since it's a school night. Thank you for having us for dinner."

Mom surprises me by wrapping me in a hug, sniffing as she nods. "I love you, Talmage. I'm glad you found someone who makes you happy."

"I love you, too, mom. And so I am."

When we get home, the girls call out a quick goodnight then head to their rooms.

I wanted to wait to tell Mack about the conversation with my mom until we were alone, so after she puts the leftovers in the fridge, we make our way downstairs.

"What did your mom say?" she asks, heading into our room.

"She wants to have lunch with us—her and my dad—so she can properly apologize."

"Oh. Okay. Is she... does she still hate me? I thought we'd made some progress tonight." Mack's shoulders slump in defeat.

I wrap my arms around her waist and squeeze her to me. "We did, Firefly. She says she's glad I found someone who makes me happy. She's still trying to figure out how to reconcile the fact I'm choosing a forever with you, rather than a forever in the church. Said she hoped I'd come back to church, but I told her it isn't going to happen."

"Do I make you happy, Tal?" she whispers.

I pull back and tip her chin so I can stare into her eyes. "I've never been happier, Mackenzie. You're the best thing to ever happen to me. I'll never regret asking you to marry me."

I dip my head, planning on only giving her a gentle kiss, but the second my lips touch hers it's like a fire ignites inside me.

Her hands claw at my back, and our kiss deepens. I thread my fingers through her hair and tilt her head the way I want so I can explore her mouth with my tongue. It feels like ages since I've tasted her, and I didn't realize how much I was craving her until now.

I don't want to say I know what addiction feels like, but the feeling I get when I'm kissing Mack has got to be pretty damn close. My skin buzzes with need when I haven't touched her in more than ten minutes.

I groan into her mouth when she nips at my bottom lip. "Why does kissing you feel like taking a deep breath, but at the same time like you've stolen all the air from my lungs?" I murmur against her.

"I don't know." *Kiss.* "I don't remember it feeling *this* good when we were kids." *Kiss.*

I reluctantly pull back from her mouth, resting my forehead against hers. "I don't think we felt as deeply back then as we do now. At least, I know I didn't. I've always loved you, but I never felt like I might die if I didn't get to touch you in some way—like you're my lifesource."

"I get it. You brought me back to life, Tal. I love you so much."

"I love you, too." I plant another kiss on her lips, reluctantly stopping because we need to have a conversation. "I wanted to talk to you about something... if you're up for it."

Mack swallows. "Is it about me not being able to get pregnant?"

"Yeah. I don't want to make you talk about it if you're not ready but..."

Mack sits on the bed, blowing out a breath. "But you deserve to know." She pats the bed next to her, and I sit down. She looks at me with tears already lining her eyes. "Promise this won't change your mind about me?"

"Cross my heart, Mack." I reach over and give her thigh a squeeze for reassurance.

"The summer before eighth grade, I went to a summer camp and met a boy. He was going into his junior year. He and I... we started flirting. Talking. We spent the week at camp nearly glued to each other's sides whenever we could, and I developed a crush on him. We exchanged numbers and texted after camp, and we realized we only lived a couple miles apart.

"We started hanging out, and my feelings deepened. He said he reciprocated them, and I believed him. He was my first kiss, and we started doing... other things, but we never had sex. Then, halfway through the school year, he ended things. He confessed our sexual sins to his bishop, who called my bishop, who made me repent. I was embarrassed and hurt, but then you and I became friends, and I started healing."

I vaguely remember thinking Mack seemed a little sad when we started hanging out at school more, but I never imagined it was because of heartbreak.

She continues, "I didn't hear from him at all, convinced he had forgotten all about me, which would have been the best case scenario. Instead, he reached out towards the end of my junior year, right after he got home from his mission, and asked to hang out. I was... kind of reckless after we broke up. I kissed a lot of boys and let them touch me because I figured the more people I could kiss, the more distance I'd put between us.

"I met up with him, and he convinced me he had changed. He told me he regretted how things ended between us and he wanted to try again. So we kept hanging out. He would pick me up and take me to the canyon or a secluded part of the lake. We'd make out and do hand stuff, but he was adamant we needed to slow down because it was wrong." Mack shakes her head like she's trying to dislodge the memory.

"We don't have to talk about this, Firefly," I whisper.

"It's important for you to know." She takes a deep breath. "Long story short, a month after school started, he coerced me into having sex with him. I gave him my virginity, and he... he gave me chlamydia. Then, two weeks later he broke up with me. I found out later it was because he was *in a relationship.* I had no idea. I was heartbroken but also kind of relieved he was done with me because he... he was mean. He'd say terrible things to me and made me feel like I was worthless. That no one would love me like he did, but then he'd use his attention as a bargaining chip."

Anger like I've never experienced bubbles in my stomach—not at Mack, never at her—but at the asshole who broke her. "Wait," I say. "He gave you chlamydia?"

Mack nods and a tear slips out. "I didn't know I had chlamydia until it was too late. I thought it was just a UTI that would go away or something, but it never did. I was too ashamed of my actions to ask my mom to take me to a clinic. I didn't want her to know what I did. One morning a few weeks later, my mom came in to wake me up, and I was burning up. She took my temperature and asked me if anything else was wrong, so I told her about the symptoms I was having, and she rushed me to the hospital. They did an STI test and confirmed it was chlamydia, but... I let it go untreated for too long. I was diagnosed with Pelvic Inflammatory Disease and they removed my fallopian tubes due to the abundance of scar tissue and damage from the infection. I could technically get pregnant through IVF, but I've never considered the possibility."

My heart drops into my stomach with every word coming out of her mouth. Mack has suffered for so long, longer than I even knew, and my heart breaks for her. She's endured so much pain.

"I'm so sorry, Firefly. That's awful. I-I had no idea. Wh-what happened with the guy?"

"Nothing. I told my mom and dad it was consensual. I couldn't handle a court case or seeing him again. But... you remember the proposal we helped with during our show on Valentine's Day senior year?"

"Please don't tell me we helped that evil man propose."

Mack gives me a sad smile. "It was one of the worst nights of my life. I got an STI and my life flipped upside down, but he got to run off into the sunset with the woman he cheated on. I didn't have the balls to tell her, so I only hope he took care of his own STI before they had sex. Who knows how many other people he was having sex with. I was already so depressed I was barely functioning, but after that night, I... I didn't want to be alive."

I don't realize I'm crying until I feel her wipe the tears away with her thumb. "Don't cry for me, Talmage. I'm okay now."

I wrap my arms around her tightly, wishing I had more than gestures for her. I can't even form the right words to tell her how sorry I am. How grateful I am she's *here* and I get to hold her.

I've never hated a stranger more than I hate him. "I'm so, so sorry, Mack. I hate you went through all of that because I—"

"No, Talmage. This wasn't your fault. It had nothing to do with you, I promise."

"But if I hadn't broken up with you—"

She puts her finger to my lips. "It's. Not. Your. Fault. There are no guarantees it wouldn't have happened. There are no guarantees we would have stayed together. There's no changing the past. We can only hope for a better future."

"I love you so much, Mack. I'm in awe of your strength, and I can't express how grateful I am to have you here."

"I love you, too, Tal. Thank you for accepting me and loving me, even if I'm a little broken."

"You're not broken, Firefly. You're one of the strongest people I know."

We spend the next twenty minutes cuddling, letting the heaviness of the conversation dissipate before we get ready for bed.

When we settle under the covers together, Mack and I are a tangle of limbs. I have other questions for her about whether or not she wants kids and what it would look like, but we can have that conversation at a later time.

Right now, I'm happy to fall asleep with the love of my life in my arms, knowing she's here with me, and she's not going anywhere.

Chapter 39

Mackenzie

24 years old...

My entire body freezes, and the police officer's words fade away as my ears ring.

This has to be a cruel, sick prank by someone who wants to hurt me.

"Hello? Miss Thorpe? Are you there?" The officer snaps me out of my spiral.

"Y-yes." I clear my throat, but it does nothing to stop the way my voice wobbles. "I can be there tomorrow."

"Your sisters' friend's mom has agreed to keep the girls until you can get here. We don't usually do that sort of thing, but considering the circumstances..." The officer trails off, leaving me to fill in the blanks.

The blanks being my parents were in a fatal car crash, and if I don't get to Utah as soon as possible, my sisters will end up in the care of the state. If I don't claim guardianship of them, they'll end up in foster care.

"Wh-who do I call when I get there?"

The officer rattles off a few numbers I shakily jot down on a scrap of receipt paper I had in my purse. When he hangs up, I let the phone fall limp at my side.

Have they told the twins? I should be there for that, right?

I don't know what I'm supposed to do other than get to Utah.

KC walks in the door, carrying a case of beer with his friends trailing behind him.

"Kenzie." I flinch at the nickname I've told him I hate. "Woah, why the tears, babe?"

I don't even know where to begin. I need to call Lizzie. I need her to tell me what to do and have her meet me tomorrow to figure out the funeral and school stuff and guardianship.

I don't know how to be a guardian. I barely know how to take care of myself.

"Babe. Hello?" KC snaps in front of my face.

"I'm leaving. I need to go home. We're done." I sound like an emotionless robot, but I don't care.

KC rears back like I've slapped him. "What, why? What did I do?"

"It's not about you. My parents—" My voice catches, and I feel the onslaught of tears waiting to burst out of me. I won't cry in front of him or his friends. I shake my head, and KC mumbles something I can't hear.

I move around the apartment, gathering my things and tossing them into the large rolling suitcases that have held basically my entire life these past five years.

I dial Lizzie as I move, regurgitating everything the officer told me. She doesn't tell me everything will be okay, because she knows it would be a lie. But she tells me she's here for me in whatever way I need her.

I don't look back when I pull away from the complex. It shouldn't have been that easy to pack up my entire life, but I guess it's a blessing in disguise.

If God exists, he can go fuck himself if it's the only blessing he has for me right now.

I told Talmage to schedule lunch with his parents sooner rather than later, so we could get it over with.

I'm still a little wary of Laurie, but she wasn't outright mean to me on Sunday, and I know having a relationship with his parents is important to Tal, so I'm going to try.

We scheduled lunch for Saturday, and the morning of—my period starts. I'm used to the debilitating cramps and nausea, and usually I can go on with my day but not before I've had pain meds.

I'm curled up in the fetal position, my insides feeling like they're trying to burst out of me when Tal comes in from taking Siren out for her morning walk.

"Good morning, I—hey, what's wrong?" He rushes over to the bed, sitting down in front of me and putting the back of his hand to my forehead.

"Nothing," I croak, but my voice comes out strained. "I just... I started my period, and I'm in a bit of pain. I just need some medicine, and I'll be fine."

Tal frowns. "I'll cancel lunch. I don't want you to go if you're sick."

I shake my head. "I'm not sick, just in pain. Nothing I haven't dealt with before. Besides, your mom already hates me. I don't want to cancel at the last minute and have her hate me even more."

"My mom will have to deal with it. I don't... tell me how to take care of you."

I sit up, wincing when my back twinges. "I'll be okay, I promise. We have to leave at eleven thirty, right?"

Tal's lips thin, and I can tell he doesn't believe me. *I* don't believe me, but I refuse to let this be a mark against me with his mom. I've suffered through work meetings and parent conferences with severe cramps, I can handle lunch with his mother.

"Let me get you some pain meds and your coffee. You'll need to take it with food, so what do you want for breakfast?"

"I can—"

"I know you can take care of yourself, but you've been taking care of everyone else for so long, you deserve to be taken care of. Let me take care of you."

I sigh. "You're not going to take no for an answer, are you?"

"Nope."

"Okay. Do we have any more of those cookies and cream overnight oats?"

"You're in luck, we have one left unless the twins got to it first."

When I'm on my period, I have a hard time figuring out what I want to eat because food rarely sounds appetizing. I have a rotation of five foods I can stomach, and those oats are the only thing that sounds remotely palatable for breakfast. I'll probably cry if one of the twins ate them.

Tal helps me up the stairs, rubbing soothing circles into my back as we go. I should ask him if he'd be willing to give me a massage later.

Kinsley and Harper are at the counter with their own breakfasts—cereal, thank God—and Tal instructs me to sit on a stool while he reheats my oats for me. While the bowl is in the microwave, he mixes up the instant espresso I use for my coffee and makes me an iced vanilla latte.

"When did you learn to make that?" Kinsley asks around a spoonful of cereal.

Talmage shrugs. "I pay attention. I wanted to know how my wife likes her coffee, so I learned."

"Ugh. You guys are so sweet you're going to make Harp's blood sugar spike." Kinsley rolls her eyes, but her smile betrays her disgust. For all her sass, I think she's happy for me—for *us*. Having Talmage as part of our family makes it feel less lonely than it was before. He doesn't replace our parents, but he adds something to our little family we were missing.

Harper chuckles and shakes her head, returning to her cereal when Tal slides my coffee and oatmeal to me. He leans back against the counter and engages the twins in a meaningful conversation about their hobbies and their friends. He's genuine about his questions and intentionally listens. The twins—Kinsley mostly—chatter on and on, and the comfortable familiarity and trust they seem to have with Tal nearly makes me cry.

I hope lunch goes well so we can grow our little family, and they can learn to trust other people.

Laurie requested we meet at Valley Baker, so we pull into the parking lot ten minutes before we're scheduled to be here. Luckily, it doesn't seem too busy.

My cramps are still insistent and painful, but the medication has taken the edge off somewhat. What I really want is a hot bath and a long nap. I'll get it as soon as we're done here.

When Tal's parents pull in next to us and wave, Tal gets out and opens my door for me before wrapping his arm around my waist. His gentle grip on my hip soothes my anxiety about what this lunch might entail.

To my shock, Laurie wraps me in a quick hug when we meet at the front of the cars, and George offers me a gentle handshake before we head inside and order.

They pay for our lunch while Tal and I grab a booth in the farthest corner, hopefully lending us a bit of privacy for the upcoming conversation.

George and Laurie slide into the booth across from us, and the ensuing awkward silence is thick around us.

Finally, Laurie clears her throat. "Mackenzie, I want to apologize for my behavior. The things I said about you—recently and when you were a teenager—were cruel and unwarranted, and I'm sorry. My worry has always been about Talmage's well-being and his spiritual health, but I couldn't see past it to notice how happy you two are." Her eyes well with tears, and she gives Tal a watery smile. "You're glowing, happier than I've ever seen you. I'm sorry for what I said to you, too, Talmage. I shouldn't have been so mean."

George grabs Laurie's hand and gives it a gentle squeeze as he picks up where she left off. "We feel awful for missing your wedding, and to make up for it, we'd like to pay for and host a reception. Whenever works best for you. We want to be part of your lives, however it looks for you two."

Laurie reaches across the table and surprises me by gripping my hands. "You have experienced so much loss, and I'm so, so sorry for that, Mackenzie. I cannot imagine—" She shakes her head. "We can't replace your parents, and we don't want to, but we hope to build trust, and maybe someday, you'll feel comfortable coming to us for whatever you need. Your sisters, too. We want to be in your corner."

Tears threaten to spill over. I may not know Laurie well, but everything she's saying sounds genuine.

"Thank you, Mom," Tal whispers from next to me, squeezing my thigh. "I really appreciate your apology and your willingness to try. We want you in our lives, too."

I nod along in agreement since I don't trust myself to speak right now.

Our food comes out, and conversation changes to lighter topics. They ask us about our reunion, and we tell them about the accident and the grocery store. The way Talmage describes it sounds like a cheesy romance novel.

Laurie asks about Harper's diabetes and says she's been researching diabetic friendly meals for when we come over for dinner. She lets me know she's happy to have the girls over any time Talmage and I want to finally go on a honeymoon.

Things feel good and easy, until George asks, "So when can we expect our first grandchild?" His tone is teasing in that dad way. The way people ask wanting an actual answer but pose it as a silly question to ease the seriousness.

Talmage looks at me with panic in his eyes, but I don't know what I'm supposed to say. The idea of disclosing my medical history and the reasons I can't have kids makes me want to hurl. Tal must be able to read the defeat on my face.

"Mack and I aren't planning on having children any-time soon, if at all."

"Why not?" Laurie's eyes bounce between me and Tal.

I clear my throat. Better to just rip off the Band-Aid. "My fallopian tubes were damaged due to an infection and had to be removed."

I don't say I've never really felt the call to be a mom the way some people do. I like kids just fine, but I've never dreamed of having my own. Maybe it's because I was thrust into the guardian role in early adulthood or because I've known since I was a teen that pregnancy isn't an easy option. Either way, I've made peace with the fact kids aren't in my future.

I fully expect Laurie and George to freak out and tell us it's our duty to have kids, spew the religious bullshit that we're being selfish.

Laurie's face softens into a sad smile. "Well, Siren's the best fur-grandbaby ever. Maybe you can have another one of those instead."

I don't think Tal or I expected that response, so we stumble through some kind of affirmation.

"If you were to decide you want to adopt or have a surrogate, we would support you," George adds. "But we respect your decisions. Your choice to have children or not doesn't involve us."

"Thanks, George," I say at the same time Tal says, "Thanks, Dad."

We end lunch with goodbye hugs and promises of Sunday dinners. Laurie wants to have lunch with just me to discuss reception plans sometime, and she wants to have a girls' day with the twins, Lauren, Lacey, and me.

I feel lighter than I have in weeks and full of more hope and happiness than I've experienced in well over a decade.

A pang of sadness hits me when I think about how my parents would feel about all of this. They loved Talmage. They would be happy I'm happy and getting along with his mom. They would be happy Kins and Harp have made friends with my in-laws and they're thriving.

I don't know what I believe about the after-life, but I hope if they're watching over me, they're content with how my life is going.

I wish they were here to be part of it.

CHAPTER 40

Talmage

26 years old...

Jamie sighs for the tenth time in fifteen minutes, so I set my drawing tools down to give her my full attention. I wish she'd just ask me to talk instead of leaving me to guess when something is wrong.

"What's up, James?" I grip her ankle lightly where it's resting next to mine on the couch.

"Are we going to talk about the email you got?"

Email?

"What email? Wait, why were you looking at my email?" I don't feel the need to hide anything from Jamie. I'd show her whatever she wants on my phone, but it feels strange for her to poke around my email without asking. I don't think I like it.

Jamie rolls her eyes. "Your phone was on the counter when the email came in, and I saw it. Were you not going to tell me you applied for a job with the Springville FD?"

"I didn't apply. They approached me with a job offer, but I don't plan on moving back to Utah."

"Maybe you should."

'You.' *Not* 'we.'

"What are you talking about?" I thought things were good. Sure, Jamie's been hesitant to set a wedding date, and she clams up whenever I ask, but... she agreed to marry me. She wouldn't say yes if she didn't want to get married.

Right?

Jamie stands from the couch, crossing her arms over chest and pacing the room. "I don't think I can do this."

"Do what?"

"I can't marry you, Talmage."

The words should feel like a sucker punch. I should be devastated and confused, but instead, I feel... a little numb. A little relieved even. Does that make me a bad person?

"Can I ask why?" I feel like it's fair to know.

"For one, your job. I don't like you putting yourself in danger. I can't live my life knowing you could die at any minute."

I don't tell her everyone *is at risk of death. It doesn't matter what their job is.*

Jamie continues, "For another, sometimes it feels like you're not fully in this. Every time I try to take things past making out, you stop it. Are you not attracted to me?"

My eyebrows shoot up to my hairline. "I'm not risking our eternal marriage just to—to get off. I thought we were on the same page about that. I thought you wanted to get married in the temple."

"I do. But I also want to feel like my fiancé is attracted to me!" Jamie lets her arms fall down to her sides, her shoulders slumping in defeat. "I think we're too different. I think you should take the job and move back to Utah. I know you want to be closer to your family, and I can't

see myself leaving California. This is my *home town. Not yours."*

"That's it? It's over? There's nothing I can do to help ease your mind?"

She shakes her head. "We deserve happiness, Talmage. I don't think we'll find that in each other. Let me know if you need help moving out."

I don't know what to say, so I nod.

Jamie slips the engagement ring off her finger and hands it to me before gathering her stuff and walking towards the door. She stops and turns to me. "I hope you find the love you're looking for, Talmage. I'm sorry it can't be me." Then, she's gone.

I sit on the couch and stare at the ring for a long while, willing myself to feel the heartbreak of my fiancée not wanting to be with me anymore, but I can't find it.

All I feel is relief. Like a weight has been lifted off my shoulders. I've been feeling apprehensive about marrying her, but I thought it was just nerves.

An image of green eyes filled with tears flashes through my mind, but I shake it away.

I shouldn't be thinking about the girl I left behind when my fiancée just left me.

I grab my computer and reply to the email from the fire chief, telling him I'd love to schedule a time to talk about the position.

Maybe the love of my life is in Utah.

The twins are gone when we get back. Off at the movies with their friends, possibly making out with boys.

Oh boy. Nope. They're too young to date.

They're not my biological children, nor are they my biological sisters, and I may have only been in their life for a short time, but they're my family, damn it. I'm going to have to beat stupid boys off with a stick if the whole Jeremy debacle is anything to go by.

Or maybe not, considering Kinsley's thirst for revenge. She can probably handle herself *and* Harper.

I can tell the pain meds Mack took are wearing off, and the weight of the emotions from lunch is making her shoulders slump.

"Go take a bath, I'm going to feed Siren and let her out to play, then I'll be down." I kiss her forehead.

"Okay. Thank you." She places the gentlest kiss on the underside of my jaw, and my dick stirs.

No. Mack's not feeling well.

She heads downstairs, and I grab Siren's food from the pantry and put it in her bowl.

The twins put her in her crate before they left, so I open the door, and she steps out, stretching her limbs like she's been cooped up in there for days instead of just two hours.

I crouch down. "Hey, girl. You hungry?"

Her caramel tail wags at the mention of eating, and I chuckle.

"Come on." She follows me to her food area, sitting like a good girl while I put the bowl down. Her tail twitches in anticipation while she waits for her command to eat. "Chow time," I say, and she digs in.

I scroll through social media while she eats, hearing the faint sound of the water running while Mack fills up the tub.

Unbidden images of Mack's naked body flash through my mind and make me hot. I love her body so much. The artwork, the hills and valleys of her lush skin, the softness of her belly, and the way it molds perfectly to mine.

I shake the thoughts away and try to think about literally anything else. I don't know if it's okay to have sex while a woman is on her period, but it doesn't seem like Mack would be up for it because she's in so much pain, and I'm not going to force anything.

Siren finishes eating, and I let her out into the backyard to chase birds or bask in the late afternoon sun. There's a dog on the other side of the fence she's become friends with, so as soon as I open the door she bolts to the fence and starts sniffing to find her friend.

My parents' thoughts about getting another dog pops into my mind. Maybe I should talk to Mack about it. Siren would love to have a buddy.

Lunch went a lot better than I expected. My parents were genuine in their apology and their desire to be in our lives, and the way they handled it made me feel... proud. They could have had a different approach, like my cousins' parents. They could have berated us and tried to guilt us into coming back to church, but they didn't.

I'm sure they're still secretly hoping we'll come back, but as long as they don't try to force us into anything or push us, I think today was the start of something good.

When Siren seems settled in the backyard, I head inside and make my way downstairs. When I get into our room, the scent of lavender and vanilla seeps through the slightly cracked bathroom door.

"Mack, did you take any more pain meds?" I call out.

"No," she answers.

I run back up the stairs to get her some water and the pills, then come back and push open the bathroom door.

Mack's got her hair up in a claw clip, copper tendrils framing her bare face. Her skin is flushed from the hot water, and the tops of her breasts are visible over the thin layer of suds.

I have to swallow twice before I can speak. Fuck, my wife is the most beautiful woman I've ever seen.

And she chose *me*.

"I brought you more meds."

"Thank you." She takes the pills and swallows them with the water before handing the glass back to me.

I set it on the counter before sitting myself on the edge of the tub. We didn't talk about what happened at lunch on the way home, and I want to know how she's feeling.

"So, how do you feel about how lunch went?"

"I think it went well. I'm... I'm cautiously optimistic we can have a good relationship with your parents."

"I feel the same way. Thank you, Firefly, for giving them a chance to apologize. It means a lot to me that you're open to it."

She gives me a small smile. "I'd do anything for you, Bear."

I lean forward and give her a kiss on the forehead. "I'll let you enjoy your bath in peace. Do you need anything else?"

Mack shakes her head, sinking farther into the water.

About forty minutes later, I hear the shower turn on and assume Mack is done with her bath. My mind wanders away from the book I'm reading, thinking about the last time we showered together. My dick perks up at the memory of her soft skin sliding against mine. The way it felt to hold her breasts in my hands.

I curse internally as she emerges from the bathroom in nothing but a towel, her skin flushed from the hot water.

She bites her plush bottom lip, her eyes roaming down my body until it comes to the tent in my sweats. I don't want to assume where her mind is, and I don't want to get my hopes up, but she's looking at me with a hunger in her eyes.

"How are you feeling?" I rasp, sitting up and swinging my legs over the side of the bed.

"Better, thank you." She comes and stands between my legs, trailing a hand down my chest. I stop her just before she reaches my erection.

"You're in pain, Firefly."

"Orgasms are supposed to help with period cramps," she whispers, letting the towel drop away from her body.

"Are they?" I murmur. My eyes are level with her breasts, and my dick twitches at being this close to my naked wife.

"Want to find out?"

I tear my gaze away from the barbells in her nipples and look up at her. "I don't want to hurt you."

Mack wiggles her hand out of my grip and slides it inside my sweat pants. The heat of her palm makes me shudder, and I release an involuntary moan. "You won't hurt me, Bear. I promise. I want you so bad." Her soft hand glides slowly up and down my length, her thumb gently swiping the sensitive spot just beneath the head.

I'm helpless to deny my wife anything. I'd give her the whole moon if she asked. I don't know how I'd accomplish it, but I'd figure out a way to get it for her if it was what she wanted.

"You take the lead, Firefly. If it hurts, we stop."

Mack nods in agreement. "Scoot back against the headboard."

I strip off my clothes and follow her directions. Mack crawls onto the bed, straddling my lap and hovering above me before gripping the base of me and slowly lowering herself down.

"Shit, you're so wet." I have to squeeze my eyes shut and count to thirty to keep myself from coming. I don't think I'll ever get over the hot, wet grip of her. I'm never going to improve my stamina when she feels this damn good.

"You fill me so well, Tal," Mack whines, circling her hips slowly on top of me. "Will you touch my clit, please?"

"Yeah. Yeah, Firefly. *Fuck.*" I don't tease my wife. I can't. Not when watching her come has become one of my favorite activities. I rub in firm circles, the way I know she likes as she undulates on my cock, taking her own pleasure.

She looks stunning like this, her lips parted, eyes fluttering closed as she bounces lightly.

"I'm right there, Tal, don't stop," Mack moans, her head falling back between her shoulders.

I lean forward and nip at her nipples before twisting my tongue around the jewelry. When I suck one into my mouth, she gasps and clenches around me. She's close—thank goodness, I'm about to burst.

I switch nipples, scraping my teeth gently over the sensitive nub, and she comes, squeezing me so tight it sets off my own orgasm. As I paint the inside of her pussy, Mack collapses into me, resting her head on my shoulder. I feel her soft, satisfied smile pressed against my neck.

I press a kiss to the side of her head, then help her off of me before we clean up. We slip into pajamas and spend the rest of the night reading next to each other.

Things are perfect.

Chapter 41

Talmage

26 years old...

Things are better since coming back to Utah. I still feel like there's something missing, but I can't pinpoint what.

I accepted the position as Captain and adopted a little golden retriever who's currently in training to be a search and rescue dog. Siren may just be the love of my life. When I looked into her big puppy eyes, I knew she was meant to be mine.

Going to church has become a struggle. I used to love putting on a suit and interacting with the other single adults. In California, there were a lot of older singles I had stuff in common with. We were at similar stages of life, and we had the same views on marriage.

Here, everyone is so young. Freshly graduated eighteen and nineteen-year-olds fill the pews, and though I know some people wouldn't balk at the age gap, I don't like it. I feel weird trying to date a woman whose peers are high schoolers.

I've heard some other guys talking about how younger women are easier to "train" or whatever, and I refuse to participate in that rhetoric. Women are not beings to be trained or used. They're humans with opinions and ideas, and they deserve to be treated with respect.

The more I listen to the men around me... the more I realize I don't think I like the way marriage or women are talked about in the church. Are women really only seen as incubators for the next generation? Are they really only supposed to go to school until they find a husband? What about their goals and aspirations?

The thought of someone teaching Lauren and Lacey their dreams aren't valid makes my skin crawl with unease.

Not for the first time, I wonder if the church isn't as great as I've been taught to believe.

Mack and I have officially been married for a little over two months, and maybe we're in the honeymoon phase, but I swear I can't get enough of her.

If I'm not at work, I'm sitting next to Mack while she clicks away on her computer. If we're home alone, our clothes are off, and we're exploring each other's bodies. I've been memorizing every line of ink on her skin, listening to her explain the stories behind them or the way it felt to be in the chair.

My favorite moments are in the post-orgasmic haze, though, when our sweaty bodies are smooshed together and I feel Mack's heartbeat racing. The connection we have has only grown stronger in the last month.

Everything's been great since lunch with my parents. Mom's even taken Mack to get her nails done to try and bridge the gap between them.

Mack said it's a bit awkward, but she can tell my mom is trying, and with time, she can see them forming a closer bond.

Thank whatever higher power exists for that.

Tonight is Hannah and Morgan's one year anniversary. Since they got married at the courthouse and didn't have a big wedding, they're having a party to celebrate.

I'm sitting on the bed in my suit, waiting for Mack to finish getting ready, when the bathroom door opens. All the air rushes from my lungs, and all the blood in my body plummets south.

I've seen my wife dressed up before, and I've seen her comfy in old sweats. I've seen her makeup done meticulously and bare-faced and perfect. I love every version of her.

But god*damn* this dress might just do me in.

"Is this dress okay? I know the invitation said 'cocktail,' but... is it too *risqué*?"

"No." My voice comes out gravelly, so I clear my throat. "No. It's perfect. You look *incredible*, Firefly."

Her hair is curled in soft ringlets and pulled half back with wispy tendrils framing her face.

The olive green dress has a corseted bust, making her breasts sit high on her chest. It's ruched on the side, giving it an asymmetrical hem and showing a glimpse of her thigh. The way it clings to her curves makes my cock stir in my slacks.

"Are you sure? I don't want to stick out anymore than I already do."

I snap my head up so I'm no longer tracing the lovely curve of her stomach pressing against the velvet. "What do you mean?"

She shrugs. "I'm worried I'll stick out like a sore thumb with the tattoos and piercings, and I don't want even more unwanted attention."

I can't help but bark out a laugh, and Mack's lips turn down into a frown.

"I'm sorry," I say, pulling up Emma's Instagram on my phone. "I clearly haven't done a good job giving you a family tree rundown. This," I turn my phone around and show an older picture of Emma that showcases the ink on her arms, "is my cousin Emma. And you already know about Elli's fiancé, Wes. They'll be there, so you won't be the only one with tattoos. You'll fit in perfectly."

"Wow, your cousin is gorgeous," she murmurs before she closes her eyes and sighs. "I'm not used to socializing with people I want to impress. At the bar, I socialized because it's what paid the bills. I want your family to like me."

I lean in and give her a gentle kiss on the forehead. "They're going to love you, I promise. Now, let's go before I peel that dress off of you and we're late."

"Don't tempt me with a good time, husband," she purrs as she runs her hand over the tent in my dress pants.

I groan, powerless to stop myself from thrusting into her grip.

She giggles as she pulls back and shakes her head, slipping on black heels so she's nearly my height.

"Let's go, Bear. The sooner we get there, the sooner you can come back and fuck me."

"I can't wait, wife."

Morgan's rented out a quaint little restaurant called The Silver Spoon. I've never heard of it, but I like the vibes so far. The tables are pushed to the side and a makeshift stage area has been decorated with arches littered in sunflowers and roses. It looks beautiful.

There are only a few tables, and I vaguely remember Hannah saying it was just going to be our cousins, Morgan's family, her brother, Jake, and a few of her friends.

"Talmage! It's so good to see you! This must be your wife. Mackenzie, right? This is my husband, Morgan." Hannah smiles, wrapping me in a hug. Morgan greets me and Mack with a friendly handshake before stepping back to stand next to his wife. He can't seem to keep his eyes off her.

"Yeah, hi. Nice to meet you. You can call me Mack—"

"WIFE?!" Emma screeches, rushing over with her boyfriend, Ben, in tow.

"*Dulzura,* give them a moment. We just got here," Ben grumbles with an amused smile on his face, wrapping an arm around her waist and tugging her into his side.

Emma rolls her eyes. "I'm sorry, but I just found out my cousin is *married* and didn't tell me!"

My cheeks flush, but then my eyes snag on something, and my smile turns into a smirk. "Oh? And when were you going to announce *your* engagement?" I nod towards her left hand displaying a large pink stone.

She brings her hand up to her chest and gives Ben a beaming smile. "Didn't he do good with the ring? We didn't want to steal Hannah and Morgan's thunder, so I wasn't going to say anything, but I couldn't bear to not wear it. Oh! Where are my manners? Hi, Mackenzie, was it? I'm Emma, and this is my fiancé, Ben. It's *so* lovely to meet you. My God, you're stunning. Good job, Tal," she says the last part in a stage whisper and tosses me a wink.

Mack's eyes are wide with so many questions as she extends her hand and lets Emma shake it. "Nice to meet you. I love your dress."

Emma's smile grows wider as she runs her hands down her hot pink ensemble. "Thank you! I love yours. The green really makes your eyes pop. And the way it hugs your curves? Perfection. Now, tell me *everything*. How did you two meet? When did you get married?"

"Who else got married?" someone gasps from behind me, and we turn to find Elli and Wes.

"Talmage, apparently! And he didn't even invite us." Emma pouts.

Elli comes around to hug Emma and Hannah while Morgan, Ben, and Wes fist bump each other.

"Well, rude," Elli teases, giving me a hug. "I'm Elli, this is Wes."

Mack's eyes widen even more, if that's possible, as Wes sticks out his hand. Sometimes, I forget my cousin is dating a very popular up-and-coming musician. Wes doesn't make a big deal out of his success, so it's easy to see him as a normal guy. He and Elli are so in love, so right for each other, and even though Elli and I haven't been super close since we were kids, I'm happy for her.

"I'm M-Mack. Nice to meet you. My sisters are big fans of your music," she says to Wes.

He dips his chin, his alabaster skin splotching red at the attention. "Thank you. It's nice to meet you, too. I'm happy to take pictures or sign autographs later if you'd like."

Mack just nods.

Emma snaps her fingers. "Hellooooo. Details, Talmage. Details. We have fifteen minutes before the ceremony starts."

"*Dulzura,* be patient," Ben chides, but it holds no heat. He looks at Emma like she's the sun. I'm glad to see they figured their stuff out. Last time they were in Utah, Emma wasn't sure she wanted to give in to the feelings between them.

Hannah chuckles. "I'm in charge, so I can push it back. I'm dying to know. Emma, we'll need an engagement story after."

Emma's cheeks turn pink. "Tal first."

"Wait! I want to hear this, too!" A brunette comes barreling into the conversation. "Sorry. I'm Sage, Hannah's best friend, and I like to know things."

We introduce ourselves, then I say, "Mack and I were high school—well, junior high—sweethearts. We fell apart, and I thought I'd lost her for good, but by some miracle, we reconnected. I knew I couldn't let her go again, so I convinced her to marry me the day after Valentine's Day."

The girls "awww," and the men nod their heads like they get it. I'm sure they can relate.

"That's so sweet. Very Mormon of you, Tal, getting married so fast." Emma winks.

"One last act before I remove my records." I chuckle. "I wouldn't have it any other way, though." I pull Mack into my side and place a kiss on her forehead.

"Ugh. Everyone's so in love in your family, Hannah. Is it my turn yet?" Sage grumbles, but there's a smile on her face.

"It'll sneak up on you and happen when you least expect it." Emma knocks her elbow into Sage's.

"Emma would know. You'll have to tell us all about your engagement after the vow ceremony. Come on, Butterfly. Let me declare my love for you in front of all our important people." Morgan takes Hannah's hand and drags her away.

We take a seat at the makeshift banquet table made up of a bunch of smaller tables mixed together and turn to give Morgan and Hannah our full attention.

CHAPTER 42

Mackenzie

26 years old...

With tears welling in my eyes, I throw myself on the bed.

Things have to get easier, right?

Two years should be enough time to get my shit together and get used to being the caretaker of two teenagers.

But I still feel like I'm drowning.

The chains of grief haven't loosened at all, and at any moment, the shackles will tighten, and the weight of everything will drag me under completely.

The only reason I've stayed is because of the twins. They've already lost their parents, if I were to give in to the hopelessness, they'd be tossed around the system for the next five years, and I can't do that to them.

As if she has a sixth sense for when everything's too much and I need her, Lizzie texts me.

LIZZIE: I'm coming over with pizza and wine.

MACK: K. Door's unlocked.

I wouldn't survive without her—wouldn't be here without her. Even in the midst of her busy schedule, she always makes time to check in. She never pushes me, never tries to get me to talk about more than I'm willing to. She's been my rock through this transition.

I feel like a shitty friend in comparison.

Wiping the tears that have surely smeared my makeup, I splash my face with cold water before I head back upstairs to wait for Lizzie.

Kinsley and Harper are in their rooms, studying or something, I don't know. We've slowly made progress and started building a foundation of trust, but I know it'll take time. Our family therapist has been a godsend with helping us learn to communicate with each other in the midst of dealing with the grief of losing our parents.

I open mail while I wait for Lizzie. Seeing my parents' names on the envelopes makes my chest pinch with devastation. They should be here. They should be opening these. They should be the ones going to Harper's doctors' appointments because I don't know what the hell I'm doing.

But they aren't here.

And they won't be coming back.

I wasn't prepared to get misty-eyed today, but witnessing Hannah—looking absolutely stunning in a white mini dress embroidered with little golden butterflies—and Morgan tearing up while reading each other their vows?

Cue the fucking waterworks.

Hannah and Morgan's three little girls are in matching pale blue dresses sitting on the laps of an older couple, who I assume are Morgan's parents. The oldest girl, who looks to be around ten, keeps wiping her eyes. From what Tal told me, Morgan and Hannah both had rough relationships prior to meeting, and their story is full of ups and downs.

I'm happy they found each other.

Emma ended up next to me and is sniffling, too. Her fiancè pulls a pack of tissues from his pocket and passes them to her, and she passes one to me.

Vows are exchanged and the couple kisses, everyone claps and cheers, then they take their seats at the head of the table.

Tal squeezes my thigh under the table, and when I look up at him, his blue gaze is a little watery. "I want to do something like this. Something small and intimate with our closest friends," he whispers.

"Me, too."

Emma leans over and points a finger at Talmage. "If you don't invite me to your vow renewal, I'm gonna be upset."

Tal grins and shakes his head. "Don't worry, you're invited. As long as we're invited to your wedding."

"Duh." Emma rolls her eyes.

"Have you set a date yet?" I ask as a server brings out the appetizers.

Emma shakes her head. "Not yet. *Someone* was impatient and proposed way earlier than I expected, so we haven't discussed a date."

"Don't set it for next June," Tal's other cousin, Elli, chimes in with a big smile.

"Ah! Did you finally decide on yours?" Emma squeals.

Elli nods. "We're sending out save the dates when we get back."

"Aw, guys, we're all going to be married. Look at us, being happy even though everyone said we wouldn't be." Emma sighs. "Mackenzie, were you Mormon?" I nod, and Emma grins. "We're happy you're part of our black sheep crew, then. Ooo, we should make T-shirts!"

Tal snorts. "I'm sure that'll go over well at the next Monson family reunion."

Everyone laughs, then the conversation shifts.

Emma, Wes, and I trade tattoo stories, and Elli and Emma tell me how they met their fiancés. Wes and Ben are a bit more reserved, letting their fiancées chatter away and catch up with everyone, but the way they look at them, it's clear they're head over heels.

Talmage keeps his hand on me in some way—on my thigh, wrapped around my own, or on my back—and when our eyes meet, the heat in them makes my whole body light up.

After dinner, the restaurant staff clears the tables to form a makeshift dance floor. Morgan's parents say goodbye so they can take their kids home for bedtime.

The songs playing are reminiscent of a high school dance, and when "Thinking Out Loud" by Ed Sheeran starts playing, Tal pulls me in, wrapping his arms around my waist and side stepping while he sings along softly to the lyrics.

I didn't realize how healing it would be, dancing with him like this, but I find myself blinking back tears. Tal and I never got to go to a dance together other than the one time. I could have asked him to a dance in high school, but I was scared of rejection. Having his arms wrapped around my waist and my arms resting on his shoulders, it stitches together another piece of my frayed heart.

"What's on your mind, Firefly?" Tal whispers against my hairline.

"How we didn't get to dance like this in high school. I'm grateful we get to now."

He squeezes my hip. "Me, too. If I could go back—"

I put a finger to his lips. "There's no point in wishing we could go back and change the past. The important thing is we're together now. Against all odds, we found our way back to each other."

Tal smiles. "And I'm never letting you go." He presses a quick kiss to my lips. "Have I told you how stunning you look in this dress?"

"Maybe once," I tease, pressing myself against him, feeling the slight bulge of his erection against my belly.

Tal groans. "That's my bad. I need to tell you a thousand more times how absolutely gorgeous you are. I've been half-hard all damn night thinking about all the things I want to do once we get home and I can peel you out of this dress."

"Why wait?"

"What?"

"Wanna be a little adventurous, Bear? Take me to the bathroom and show me how much you want me." I graze a knuckle over his cock, and he shudders.

The song is about to end, and a quick glance around the room shows everyone is distracted.

Tal doesn't say anything, just grabs my hand and quickly walks towards the sign pointing to the restroom.

I can't help the giggle that breaks free when he opens the door to the family restroom and drags me in, locking the door and immediately pinning me against it.

"Is this okay?" he rasps, his lips a breath away from mine.

"Yeah, Bear. Show me how much you want me."

Tal's lips crash against mine desperately, like he's been waiting all night to kiss me. I love how needy he can be, how unabashed he is with his desire. How wanted he makes me feel.

He trails kisses down my jaw and neck, running his nose along my jawline and inhaling. "Why do you always smell so good? I swear I could live off your scent alone," he moans, nipping at the juncture where my neck meets my shoulder.

He doesn't let me answer, though. He kisses me again, invading my mouth with his tongue and rucking the skirt of my dress around my hips before cupping my pussy through my underwear. He pulls my panties to the side and runs one finger through my lips, teasing my clit with slow circles.

When he pulls away to watch where he's touching me, I let out a soft moan. "Are you going to fuck me against the door, Tal? Can you be quiet while you fill me with your cock? We wouldn't want anyone to hear us."

Tal whimpers as his fingers falter. "I need to taste you first." He drops to his knees, helps me out of my panties, then shoves them in his pocket.

My head hits the bathroom door as his mouth latches onto my pussy, swirling his tongue through the wetness like he's lapping up his favorite dessert. I thread my fingers through his hair, keeping his mouth where I need it. He groans against me when I tug gently on the silky strands.

"Yes, Tal, right there," I moan as he suctions his lips around my clit and sucks gently as his fingers tease me. He breaches my entrance, shallowly thrusting his fingers. God, I want him to take his time, but I don't want anyone to come looking for us.

I pull him off, and he looks up at me, groaning in protest. "I wasn't done," he whines.

"We need to be fast, Bear. Give me your cock now, and you can take your time later."

Talmage sighs but rises from his knees and undoes the buckle on his belt, hastily shoving his pants and underwear down just enough to free his cock. Tal looks around, motioning towards the sink. "Bend over, Firefly, and hold on because this is going to be fast."

I move to the sink and bend over. In my heels, I'm the perfect height. Tal runs the head of his cock through my wetness before thrusting into me in one go, jolting my body forward as we both moan.

Tal sets a steady, rough pace that has the head of him stroking my G-spot with every forceful thrust, quickly ramping up my orgasm. I shove one hand underneath my stomach to rub circles on my clit so I can get there faster, and the first pass of my fingers has my pussy clenching around him.

"*Shit,* Mack, if you don't come, I'll make it up to you later, I swear. I'm so fucking close," Tal grinds out.

"I'm close. Don't stop." I pick up my pace, matching the speed of Tal's thrusts.

When he groans my name quietly, I feel the first pulse of his cock as he comes, my orgasm crashes through me.

Tal stays seated inside me while we catch our breath, and when he pulls out a rush of his cum trickles down my thigh. I glance back to see Tal's gaze fixed on the pearly liquid.

"Am I supposed to like seeing myself drip out of you so much?" he whispers in awe. "Because I *really* like it."

I can't help but giggle. "I don't know, but I like feeling it. I don't want to be dripping while we talk to your family, though, so..."

"Right." He grabs some paper towels and gingerly wipes the mess from between my thighs, then wipes his cock before tucking himself back into his pants. He helps me slip my panties back on with a pout on his face, like it kills him to cover me back up.

I place a gentle kiss on his lips before we peek out the bathroom door. There's no one out there, so we walk down the hall. When we pass by what looks to be a storage closet, we hear whispered voices and what sounds like... kissing?

Looks like we weren't the only ones who couldn't keep their hands off each other.

Emma gives me a knowing smirk when I stand next to her. "You need to send me the lipstick you're wearing."

Heat flushes my cheeks, but Tal rattles off the name of the brand and the shade. "It's smudge-proof." He grins proudly.

"I can tell," Emma deadpans. The tips of Tal's ears turn pink, but the small smile doesn't move from his face.

"How do you know what brand and shade it is?" I whisper when the conversation moves on from my lipstick.

"I pay attention to all the products you use in case I need to pick something up. I have a running list in my notes app."

My heart is going to burst right out of my chest. Marrying Talmage may have been out of desperation and buried feelings, but I lucked out with the best, kindest, most genuine man a girl could ask for.

And he chose *me*.

"You're the best husband ever," I whisper.

Tal smiles at me. "And you're the best wife. I love you, Firefly."

"I love you, too."

Tal and I linger a little while longer, talking to Elli and Wes about our upcoming trip to San Antonio. The twins are going to *freak out* over Wes Jones hanging out with us while we're there. We talk with Emma and Ben about a trip to San Diego. Emma chatters on about all the things we need to do while we're there and offers to hang out with the twins so Tal and I can have a romantic night out.

Hannah and Morgan give us an open invitation for dinner, saying they want to get to know me better, and my heart is full of gratitude and love for these near-strangers who have shown me such compassion and kindness after only knowing me a few hours.

After mending things with Talmage's parents, knowing the twins have formed a connection with his siblings, and now meeting his cousins, my life is full of so many good connections. Connections I didn't realize I was missing until now.

Life doesn't seem so bleak anymore. Marrying Talmage was the best thing I've ever done, and I'll never regret it.

EPILOGUE

Talmage

4 years later...

"Arson, stop trying to bury your sister!" Mack scolds.

Arson, our six-year-old beagle, is currently spraying dirt at Siren as he digs for... something.

We should have named him something related to excavation considering how many holes are in our backyard. We adopted him three years ago, and while he and Siren get along most of the time, Arson likes to antagonize her.

He pops his head up and gives Mack his best "I'm innocent" head tilt, but my wife is immune to his manipulations.

"Don't give me that look, buddy. I'll give you a bath without the bubbles if you keep it up."

Arson barks in protest but abandons his half-dug hole in order to sniff Siren and make sure she's not mad at him.

I just woke up after sleeping off a difficult shift where we had to fight a small brush fire at an abandoned field.

No one was injured, thank goodness, but it was still taxing. I'm just grateful we were able to put it out in time so I wouldn't be dead on my feet for today.

Mack's standing at the stove in nothing but a satin robe barely covering her ass, and I suppress a groan. It's a big day for her, and we can't waste any time by fucking.

Even if I'm dying to have the taste of her on my tongue.

I press my body against hers, wrapping her up from behind and placing a kiss on her shoulder. "Good morning, Firefly. Are you excited for today?"

Mack turns her head and kisses me quickly. "Yes. I'm ready to be actively helping instead of simply learning about it."

Right after we renewed our vows, Mack sat me down and asked if we could discuss the possibility of her going back to school to become a victims' advocate. I was immediately on board. She quit her job and started taking shifts at Great and Spacious again for some extra cash. She enrolled in online classes that fall. Today is her graduation, and she'll be working with the city as a victims' advocate.

Harper and Kinsley decided to attend the university in Logan to study music and bio science. It's been weird not having them at the house all the time, but it's also been nice to be able to fuck Mack wherever and whenever I want.

The twins are driving down today to celebrate Mack's graduation. All of my siblings, their partners, Hannah and Morgan, Lizzie and Enoch, and Joanna will be there to cheer my wife on as she walks across the stage.

"Have I told you how proud I am?" I murmur against her head.

"Only a few hundred times."

"That's not enough, Firefly. It should be in the thousands."

I step back to turn the coffee machine on, then help Mack plate our eggs-in-the-hole. When the coffee is done brewing, I fix hers with caramel syrup and a splash of heavy cream, and mine with white chocolate creamer. It took a while to find a coffee combo I like, but now it's a daily occurrence.

I officially removed my records six months after we got married, and life has been blissful. Not carrying around the weight of the church's expectations and rules has given me room to grow in ways I never thought I would.

To my shock, Lauren asked me to go to lunch one day and peppered me with questions about leaving. Ultimately, she decided to remove her records, too. She came out as a lesbian shortly after and is now living with her wife in Colorado teaching music. Lacey removed her records as soon as she turned eighteen.

Thomas and Tim don't understand why, but maybe someday they will. My parents were a little hurt when my sisters made the choice to leave, but they haven't treated them any differently. Lauren's wife was welcomed with open arms and fits in perfectly with our family.

My parents have made a point to not talk about church related stuff with us. It's difficult for them to know most of their kids won't be with them in the heaven they believe in, but I'm proud of them for trying to make sure we still feel welcome in this life.

Mack and the twins' relationship has flourished in the last few years. Kinsley dominated every science fair project she entered, taking state and even placing at nationals. Her hard work opened every opportunity for her, and she had her pick of colleges, but she still chose to stay close to us and Harper.

Life has been full of laughter, love, and light over the last four years. I never realized life outside of the church could be this way, since we're taught the opposite. We're told people who leave are unhappy and directionless; they just want to sin without consequences, or they didn't try hard enough to understand the gospel.

I can say with one hundred percent certainty they're lying.

Looking at how far my cousins and I have come after leaving is proof happiness doesn't have to be found in organized religion. Happiness comes from living an authentic life filled with love—both romantic and platonic.

Happiness can come from enjoying a cup of coffee or a mimosa at brunch on a Sunday. From enjoying the sting of a tattoo needle etching artwork into your skin.

For some, happiness comes from having adventurous, kinky sex. Others find joy in raising their kids without the pressure of the rules of the church. Some people find peace in knowing they get to choose whether or not they have kids at all.

I'll forever be grateful for running into Mack on that chilly winter day. I'm grateful she said yes to being my wife, even if the reasons for it were slightly unhinged.

My life is brighter with my Firefly in it, and it's only going to continue to improve. Sure, we've faced challenges, and we'll continue to do so, but choosing her and choosing my own forever outside of the church will always be the best thing I've ever done.

THE END

Acknowledgements

The end of this series is so bittersweet. I've spent the better part of two years writing the characters of *Broken Shelves* and without the support of my readers, I wouldn't have accomplished this.

So thank you, readers. For taking a chance on my silly romances about traumatized people healing after leaving religion.

Thank you to my BETA team, Kristi, Winter, Mercy, Taylor, and Samm. You all helped me bring this story to life.

Special shoutout to Samm for helping me make Tal's job as authentic as possible.

Thank you to my editors, Brit and Jen, as always, for being on my team and helping me make Tal and Mack's story the best it could be.

To Lemmy with Luna Literary: your hype is greatly appreciated and I adore you.

Thank you to my husband for holding me when I cried over the plot twists and lack of creativity sometimes. And for being my biggest fan and pedaling my books at your job.

And finally, thank you, to JJJ. You'll never know I wrote this (hopefully) but without the agonizing heartbreak I experienced from fifteen year old you, I wouldn't have come up with this idea.

If you've read this far, thank you! Here's a peek into the future.

What's next in the Daisy Wren-iverse?

Love Under the Hood, a Valentine's Day romcom will be out by the end of 2025, and after that... sapphic cowgirls.

Then... rugby! My *Utah Knights* series will be six books (for now. I keep adding things lol) and will have things like marriage in trouble, a Vegas wedding, why choose, ex-fiance's brother, and so much more. Make sure you're signed up for my newsletter or following me on social media to learn more!

About the Author

Daisy Wren lives in the Utah Valley with her husband and three kids. When she's not writing her next book (or working her corporate job), she's reading, cooking, and spending time with her family. Daisy's love of writing has been prominent since childhood, and she's always felt a call to share her stories. A hopeless romantic since she first saw *The Phantom of the Opera* at age eight, she's been writing her own love stories ever since. Daisy is a former member of a high demand religion and hopes to bring light to the issues of the church she was raised in, while also telling beautiful stories about life after leaving. Please visit her at www.DasiyWren.com, or on social media for updates about upcoming releases and for bonus content!

Tiktok: @daisywrenauthor

Instagram: @daisywrenauthor

Threads: @daisywrenauthor